Praise for
A Conspiracy of Alchemists

"Oh my Steampunk God! . . . If you like steampunk you definitely have to give this jewel a try. It would be a sin not to, really."
—Butterfly-o-Meter Books

"A wonderful sense of fun on every page . . . Visit [your] nearest bibliographic emporium and seek this rather magnificent tome out."
—The Eloquent Page

"I truly enjoyed this novel and strongly suggest it to Steampunk fans. I'm convinced *A Conspiracy of Alchemists* will rock your world!"
—Tynga's Reviews

"Pure fun to read."
—Karissa's Reading Review

By Liesel Schwarz

A Conspiracy of Alchemists
A Clockwork Heart

A CONSPIRACY of ALCHEMISTS

LIESEL SCHWARZ

DEL REY • NEW YORK

2013 Del Rey Mass Market Edition

Copyright © 2013 by Liesel Schwarz

Excerpt from *A Clockwork Heart* copyright © 2013 by Liesel Schwarz

All rights reserved.

Published in the United States by Del Rey Books, an imprint of The Random House Publishing Group, a division of Random House, Inc., New York.

DEL REY and the HOUSE colophon are registered trademarks and the Del Rey colophon is a trademark of Random House, Inc.

Originally published in the United Kingdom by Del Rey, an imprint of Ebury Publishing, a Random House Group Company, London, and subsequently in the United States by Del Rey Books, an imprint of The Random House Publishing Group, a division of Random House, Inc., in 2013.

This book contains an excerpt from the forthcoming hardcover edition of *A Clockwork Heart* by Liesel Schwarz. This excerpt has been set for this edition only and may not reflect the final content of the forthcoming edition.

ISBN 978-0-345-54826-9
eBook ISBN 978-0-345-54127-7

Printed in the United States of America

www.delreybooks.com

9 8 7 6 5 4 3 2 1

Del Rey mass market edition: August 2013

A CONSPIRACY of ALCHEMISTS

PART I

PARIS

This was the place where people came to give their souls to fairies. I watched her step into the café and close the door, at once sealing out the noise and stench of the Latin Quarter behind her. It was still early in the afternoon and the café was empty.

She blinked as her eyes adjusted to the dim interior of this place. The battered paneling of oak trees long dead is always a little disconcerting after the bright crowded streets.

The one they called Aleix unfolded from the shadows behind the counter. He wore his long hair bound in a simple braid that made him look slightly Oriental in appearance, but to even the most ignorant there could be no mistaking his race. He was a Nightwalker.

They studied one another for a moment.

"Are you Aleix?" she said.

"Who wants to know?" It was more of a command than a question. He narrowed his eyes as he assessed her, carefully noting the jodhpurs and man's shirt she wore under her leather coat. Whether she was peer or prey would be measured, considered carefully before he spoke, for that was the Nightwalker way.

"I'm looking for Patrice. My name is Elle—Eleanor Chance. The pilot." Her breath caught in her throat as she spoke, as if the words had come faster than she had expected.

He relaxed his shoulders. "Upstairs. The flower house," he said with the briefest of nods.

To the side of the counter a heavy crimson curtain partly covered the curves of a cast-iron staircase.

"Shall I go up?" she said.

He shrugged as if what she did was of no interest to him,

but I knew she had been expected. For no Nightwalker would rise at this hour for the sole purpose of seeing to the task of polishing glasses.

The soles of her boots left a trail of sawdust from the floor below. I sensed the whispers of pine and beech rise up from the resonating stairs as she moved over them. It was a clever thing, this wrought, twisted staircase. Designed to allow the patrons who frequented this place to enter and leave at will, it held those of us who worked here caged within its iron bars and scrolls. For few creatures with the old blood in their veins could cross pure iron unharmed.

When I was still young and living among my people, the Dryad, I once had a different name. But that was many years ago, at a time when anise and wormwood were nothing more than plants that made up my world. A time before sacred dreams could be bought for a few sugar cubes.

My real name is long since forgotten along with so many memories of green. All that remains of me now is what you see here amongst the coal-fire, stone and dead glass. For I am *La Fée Verte,* the keeper of the absinthe drinkers. But you may call me Adele if you must.

I saw her for what she was, this young woman with the clear blue eyes and hair like the leaves of the horse chestnut when the season turns. I saw that she would one day cast no shadow on the narrow path between Shadow and Light.

Isn't it strange how not even pure iron can stay events once they have been set in motion? I knew from the moment I saw her she would offer salvation. But salvation often comes at a price. Perhaps a price I might have paused to consider a little more closely at the time. But I was too caught up in my own thoughts to pay heed to the signs. All I knew was that for the first time in years, I felt hope.

CHAPTER 1

SEPTEMBER 4, 1903

The opium den above the Café du Aleix smelled of clove incense and oblivion.

"Eleanor! Welcome to Paris. I am so glad you came." Patrice, her docking agent, rose up from the sofa and gripped her shoulders fondly. He was a big bear of a man and the little shake he gave her almost lifted her off her feet.

"Patrice," Elle said in her best French. "Always a pleasure to see you." The sweet scent of opium rose up from his clothes as she kissed him—twice on each side, as was the custom on the Continent.

"Sit. Sit. Rest for a moment. I'll go and see if I can get us some refreshments. Watch my seat for me." He swayed down the staircase on legs that were not entirely steady.

Elle slung her holdall over the back of a chair where she could keep an eye on it and sank into one of the linen-covered settees that lined the walls. The windows of the café were all sealed up so no sunlight could penetrate its sanctuary. Ornate brass lamps sat against the red chinoiserie wallpaper. The warm glow of their spark cores softened the sordid purpose of this place.

The only other patron in the den was a brawny man in a gray jacket. He hunched over a journal, scribbling furious lines of verse over the pages, pausing only to slam down gulps of absinthe from a greasy glass at his side without even bothering to mix it properly. The murky liquid swirled inside the glass, like an artist's water jar after too many paintbrushes had been dipped into it.

Next to the poet, a green absinthe fairy balanced *en pointe* upon the edge of the low table. She arched her arm and swung her leg to and fro, like a little dancer at the barre. The poet cursed, crumpled the page and flung it across the room, where it burst into flames and disappeared.

Poets, Elle thought with annoyance. The poetry had to be supremely rubbish, for the fairy-muse to look that bored. It was almost cruel to watch the poor thing suffer like that.

The man looked up from his work and their eyes met. He smiled at her, his expression lush and predatory.

Elle looked away, denying him the satisfaction of seeing her shudder. A desperate need to rush outside for fresh air and light filled her, but she remained in her seat. To reassure herself, she touched the row of buttons on the front of her shirt. The slim hilt of the stiletto she kept tucked into the front laces of her corset was still there.

She sighed and looked up at the roof. Hopefully this business with Patrice would be brief, so she could be on her way. She hated stepping into the Shadow side. It was odd that even in this day and age there were still places in this world where Reason and Enlightenment had not reached.

Patrice appeared with a tray at the top of the stairs. He walked carefully over to the table and set it down on a clear space with exaggerated care. The floorboards groaned briefly as he sank into the upholstery opposite her.

"I brought tea. Oolong. Have some." He lifted the

teapot and poured the steaming liquid into small ceramic cups. There were dark crescents of dirt at the base of his fingernails when he handed her one.

"So tell me, my dear, did you have a pleasant flight over the Channel?" he said.

"It was fine. Windy, but nothing unusual for this time of year." She wanted to ask about the assignment, but Patrice was not a man who could be rushed. She would have to go through the ritual of negotiation with him first.

"Would you like a pipe?" He rummaged around the opium paraphernalia on the table. "I'm sure I have a made one here somewhere."

She shook her head. "Better not. Wouldn't want to crash my ship and your cargo into the sea, now would I?"

He fiddled with one of the carved pipe stems in a moment of indecision. "I suppose you are right. Might as well do this with a clear head." He gave her a knowing smile.

"Patrice, what is this all about?" She sat forward, unable to contain her curiosity. "The telegram said that the charter is urgent and to meet you here, but nothing else. Paris is a long way to travel on speculation, so I hope I haven't travelled here unnecessarily."

Patrice's laugh was a sudden burst of noise, swallowed up by the paper screens and furnishings. "Always straight to business, little one. That's what I like about you. You never get distracted when there's work to be done."

At the sound of Patrice's laughter, the absinthe fairy looked up. She flexed her wings and wisped over to where Elle and Patrice were sitting. Elle averted her eyes. The fairy-muses of Paris were elegant from afar, but, like dragonflies or the prostitutes who prowled dark alleys, they were quite ugly if one looked at them too closely. They said the fairies brought brightly colored dreams from which one never wanted to wake up and which brought descent into complete madness. Much was said about the hideous things they did to their charges—the absinthe drinkers—once held in their spell. And Elle had no desire to be caught by the charms of *La Fée Verte*.

The fairy shifted form until she was nothing but a knot of gray-green light rising in the direction of the bamboo fairycote that hung from the ceiling. The sound of fairies whispering in the air above washed over Elle. She felt their attention like a whisper of breath against her skin and she shivered.

"So, on to business." Patrice stroked his broom moustache slowly as he spoke.

"I'm listening." She was careful to keep her voice even. She needed this charter. She would not have bothered coming to this dreadful place if she didn't. Patrice was one of the few agents who didn't mind that she was a woman. She had managed to log some valuable flight hours thanks to the official work he sent her way. In return, she did some of his off-the-books business for him. She owed him that. It was the way the world worked: Everyone owed somebody something in the end and it helped if those you owed were friends.

"Tonight's charter is a rather delicate matter," Patrice said, interrupting her thoughts. "The utmost discretion is required. It concerns the conveyance of a very important parcel. You are to fly to England. Someone will be waiting to collect the freight at the Aerodrome. You will receive further instructions upon your arrival."

"That shouldn't be too difficult. But . . . ?" There was bound to be a catch somewhere. There invariably was when it came to dealing with Patrice.

Patrice nodded and smiled as if he had read her thoughts. "I need you to look after part of the freight for me this afternoon. Only for a few hours, until you fly tonight. It shouldn't cause you too much trouble. There is a reason I told you to watch my seat. See, I have it right here."

He pulled a polished wooden box out from between the cushions behind him and put it on the table between the teapot and the pipes. "No one will even know you have it."

"That can't be all of it, surely? They wouldn't have chartered a whole airship for one little box, would they?"

He shrugged. "It's an important parcel."

She frowned and ran her finger along the brass-edged corner of the box. It was roughly the size of a book— a solid block of wood with no obvious hinges or opening. A fine pattern of ancient-looking symbols was laid into the surface.

"Patrice, I am just a pilot. I fly the freight. I deliver it. I get paid. That is all and you know it. You cannot ask me to start carting things around Paris for you. That has never been part of our agreement."

"Make an exception this one time, please. It's not as if I'm asking you to guard a warehouse. It's just one small box."

Elle looked over her shoulder. The poet on the other side of the room had fallen asleep with his pencil still in his hand. A soft snore emanated from somewhere at the back of his throat.

"What's inside the box?" she said in a fierce whisper. "There has to be a reason why it can't be opened, and I'm not going to carry it around in my holdall unless I know what that is."

Patrice shook his head. "I cannot tell you what is inside the box. I am bound by an oath of secrecy. All you need to know is that it's extremely valuable, but completely safe. And you are not to let it out of your sight until you get to England."

"And where is the rest of the freight?"

"The rest of the freight will be waiting for you at the airfield."

"You will be aware, of course, that this is going to increase the risks I have to take. What if I am searched and they find the box?"

Patrice rested his moustache on his knuckles in measured exasperation. "Anyone who sees it will simply think it's a jewelry box. My client, Viscount Greychester, is a very powerful man. If anything does happen, he will take care of matters. Just mention his name and all will be smoothed over. Just like that." Patrice tried to snap his fingers, but no sound came from them. He looked at his hand with the slight surprise of the uncoordinated.

"It's going to cost more. I'm not doing this for charity, you know."

That wasn't completely true. She loved to fly more than anything and she would do it for free if she could, but dreams and dirigibles cost money.

He sat forward and took hold of her hands. "All I need is a standard Channel crossing. Nothing unusual. I am asking that you do this for me. For all the times I have helped you."

He had a point. There was no arguing with him on that. She gave Patrice a look of extreme dubiousness.

"And before you start complaining about it, here is your fee." He pulled a dark blue velvet pouch out of the pocket in his waistcoat and placed it on her palm.

Elle's eyes widened with surprise. It was an eternity bracelet inlaid with gems. Brilliant cut stones, the size of peas, set in a neat row ten or eleven inches long. At each end was one half of a clasp that intertwined in a Celtic knot.

"Patrice, are those diamonds?"

He nodded. "They are indeed. Your preferred mode of payment, I believe?"

Elle pulled her combobulator optic loupe from her holdall, clicked it open and held the lens up to her eye. The tiny gears whirred and clicked as the image came into focus. She studied the bracelet between her fingers. Even in the dim light of the spark-lamps, she could see that the diamonds were flawless. They shone with a strange but exquisite shade of blue. She would have to take them to a jeweler to be valued, but the bracelet would fetch quite a price if she used the right people.

She had found that jewelry was the perfect form of payment for her services. Diamonds were far preferable to bills that needed her father's signature for her to draw upon them. Gold was too heavy to carry and too hard to sell when it came to it. But no one asked questions when a lady sought to sell jewelry discreetly. Elle had become very good at spotting paste gems from real ones.

She put away her optics, taking care not to seem too pleased.

"So do we have an agreement?" Patrice picked up his tea and sat back against the cushions.

Curiosity bubbled up inside her. She lifted the box up and gave it a wiggle. It had a heavy, solid feel to it that spelled trouble. She should say no to this charter. She felt the little voice inside her whisper the warning. But doing exactly what she ought not to was one of her very worst habits. And now was not the time to break old habits. Not when her ship needed mending.

"All right, Patrice, I'll do it," she said. "But only because it's you who is asking." She slipped the box into her holdall and set it on the floor next to her feet.

Patrice raised his cup and smiled. "To a successful flight, then."

To wealthy eccentric clients with more money than brains, Elle thought to herself as she took a sip of fragrant tea.

"Try the bracelet," Patrice said. He gestured with his hand for her to try.

She flicked the diamonds over her wrist. They wound around it and the clasp shut with a click. "It's rather early in the afternoon for diamonds, don't you think?" She held it up to admire it in the light.

The absinthe fairy drifted down from the rafters and hovered before Elle, as if she was trying to get a better look.

"You like shiny things, don't you?" she said to the fairy.

The fairy moved up and down in what appeared to be the affirmative. Then, in a green flash almost too quick for the eye to see, the knot of light disappeared into the bracelet.

"Hey! Where do you think you're going?" Elle wiggled her arm, but the fairy refused to budge. Elle tried to undo the clasp, but it was stuck. "Patrice, I think my stowaway has broken the clasp. Can you help me, please?" She held her wrist out to him.

"Oh! That can't be good—" Patrice started to say but something beyond her shoulder caught his attention.

"Patrice, there you are!" A man said in English behind her.

"Marsh. You have found us!" Patrice flushed red and half rose up from his seat.

Marsh turned out to be a tall man wrapped in a black carriage cloak despite the mild weather. His dark hair was just that little too long and messy to be fashionable and the finely tailored black shantung waistcoat, visible from between the folds of his cloak, was too expensive to match the rest of him.

"This is Miss Eleanor Chance. The *pilot*," Patrice said, emphasizing the last word.

"How do you do." She hid her arm behind her back.

It was never wise to advertise in this type of establishment that one was wearing diamonds.

Marsh barely nodded in reply as he looked her up and down. His fine, regular features creased into a frown. "Patrice, surely you can't be serious?" he said.

Patrice started to stammer an answer, but Marsh turned on him. "And iron? What were you thinking? Do you realize that I have been looking for you for three hours?"

"It was the safest place I could think of to wait. Besides, there is nothing to worry about. This was merely a diversion, nothing you wouldn't be able to overcome." A tinge of obstinacy crept into his tone. "Miss Chance is an excellent pilot. She has top-notch credentials. I can assure you that all will be well."

"I honestly don't give a damn about her credentials," Marsh said, "but I do care about the fact that we need to leave this place. Immediately."

Elle felt a tight little bud of anger unfurl inside her. "*Mister* Marsh," she said. "If the fact that I am a woman is not to your liking, then please, by all means, go and find someone else to fly your cargo. But I am keeping the diamonds for my efforts."

"Please tell me you're not one of those tedious Suffragettes as well. Good work, Patrice," Marsh sighed, and rolled his eyes.

Being called a Suffragette in such unfair and unflattering terms was one thing; being called tedious was another, and Elle wasn't going to dignify his insufferable remark with an answer. Instead, she gathered her holdall to return the box.

Patrice placed a hand on her arm. "Please, if I may. My associate is not himself today. We really do need your assistance." He gave Marsh a pointed look as he spoke.

Marsh rubbed his hand over his face in a gesture of resignation. "Very well, but this is on your head, *mon ami*."

Patrice turned to Elle. "Allow us to hail you a cab. It will take you back to the airfield. Wait there for further instructions. I do hope you would forgive this imposition while Mr. Marsh and I attend to a few last-minute items of business." He paused for a meaningful moment as he pleaded with her in silence to play along.

"I can walk, you know. The airfield is not that far from here."

"I would feel better if I saw you off safely." He inclined his head toward the contents of her holdall.

She tightened her grip on the strap. Let them waste money on a cab if it mattered that much. "Very well, then, Patrice, I'll see you at the airfield for takeoff. We depart at six. Don't be late," she added with as much hauteur as she could muster.

Marsh rolled his eyes. "I'll be downstairs," he grumbled as he stalked off.

CHAPTER 2

Outside the café, Patrice handed Elle into an old hansom carriage, recently converted and fitted with an engine. Horseless carriages were all the rage in Paris these days. The spark reactor and steam engine were attached to the front of the carriage underneath the driver's seat. The dome of the reactor gleamed blue-green and the pistons huffed and hissed. Little puffs of steam escaped while the engine idled. The cab driver, seated on the front of the carriage, held on to the lever brake to stop the cab from lurching forward.

Patrice had a word with the driver and handed him money. Then he poked his head into the window. "Take care of yourself until we meet again. And don't worry about Mr. Marsh. I will see to him. Just make sure you look after the box." He pulled up the window and snapped it shut.

Elle nearly fell over in her seat as the cab pulled off over the cobbles. The driver did not seem very skilled in his command of the machine. And if there was one thing Elle knew about, it was spark-powered engines. They took finesse to master and this was clearly a skill the cab driver had not quite acquired yet.

They trundled down the street and took a right turn. She caught a glimpse of the Eiffel Tower. *La Dame de Fer* rose up over the city bathed in afternoon light.

She frowned. She knew Paris well enough to know that they were going in the wrong direction.

"Excuse me!" She banged on the hatch door that opened up next to the driver so passengers could give directions. He didn't seem to hear her so she leaned forward to open the window. It was stuck. She rattled the frame and wrenched at it until she managed to drag it open slightly.

"Excuse me. This is the wrong way," she called out to the driver.

There was no answer. She tried the door handle, but it too was firmly locked. The cab sped up. Something was very wrong. There was no way of telling where this man was taking her. Paris was rife with occultists and libertines in need of quarry. And that was without counting the Nightwalkers and the other creatures of Shadow. This city could be a dangerous place for a woman on her own and she had no intention of ending up on some dark altar or a dinner platter in a dungeon somewhere. And there was the box to consider. She needed to do something. Quickly.

Elle gripped the door handle and shoved at it. It budged slightly, but held firm. The buildings started whirring by with nauseating speed. She swallowed down the urge to panic and hitched her holdall across her body so the leather strap nestled between her breasts. With her bag in front of her, she turned sideways and gave the door a kick with both legs.

Cab doors are by their nature rather flimsy and not designed to be kicked. The cab shuddered. She kicked it again. The leather-padded plywood door split next to the handle. She leaned back and kicked the door again with all her strength. With the sound of tearing upholstery, the door flew open.

The driver looked down in surprise and let go of the brake. The cab lurched forward, almost out of control.

Elle closed her eyes and launched herself out of the moving cab. She landed on the pavement, hitting her elbow on the cobbles. She rolled and sat up, looking about to get her bearings so she could see which way to run.

The cab slowed down and the engine shuddered to a halt as the driver let it stall. He yelled and leapt off the machine after her.

She stood up to run, but out of nowhere someone stepped from behind and grabbed her. Before she could react, Elle felt the cool graze of sharp-edged steel press against her throat and it made her stop in her tracks. "Don't move, or I will slit your throat from end to end," a voice behind her said. The smell of licorice laced his breath as he held her in his grip. Absinthe. That meant it was quite likely the man was deranged.

Elle held very still as the blade edge scraped against her skin. If he was away with the fairies, there was no telling what he might do. One wrong move and she would be dead for sure.

"Go restart the cab," her captor said to the driver. He tightened his grip on her. "Now, very slowly, let go of that bag of yours." His damp breath filled her ear. "Go on, hand it over . . . there's a good girl." His fingers crawled up her arm and over her shoulder. They dug into her neck as he gripped the strap of her holdall. In a violent move, he dragged it over her head, taking several strands of her hair with it.

Elle gasped with pain and revulsion. She tried to move away, but his fingers dug into her throat, threatening to choke her.

"There you go. Now you and I are going for a little ride. And don't you dare scream, or I'll make sure you will be sorry."

Fury rose up inside her. She was not going to let this man drag her off to do who-knows-what with her. And she certainly wasn't going to let him get away with her holdall.

"No, you will not," she croaked. She brought her foot up and shoved her heel into her attacker's groin. Elle was slim, but years of helping her father in his workshop building engines had made her lithe and strong. It was a lucky shot, but her boot sank into his crotch with satisfying force.

Her attacker wailed and doubled over.

Elle twisted out of his grip and kicked him in the knee. He went down onto the pavement, clutching his groin. She caught sight of his face and gasped. It was the poet from the café.

How? Why? She didn't have much time to wonder. The driver yelled and jumped off the cab, where he had been restarting the engine.

She drew her stiletto out of her bodice and balanced it in her hand, ready to defend herself.

The driver just laughed when he saw her weapon. In reply, he drew out a long metal rod and flicked it. An electric-blue charge started crackling at one end of the stick. Elle swallowed with dismay. It was a Tesla spark prod—the type policemen used to subdue unruly mobs and anarchists. One buzz from that and she would be immobile and drooling on the floor for hours. The driver stood in the road, blocking her way. The spark prod in his hand crackled ominously.

She glanced down at the squirming poet. She only had a few moments before he recovered enough to come after her again.

Together, the two men were more trouble than she could manage. She turned to run, but the poet grabbed her ankle and tripped her. For the second time she fell hard on the cobbles. She held the blade up, ready to stab whoever touched her next.

"Let go of her!"

A pair of boots appeared next to her face. She looked up and realized with a rush of surprise that it was Mr.

Marsh. Before she could protest, he hauled her to her feet. She found herself face-to-face with his solid chest as he slipped his arm around her waist to stop her from falling.

The poet cursed and spun round. And slashed at Marsh's calf. Marsh cried out and swiveled Elle out of the way as he held her to him.

The poet dragged himself up to face them. His stubbly cheeks glistened with sweat. He started laughing and held the holdall up before him.

Elle lunged at it, stumbling out of Marsh's grip. For the third time in as many minutes she landed on the ground, winded.

Marsh and the poet squared up to face each other.

"Come on, then. Let's have it," Marsh said in a low voice. He leaned forward, ready to fight.

The poet grinned at him and shook his head. "Oh no." He spoke English with a heavy Cockney accent. "Not that way, Gov. I ain't that stupid." He drew something from inside his pocket and hurled it at Marsh. There was a bright flash of light as the projectile hit Marsh square in the chest. The air filled with the acrid smell of alchemy.

Before anyone could do anything, the poet disappeared in a cloud of smoke.

Patrice ran up to them. He was panting and rubbing his fist. "Are you hurt?"

Marsh was bent over at the waist. He was taking long steady breaths. His hair had flopped forward into his eyes and his hat lay forgotten on its side on the cobbles.

"Did you get him?" he asked Patrice.

Patrice shook his head and pulled a slim black cigar from his pocket. He lit it and took a deep draw. The end glowed red in reply. "No, he got away," he said as he exhaled. "I grabbed him, but he was too fast. Managed to get a good punch in though."

"What are you doing here?" Elle said. She rubbed her palm. A dusty bruise was already forming from landing on the cobbles. "Have you been following me?"

Marsh straightened up with a groan. "I noticed that your cab drove off in the wrong direction and decided to investigate. We were lucky that another cab was to hand and so we were able to follow you. And a good thing we did too, by the looks of things." He bent over and examined his leg. The leather of his boot was marred with a long gash where the knife had split it. "I seem to have had a lucky escape." He stood up straight. "Just ruined a good pair of flannels. Thank you for asking." He gave her a pointed look.

Elle realized she was holding her breath and let it out slowly. "I could have managed on my own, you know," she said.

Marsh snorted. "With that brooch pin?" He gestured at the stiletto she was still holding.

"This is a deadly razor-sharp weapon, if you don't mind." She turned her back to him and tucked the blade into its place inside her shirt.

"Well then, you should mind that you don't cut yourself or your laces," he observed.

With her buttons done up, she faced him. "That was the poet—the one from the café. And he's gotten away with my holdall, and the viscount's box."

"That was no poet." Marsh retrieved his hat from the cobbles. "Patrice, I am hoping with everything I am that the box Miss Chance is referring to isn't our box. It's not, is it?" he asked between gritted teeth.

"I thought it would be the safest place. No one would look in a lady's luggage, surely?" Contrite, Patrice looked down at the ground.

Marsh said something into the air above him in a language Elle did not know. She guessed from the inflection that the words were not fit for polite conversation. Then he turned to her and gripped the tops of her arms. "What else was in the holdall?" He gave her a little shake.

The ferocity of his question sent her heart racing. "J-just my things, the flight papers . . . and the box," she stammered. She liked to think of herself as robust, but such manhandling was quite unacceptable and her blood was still pounding through her veins from the shock. "Now let go of me, this very instant, you big lout." She kicked his shin and started wriggling furiously to escape his grasp.

Marsh cried out as her boot connected with his shin. He straightened up and loosened his grip. "Damn it, that hurt." His eyes were winter-cold.

"Well, you deserved it," she said.

Marsh did not respond. Instead, he looked away before he spoke. "It seems that the men Patrice and I initially had business with now have business with you. And for that, I am truly sorry." His expression softened as he spoke.

Elle found herself at a loss for words. Physical shock and delayed reaction were sending her whole body into shakes. She swallowed the lump that was building in her throat and looked away.

"Very well, if you insist on pouting, we shall share pleasantries first. Tell me, madam, are you harmed? Any broken bones? No gaping injuries?"

He was mistaking her silence for petulance. "No, I'm sorry, I didn't mean to pout. I mean, I'm fine. A few scrapes perhaps, but no harm done." It was a ridiculous answer and she found herself casting about for a better one, but his attention was already elsewhere.

"Patrice, this has been a most unfortunate turn of events. I fear that matters have become rather complicated by this little episode. We need to get back to London as soon as we can." He pulled out his pocket watch and looked at it. "We must make for the airfield immediately, before they decide to come back."

"I think we need to call the authorities," Elle said, recovering some of her composure.

Marsh shook his head. "You may take it from me that the police will be of no assistance in these circumstances. In my experience, involving the authorities will be far more trouble than it's worth."

Elle stared at him. She did not move.

"Come along, then, Miss Chance." Marsh nodded at her.

"I beg your pardon!" she said, bristling at his presumptuousness. "I'm not moving from this spot until I get an explanation as to what just happened here."

Marsh turned round and faced her. She was beginning to realize that this was not a man who was used to being contradicted. "An explanation? Very well," he said in a low voice. "By deviating from our plan, your friend over there has just placed all of our lives in danger. You now know too much and so do the men who attacked you. Is that enough?"

"Not even close."

His expression grew darker. "You may trust me on this: The less you know about the matter, the less they'll be able to torture out of you later."

Elle crossed her arms over her chest. "And why should I trust you?"

"Because, Miss Chance, *I* am the freight you have been hired to carry to England tonight."

"You're the freight?" She frowned.

"That box was too important to be left in the hands of a stranger. Something Patrice did not appreciate fully, I see."

Elle shook her head. "Even if I agreed, the ground crew would spot you and they would never let you board."

"That's why I told Patrice to hire a *resourceful* pilot.

Unfortunately, as we are now landed with one another, I'll happily hide in a crate if it would assist." The corners of his mouth twitched. "You see, I am now in your hands as much as you are in mine. A rather unfortunate situation, but seeing as we all want to go home tonight, I suggest that we stop messing about and get on with it."

He was right, which was utterly annoying. She didn't want to wander the streets of Paris on her own for the next few hours either. Not with the knowledge that those men were out there and intent on capturing her. She could bid good-bye to Mr. Marsh and this whole unhappy business the minute they landed in England. It seemed a sensible enough trade under the circumstances.

"Fair enough, Mr. Marsh. I will take you back to London with me. But I'm only doing this because I promised Patrice that I would. And I believe in keeping my promises."

"As do I, Miss Chance. As do I." He turned his attention back to Patrice. "Patrice, let's see if we can start that machine, shall we?"

Patrice touched the rim of his hat and climbed onto the driver's seat. Marsh took hold of the engine crank and gave it two turns. The spark reactor glowed blue-green. The machine started huffing and puttering as the water boiled in the tanks.

Elle climbed into the cab. Marsh followed and suddenly she found herself very close to him on the black leather seat. She lowered her lashes and sat back as primly as she could.

"Oh, there is no need for that. Your virtue is quite safe with me, madam. For the moment at least." His mouth quirked with arrogant amusement. Then slowly and quite deliberately he leaned over her to wedge the broken carriage door shut. She caught the faint scent of sandalwood that drifted off his skin as he brushed past her. The deliberateness of it set her teeth on edge.

Marsh sat back in his seat and banged on the driver's window. Patrice nodded and let go of the brake. The cab lurched through the backstreets toward the Jardin du Luxembourg airfield, where a small air freighter known as the *Water Lily* waited.

CHAPTER 3

In a shaded alley, not far from where the cab with the broken door had disappeared around the corner, another carriage waited. No driver held the reins of the dripping black horse harnessed before it. Rivulets of water ran down the creature's sleek body and over the knobbly bits of water grass tangled in its mane.

The poet stepped out from the doorway, where he had materialized a few moments before, and brushed the yellow dust off his lapels. He wrinkled his nose at the smell of the transporter compound. He hated the smell of alchemist sulfur. It made him itch.

He eyed the horse warily. It stared back at him with a mixture of hatred and anguish. Definitely none too pleased about being so far from the river. Open cuts along its neck turned the water pink as it trickled down its legs and pooled around the black hooves. The poet's master had been at work. He could tell.

He edged along the wall to ensure that there was as much distance between the horse and himself as possible and climbed into the carriage.

"Nice horse," the poet said as he sat down.

"Indeed." The occupant was hidden in the gloom of the interior. "She was trying to lure some sailors into the water near the docks when I caught her. The thought of owning one amused me. She's proven to be wonderfully submissive under my hand. I shall miss her when her spirit breaks." He paused for a moment. "Well, Feathers, did you get it?"

Feathers broke out of his reverie about beautiful naked river women who turned into horses. "I have it." He held up Elle's holdall. "Mr. Chunk was waiting in the cab and picked the lady up just as you ordered. It's a good thing I followed them from the café. Lucky I knew the way he was going or else Mr. Chunk might've lost them." He pulled the box from the holdall and handed it into the shadows. "Sir Eustace, may I present the box. George Feathers at your service."

Sir Eustace Abercrombie reached out and took it from him with a gloved hand. "Oh, it is something, isn't it? Well done, Feathers. Well done indeed."

Feathers watched his master turn the box over and examine the brass edging.

"Did you get the key?"

"Key?" Feathers blanched. "With respect, sir, you never said nothing about a key."

Without warning, Abercrombie struck Feathers in the face. The ferocity of the blow was barely contained within the confined space and the carriage rocked briefly on its springs. Feathers felt his eyes fill with water and he did his best to remain impassive. The seat was also not helping his aching groin, but he held firm. It was the mark of a good henchman to show no pain. It would do him no favors if he showed weakness.

"The key," Abercrombie growled. "How do you propose we open this?" He leaned forward and shook the box.

Feathers averted his gaze. He had never quite managed to become accustomed to his master's face. Abercrombie was clean-shaven—right to the very hair on his head. When the light touched him in a certain way, it was as if a series of dark runes and glyphs moved underneath the skin that covered his face and skull. The marks of the Sacred Guild of Alchemists. And right now Abercrombie was so livid that the runes seemed to have a life all of their own.

"Don't be such a fool. The box will only open if it is in contact with the key." Abercrombie spat. "Give me that." He grabbed the leather holdall from Feathers and started rummaging through it. "Nothing. Do you even know who has it?"

"The girl must have it. Mr. Chunk was supposed to take her to the temple in the cab, like you ordered, but things didn't quite work out as planned." Feathers proffered the excuse timidly. She'd had a lovely throat though. It was slender and the skin was smooth like milk. He loved the feel of ladies' throats under his fingers. The sound they made when he squeezed.

"What have we here?" Abercrombie drew a bundle of papers out of the holdall. A sliver of light appeared and illuminated the inside of the carriage. His master held the papers up to the light. "The British Imperial Flight Company. Scheduled flight to London. Takes off at six. Pilot: Miss E. Chance. Cargo: To Be Confirmed. Now, that is an interesting development."

The light went out and Feathers blinked in the gloom.

"I think that you should be the one to go after them, seeing as you were the one who let them escape. Now, don't you, Mr. Feathers?" He could feel Abercrombie's stare reaching out to him from the gloom. "All the way to London and beyond, if need be."

"Yes, sir." Feathers bit his tongue. London was not his favorite place on account of the fact that they would hang him if they ever caught him there. Too many ways to get into trouble in London Town. What he wanted was to stay in Paris and work on his poems, but the odds of being caught and hanged in London were still more attractive than risking the wrath of his master. Sir Eustace's penchant for inflicting pain made his own proclivities pale by comparison. There were few things in the world that brought his master more satisfaction than binding those who served him into submission. Feathers had seen with his own eyes the elaborate chains and straps his master maintained for such purpose. The plight of the water horse suddenly came to mind.

"Bring me the girl alive. Without delay."

"Yes, sir." Feathers inclined his head as far forward as he dared within the small space.

"Now get out. I need to speak to the Guild. And our friend on the other side of the Channel after that. There is much that has to be done and little time to do it."

Abercrombie lifted his hands and motioned in the air as if he was taking hold of a set of reins. The horse raised her head and snorted in response.

Feathers opened the carriage door and got out.

"And Feathers, do not fail me this time." Abercrombie's voice followed him from the carriage.

"Yes, sir," Feathers turned to say, but the carriage had already moved down the alley.

CHAPTER 4

Inside the cab with the broken door, Elle waited with Marsh and Patrice for the afternoon to pass into evening. She watched two electromancers dressed in gray habits as they strolled down the Boulevard Saint-Michel. Behind them, the streetlights blinked on one by one as the little hermits ignited the glass-covered spark cores on top of the lampposts. Paris was readying herself for the night.

A gaggle of prostitutes cackled and called out to the electromancers in guttural tones as they passed them by. Their crude words echoed against the buildings. Horrified at the lewdness of the women, the little monks shuffled on. A horse clop-clopped as it made its way up the road to the Sorbonne.

The bracelet was safely tucked away under her shirt cuff. She squeezed her coat sleeve at the wrist and felt it dig into her skin with a reassuring hardness. She knew a jeweler just off Fleet Street who specialized in jewels and pendants from the Shadow side. He would certainly know how to exorcise a fairy and undo a clasp spell for sure. She would go there tomorrow without delay. In the meantime, she only hoped none of the Shadow magic rubbed off on her. Absinthe fairies were creatures to be treated with the utmost circumspection.

Patrice chewed on the decidedly soggy-looking end of his cigar stub. It had gone out some time before—a small mercy in the stuffy warmth of the cab. Marsh pulled his pocket watch out and flipped it open. It was the seventh time he had done that in the last hour.

Elle studied his hands as he snapped the front of the watch shut and then flicked it open again. Mr. Marsh had the long elegant fingers of a confidence trickster. She wondered how many shady characters the viscount had in his employ. She was one of them now, she realized.

"I think it's time to go," Marsh said.

They left the cab where it stood in the alley and crossed the road to reach the airfield behind its neat black railing fence.

"I don't have a departure permit, and the docking papers were in my holdall," Elle said as they entered the ornate side gate.

Marsh felt inside his waistcoat and pulled out a bill folder. He handed a few notes to Patrice. "See if you can persuade someone to give us papers with that."

Patrice nodded and walked over to the row of buildings that housed the administrative offices.

Outside the departure pagoda, passengers milled amongst leather-clad steamer trunks. A small gray poodle yapped at a man with extraordinarily hairy ears, who looked very much like he was a werewolf. A clutch of children escaped from their governess and disappeared amongst the crates and trunks. Here, in this public place, the worlds of Shadow and Light merged in harmony.

Two dove-chested ladies in large hats trimmed with feathers passed them. Behind them, a valet grunted as he lumbered under a mountain of luggage. The ladies gave Elle's jodhpurs and riding boots a disdainful look as they passed. Elle dismissed them with a matching stare. Let them think she was one of Monsieur de Toulouse-Lautrec's kissing-ladies as much as they wished. Women dressed as men might be daring and sometimes scandalous, but there was no arguing the fact that trousers were far more comfortable and practical than the petticoats and stays she wore when she wasn't flying.

Marsh touched the rim of his hat and smiled at them. The ladies tittered at each other and cast long glances at him from behind their lace gloves as they made their way to the row of ornate passenger dirigibles that sat urging against their moorings in the fading light.

"Do try not to attract too much attention to yourself, Mr. Marsh," Elle said.

"Easier said than done," he responded without taking his eyes off the ladies.

Elle took a deep breath to dispel her annoyance.

"Now, while no one is looking, if I might tear you away for a moment?"

"I'm at your service, madam." Marsh touched the rim of his hat and they strode across the lawn to the other side of the airfield, where the *Water Lily* waited. Elle inhaled the smell of river and hot metal mixed with the scent of freshly cut grass. She loved the way Paris smelled.

To her relief, they reached the airship without anyone paying them much heed. In a practiced motion, she climbed the rope ladder and hoisted herself into the cockpit. The *Water Lily* was nowhere near as big as the cathedral-sized passenger dirigibles that crossed oceans. She was a 40-footer, with double thrusters, which made her fast and maneuverable. The cockpit windows ran in elegant lines from halfway up the hull to the ceiling, allowing the pilot a panoramic view. At the corners of the windowpanes were pink and white water lilies inlaid into the glass. Elle loved those lilies. Wire grate doors designed to protect the pilot from flying cargo in rough weather separated the cockpit from the freight hold. Elle ran her hand over the varnished woodwork and the brass railing of the interior. The *Water Lily* was beautiful even if she was only a freighter.

"The freight area has no seats, so you are going to

have to take the copilot seat," she said as Marsh appeared through the hatch.

Marsh winced slightly as he settled against the russet leather seat.

"I have some bandages in the back, if you need one," Elle said.

"It's just a bruise." He waved her off. "He caught me in the ribs. A lucky shot, I dare say."

She leaned over and pulled a half jack of brandy from one of the cubbyholes. "Um . . . thank you." She uncorked the bottle and handed it to him.

"For what?"

"Well, you did chase away that Warlock who attacked me earlier. And I wanted to say that I am grateful for that."

He took a swig from the bottle. "That was no Warlock." He swallowed and grimaced.

"How can you tell?" she said.

He took a smaller, more cautious sip from the bottle and handed it back to her. "I just can. Whatever he used, it wasn't Warlock magic."

She snorted. "Even to me, the most uninformed of people, that blast looked lethal." She raised her eyebrow at him. "Come to think of it, why aren't you dead?"

Marsh sat up. "Thanks be to the Shadow, I'm generally more blast-proof than most, which comes in rather handy sometimes."

"So you're an occultist?" Elle snorted. "You'll have to forgive me, Mr. Marsh, but if you ask me, all the hullabaloo about the great divide and the two realms is a load of nonsense. Now stop pretending to be all noble and let's see if you're hurt." She leaned forward to look at him.

"Thank you, but that really is not necessary." He studied her for a moment. "But tell me, are you really a nonbeliever? Surely you must believe in the electromancers. They are after all the ones who produce the spark that powers the machines of the Light side of the world?"

"Electromancers can be explained by science. As for the rest, I could be called a skeptic at best," she said. "I don't deny the existence of the Shadow realm, but I do believe that people should not be dabbling in things they have no business with." She fiddled with the door catch of the cubbyhole. "The organized occult has been the root of the most atrocious evil in the world and so I cannot abide it. Just look at what happened with the Emperor Napoleon and the wars. Not to mention the awful wars in Africa. One only has to open the papers for it to be plain," she said.

He didn't answer, but she could see his jaw muscles move as he clenched it. "One should never say *never*, Miss Chance," he said softly.

What a strange man he was.

The clock embedded in the flight console pinged. Five minutes to six. Time to go.

She knocked the cork back into the brandy bottle and put it away. "And so to conclude our eventful afternoon, I think we should make ready for takeoff." She climbed into the pilot seat and pushed forward the lever switch that controlled the ship's spark reactor.

The glass dome over it glowed blue-green as the reactor hummed to life. They listened to the boiler tick as hot water boiled and turned to steam. A light blinked on in the flight console. With both hands, Elle grabbed hold of the porcelain-handled crank that turned over the engine. It spluttered into life and the hull creaked as steam filled the tank that fed the thrusters. Pressure gauges thrummed and needles quivered, moving slowly upward to the proper levels needed for takeoff.

Elle unfurled the signal flag to show the ground crew that the ship was ready.

The moment the flag went up, men in white coveralls

appeared below them. They unpegged the ropes that held the *Water Lily* to the ground.

"Where is Patrice?" Marsh sounded irritated.

"He'd better be here soon if he wants to go to London tonight," Elle said.

A shrill whistle pierced the air and they both looked up.

"Stop! Cease takeoff immediately. You are ordered to stop and stay where you are!"

There was a commotion on the ground. Docking crewmen scattered before a group of policemen who were running across the field. The constable at the back was the source of the whistle. He was shouting orders through a brass speaking-trumpet.

"Perhaps we should see what the police want," Elle said.

Just then, a figure stepped out from behind the constable. Even in the fading afternoon light, there was no mistaking his meaty frame. It was the poet from the café. Elle stared at him, transfixed. "It's the man who attacked me . . . the poet," she said.

"We have to leave. Before they reach the ship." Marsh was next to her at the window.

A whistle sounded in the cockpit, signaling optimal pressure had been reached in the chambers.

"What about Patrice?" Elle asked.

Marsh peered out of the window in the direction of the docking office. "I'm sorry, but we have to leave him behind. He can take care of himself."

"Wait!" Elle pointed at the ground. Patrice was charging across the grass like an angry rhinoceros, dodging passengers and policemen as he went.

"Cast off!" Elle yelled out through the communication tube to the ground crew, who were all looking around in confusion. "Cast off now! That's an order!"

To her relief one of the crewmen started lifting the tether ropes off their pegs. Elle held the thruster-controls to keep the ship steady as the ropes were released one by one.

"He's too slow. We are going to crash." The ship lunged and veered dangerously close to the ground as it was dragged off balance. Elle looked out of the window and almost swore aloud. The last straining tether rope was tangled in a mooring trellis. A few of the ground crewmen were tugging at the rope to free it. "Leave it! You'll lose a hand on that!" she shouted into the communication tube.

She opened the throttle and the ship lurched in the opposite direction. The *Water Lily* groaned and strained as she tried to break free from the bonds that held her to the ground. Elle heard the crack of a splitting trellis and then, suddenly, the *Water Lily* was floating free. She started rising up gently as the billowing canvas balloon took the weight of the hull.

Elle grabbed hold of both thruster-controls and dragged them into reverse to keep the ship from launching. The ship bobbed out of her berth and across the field, toward the departure pagoda. Tether ropes trailed behind her like the tentacles of an ocean creature. A woman shrieked as a flailing rope nearly hit her. Two policemen tried to grab it, but they collided with each other instead and crashed to the ground.

"Open the cargo doors. It's that lever to the left. I can't hold her for much longer," Elle called to Marsh.

He wrenched the freight doors open. "Jump," he shouted at Patrice.

Patrice shoved a policeman out of the way and caught hold of one of the ropes as the ship lurched up into the air.

The policemen pulled out their service revolvers and started firing. A bullet whizzed past the ship's front window and pinged off the metal frame, cracking one of the lily-inlaid panes.

"Oh no, you're not shooting holes in my baby!" Elle steered sharply to the left. With a gush of steam, the airship glided up diagonally like a big air bubble rising through water. More bullets whizzed past, a few flew straight through the balloon. Others hit and splintered the hull.

Marsh looked at Elle in alarm. "Helium and double canvas," she said. "Bullet holes are too small to make a difference. Now take cover before you get shot."

Elle gritted her teeth. She hoped they had enough spare gas to get home. It was not a happy thought.

She maintained the ascent path until the whizzing of bullets died away, before she eased back on the thrusters. The ship leveled into cruising position with a gentle gush of steam as they left Luxembourg airfield behind.

Marsh finished hauling Patrice into the hold and they both collapsed against the hull, panting as the roofs and chimney pots of Paris floated by below them. Both men were looking somewhat wide-eyed.

Marsh retrieved his hat. "Do try to be punctual next time, old chap." He started laughing, but the laughter seemed to set off pain in his ribs. He coughed and patted his stomach.

Patrice stood up, balanced against the hull and dusted his lapels. "Departure permit." He handed the document to Elle. "You have no idea how far away from the departure pagoda the ship is when one is in a hurry."

"Was that resourceful enough for you, Mr. Marsh?" Elle asked with a little smile. She started cranking the reel that hauled up the tether ropes.

"I think you'll do," he said as he settled into the copilot seat. He smiled at her.

She looked away and focused her attention on the clouds ahead of her.

"I suppose we won't be going back to Paris for a while,"

Patrice said as they watched the streets and houses of Paris slip by below.

"That might probably be for the best." On impulse Elle reached over and pulled the cord that operated the ship's foghorn. The horn blared out over the clouds as the *Water Lily* slipped off into the sunset. "Next stop, Croydon Aerodrome."

CHAPTER 5

I dreamed of night-gray clouds shifting as I slumbered. Below, my saltwater sisters, the selkies, sang to me as we passed high in the sky over them.

Perhaps I should have roused and made myself known to the girl, but I was so weary. And she had the other to rely on. He would see that she would come to no harm. Of that at least, I was sure.

We were a proud people once. We stood at the side of the phyllomancers in the days when the sun scented the earth with sage and rosemary. In the study of the leaves, we helped them see what would come to pass. But that was a long time ago. Mankind no longer concerns itself with what might be tomorrow. Instead, they spend their short, brutish lives burning and wasting, without sparing a thought for what might happen once they are gone. They call themselves scientists and "enlightened," while we, the ones who have seen the seasons turn a thousand times over are denigrated to dwell in the Shadows.

There are those who believe that humans are beyond the assistance that any of my kind might give. There are those of us who have hardened our hearts. But I embrace neither of these thoughts completely.

The girl with the horse-chestnut hair did not know the danger she would face. She was blissfully unaware of the clouds that gathered from behind. And so I slept on, dreaming of the serenity found only at the feet of trees.

The clouds before the headlights of the *Water Lily* parted for a moment. Elle caught a glimpse of the quartz-black sea of the English Channel as it shifted below them.

She checked the clock on the instrument panel. It was past midnight; they had been flying for almost seven hours.

She yawned, put the steering lock in place to keep the ship on course and reached up to stretch her shoulders. Out of habit, she glanced at her compass to check the ship's bearings and smiled with satisfaction. Apart from being a bit low on balloon gas, they were steady on course.

The ship was pulling a little to one side as helium seeped from the bullet holes, but they didn't have far to go now, so they would be all right. She would need to book the *Water Lily* in for an overhaul after they landed though. She was also now going to need her canvas patched and refilled. That was annoying. A quick charter across the Channel did not usually include being shot at. She fiddled with the bracelet around her wrist. She should have known there would be problems the moment Patrice gave her this bracelet. What could possibly have been inside the box that would have caused such a fracas? She shrugged. If she'd learned anything in the past few years as a pilot, it was that sometimes it was better not to ask questions.

She glanced over at her travel companions. Patrice was asleep on a bale of cotton packing bags, judging by the soft snores that were emanating from the back. Marsh was in the seat next to her, hunched up in his cloak with his eyes closed. He had a fine face, etched out in profile by the lights of the flight console. It was a pity that it belonged to a man who was so ill-tempered.

"That must be England," he said, opening his eyes as if in reply to her thoughts.

She looked away and cleared her throat. "Yes. I took the long way round across the Channel from Dieppe. The moon is out, so if you look carefully, you should see the white cliffs and the lights of Eastbourne in a few minutes."

He leaned forward to look out of the window. "Interesting. I've never flown in the front seat before. Look at all those stars."

"It's what I love best about flying. Up here everything is so quiet. Peaceful." She thought better of telling him why they were still in the air. The fact that she had to fly at slow speed to conserve balloon gas and that she'd taken the long way to avoid air patrol ships did not make for tranquil flying.

She spotted the lighthouse that signaled landfall in the distance. "See those lights to the left of that bank of clouds? Those are just off the white cliffs at Beachy Head. We're nearly home."

"And where would home be, Miss Chance? London?" he asked.

"Oxford actually, but I stay with my uncle and aunt in London when I am flying. They have a house off Grosvenor Square."

"And your uncle is?"

"Lord Geoffrey Chance. My father, Charles, is his younger brother."

"Professor Charles Chance?" Marsh considered the matter for a moment. "The spark-reactor scientist? *He* is your father?"

"Professor of science and engineering. Hydro-thermal combustion thaumaturgy and propulsion engines, to be precise."

"And your mother?"

She studied the cloud formations in front of her. It was a difficult question to answer. "My mother died when I was very young. That's all there is to say about her."

"And is it because of your father that you like to fly?"

Elle bristled. Her family was not a subject she liked to discuss. Especially not with strangers. "Something like that. But what about you? Where is home for you, Mr. Marsh?" she asked, turning the conversation away from herself.

"Cornwall."

She waited for him to elaborate, but he remained quiet. It was probably better that way. She wasn't sure how much she really wanted to know about him . . . or what he and Patrice were up to. All she wanted right now was a hot breakfast and a good sleep.

She stretched again. "I don't know about you, but I could do with a nice cup of tea."

"I think I could be persuaded." His face brightened at the prospect.

She reached down into one of the cabinets for the wicker basket that held her tea things and pulled out a teapot. She dropped a handful of tea leaves into it and handed it to Marsh. "Do us a favor and fill this. You'll find hot water in the samovar that runs off the reactor."

He rose and moved stiffly across the cabin to the brass samovar, clearly not as unaffected by their escape earlier as he'd let on. Elle smiled to herself. So Mr. Marsh was human after all.

Marsh put the filled teapot down on the counter between them. "This is a handsome ship," he said, eyeing the interior.

"She is lovely, isn't she?" Elle poured the tea into enameled tin mugs and spooned a liberal helping of sugar into each. The tea was strong and dark, with a swirl of leaves clouding the bottom. A freight ship was no place for fancy china.

"Who owns her?"

Elle straightened. "That would be me," she said with a touch of pride. "She's an independent charter and I hold her lease, but the British Flying Company subcontracts us for now. At least until I have enough capital to start up on my own."

He looked slightly impressed. "A woman with her own charter company. How fascinating."

"There is no reason why there shouldn't be," she said, annoyed at his tone.

He rolled his eyes. "Are we about to enter into a debate on suffrage, Miss Chance?"

"We might, if you provoke me," Elle said.

Marsh sighed. "As admirable as the movement is, you may take it from me that the Suffragettes know nothing of the true power of women."

"Oh, and I suppose you are an expert on the subject?" she said.

"Actually, I am."

"Is that a fact, now?"

"All I'm saying is that forcing the issue by way of the right to vote will never be helpful. It simply goes against that which is natural. And the loss of belief in the old ways is something we can ill afford these days."

He was being serious, she realized. She pressed her lips together to hide her disappointment. He was lovely to look at and mildly charming, but under the surface was nothing but shallow, smug arrogance. And she was not going to give him the satisfaction of becoming angry. "For Patrice." She shoved a mug at him and nodded at their softly snoring companion.

Marsh walked over to him and nudged his shoulder. Patrice sat up. He was red-cheeked and disorientated as he took hold of the mug. He muttered something in French about it not being coffee.

Elle pulled a tin of biscuits from the basket. "Here, have a bit of shortbread. Our housekeeper makes them. She is the unrivaled queen of biscuits," she said as she handed the tin around.

They drank their tea and bit into the buttery short-bread. Around them, the *Water Lily* groaned and creaked as she limped across the sky. Elle risked another sideways glance at Marsh. Yes, he was definitely a fine-looking man. He was also most certainly trouble—the kind she would do well to avoid.

The communications console rattled and spewed out a thin strip of paper tape. Elle tore it off and looked at the Morse code tapped onto it.

"Airfield coming up. They've cleared us for landing," she said with some relief. "You chaps had better finish your tea. And keep your heads down. I've seen enough trouble for one trip."

The lights of the airfield loomed into view. Elle brushed biscuit crumbs off her coat and stowed the tea things away. It was time to ready the ship for landing.

The airfield opened up below them. To the side were the gargantuan airship hangars where the biggest air-ships could be overhauled. A row of spark lights lit up on the ground, indicating a landing berth to the left.

Gently she eased off on the throttle and the *Water Lily* aligned herself with the wooden landing platform below. The thrusters spluttered into reverse. With a wheeze of steam, the dirigible berthed. Her slightly flaccid balloon keeled to one side as she shuddered against the mooring trellises. To Elle's relief, the tether ropes released when she pulled the operating lever. Patrice's circus act on takeoff hadn't entangled them as badly as she'd feared.

The night crew ran out and grabbed hold of the tether ropes. A few moments later the whistle sounded to signal that the ship was secure for disembarkation. She took a deep breath. They had made it.

Elle was about to reach for her holdall when she remembered it was gone. The loss of it made her insides lurch. The thought of some greasy absinthe-soaked lout pawing through her possessions made her nauseous, but there was nothing she could do about it. She sighed and tucked her pilot license and the ship's departure permit into her coat pocket. The holdall had been her favorite. It would take a lot of searching to find another one that she'd love as much.

They waited until the ground crew had finished tying the last ropes before Elle opened the hatch and let the rope ladder tumble down.

It had been raining and the ground squelched a muddy welcome under her boots when she stepped off the bottom rung of the ladder. She smiled. It was good to be home.

"Well, we've reached the end of our journey," she said when her passengers stepped into the mud beside her. "The freight-ship berths are miles away from the departure hall, so if you keep your heads and don't act suspiciously, no one will notice you leaving. You may have to tramp through a field or two to get to the main road though. It's that way." She gestured into the darkness. "I wish you best of luck, chaps. And Patrice, I do hope you find the man who took the viscount's box." She turned to Marsh and extended her hand.

He took it and looked into her eyes. "Thank you. For everything." She felt another jolt. What is it about this man's stare that affected her so? It really was most disconcerting.

"We really should see you through the arrivals terminal safely. In fact, I insist on it," Patrice said.

"Oh, that won't be necessary." She was in no mood to explain her unscheduled passengers to the authorities.

"Miss Chance!"

She turned at the sound of her name shouted in the distance. A lad of about ten or eleven was running across the field to meet her.

"Quick. Hide!" she said.

Marsh and Patrice stepped into the shadows.

"Miss Chance." The boy panted as he came to a stop before her. "The night superintendent wants to see you in his office as soon as you've cleared customs. He said I am to go with you. This way, please, miss," the boy said. He took off in the direction of the buildings.

Elle motioned behind her back for Marsh and Patrice to stay out of sight and then followed the boy. She had been dreading the explanations she was going to need when they discovered that she had no docking papers from Paris with her. And that was without having the Airfield Superintendent involved. She put her hands in her pockets and huddled into her coat in the crisp night air as she followed the boy across the airfield to the buildings.

Light from the arrivals hangar spilled out onto the airfield as they entered the deserted customs office. A single spark-lamp cast a lonely, bluish glow over the counters. Four rings of the counter bell eventually procured a sleepy clerk from the back. He shuffled up to one of the little windows and blinked at them in the bright light.

"No freight. Empty cargo freighter returning to home-port. The docking papers have been sent to the British Flying Company direct." She slipped the Paris departure permit across the counter. "And I need a repair and maintenance form, please. The old girl needs a good solid overhaul."

To her relief, the clerk just yawned as he found the *Water Lily* in his ledger. He stamped the arrival papers without any further questions and waved them off, intent on getting back to his nap as soon as possible.

On the other side of the customs gate, the passenger hall was also deserted. Only freight flights landed and took off at this uncivilized hour.

"This way, miss," the boy said. "Airfield Superintendent says I'm to make sure I deliver you straight to his door." They walked through the deserted building toward a row of administrative-looking doors. They followed the corridor, their boots echoing in the hollow hallway until they reached a set of doors with the words *Airfield Superintendent* painted in gold letters on them. The boy puffed out his chest and knocked on the door.

Elle took a deep breath. Now to face the music, she thought.

"Enter," someone said from within.

Elle hoped Marsh and Patrice had managed to disappear without anyone seeing them. She was going to have a serious word with Patrice the next time she saw him. A few hours' sleep in one of the airfield barracks and then the train to London sounded most attractive right now. But first there was the Superintendent to placate.

CHAPTER 6

The humid warmth of the superintendent's office enveloped Elle as she stepped inside.

"Ah, Miss Chance. Thank you for coming in. Do sit down." Airfield Superintendent Briggs beamed at her from behind his desk. He was a red-faced man in his forties who looked more as if he should be farming apples than running the night shift. He heaved himself round his desk and ushered her to a chair. "I am sorry to call you in at this hour and after your long flight, but well, ah, the matter can't really wait."

Briggs shuffled round the table to put a few logs into the cast-iron stove that squatted in the corner of his office. He jabbed at the coals with a fire poker and then closed the grate. Heat surged and the room was suddenly stifling. "That's better," he said. "Do sit down, my dear."

She caught a slight movement from the corner of her eye as she took a seat. Elle felt the hairs on the back of her neck rise slowly. Someone else was in this office, hidden in the cluttered shadows that fringed the lamplight.

The airfield master flopped back down in his chair. "Ahem, yes, Miss Chance, may I introduce Viscount Greychester." He motioned the shadow forward. "Your lordship, may I present Miss Chance."

Marsh stepped into the pool of lamplight. "How do you do, Miss Chance," he extended his hand with a formal nod.

"How . . . How do you do." Nonplussed as to how he'd managed to reach the superintendent before her, she reached out and shook his hand. His fingers were cold around hers, as if he had just come in from outside.

He released her hand and leaned against the edge of the desk, narrowing his eyes very briefly as if he was giving her a warning.

"Ahem . . . We are fortunate that his lordship happened to be waiting at the airfield for his charter when we needed him," Briggs said.

"Yes, fortunate indeed." Elle felt slightly faint. Marsh was the viscount. She should have realized it the moment she laid eyes on that fancy waistcoat of his.

He folded his arms. "Airfield Superintendent Briggs has just informed me that he received a rather disturbing cross-Channel message from Paris. Something about difficulties with the *Water Lily*?"

Briggs coughed and motioned at the spectrogram telegraph box that was perched on a bracket attached to the wall behind his desk. The ribbed rubber tubes that stuck out of the box were tangled, as if the machine had been answered in a hurry. "The French air authorities say your ship took off without proper clearance and that you were carrying contraband goods and passengers on board. They want to charge you for breach of the Aeronautical Treaty. I'm afraid that they have threatened to notify the British Flying Company of this. But I am sure it must all be a misunderstanding?"

Elle felt her insides grow cold. "They can't be serious. I had a valid departure permit."

"I'm afraid they are serious." Briggs started wringing his hands. "They say you fled from Luxembourg Airfield, resisting arrest."

"But I'm innocent. They attacked *me*!" Elle said.

Marsh interjected. "This is precisely the reason I have come to meet with you this morning, sir. I too was made aware of the matter in the course of last night and it is imperative that I intervene." He straightened to his full height. "You see, this was *my* charter flight. Miss Chance and my Paris man, Mr. Chevalier, acted on my express instructions. This is official business, the nature of which I am not at liberty to disclose at this point in time."

Briggs patted his forehead with his handkerchief. "The French authorities are seeking the immediate suspension of Miss Chance's license and I don't see how we would be able to refuse their request. At least not without creating a rather unpleasant international incident, that is."

"But that is ridiculous! I had to take off. They were shooting at my ship!" She gave Marsh a sharp look, not sure if she should say more. He shook his head ever so slightly and looked away.

"I'm sorry, I can see their point entirely," Briggs said, suddenly officious. "We can't have airships taking off and flying about at will. It would give rise to chaos and anarchy. The rules must be obeyed."

Marsh was silent.

Elle closed her eyes in despair. There was no way she could charm her way out of this mess. She was completely on her own. And her father and uncle would find out that she was flying bootleg freight on the quiet. There would be long lectures. There would be "I told you so"s and a lot of "flying is no business for a woman"s. She'd have to give up the lease on the *Water Lily*. Everything she had worked for would be lost.

She was suddenly very angry. Despite herself, her throat thickened with the urge to cry. But tears would only confirm everything these men already thought. And she was not going to let them have that pleasure. She swallowed hard at the lump of humiliation that was threatening to choke her.

Marsh cleared his throat. "Mr. Briggs, if you would

perhaps be so kind as to hand over the communication from Paris. I shall see that it is sent straight to the Ministry so we may resolve this matter along diplomatic channels." He motioned to Elle. "And if you'll allow us a moment. Perhaps a cup of tea for the lady might be appropriate?"

"Yes, of course." Briggs nodded. He shuffled off, looking distinctly grateful for Marsh's intervention in the matter.

As soon as Briggs was out the door, Marsh put his hand on her arm. "I am so sorry for putting you through this charade. I didn't think the French authorities would move so fast. I had hoped that my contacts would resolve any difficulties before there were problems." His voice was low and conspiratorial.

Elle swatted his hand away. "I am not taking the fall for this, Mr. Marsh. You dragged me into this mess and you had better get me out of it." She poked at his chest with her forefinger. "That is what Patrice promised, and a deal is a deal. So you better start by telling me the truth, or we are both going to end up in jail before the sun rises."

He leaned closer to her. "It's not safe to speak here. I will explain more later, but the truth is that we needed someone anonymous to transport us back to London. Patrice was in charge of the arrangements, which is why I think he recruited you. We were going to meet you at the airfield and I was to travel on your cargo flight, but Patrice deviated from the plan. He disappeared shortly before lunch yesterday afternoon and I spent far too long looking for him. I was rather fortunate to have found him in that café when I did. I'd thought it best to leave you ignorant about matters for your own protection. You really shouldn't have run off like that when we landed, before I had a chance to explain things. When we overheard the attendant telling you that Briggs wanted to see you, I slipped round the back while you were clearing customs. He was ready to take you into custody a few minutes ago."

She paled. "I told Patrice that I am just the pilot. He promised me there would be no trouble."

"We will resolve this. I give you my word," Marsh said.

She sat back in her seat. "And how are you planning to do that? Send a telegram to the prime minister? Petition the King?"

"If I have to. But for now, we need to keep what happened in Paris between us. Until I have spoken with my contacts. Would you mind terribly if we did that?"

Elle's despair turned to anger. "Which part would you like to keep between us, Mr. Marsh? The bit about how you lied to me, tricked me, and then almost got me killed? Or is it perhaps that the criminals and cab drivers who frequent the streets of Paris now have command of illegal alchemy that allows them to disappear in plumes of smoke? All I did was try to help you, and look where it has got me. I should have known all this was too good to be true. And besides, who exactly are you? Are you a spy or something?"

"Or something," he said. "But you have to believe this is not what you think. I have very good reasons for doing what I did."

"I don't very much care for your reasons, Mr. Marsh . . . or Lord Greychester . . . or whoever you are. I have absolutely no reason to trust you."

A look of exasperation crossed his face and he pressed his lips together. "As I see it, your options are rather limited at present. You can either trust me to get you out of this situation discreetly, or I can walk out of here and leave you to face our ruddy-cheeked friend on your own. The latter option will, more likely than not, end in your incarceration."

Elle felt her argument crumble away. She didn't want

to go to jail. And she definitely did not want her father or uncle to find out about this.

"So what's it going to be?" He drew his lips in a thin line.

"Very well, I will keep your secret," she said. "I don't see how I have any choice in the matter. And right now I just want to go home, so if you'll excuse me, I think I'll do that." Her words sounded more petulant than she had intended. Still, she pushed herself out of her seat and made for the door. She yanked at the brass door-knob just as Mr. Briggs came into the office with a cup of tea.

"Oh, Miss Chance. So close to the door," Mr. Briggs said. He sloshed the tea into the saucer as he handed her the cup of grayish brew. "Here you go, my dear. That'll perk you right up. Such a terrible shock you've had this evening."

"Mr. Briggs, I have a motor with a driver waiting. You may release Miss Chance into my care as soon as she has finished her tea," Marsh announced. He picked up his gloves. "Until this misunderstanding has been resolved, I am taking the lady into my custody."

Elle spluttered into her tea. "Excuse me? You are going to do what?"

"I am taking you into my custody until the matter is settled with the authorities. You are not to leave my sight until then."

Mr. Briggs was nodding in agreement. "I will make a note in the records, my lord."

"B-but you can't do that. Can you?" Elle said.

Marsh looked at her and his well-formed mouth curled up into a triumphant little smile. "Oh, but I can and I just did. And it's a task I take very seriously."

"Ahem, there is also the matter of your ship's repair and mooring fees," Mr. Briggs said.

"I am taking charge of the *Water Lily* as well. I will

send someone to attend to the repairs tomorrow. She can be stored in one of the hangars here in the short term. Please arrange to have the accounts sent to my secretary," Marsh said. He held up his hand to stop Elle before she could speak. "And I'll not hear another word on the matter. The mooring fees are for my account too. I insist. It's the least I can do." There was a little gleam in his eye warning her not to push the point.

Elle felt the urge to smack him. The man was unbelievable, but now was not the time to fight that battle. She would do much better if she bided her time. Enemies kept close are enemies known.

Elle set the cup in its swampy saucer down on the desk, where it would leave a mark on the wood; a gift for Mr. Briggs to find later. She straightened her coat and lifted her chin "Very well, then, Lord Greychester. We had better be off. We have quite a way to travel yet."

He held the door for her and they walked down the corridor in silence.

Outside, Patrice had collected Marsh's car from one of the private stables at the airfield. The motor gleamed in the light of the airfield terminus, in all its white paint and silver-riveted loveliness.

"Beautiful, isn't she?" Marsh said. "It's a Stanley."

She turned on him. "I don't know who you think you are, Mr. Marsh, but if you think you are going to use this situation to get your hands on my ship, you are very seriously mistaken. Don't think I didn't see you eyeing her while we were in the air."

"Ah yes, the little airship. I give you my word that she will be safe. As long as you do what I say."

"Your word? How am I supposed to accept that?"

He sighed and took her by the elbow. "Well, as I see it, my word is the best you are going to get for now." He swiveled her round to face the doors they had just left.

"But we could always go back to the superintendent's office if you prefer."

Elle clenched her molars together so tightly she felt her jaw creak. "Fine." She turned back so she faced the car again. His body moved in time with hers as if they were dancing. "I will go with you, but don't think for one moment that this discussion is over."

"Oh, I don't doubt that. But in time you will come to see that I am quite an honorable fellow. Isn't that right, Patrice?"

Patrice just shook his head and chuckled at them from where he was sitting in the driver's seat.

Marsh opened the door for her. "After you, madam."

Elle glared at him as she got into the machine. Grudgingly, she had to admit that the motor really was a thing of beauty. The outside gleamed with white paintwork and brass tubing. Dual reactors, by the looks of it.

She allowed herself to sink into the plush seat. And though she would never admit it, she was secretly relieved to be going straight home. The bunks in the pilot quarters at the airfield were not always that pleasant, and it would be hours before the first trains to London started running. Home was where she wanted to be right now. The edge of the bracelet slipped from beneath her sleeve as she sat down. Quickly she tucked it away. Hopefully the fairy would stay asleep until then.

Marsh sat beside her. He ran his hand over the seat. "I quite like the new shape, don't you? Six-point-five horsepower. Fast as a bullet, she is. With the dual reactor and new patented micro-condensers, we get about twenty miles to a gallon of water. It helps that the canals are close by though."

"If you like that kind of thing," Elle said. She had no intention of paying his stupid motor compliments.

He didn't respond. Instead, he said to Patrice, "Shall we, old man?"

Patrice took a last puff of his little black cigar and flicked the glowing ember into the night. He eased the accelerator lever forward and the steam car slid into motion. They were going to Oxford.

The car prattled and huffed as it sped along the dark country lanes. Elle watched Marsh surreptitiously from her corner of the backseat. His eyes were closed as he rested his head against the leather. Lord Greychester. She was sure she'd heard that name before.

"It's not polite to stare, you know," he drawled after a few minutes.

Elle bit her lip. He'd caught her. Again. To hide her embarrassment, she pulled the travel rug on her lap around her and closed her eyes, quietly grateful that her glowing cheeks would not be that obvious in the dark.

He chuckled softly.

He would need watching. She would have to keep her eye on him every step of the way, she thought as the rocking of the car lulled her into an exhausted sleep.

CHAPTER 7

Marsh watched Elle sleep, wrapped up in a mohair travel rug. Vivienne Chance's daughter. He only made the connection once they were in the air. And with her surname as plain as it was before him.

Miss Chance was a difficult woman, that was plain. She was monstrously stubborn, with a tongue as sharp to match. But he had to admit there was something about her.

He studied the fine curve of her nose. She was very pretty. He bristled at the thought. He'd learned his lessons on the subject of beautiful women well enough. And bitter lessons they were; bitter enough for him to know better.

He sighed and pinched the bridge of his nose in an attempt to drive away the tiredness that was threatening to swallow him whole. The loss of the box was a blow to their cause. He should never have allowed Patrice to deviate from their plan. And now he had to deal with the added complication of this woman.

Elle shifted position and nestled her head against the leather of the seat in search of a more comfortable spot. A few strands of her hair had worked their way out of the low knot at the base of her neck. They were draped across her cheek as she slept, gently moving in the breeze that the motor stirred up. Marsh resisted the urge to lift them out of the way.

Careful not to wake her, he placed his bare fingers

against her temple and focused his energies on her. As a general rule, he had serious moral objections to using his abilities on people. It was not the way of the Brotherhood, but he needed to make sure this was really Vivienne's daughter. And this was the quickest way. He felt the tiny facial muscles under her skin relax beneath his fingertips. Then he closed his own eyes and allowed himself to drift away as he synchronized his mind with the velvety luxury of her sleep patterns.

He felt a sudden shift. He drew back in surprise and stared at his fingers. They were tingling. He reached out and touched her temple again. A jolt of energy crackled under his fingertips. She was pushing him away. In her sleep.

Marsh blinked in the dark. Was it even possible? After all these years? He sat back in his seat and stared out before him; his mind reeling with the implications of what he had discovered. Forget the Ministry. They were a bunch of impotent bureaucrats. He needed to speak to the Council about this. But first he needed more proof. And extracting it was going to be a delicate task, if today was anything to go by.

He rubbed his eyes again. This mess was becoming more complicated by the minute.

When they reached the outskirts of the town of Windsor, they stopped to refill the water tanks.

"She all right?" Patrice asked. He had a smoldering cigar clasped between his lips as he helped Marsh haul the hoses and the hand pump out from the hatch behind the boot.

"Fine. She's asleep. It's been a long day."

They dragged the hoses to the canal.

"You picked her for more than her flying skills, didn't you? What are you not telling me, Patrice?"

His companion just shrugged as he puffed at his ubiquitous little black cigar, in a very Gallic, "I have no idea what you are on about" gesture. Patrice could be a stubborn bugger when he wanted to be. "Word on the street is that she has talents other than flying freight. I thought it might be fun if we used her. And she has a pretty face. I thought you might like that. It's not my fault she didn't take to you."

"We both know that's not what this is about."

Patrice's eyes glittered sharp for a moment in the light of the lantern. "Why? Have you found something?" Somewhere in the distance an owl called out in the black night.

"I'm not certain," Marsh said.

"So you did find something in her."

"Perhaps. I can't tell for sure."

"Then we should find out. This could be important."

"All in good time. I'm not about to wake our young lady on the suspicion that she might be special. I think I have faced her temper enough times for one day. There is always tomorrow."

"If you say so." Patrice shrugged and they cranked water into the tank in silence for a few moments.

"You think he's home?" He inclined his chin in the direction of the looming shape of Windsor Castle, darker against the night sky in the distance.

"He, *mon ami*, should be referred to as his majesty, the King of England. And no, I believe the King has already left for his annual visit to his favorite spa in Switzerland. His majesty adheres to a very regular routine." Marsh closed the water tank with more force than was strictly necessary. "That should do it, don't you think?"

Patrice puffed at the last of his cigar and flicked it aside. The butt glowed orange where it fell in the wet grass.

They rolled up the dripping hoses and stored them in the compartment under the steam car.

"Here, let me have a go. You've been driving for hours and I'm bored in the back," Marsh said.

Patrice shrugged and settled in the front passenger seat, next to Marsh. He pulled his hat over his eyes and flipped his coat collar up against the crisp night air. Marsh took hold of the steering lever, engaged the gears and eased the accelerator lever forward. The spark reactor glowed and the automobile trundled off into the night.

PART II

OXFORD

CHAPTER 8

The famous spires of Oxford glimmered through the morning haze shortly after eight o'clock that morning. Elle straightened up from underneath her travel blanket and looked about. The morning sun flickered on the river and bounced off damp leaves as they passed Iffley Lock and the part of the river they called the Isis. Her spirits rose; she would be home soon.

"Good morning." Marsh turned round from where he was sitting in the front passenger seat and smiled at her. Dark stubble covered his chin.

"Oh, good morning. Have I slept the whole way?" She straightened her shirt and tucked her hair back into its knot.

"The whole way," Patrice said over his shoulder without taking his hands off the steering lever.

"Did we stop?"

"Indeed we did. Twice. You even missed the part where I drove," Marsh said. "But if you'd oblige us with a few directions, we shall stop for a third time to deliver you home safe and sound."

Soon the steam car pulled up outside the house she shared with her father. Situated on the outskirts of town, it was a new house as far as houses in Oxford went. It had been built in the style the King's mother, Queen Victoria, had favored some thirty years before. Elle loved the redbrick front and the white stonework around the windows. It reminded her of the gingerbread houses one saw around Christmastime.

"Pull into the coach yard behind the house, if you don't mind," she said. "It will be easier to turn the car around that way."

The steam car shook to a halt on the gravel behind the house. It hissed as Patrice released the steam in the engine pressure tanks. Startled by the noise, a fat wood pigeon flew off the lead-roofed spire, an acknowledgment of their arrival at a house that was otherwise silent.

Elle stretched her back as she stepped onto gravel. Her body ached all over from sleeping upright. She stopped mid-stretch and gripped Marsh by the arm.

"What?" he said.

She raised a finger to her lips for them to be silent and pointed at the back door. It was ajar.

"Something's wrong," she whispered.

Marsh motioned for her and Patrice to take up positions on either side of the door frame. The sound of gravel crunching underfoot as they tried to be quiet was excruciating.

The brickwork pressed against Elle's back as she flattened herself to the wall. Marsh leaned forward and pushed the door with his boot. The old wooden door creaked open to reveal a patch of red tile kitchen floor.

Silence. The house was quiet . . . and dark.

Elle held her breath in an attempt to still her heart as it hammered against the inside of her rib cage. She craned her neck forward to get a better look, but Marsh pushed her back against the wall. His hand felt heavy and warm against her stomach. Silently he mouthed the word *stay.*

With slow, deliberate movements, the two men entered the kitchen.

Seconds ticked by in time with the pulse of blood through Elle's veins.

A woman screamed, followed by a flash of light and a loud metallic clang that ended the silence.

"Oh my goodness—Mrs. Hinges!" Elle ran into the kitchen.

Patrice was on his knees on the floor, holding the side of his head. Marsh stood over Mrs. Hinges, who was armed with a large cast-iron frying pan.

"No, don't hurt her!" Elle shouted.

Everyone looked at her.

"Eleanor!" Mrs. Hinges pushed Marsh out of the way and folded Elle into a big hug that pressed the pan handle into Elle's back. "Oh, my darling girl, I've been beside myself with worry. Thank heavens you are all safe. Now, get away from us, you devils!" Up went the frying pan to its former defensive position.

"There is no need for any of that." Elle disentangled herself from Mrs. Hinges and pushed the frying pan down. "Mr. Marsh over there was kind enough to bring me all the way home from the airfield. I'm so sorry to have startled you. What on earth is going on here? Why is the house so dark?"

"Get back, I say!" Mrs. Hinges glared at the men with wild eyes. Her long salt-and-pepper hair was hanging down her back in a braid and her normally immaculate starched apron was stained and crumpled.

Elle gave Marsh a warning look. "I think we should all take a moment to calm down, don't you?"

Marsh nodded at Patrice and they both took a step back.

"Mrs. Hinges, this is Mr. Marsh—I mean Viscount Greychester—and this is Patrice Chevalier, my docking agent and his lordship's man."

The older woman's eyebrows shot up and the frying pan wavered.

"Gentlemen, may I present Mrs. Mathilda Hinges, our housekeeper and dear friend."

"Ah, the unrivaled queen of shortbread biscuits. How do you do, madam." Marsh bowed politely.

Mrs. Hinges nodded at Patrice suspiciously and turned to Marsh.

"How do you do, my lord." Her free hand fluttered to the base of her neck and she bobbed an unsteady curtsey.

She turned to Elle and gave her a stern look. "Eleanor, what on earth are you doing, bringing important guests into the house through the back door, like thieves? Do you realize that I could have killed them?"

"I'm sure you could have. But more importantly why were you hiding in the kitchen armed with the frying pan?"

In answer, tears welled up and collected in the crinkles around the older woman's eyes. "Oh, it was terrible. I've not slept a wink all night. They came into the house after midnight and took him. You know how he likes to work late sometimes. Grabbed him out of his study. I was fast asleep when— The commotion woke me." She wiped at her face.

Elle frowned. "Who? Who came?"

"Oh, they were like devils, they were. All wrapped up in cloaks." She eyed Marsh's carriage cloak. "They came into the house through the front door and grabbed the professor, right where he was in his study. They didn't even let him put on his coat." She sniffed and rubbed her eyes.

"My father has been abducted?"

"Constable Pierce only left about an hour ago. A proper case has been opened and everything, but what do the local lads know about such a crime? This is the work of Shadow, I tell you." She shook her head and set the frying pan down on the kitchen table. "What has the world come to that we're not even safe in our own beds anymore? That's what I'd like to know."

"No!" Elle strode past Mrs. Hinges, through the kitchen and into the house. She tore up the stairs, flinging open doors on the second floor until she reached the professor's bedroom. The bed was made. No one had slept in it.

She bounded down the stairs and into her father's study. It too was empty. The professor's chair lay on its side and books and papers were scattered across the parquet floor.

Shock enveloped Elle like a wet wool blanket and she sank to her knees. The others found her there a few minutes later.

"Oh, my dear girl. I'm so sorry. I should have watched over him more carefully." Mrs. Hinges put her arm around Elle.

Marsh spoke. "Mrs. Hinges, Miss Chance is currently in my charge and so it falls to me to assist in these circumstances." There was quiet authority in his voice.

Mrs. Hinges rubbed her eyes again. "In your charge? But I don't understand."

"It's all a silly misunderstanding. Nothing to be concerned over. *Mr.* Marsh was just about to leave," Elle said.

"On the contrary. I think my stay here has just begun," Marsh said.

"I said, you are leaving."

"And I said I am not going anywhere—not until I know what has happened here."

They glared at one another. Neither blinked.

"Perhaps we should hear what his lordship thinks," Mrs. Hinges said.

"I don't really care what he thinks. This is none of his business."

"Oh, but I think it is," he said. "Especially since I so recently find myself in charge of a certain freight ship, currently moored in Croydon." There was a dangerous edge to his voice.

"Eleanor. Where are your manners?" said Mrs. Hinges, now fully composed. "And if you are going to insist on wearing that terrible shirt, at least make sure that it is tucked in properly."

Elle suppressed a sigh as she straightened her shirt. Mrs. Hinges was a formidable woman; there was no arguing with her once her mind was made up. And she supposed it wouldn't hurt to have Mr. Marsh where she could keep an eye on him. "Very well, you can stay. But don't get too comfortable."

"Oh, I will do my best not to." Marsh gave her one of his irritating little smiles.

Mrs. Hinges straightened her apron, fished a handkerchief from her pocket and dabbed her eyes. "Well, gentlemen, I had better take your coats, then. Perhaps a spot of breakfast is called for. You must be hungry after your long journey. If you'll follow me, I'll show you to the guest rooms, where you may wash up. This way, if you please."

Elle glared at Marsh as he followed Mrs. Hinges from the room. But she had her ship to think of and so she would have to play his strange little game a little longer.

"Don't worry, little one. I am here to help. I won't let him take the *Water Lily*, you have my word on that," Patrice whispered as he walked past.

"Thank you. You are a gallant and true friend," Elle said. "It's good to know that I have someone I can rely on."

CHAPTER 9

About an hour later, Elle had swapped her flying clothes
for a demure gray skirt and white blouse with a brooch
at the throat. She had even taken the time to pin her hair
up in a rather fetching Gibson Girl knot. Ready to face
them as the model of poised sensibility, she squared her
shoulders as she strode downstairs. This time she was
not going to let Marsh get under her skin like he had in
the Superintendent's offices at the airfield.

Marsh and Patrice were in the dining room. Mrs.
Hinges had set the table on damask and was busy pouring tea into the good teacups.

"Ah, the aviatrix transforms into an elegant lady," Patrice said with some appreciation as he and Marsh rose
from the table.

"Please sit." She waved them down. "Mrs. Hinges,
may I see you for a moment?"

"Of course, dear."

Elle followed the housekeeper through to the kitchen.
"What are you doing?" she asked the moment she closed
the door behind them.

"Why, I was busy pouring tea for his lordship before
you dragged me away." Mrs. Hinges set the teapot down
on the kitchen table. "I've been saving a bit of ham for
your father's tea, but it seems like he's not going to be
needing it for the minute, so I thought I would let his
lordship have it with a fried egg."

"Mrs. Hinges, you must tell me everything about my

father's disappearance. I need to know what happened." Elle glanced over her shoulder at the closed door that led to the dining room. "I've had nothing but trouble since I met Mr. Marsh. And he may have dragged Patrice into this mess too. I don't want them to get too comfortable. Not until I know who is behind all this."

"Oh, I wouldn't have thought it was as bad as that, dear. I've read about Lord Greychester in the society pages." She tapped the side of her nose. "They say his family is descended from old money. They say he has a touch of the old blood in him. Very well known in Shadow circles."

"I don't care how much money he has. Shadow or not, the man is nothing but trouble."

Mrs. Hinges pressed her lips together in a firm line. "I think we are very lucky to have his lordship here to help us. You should be grateful that he is taking an interest in you. You won't see many gentlemen of his caliber about these days. Especially not ones willing to help silly girls out of a pickle." From the drying rack, she picked up the frying pan that had so recently made its acquaintance with the side of Patrice's head and placed it on the stove. The fact that Elle had chosen a life of flying over the respectability of a good husband and children was a tender issue.

"Please, Mrs. Hinges, don't be like that," Elle pleaded.

Mrs. Hinges looked at her sharply. "Your father hired me all those years ago to help him raise you after your mother died. I have known you all your life and I know what silly thoughts you have in that head of yours sometimes." She waved the egg lifter at her. "The thought of someone like his lordship involved in a despicable crime like your father's disappearance is just about one of the silliest ideas you've ever had. For every finger pointed forward there are usually three fingers pointed back."

The older woman let the accusation hang in the air between them.

"So what you're saying is that this is all *my* fault?"

Mrs. Hinges tutted and broke an egg into the pan. It crackled and sizzled as it hit the hot fat. "I'm saying nothing of the sort. And don't you go thinking that either. But there is nothing wrong with accepting a helping hand offered in friendship. You would do well to remember that instead of pointing a finger at anyone."

"Let's send a telegram to Uncle Geoffrey. He'll know what to do."

"You know how things are between them. If there is anyone powerful and influential enough to find your father quickly, then it is his lordship. Now go and sit down at the table and mind your manners."

Elle sighed and went to the dining room.

Marsh and Patrice were busy helping themselves to a stack of freshly buttered toast from the bread-toaster apparatus perched on the sideboard. The toast-maker was a metal box fashioned in the shape of a castle, complete with turrets. It was fitted with a tiny spark reactor under the keep. A small conveyor belt fed the sliced bread into the machine, where it was toasted by the heat from the reactor before being dropped out from the portcullis and onto the recipient's plate, amidst the whirring and ticking sound of tiny gears.

"What a clever machine!" Patrice pulled a perfectly toasted slice of bread from the conveyor belt with a pair of silver tongs and added it to the growing pile of toast on his plate.

"Yes, it is, isn't it? No more burnt fingers from holding toasting forks in front of the fire. Or cold toast arriving on a tray." Elle helped herself to two slices from Patrice's stack and sat down at the table.

Mrs. Hinges was right. What she really wanted to know was if this business with her father had been her fault. The possibility was almost too much to bear thinking about. Her poor father. Where was he? What was she going to do?

"Miss Chance, are you quite well?" Marsh asked.

Elle blinked. "Yes. I'm fine."

Mrs. Hinges bustled into the dining room and set plates of fried eggs and ham in front of them. The eggs looked and smelled ravishing. Elle's insides gurgled at the smell of the food. She realized that the queasy feeling in her stomach was hunger. She picked up a piece of toast and dipped it into her egg.

Marsh sat next to her, eating and making notes in a notebook with a pencil, oblivious to the offense he was causing.

She bit into her toast in resentful silence.

Eventually, Patrice set his fork down. "My head hurts like the devil is dancing upon it," he muttered. He explored the angry purple lump on the side of his head in the reflection of the silver milk jug.

Marsh looked up and smiled. "Looks like Mrs. Hinges got the better of you, old chap."

"Mr. Chevalier, perhaps you should lie down and rest for a while. I think a cold compress might take that swelling down, hmm?" Mrs. Hinges said.

"The prospect of a nap does sound appealing. It's been a long night," Patrice said.

"Well, why don't you go upstairs and lie down. I will bring you a compress and some headache powders in a minute," Mrs. Hinges said.

Patrice allowed himself to be led away while Mrs. Hinges fussed over him.

"Patrice appears to have had a lucky escape this morning. Some parts of Oxford are more perilous than the backstreets of Paris, it seems." Marsh gave Elle an amused look.

Elle set her fork down. "Mrs. Hinges is a good woman

and she was only trying to defend herself. I would have done exactly the same if it were me. In fact, I'm minded to fetch that frying pan right now."

Marsh looked at her with surprise. "I beg your pardon?"

"Mr. Marsh, you may sit here at your leisure, having your tea and eggs as it pleases you, but I cannot. Not while I know that my father is out there somewhere. Alone."

Marsh set his fork down. "You are quite correct. Forgive me for considering your comfort and welfare before launching into a major search operation." He set his mouth in a grim line.

"My comfort and welfare?" she snapped. "My father could be dying or worse as we speak!"

"That may be so, but there is much we need to consider before we proceed."

Her temper flared. "Consider? There is nothing to consider." She pointed at him. "You, sir, have been nothing but trouble since we met. I've been attacked, nearly killed, you've stolen my ship and my father has gone missing. And you didn't even have the decency to tell me your real name and title!" She paused to draw a little exasperated breath. "If I were a betting woman, I would wager that none of this is a coincidence, so why on earth should I believe anything you say?"

"Are you quite finished?"

"I am not. I would very much like to know the real reason you are here. What do you want with us? I will need this information for the police constable when I go to see him later."

He stared at her for a long moment. "Attacks on my character, Miss Chance, do not sit well with me." His voice held that dangerous edge again. "And I'll not have you blundering into this matter, only to destroy all hope of rescuing the professor alive. If your father's abductors are who I suspect they are, then they're not men one should wish to trifle with. Their network spreads everywhere. They operate with calculated force and precision. I, for one, have no wish to run after these men unprepared. Now oblige me and finish your breakfast. Please."

Elle picked up her fork and spooned some egg into her mouth with as much nonchalance as she could muster. She hated to admit it, but he was right. He always seemed to be right—something that was becoming most annoying. "Well then, what do you propose we do?"

"*We* are not going to do anything. *I* am going to make sure that *you* are safe, and once that is accomplished, Patrice and I will find these men. We have ways to make them tell us what they've done with your father. And once I have established your father's whereabouts, then he and I will rescue him."

"And what am I supposed to do in the meantime?"

"I don't know. Staying alive might be a good start."

"Very well, then, I shall go back to work and ask for a new assignment. I am taking my ship back."

His face grew stern. "Absolutely not. I forbid it." He placed his palm on the table.

Elle's temper raged. "How dare you forbid me to do anything? You are not my father or my husband!" So much for the model of poise and sensibility.

"I might not be, yet here I find myself in charge of you. Again." He gestured in exasperation. "What will you have me do? Shall I marry you so I can force you to listen to me?"

"I'd rather eat my own foot than marry a man like you."

He leaned toward her. "I should propose to you right now, just to see you try."

She leaned forward to reply, but realized her mistake almost immediately. Her face was suddenly only inches away from his.

His eyes darkened. The reaction was animalistic, almost predatory. Very gently he reached over to trace the line of her jaw, lifting her face even closer. His touch made little tremors sift through her. She closed her eyes, lost in the sensation.

But the sound of Mrs. Hinges thumping down the stairs, humming loudly, tore the moment apart.

Marsh let go of Elle and sat back in his chair. He pinched the bridge of his nose and closed his eyes. "Please forgive me. That was entirely inappropriate. It has been two days since I've slept properly and my patience is worn somewhat thin."

She stared at him, too mesmerized to speak.

"I am not a man who was blessed with deep reserves of patience. You would do well not to provoke me like that again."

Elle blinked, breaking out of her trance. "Right, then. We will rest a while and then set out to find my father. But I am still coming with you, Mr. Marsh, and there is nothing you can do about it."

A shuffling sound preceded Mrs. Hinges as she made her way toward the dining room. "Let's not upset Mrs. Hinges any further by fighting. She's had quite enough shocks for one day, don't you think?" Elle said.

"Agreed." His voice was soft, intimate.

Elle turned back to her now cool eggs and toast just as Mrs. Hinges entered the room.

"My lord, I just wanted to let you know that Mr. Chevalier is resting. He says he should be back on his feet in an hour or two."

Marsh smiled. "That's wonderful, Mrs. Hinges. But let him rest. I think we are all a little tired." He cast a quick look at Elle.

Mrs. Hinges nodded. "Indeed so, my lord. Indeed so."

"And, Mrs. Hinges . . ."

"Yes, my lord?"

"Thank you for taking us in. That was very kind of you." He gave her one of his special smiles.

A red flush crept up over the housekeeper's cheeks. "Oh, no need to thank me, my lord. It's the least we can do. But I did think that once your lordship is finished with breakfast, we should take a look at the professor's study to look for clues. The police have already been but I insisted the constable leave everything the way he found it. I read in the papers that this is what one should do."

"Excellent work, Mrs. Hinges. That is exactly what I intend to do, as soon as Miss Chance has finished her toast."

Elle swallowed the bite of toast she had been chewing. Did he have to sound so assured? It really was most annoying.

CHAPTER 10

Elle's father's study was on the other side of the house—away from the *domesticity,* as he liked to call it. It was a well-proportioned room, dominated by a large drawing table that stood in the middle of the parquet floor. The tabletop was littered with rolled-up bits of wax paper and drawings. Schematics were pinned open on it, held down by brass gear disks or hunks of metal that looked like they had once been part of a machine at some point. A morose fern sat in a brass bucket on a pedestal in the corner.

Someone had picked up the overturned chair, but papers were still strewn all over the floor. But then again, the professor was so messy, it would have been entirely possible to ransack the place without anyone noticing.

Elle watched Marsh survey the professor's clutter. He made a note in his pocketbook as he examined the rows of leather-bound books neatly lined up along the shelves. He looked over at the plans on the table. "Interesting," he murmured.

"Oh, he's been working on those for years." Elle ran her fingers over the papers with affection. "He has this theory that it is possible to build aerodyne flying machines. You know, ones that propel themselves and don't require a float like the dirigibles do. He keeps his research secret though. There are many who want to know his ideas."

Marsh leafed through the plans. "I believe this is not

dissimilar to the work of Mr. Wright and his brother in America."

"My father corresponds with them. I think the current topic of debate is steering mechanisms."

She sat down in her father's battered high-back leather chair. The professor had modified the seat at some stage so it could swivel round. Little brass pistons could be manipulated to achieve the correct height and pitch of the chair. He had also replaced the feet with brass wheels so he could move across the room without getting up. The chair wobbled and skidded as it adjusted to Elle's body. The leather smelled like her father, a mixture of engine grease and tobacco. She suddenly felt very lonely and small.

Marsh was staring down at her. "Are you all right?" He looked concerned.

"I'm so worried about him. Do you think his abductor might have been someone who wanted the designs for the flight machines?"

"I don't know. But we will find the professor. I promise."

She nodded and bit her lip. It was proving to be quite difficult to hate Mr. Marsh when he was being this kind to her. Her eyes prickled with the urge to cry again.

"Do you think he'll mind if we go through his papers?" Marsh opened one of the drawers in the professor's writing desk.

"I'm sure he won't, given his current plight."

"You take that side. I'll take this one. We might find something among all this stuff." He swiveled her chair around so she faced the desk.

The desk was crammed with bits of paper. Old accounts and invoices and scraps of paper with mathematical equations scribbled over them were shoved into every conceivable crevice.

"This is like looking for a needle in a haystack," Elle said after a few minutes of rifling.

He nodded and pulled out another wad of papers from one of the cubbyholes. "I think your father might need an assistant." He leafed through the sheets.

"The state of this study is a lost cause. Trust me, we've tried." She sat back in the chair. "It's always been like this. I remember, when I was little he used to pull out the side panels of the desk so I could sit next to him. We would do sums together for hours." Those had been the days when her father could ignore the fact that she was a girl. "Look. It opens up if you undo this latch." She reached over and unhitched the latch that held the wood panel of the desk in place and slid it out. An envelope fell out and onto the floor.

Marsh picked it up. "I believe this might be for you." He handed her the envelope.

Her name was scrawled on the face of it in her father's eccentric copperplate handwriting, along with the words *In case they come*. She stuck her finger into the corner and ripped the paper open.

"Bravo, professor," Marsh said.

Inside was a key. She held it up and examined it. "I know what this opens!" she said with a sudden wave of inspiration. She jumped out of the chair. It wobbled dangerously, but stayed upright.

"Come with me. It's this way." She opened the French doors that led from the study into the garden. At the bottom of the garden was a stone wall with a gate. In the middle of the field that lay behind the gate was a barn. Elle ran across the garden and opened the gate. Marsh caught up with her outside the wooden doors of the barn.

"This is my father's other workshop." She was out of breath from running in her skirts and stays. She slid the key into the padlock and swung the doors open.

Elle and Marsh blinked into the windowless gloom.

"There is a switch over here somewhere." She fumbled around until she found the lever that activated the spark lights. "Ta-daa!" she said with a flourish. The barn filled with dusty light. To one side were a workbench and a lathe. Rows of tools and instruments lined the lime-washed walls.

"What on earth is that?" Marsh pointed at a contraption that was partly covered by a large piece of canvas. It took up more than half of the workshop.

Elle pulled away the canvas. "He's built it! He's actually finished one of his flying machines," she said as the canvas slid off to reveal a set of sleek brass-and-steel rotor blades that drooped ever so slightly as they hung from the cockpit.

"Do you know how to fly one of these things?" Marsh said.

"I'm not sure. I don't think anyone has ever flown one before, but I am familiar with its dynamics. I'd certainly love to try." She walked round the machine and stared at the exposed engine, situated between the tail and the cockpit. "Just look at those spark reactors!"

"And how far do you think it could fly?"

"Oh, I don't know. As far as we want it to." Elle ran her hand over the polished surface and smiled to herself. She had a plan.

CHAPTER 11

"His lordship said for me to tell you that he had some business to attend to in town and that he'd be back later. The fishmonger's been round this morning and I've got a nice bit of plaice for tonight's dinner," Mrs. Hinges said when Elle wandered into the kitchen shortly before noon. She was furiously scrubbing potatoes in a bowl of water. Elle felt a little sorry for the poor potatoes.

Elle sat down beside her. "Mrs. Hinges, are you all right?"

The older woman gave her a sad smile. "Busy hands make the time pass. There is no sense in sitting around feeling sorry for oneself, now is there? It won't bring the professor back, now will it? One must carry on, no matter how hard it might be sometimes." She picked up another potato and plunged it into the basin.

"Why do you think they took him?" she said.

Mrs. Hinges stopped working and looked at her. "I honestly don't know, dear." There was a slight tremor in the older woman's voice. "There are many who would pay a lot of money to be privy to his work."

Elle felt a profound sense of anxiety and dread as she considered this. There had to be more to it than that, and she didn't like the direction her thoughts were taking.

She picked one of Mrs. Hinges' excellent strawberry tarts off the plate before her and straightened up. Sitting here at the kitchen table brooding wasn't going to make matters better. "Mrs. Hinges, I will be in the workshop if you need me."

"Oh, do be careful, my dear. His lordship said that we shouldn't go wandering off by ourselves. He said to stay indoors, where it is safe. It's best not to take any chances." Mrs. Hinges sounded quite distressed at the thought.

"Blast what that man says. I have some business of my own to attend to," Elle said as she left the kitchen.

The reassuring smell of engine grease and dust greeted her as she opened the doors of the workshop. She was keen to have a closer look at the flying machine, but the first order of business was to see if she could do something about the bracelet around her wrist. She picked up a pair of sturdy pliers. It seemed a pity ruining such a fine piece, but needs must. And the sooner she was rid of the creepy thing, the better. She tightened the pliers around the metal, close to the clasp, and pressed down with all her might. The bracelet started writhing and wriggling as if it were in pain. Startled, she let go of the pliers and examined it with her optic, but apart from a soft green glow of the diamonds which was presumably the fairy, there was not a mark on it—not even a scratch.

She tried again to separate the clasp, this time by clamping the bracelet in the vice and hitting it with a hammer. Once again it started vibrating, and this time also let out a bolt of energy, which was so potent, it nearly knocked Elle off her feet.

"Ow!" She rubbed her wrist, where the skin was now red, and promptly dismissed the use of her father's spark-welding torch. Clearly the bracelet had no intention of going anywhere for the foreseeable future. She sighed and stood up from the workbench. She was going to have to ask her father for help with this as soon as he was home safely. And finding him was her first priority now.

She glanced over to the other side of the workshop.

The flying machine glowed brown and bronze under the light of the naked spark globes. Disturbed dust particles shimmered in the light around it.

Elle picked up a wrench and eyed the fuselage critically. The brass-smiths her father used to manufacture his inventions had done good work here. It was a beautifully crafted piece of machinery. She could hardly believe that her father had built the entire design without telling her about it.

The elegant lines of the machine reminded her of a dragonfly ready to take flight. It sat on four small wheels that could move independently from one another in order to maneuver the machine about on the ground. A glass-paned dome with red velvet seats inside rested on top of the wheels. At the back of the dome a metal cage held the spark reactor and water tanks. The cage tapered off into the tail. On top of the glass dome, a large propeller drooped downward in a slight curve. Another smaller propeller sat at the tail end.

"Let's see what's inside you," she said to the machine. She opened the engine compartment and started tinkering with the reactor. The faint blue-green of a spark reactor under her hands always had a way of soothing her. This was the heart of the machine—its essence. And this one was particularly lovely. Her father had used a configuration she had not seen before.

Elle liked working on machines. They had specific rules, and best of all, they were predictable. Safe. Unlike people, who were just the opposite.

With her curiosity aroused, she started following the brass tubes and connectors to the various parts that made the engine work. Within minutes, she was under the spell that only a finely made machine could cast.

She was so deeply engrossed in the inner workings that she did not hear Marsh approach.

"Now, that's something one doesn't see every day," he said behind her.

Elle froze. She was bent over with her head inside the spark reactor, trying to reach a connection at the bottom of it. In a pang of acute mortification she realized that her bottom was, at that very moment, raised up and poking out of the cage. The gentle curves of her *derrière* would be quite clearly visible through her coveralls that were drawn tight from stretching for the connection she was inspecting.

She clipped the connection into place and dragged herself out of the machine with as much dignity as she could muster.

"Lord Greychester. Good afternoon to you," she said, tucking an escaped strand of hair behind her ear.

"Ah, now it's 'Lord Greychester.'" He adjusted the angle of his head to meet her gaze. "What happened to 'Marsh'?"

He was enjoying the moment far more than was appropriate, Elle thought. She crossed her arms across her chest and raised her chin. "And how may I assist you?" she said, cooling her tone. It was all she could do to hide her embarrassment.

His smile faded and he shrugged. "I am pleased to see that you have recovered from last night's ordeal. Mrs. Hinges was most concerned about you. She asked me to tell you that it is time for you to dress for dinner. I felt like a bit of a walk, so here I am. I find that fresh air does wonders for the constitution. It has been lovely weather we've been having of late." He looked up at the darkening sky. "Most unusual for this time of year, don't you think?"

"Is it that late already?" She glanced at the clock on the other side of the workshop, ignoring his strange comment about the weather.

He walked up to the machine and ran his hand over

the gleaming brass-work, not unlike one would when inspecting a finely bred horse. Elle found herself distracted by the elegant taper of his fingers as they glided over the gleaming wood.

"Any news?" she said.

"The police know very little."

"So where do we start?" She put down the rag she'd used to wipe the grease from her hands.

"I have a few suspicions, but I honestly don't know. I suspect we will have to wait until we hear from the kidnappers." He looked troubled.

Elle ran her hand over her forehead. "Surely there must be more we can do?"

Marsh sighed. "At least we know that they want him alive. They wouldn't have gone to all the trouble of taking him if they didn't. So all we can do for the moment is wait."

To distract herself, Elle picked up the wrench and screwdrivers she'd been using and put them back into the toolbox.

"That really is a fascinating-looking machine," Marsh said, pointing at the contraption.

Elle nodded. "I've decided I shall name this machine a gyrocopter."

"A gyrocopter," he said. "Nice name. How far do you think you would be able to fly this thing?"

She turned her head to one side and contemplated the question. "I think I might need to practice, but if the mechanics are sound and there is enough water for steam, I see no reason why we couldn't fly as far as we wished. And look," she pointed at the wheels. "It's designed to be maneuverable. It can go and land wherever one wants. No more timetables or delays."

"Miss Chance, you are truly a most surprising woman." He touched the rim of his hat. "Mrs. Hinges says dinner is in an hour and I shall leave you to finish your examination of the mechanics in private." He turned away and left the workshop.

She watched him walk away with the strange sense that there was something more to that invitation. As if she needed his approval.

CHAPTER 12

Dinner that evening, as promised, was fish followed by a large roast hen that Mrs. Hinges had procured from her friend at the butcher's. Normally roast chicken was reserved for Sunday luncheon, but the housekeeper would hear nothing of Elle's protestations.

"I don't know why you are making such a fuss," Elle scoffed.

"There's nothing wrong with putting one's best foot forward. Whatever would people say if we did not look after our guests properly?" Mrs. Hinges hoisted a roasting tray out of the oven and shuffled the potatoes about. They sizzled in reply.

"Oh, tosh. Viscount or not, he's quite the confidence trickster when it suits him." Elle popped a piece of carrot into her mouth. "Besides," she said between crunches of carrot, "we can't be certain he's not the one who's behind all of this. All this is far too much of a coincidence for my liking. Mr. Marsh might be charming, but mark my words, the man is not to be trusted."

Mrs. Hinges gave her a dubious look. "I haven't exactly seen anyone else rush forth to aid us. If I've said it once, I'll say it a thousand times: I think we are very lucky that his lordship has taken an interest in us."

"I don't see why we should wait around for some hero on a white horse to help us. I'm perfectly capable of finding my father on my own."

"There is no shame in sometimes asking for help, my

dear. Pride cometh before the fall. In time you will come to see that." Mrs. Hinges shook her head in disapproval. "And stop eating off the counter and speaking with your mouth full. Where are your manners?" She spooned basting juices over the chicken and a cloud of thyme-flavored steam rose from the pan.

Elle stood away from the counter and folded her arms. It was so much easier being a man sometimes.

"Why don't you do something useful like go upstairs to dress for dinner?" Mrs. Hinges stoked the coals in the cooker. "His lordship is upstairs in the guest room and said he would be down soon. And I've set the boiler heating, so there should be a nice hot bath waiting for you." She closed the oven and gave Elle a friendly pat. "Now off you go."

"All right, I'm going." She stomped up the servants' staircase that ran upstairs from the kitchen. It was the shortcut she had used to get to her room for years.

The house was not stately or particularly grand, but it was eminently comfortable and well appointed. Most houses employed brownies or house-goblins to assist in the cleaning and housework, but her father had always felt strongly about the abuse of creatures of Shadow and so theirs was entirely devoid of magic.

However, in what had been one of the guest rooms, they did install one of the new modern bathrooms that were becoming fashionable. A good long soak in the cast-iron tub was an indulgence Elle relished.

Back in her bedroom, Elle stared at the contents of her wardrobe. They didn't socialize much, which was a good thing, because dressing for dinner was such a bore. Her uncle and aunt, in London, were far better at attending society. She shuddered when she thought about her coming out season a few years before. It had been an unmitigated disaster. Her well-meaning aunt had taken her under her wing, had done her best to give Elle a proper debut, but all those parties and balls . . . It was enough to drive anyone mad. Most of her suitors had been either dull or stupid or both, and she'd been quite forthright in her opinions. Until she made friends with Ducky Richardson, that is.

Ducky was enrolled in the Royal Flight Academy and had been drafted into the Dirigible Flying Corps. He was training to pilot one of the giant war dirigibles that made up the Royal fleet. It was good old Ducks who had filled Elle's head with tales of dashing adventure high up in the sky. And Elle was sold. She'd wanted to be the pilot of her own airship more than anything, and all thoughts of suitors and proposals of marriage promptly flew out of the window.

Eventually her aunt had caught her smoking cigars with Ducky and some of his fellow flight recruits under the stairs at a ball. That was the last straw for her long-suffering aunt, and Elle was returned to Oxford in short order, along with the news that a well-brokered marriage was most unlikely. Her father was so caught up in his work that he barely registered she was home. It was only after she'd sold some of her mother's jewelry to pay for flight school that things became bothersome.

He had ranted and despaired, shouted at her for days. But Elle had dug in her heels. In the end, mostly because it was less of an effort to agree with Elle than it was to fight with her, her father had relented. Strings were pulled and favors were asked and so she went off to train as a pilot. These days, she was either flying or too tired to bother going out. The professor was generally so engrossed in whatever he was working on that he hardly noticed her and it was not long after that that she had stopped bothering to dress for dinner when it was only the two of them.

She flicked through her wardrobe. She had better

make an effort to honor the roast chicken or else Mrs. Hinges would never let her hear the end of it. She pulled out a blue dinner gown and held it before her, looking at herself in the cheval mirror. She had bought it on impulse straight from a shop window in Paris and, much to the dismay of the shopkeeper, without a proper fitting. But Elle hadn't cared. She liked the neckline and the way the dress draped around her. It reminded her of one of the Mucha posters that were all around Paris. And for Elle, that was good enough.

She towel-dried her hair and pinned it into a knot that made her neck look long and elegant. The dress was a little bit showy for dinner at home, but it would have to do. She only hoped they didn't think that she was trying too hard.

As she worked at taming her hair, the diamonds around her wrist caught the light and she stopped to examine them. "I promise that if you behave, I will find you a lovely bottle of absinthe to bathe in tomorrow. Only please don't hex me so I become insane, or turn me into something hideous," she whispered at the bracelet. There was no answer. Fairies were strange creatures that lived by their own code. No one could make a fairy do anything it didn't want to do.

The sudden clanging sound of a hammer against metal emanating from downstairs caught her attention. For the first time in years, Mrs. Hinges was actually ringing the dinner gong in the dining room. Elle suppressed a giggle. Soon they would be hosting polo tournaments in the back garden if things carried on this way.

Marsh and Patrice rose as she walked into the drawing room. They looked as if they had been deep in conversation before she arrived. She felt Marsh's gaze flick over her as he took in her dress. "Lord Greychester, Patrice. Good evening," she said formally.

"Miss Chance, you look lovely," Marsh said as he led her to her seat. He handed her a glass of sherry.

"Thank you." She took a sip from her glass and felt the wine warm her throat. His stare was making her nervous, which was rather silly.

Mrs. Hinges rang the bell again. Marsh and Patrice were both looking at her expectantly. Marsh had an odd little smile on his face as he inclined his head to the door. It took Elle a moment to remember that with her father absent, she was the host. Her cheeks flushed and she rose quickly from her seat. "Um, gentlemen, shall we go in to dinner?" she said quickly.

"We would be delighted," Patrice said. He fell in step next to her and escorted her into the dining room, leaving Marsh to follow behind, unaccompanied.

Dinner commenced with a bowl of fine leek and potato soup, followed by the fish. With a pang of regret, Elle listened to Mrs. Hinges fuss and clatter in the kitchen. Their home was too modest for footmen, and Mrs. Hinges hired maids and knife boys only when needed. The rest of the time she did all the work herself. And so, instead of sitting in the kitchen all by herself, the professor had insisted years ago that Mrs. Hinges take her meals with them. It was quite odd to see her so formally in service. This evening, Eric from down the road had been roped in to carry platters. He looked freshly scrubbed and slightly anxious as he entered the dining room.

"How are you feeling this evening, Patrice?" Elle asked once the first course had been cleared away.

"I am much better, thank you, little one. A good rest does wonders for the body. And madame's poultices worked wonders." He bit into a chunk of Mrs. Hinges' excellent bread and chewed with gusto. "We French are much tougher than you believe us to be."

The chicken arrived in all its roasted and glorious splendor. Eric shuffled off to fetch the platters of roast potatoes and vegetables, while Mrs. Hinges served. Normally this was the task of the butler, but as they had no butler to command, the housekeeper took it upon herself to step in.

"I wouldn't dare trifle with Mrs. Hinges." Marsh winked at the housekeeper as she set about carving the meat. Mrs. Hinges looked at him sternly, but Elle could tell as the meal progressed that the older woman was completely in his thrall.

"I must tell you about my latest discovery." Patrice looked up from his pudding of apple sponge baked with sugar, cinnamon and sultanas. He pulled a newspaper clipping from his waistcoat and spread it open on the table before him, all manners and decorum forgotten. "It is a new machine that can emulate the workings of the human heart. The machine has a tiny spark core and runs on clockwork gears. Within this generation, people from the Light side will have employed science to achieve immortality," he announced.

"And how would they go about inserting said mechanical heart?" Marsh made a face.

"Actually, I don't think I want to know. Especially not at the dinner table," Elle said. She wasn't usually this squeamish, but this evening, she found herself feeling tired and hollow. A soft throbbing just inside her temple was threatening to erupt into an almighty headache. She did her best to smile and maintain the conversation, but her mood sank and dwindled as dinner wore on. It was as if an oppressive weight was bearing down on her and nothing she did seemed to make it go away.

Eventually she sighed and set down her spoon. "I fear that I am terribly tired. It has been a very long day and I am quite exhausted. If you'll excuse me, I think I shall retire for the night. In my absence, please make yourselves at home with brandies and cigars in the drawing room." She rose and they stood in response. Marsh frowned but he said nothing.

"If you need anything, please ask Mrs. Hinges," Elle continued. "She will see to your needs."

She took herself back to her room before anyone made a fuss. Mrs. Hinges would have words with her tomorrow for being rude and abandoning their guests, but the overwhelming urge to run away as fast as she could was so strong, she could not fight it any longer.

CHAPTER 13

The girl was being followed by ghosts. I knew those ghosts once. They were not malevolent—at least not to her. They were wise ghosts, with the knowledge of the ages within them.

I heard them whisper. They chattered amongst themselves in wonderment. Could it be that the girl was finally free of the constraints that kept her away from them and her true self? The ghosts were excited at the thought. There was much they needed to teach the girl. Would she listen to them?

I was not so sure. The years spent separated from the tethers that held them to this world had made the ghosts naïve. But ghosts rarely worry about the fate of the living, unless, of course, the living had something to offer that directly benefitted them. These ghosts had been silent for half a generation, existing like cowards in the realm of Shadow alone. It takes much to prompt them to rise up from the folds of reality where they dwell, for they care little about progress and science. Those already dead feel little for those of us who must face the awful truths of our shrinking world.

But, these were matters of which the girl had no awareness. I could tell that she sensed that something was amiss. That something would change within her, very soon.

Back in her room, Elle pulled at laces and layers of clothes until she stood naked in the half-light of the lamp. Grateful for the release from her stays, she took a few liberating breaths before throwing her cotton night-dress over her head. She padded over to the window and pushed it open. Cold air flooded around her and she shivered. In the moonlit garden, the plants and trees stood serene in the dark, their limbs stretched out in a silent invitation to her to run into the foliage where she could conceal herself, a place where no one would find her.

He's coming for you. You had better run. Before it's too late, something whispered inside her. It made her shiver. She lifted the bracelet, still tethered around her wrist. "Is that you, little fairy?" she whispered back. No answer. She looked about, feeling decidedly foolish. Now she was talking to fairies too.

Annoyed, Elle closed the window with a thump. Lack of sleep was starting to unhinge her mind. She smothered her bedside lamp and bundled herself up under the covers. The greasy-metallic smell of lamp oil hung in the dark. Downstairs had spark lighting, but upstairs they made do with more traditional lamps and candles. Her father said that there was no need for expensive lighting in bedrooms, because they had their eyes closed for most of the time spent there anyway. Elle sighed and closed her eyes, willing herself to sleep. She would be of no use in the search tomorrow unless she got some rest.

. . . Darkness. Nothingness stretched above and below . . . A shiver ran through her. She was not alone. Cloaked shadows soared through the darkness. Rows of runelike symbols glowed against the black.

The image shifted. Marsh stood in the sunshine in a garden. She raised her hand to wave at him. He smiled at her and disappeared.

Then the shadows were back. Their awful eyes probed and searched for her. Their faces covered in symbols that scarred their skin. They swirled around her; faster and faster they moved until they were nothing but a gray blur. Above the swirling shadow she saw Marsh. He was looking for something, peering down into the darkness. The maelstrom of the gray shadows gained momentum. They threatened to draw her into their midst. She screamed, but no sound came . . .

Elle sat up in bed. It was very dark and quiet. Too quiet. A floorboard creaked. Something in the dark made her skin prickle. She strained her eyes and blinked, but it was so dark it felt as if her eyes weren't working. Her fingers found the box of matches kept on the table beside her bed. A little flame sprang to life in a sulfurous burst as she struck a match and lit the lamp. The small pool of light that formed on the wick made the farther reaches of the room seem much darker.

Without warning, someone grabbed her by the throat. She felt her attacker's fingers dig into her flesh. She tried to scream, but his palm slipped over her mouth to silence her.

"'Ello, my lovely. You might remember me from Paris." It was the poet from the Café du Aleix. "I can see you do." He sneered at her. "Now, where were we, before we were so rudely interrupted?"

Elle felt a horrible choking sound escape from her mouth. She writhed and struggled against the man. They dipped to the side and she hit her head against the side of the little table beside the bed. Dazed, her fingers closed around the lamp she had just lit. She lifted it and smashed it against her attacker's head. Time slowed down as glass shattered and she watched with fascination as flames leapt up where oil and flame and bedcovers met. And in the burst of light, she saw his face.

She opened her mouth and took a strangled breath to scream, but smoke filled her lungs and all she could do was gasp and cough. Flames sprung up everywhere around her. The poet's face contorted with fear and horror as his coat burst into flame. He let go of her and staggered across the room, flames licking over his back and dripping onto the floor behind him. He flailed his arms, but the movement only made the flames roar even higher as they consumed him. Acrid smoke swirled all around. Elle coughed and stumbled out of bed. She dragged one of the blankets along with her, to throw over the man in order to put the flames out, but the poet howled and, with the crash of breaking glass, threw himself out of the window. She heard an awful bone-crunching thump and then everything went silent.

Elle buried her face in the blanket and stumbled toward the door.

"Eleanor—Miss Chance!" Marsh burst into the room, nearly knocking her over.

"Here, take this. Help me put out the flames," she said, shoving the blanket at him.

She grabbed the water jug from the nightstand and poured it over the flames, stamping and patting the fabric with the base of the jug as she went.

"Are you hurt? What on earth happened?" Marsh said between coughs as they put out the last smoldering patches on the bed.

"I'm fine. I hit him with the lamp . . . and then . . . fire . . . he fell through the window," she managed to croak.

He went over to the window, cursing as his toe nudged some of the broken glass on the floorboards. In her daze, she realized he wasn't wearing shoes.

"Oh, my darling!" Mrs. Hinges said from the doorway. She started coughing.

"Careful, Mrs. Hinges. There is broken glass everywhere. Would you be kind enough to wake Patrice for us?" Marsh commanded.

"I am here," Patrice said, peeking out from behind Mrs. Hinges.

"Patrice. Good, you're up. Mrs. Hinges, please take

Miss Chance downstairs. Perhaps a cup of tea with lots of sugar might help. Patrice, come with me," Marsh said. "But first I think I need to find a pair of shoes." He bundled them out of the room.

Downstairs, Mrs. Hinges wrapped an old paisley shawl around Elle. She set about stoking the range cooker back to life, from where it had been banked down for the night. "Let's get a pot of tea brewing, shall we?"

"I need to see what happened," Elle said.

"Let the gentlemen sort it out," Mrs. Hinges said, but she was speaking to an empty kitchen. Elle had already disappeared out the door.

"What happened?" Elle said as she walked up behind Marsh and Patrice. Both looked up at her in surprise. In front of them, in a crumpled heap was what had once been her attacker.

"You shouldn't be outside like this," Marsh said.

"I'm quite all right, thank you very much. See, I have a shawl." She lifted the fringed edge and stepped closer. "Let's have a look, shall we?" Her voice was raspy and her throat ached from the smoke, and from the poet's death grip.

Marsh shook his head in resignation and they turned to the body on the ground before them. Patrice held the lamp aloft. Horrible wisps of smoke and steam rose up from the center of the smoldering mass.

"Hmm, not much left of him, is there?" Marsh muttered. He lifted a strip of charred cloth off the body with the back of his pencil. The scrap of fabric fluttered to the ground.

"It's him. The same man from Aleix's Café in Paris," Elle said.

They both looked at her.

"He was in my room. I don't know how he got in, but there he was. Something woke me. It was like something was whispering to me in the dark. It was all very confusing. He was choking me. I reached out for something I could use to fend him off. And the lamp smashed . . . " Her hand went to her throat and she rubbed her bruises. " . . . then he went up in flames. I couldn't do anything. He just leapt out of the window."

"Good thing your father didn't install spark lights across the whole house," Marsh said drily.

"Now he's dead." She stared at the body before her. Small wisps of smoke still rose up from the bits that had been on fire. The smell was overwhelming. Elle turned her head to the side to stop herself from retching.

"Patrice, please keep an eye on things out here while I see Miss Chance inside. We need to clear this mess away. I don't want the police poking their noses into the matter quite yet. Not until we've finished our investigations at least. When we are done here, I must contact the Council. But first, we need to find a shovel."

Patrice nodded and lit his cigar. For once the sweet smell of good tobacco leaf was welcome, as it covered the stench of charred flesh.

With gentle hands, Marsh steered Elle indoors. She looked back only to see Patrice run his fingers round the inside of the neck of the body. In a quick movement he pulled a silver pendant on a chain out from underneath the charred layers of skin and cloth. Carefully he wrapped it in a handkerchief and dropped it into his pocket.

CHAPTER 14

"Abercrombie," Marsh said. He handed her a large brandy and poured one for himself.

Elle stared at him. "Aber-what?" She wrinkled her nose. It was very late and they were sitting on the dust sheets Mrs. Hinges had insisted on draping over the furniture in the front drawing room before going to bed. Even here, the smell of burnt things hung in the air.

"Sir Eustace Abercrombie. Industrialist and entrepreneur. Owns a chocolate factory near Manchester. Lovely chocolate, terrible place to work. Or so I am told. Apparently, he dabbles in exotic flavors derived from the Shadow side. He is also an Alchemist. A very powerful one." Marsh rubbed the back of his neck and examined the dirt and soot on his fingers from the fire and the impromptu burial they had just undertaken.

"That sounds fascinating, but why are you telling me this?" Elle said. Her impatience was growing by the minute. It had taken forever to calm Mrs. Hinges down enough to send her to bed, but they were finally alone. She took a big sip of brandy and felt the liquor burn as it slid down her tender throat. "I want proper answers and no one is leaving this room until I know the truth about what has been happening."

She saw a look pass between Marsh and Patrice as Marsh handed him a brandy.

The Frenchman shrugged and flicked a bit of soil off

his coat lapel. "You might as well tell her. She is not going to give up until you do. Are you, little one?"

Marsh sighed and rubbed his eyes. "I believe Abercrombie happens to be the man behind the attack on your person last night. And, if I were a betting man, I would wager he is also behind your father's disappearance."

Elle blinked. "But why? My father and I are nothing to this man. We don't even know him."

"Have a look at this." Marsh lifted a silver chain and pendant from his waistcoat and laid it on Elle's palm. "It's a talisman. Patrice found it on the body last night. It's designed to give the wearer extra strength, which might explain the extent of those bruises." He gestured at her throat.

Elle eyed the chunk of silver as it lay in her hand. The metal felt alive against her skin. For a moment the dark images she had seen in her dream flickered before her eyes. Strange things started whispering around the edges of her mind. "Urgh . . . that's creepy." Repulsed, she dropped the talisman on the occasional table beside her.

"I always thought Alchemists were just old men with dreams of turning lead into gold," she said, wiping her hands with her handkerchief.

Marsh narrowed his eyes. "No one fully understands the true origins of alchemy, but it is thought that their order is as old as humanity itself. Some believe that the Alchemists' knowledge was handed to them by a supreme being or force before the world split into Light and Shadow. We will never know. But what we do know for certain is that Alchemists have always drawn their strength from the power of darkness."

She snorted. "What nonsense. If they were so powerful, why do they hide and skulk around like that?"

Marsh shook his head. "You underestimate these people at your own peril. They are more powerful than you could ever imagine." He rubbed his chin. "Our recently departed friend used alchemy to disappear from the streets in Paris, when we ran into him yesterday, so I decided to contact my sources in London shortly after we arrived this morning to see what the Alchemists were up to. They have been watching the Guild for some time now. Blood ritual sites have recently been discovered. Some freshly used."

"Blood ritual?" Elle frowned.

"Blood alchemy is powerful magic," Patrice said. He puffed on his cigar. "They do terrible things to animals in their rituals and experiments, sometimes flaying them alive in order to capture the essence of the creature."

She paled. "Do you think my father—" The question was too awful to ask. She shuddered. "Surely they wouldn't do that to a human, would they?"

"We can only hope not." Marsh's voice softened. "Patrice is right. The craft of blood alchemy is not for the fainthearted."

"But you don't think the professor is in any way involved with all this, do you?" Patrice said.

"As I said, there have been a number of reports involving strange happenings and we have been keeping an eye on them for quite some time now." Marsh sipped his brandy. "I believe that it is no coincidence that the henchman of such a prominent Alchemist was found smoldering on the garden path last night."

"My father would never condone such things." Elle suddenly felt sick with worry.

Marsh smiled tightly. "I made no suggestion that I think he would. But the Alchemists are definitely up to something. There are whispers about trouble with the Nightwalker treatise."

"Nightwalker treatise?" Elle was out of her depth. She knew almost nothing about what went on in the Shadows.

"Alchemists are a strange breed. They are bound to

serve Nightwalkers for all eternity, yet they behave with an arrogance that belies the fact that they are no more than slaves," Marsh said.

"The treatise is still honored among certain of the more fanatical Nightwalker sects. The Alchemists have been the daylight keepers of the Nightwalkers for thousands of years," Patrice said. "In recent years, a number of enlightened Nightwalkers have crossed over from the Shadow to the Light. They have severed the ties that bound them to the Alchemists in favor of their own private arrangements, but many hold on to the old ways."

"Blood alchemy, summoning rituals, the disappearance of spark scientists." Marsh shook his head. "None of this is good news."

Elle felt a chill run up her spine. "What do you think it means?"

Marsh stared into his brandy. "I'm not sure, but I have a few good guesses."

"And they have the box," Patrice said. Marsh gave him a sharp look and Patrice shrugged. "Might as well tell her."

"Quite right too. What exactly was in that box?" Elle said, seizing the opportunity to change the subject. "I am part of this now, whether you like it or not, Marsh."

Marsh sighed. "The box contains a chunk of pure carmot."

"And what exactly is carmot?" Elle said.

"Carmot. *Lapis philosophorum*," Marsh said grimly. "The base element that constitutes what Alchemists call the Philosopher's stone. It's not *the* stone, per se, but in the wrong hands it could be used to forge such a stone. And with it, the holder could achieve any number of miracles. They could turn lead to gold. They could use it to brew the elixir of life. In fact, they could end up controlling the very time and space that holds our existence together.

"The search for pure carmot is as old as mankind. Many legends about its existence exist. Quite by chance, the box that was taken from you in Paris was discovered in the vault of an abbey in France a few months ago. It had been hidden there by Templars who took it from Jerusalem during the Crusades. Patrice and I liberated the box from the abbey and we were set to bring it back here so it could be placed in safe hands. We thought a discreet charter flight would be the safest way to achieve this. And so you were recruited for the task."

"And you let someone in a café carry it around in their holdall?" Elle glared at Patrice.

"No one can open the box without the key. And it is the key that the Alchemists now seek," Patrice said, eager to defend himself.

"And they think I have it, because I was the last one to hold the box?"

"My dear Miss Chance, you *are* the key," Marsh explained.

"What do you mean I am the key?"

"The diamond bracelet you wear is the key. The bracelet is spell-wrought. Once fastened around the wrist, it cannot be removed until it is used to open the box."

"You were only supposed to take his lordship and the box to London. We were going to remove the carmot from the box and let you keep the diamonds once we'd destroyed the box at the airfield. You were never supposed to even know what you were carrying," Patrice said.

"Well, thank you very much, Patrice." She was more than a little annoyed now.

"Patrice forgot to tell me about the little payment scheme the two of you operate. Perhaps now you might understand why I was so surprised to see you wearing the diamonds when we met in the café," Marsh said.

So he had seen the bracelet. Elle felt herself cringe for being so silly.

"I will of course ensure that you are paid in full for your services once your father has been returned," Marsh said.

"Isn't there some way that I can just take off the bracelet? You can lock it away in a vault and then no one will be able to open the box?"

"Unfortunately, it's not that simple. The bracelet and the box are designed to seek one another out. There is no stopping the process once they are separated."

Need she tell Marsh about the absinthe fairy? It was probably better not to. This business was complicated enough as it was. And, for all she knew, by now the fairy was dead or long gone. Despite herself, she felt a little twinge of worry at the fate of the fairy. The poor thing must have had no idea what she was flying into when she decided to inhabit the bracelet.

"I need to meet with the Council urgently. If anyone knows what the Alchemists are up to, it would be them. They are gathered in Venice at the moment."

"The Council?" Elle said.

"His lordship is a Warlock and a member of the Advisory Council of Nations," Patrice said.

She looked at Marsh in surprise. "And when exactly were you going to tell me *that* little fact?"

Marsh shrugged. "You never gave me a chance. I'm almost certain that if we find the box, we will find the professor. And so I must take the first airship bound for Italy without delay."

Elle shook her head. "Why not take the gyrocopter? If this machine can do what I think it can, then I could fly you there in a few days. If you went by airship or train it could take over a week."

He considered this for a moment. "Do you think that thing could really fly?" he asked.

"Yes, I really do. I spent all afternoon looking at it and I think I've discovered most of its inner workings."

"Well, it's a terribly long way to go in an untested machine. Do you think it is even possible?" Marsh looked doubtful.

Elle felt herself become excited about the idea. "Absolutely. If we limit our luggage so we may carry extra water for the boilers, I believe we can."

Patrice shook his head. "I don't think that it is a good idea. No one has ever achieved a flight such as that which you are planning."

"Just because it hasn't been done before, does not mean that it is not possible," Elle said.

"No, I think you should stay here in Oxford where it is safe, little one. I can remain behind and make sure that you come to no harm. His lordship could go by airship to meet with the Council. Once he has spoken to them, he could send us a telegram. I could never live with myself if anything happened to you." He smiled at Elle. "Not after what happened in Paris."

"No, Patrice," Marsh said. "We need the speed of the flying machine. We have already spent more time here than we should have. And besides, Miss Chance is safer under my protection. It is clear that the Alchemists are able to infiltrate this house. We cannot risk another attack like last night."

"Surely they wouldn't dream of sending another man, would they? That would be insane," Patrice said.

Marsh shook his head. "Insanity is exactly what we are dealing with when it comes to Alchemists. Miss Chance must remain with me. I will not be moved on the point."

"I will go," Elle said. "He is my father and I am not going to sit around and do nothing. I'm sorry."

"No! I cannot allow it." Patrice's anger was quite disconcerting.

Elle placed a conciliatory hand on his shoulder. "Patrice, you are very sweet, but I can make up my own mind in this matter. If using the flying machine will help save my father, then I say we should use this opportunity. I will be perfectly safe with you and Marsh to protect me. And besides, I do believe that it would be more difficult for them to catch me if I don't remain in one place."

"For once, it seems as if you and I are in perfect agreement," Marsh said. "Patrice, you have been outvoted on this one, old chap." He winked at Elle. "See, I do believe in giving women the vote."

Elle rolled her eyes at him and did her best to ignore the strange quickening she felt in her chest when he smiled at her.

Patrice shook his head. "This is madness. We cannot take her with us. And we don't even know if that thing can fly. We could all crash to our deaths!" He was almost shouting now.

"Oh, don't be such a baby, Patrice," Elle said. The gyrocopter had solved her problem most admirably. She still was not completely sure whether joining forces with Marsh and Patrice was the right thing to do, but there was never any real possibility that she would have stayed at home while Marsh went looking for her father alone. It still meant that she would have to watch Marsh and Patrice every step of the way, but Mrs. Hinges was right: doing something seemed far better than doing nothing.

"Then it is decided," said Marsh. "We leave tomorrow. Of course, all pilot's expenses and incidentals would be paid."

"Agreed," Elle said. And as she did, she sent silent prayer that the gyrocopter would fly.

CHAPTER 15

Elle woke and stretched under the covers. She had finally fallen asleep in one of the narrow cots in one of the attic rooms, but even here, the place smelled of smoke. It was still early and the sunlight was just starting to edge through the curtains. She groaned and pulled the covers over her head. Her eyes felt puffy and swollen and her head ached from smoke, lack of sleep and late night brandy. She wanted to roll over and give herself over to sweet luscious sleep where none of the terrible events of the last two days existed.

Irritated with herself, she sat up and rubbed her face. This was not the time to be feeling sorry for oneself. She needed to concentrate on finding her father.

In the distance, a bell started to toll in time to her thoughts. It was Sunday morning in Oxford and the dreaming spires were singing.

There was a soft knock at the door and Mrs. Hinges entered, carrying a tray. "I've brought you tea and toast, my dear. How are you feeling?"

Elle sat up and took the tray from her. "It's so early. Mrs. Hinges, you needn't have bothered."

Mrs. Hinges busied herself with opening the curtains. "Oh, it's no bother. Best you start this adventure properly fed. His lordship and Patrice are downstairs, waiting. His lordship says to tell you that they are ready to leave as soon as you are."

"Mrs. Hinges?"

"Yes, dear?"

"Do you think I am being foolish?"

"Foolish about what, dear?"

"Going after my father. And with a stranger like Marsh. I honestly don't know if he can be trusted."

Mrs. Hinges smoothed her hands over her apron. "I think you are being ever so brave. And his lordship is a good man. I can tell these things. I wouldn't have let you go if I'd thought otherwise. That French fellow, on the other hand . . . " She drew her lips into a straight line.

"Don't be silly. I trust Patrice."

"Well, I can't say anything about that. All I can say is what I see with my own eyes. Now have your tea. It's time to make ready."

Elle sighed and tucked the curls around her face behind her ears.

"His lordship will find your father. I'm sure of it. He promised he would. A gentleman's word is his bond," Mrs. Hinges observed as she fussed about the room, dusting imaginary bits of fluff off the mantelpiece as Elle ate her toast.

"I shall let you get on with things, then, shall I?" she said after a while. "I am sure the gentlemen will need more tea before they finish their breakfast. I've put clean towels in the bathroom for you," Mrs. Hinges said as she bustled out of the room and down the hallway, humming to herself.

Half an hour later, Elle stood in her underwear and surveyed the proposed contents of her bag laid out on the bed before her. Her own room had been swept and cleaned between the time they went to bed and the time she emerged from the bathroom. Mrs. Hinges never ceased to amaze when it came to cleaning, but the smell of smoke still lingered. She tried her best to ignore the gentle breeze coming from the broken window behind her and concentrated on her belongings, ticking them off on the list in her head as she packed them into her carpet-bag. She had been lucky; her clothespress and chest of drawers had escaped the worst of the soot.

She reached into the back of the clothespress and pulled out a parcel. She unwrapped the oily layers of brown paper and cloth to reveal a Colt 1878 Frontier revolver. She rubbed her thumb over the mother-of-pearl grip as she weighed the gun on her outstretched palm. Her father had bought it for her when she'd graduated from the flight academy. "If you are going to be a pilot, then you had jolly well better learn to take care of yourself," he had said.

Her fingers trembled slightly as she picked out the rounds from the paper box of ammunition wrapped in the folds of the cloth, and loaded the gun. The chamber slipped shut with a satisfying click. She moved the safety lock into place. She had been silly to leave it behind on the last trip, but she would not make the same mistake again. The next time someone tried to grab her, she would be ready for them.

She pulled on a clean pair of jodhpurs and tucked in her freshly starched shirt. Then she slipped her corset on and tightened the laces. It was a hunting corset, made shorter and wider than the ones she wore under her dresses. Worn as part of a riding habit, it allowed the wearer to move and breathe more naturally.

Elle had instantly liked the paisley print panels in the front of the corset when the shopkeeper had shown it to her. It was pretty enough to be worn on the outside of her clothes. It was a radical idea, but she liked it. And for a fee, she had persuaded the corset-maker to stitch in a few custom modifications. A small holster was strapped onto her left side. She fitted the revolver into the holster so it would be accessible, but hidden from sight if she wore her coat. She slipped her stiletto into the loops fitted behind the front laces, and tucked a small purse with her emergency money, along with a particularly fine pair of diamond earrings she had earned from one of her trips, inside the removable lining.

Suitably armed, she slipped a dark red brocade waistcoat over the corset and buttoned it. She pulled on her boots and, as a last touch, traced a line of perfume oil onto the skin above her breasts, which were visible in the opening of the shirt. The scent of freesias filled the room.

She gave herself a last once-over in the mirror and then folded up her white silk scarf with the frond-trim around the dark bruises on her neck. With a last look behind her, she hoisted up her carpetbag and went downstairs.

"Good morning." She dropped her bag by the door of the front parlor.

Marsh looked up from his newspaper. The smallest flicker of color played across his cheeks before he answered. "Miss Chance. A good morning to you too. Ready?"

His look sent a ripple of apprehension through her, right to the tips of her fingers. "I'm as ready as I'll ever be," she said, keeping her voice even.

"Well then, without further ado shall we be on our way?" Marsh folded his newspaper, making sure that all the corners lined up. His eyes were calm, even cold. Elle shrugged off her untoward thoughts. She would deal with those later.

Patrice started gathering the travel bags. He was without a shirt collar and his sleeves were rolled up to the elbows, showing his beefy forearms.

"Patrice, why are you not dressed?" she said.

"I have asked Patrice to stay behind to look after Mrs. Hinges. We don't want anyone bothering the good lady while we are away. Besides, with one less person, we can carry more water for the boiler."

He took up his gloves and hat from the sideboard. "Mrs. Hinges has kindly packed us a spot of lunch for our journey. Jolly good of her, don't you think?"

Patrice muttered something very rude in French about how their plan was ill-considered and something about the nether regions of a goat as he hoisted the bags over his shoulder.

"Are you sure about this?" Elle asked Marsh.

"Positive," Marsh said.

"Don't worry, little one. This will be over before you know it and we will see each other again very soon." Despite his light tone, Patrice's face was drawn tight with anger.

"Oh, Patrice, I promise we will celebrate together as soon as we get this stupid bracelet off my wrist and bring my father home," Elle said.

Patrice gave her a thin smile. "Yes. We will celebrate."

"Shall we be on our way, then?" Marsh held open the French doors that led from the parlor into the garden.

She caught the slight scent of sandalwood as she passed him. He gave her an amused look but, apart from that, he seemed quite unaffected by her.

"Now, that's an impressive-looking contraption." Mrs. Hinges surveyed the gyrocopter with her hands resting on her hips as Marsh and Patrice wheeled it out of the workshop.

"Heavy too," Patrice huffed.

Elle did a quick check on the spark reactor and pulled out the brass crank-handle attached to the engine.

"My lord, would you be so good as to crank the handle when I tell you to?"

Marsh cranked the handle, and the reactor came to life with a low hum.

"Is it working?" Marsh said as Elle emerged from the cockpit.

"Just waiting for the water to boil." She smiled at him. "From what I can see, my father has designed a closed-circuit system, which means less steam escapes from the pistons as they move."

"Ingenious," Marsh said drily.

"It means the machine needs less water and steam to run, which in turn allows for the unit to be sufficiently light to be airborne. Or that is the idea, in case you were wondering." She let her voice trail off.

Steam started hissing through the pipes and valves. Elle pulled a new pair of goggles out of her coat. They were a spare pair she had picked up on impulse. She handed them to him. "To wish you well on your first flight," she said, feeling suddenly shy and awkward.

His face lit up as he took the goggles from her. "Thank you. How very thoughtful of you. I shall cherish them always." He slipped the goggles round his hat.

Elle felt her cheeks grow warm and she quickly shoved a folder of papers at him. "You, sir, are navigating. These are my father's maps of the Continent. I am not sure how well we'll do with them, but it wouldn't hurt to have them handy. You will find a compass in the pouch as well."

The standby valves started whistling, signaling that the machine was ready.

He smiled at her. "Well, Miss Chance, I do believe that it is time to go."

"I had better try this first before you get in." She slid into the pilot seat and strapped herself in.

He slid into the seat next to her. "Oh, no, you're not. We are going to make history together, you and I."

A little distance away, Mrs. Hinges stood next to a scowling Patrice. She waved a lace handkerchief as she watched them.

Elle closed her eyes and said a silent prayer.

"Stand back!" she yelled. She flicked the switch that operated the propellers, and they came alive with a slow whirr. Faster and faster they turned, churning up bits of sticks and dust.

She took hold of the steering column and slowly eased the controls forward. The propellers whirred faster and faster, and Mrs. Hinges had to grab hold of Patrice to steady herself against the updrafts of air that formed around them. More bits of debris flew about. Patrice had to duck as an old newspaper nearly hit him in the face. The propeller blades gained critical momentum and, with a shudder, the gyrocopter lifted off the ground. It rose up into the air.

Somewhere down the road, a neighbor's dogs started howling and Marsh let out an excited whoop in reply.

Elle looked down at the ground. "Put that in your pipe and smoke it, Orville Wright!" she yelled.

The gyrocopter hovered in the air. They were flying.

"Let's make a loop around the field first!" She had to shout over the noise of the propeller blades.

He nodded and made a gesture to indicate a circle. She eased the controls upwards and the gyrocopter gained altitude. It lurched slightly, and then banked to make a big loop through the air.

Marsh smiled and he gave Elle a thumbs-up.

"Now let's see if we can land this thing!" she yelled.

She made the 'copter hover over a patch of ground outside the workshop and eased the steering downward. The 'copter bucked, wobbled and set itself down on the ground with a thump. Elle shut down the engine. They stared at one another in amazement as above them the whirring blades turned slower and slower.

Elle suddenly realized that her fingers were aching, and she let go of the steering lever. She sat back in the seat, and smiled a great big triumphant smile. They had been flying, high up in the air in a machine that no person had ever thought possible. And there was no better feeling in the world than that.

Marsh smiled at her.

"I think we should have a range of about two hundred miles with the water we have on board," she said.

Marsh nodded. "I will keep an eye on the distance." He made a mark in the margin of the map with his pencil. "I can't believe we just did that," he said.

Patrice and Mrs. Hinges ran up to the gyrocopter. Mrs. Hinges was laughing and dabbing the corners of her eyes with her handkerchief. "Oh, your father is such a clever man. I am so proud. I wish he were here to see it."

"Are you ready, my lord?" Elle said.

"I think I am." He smiled at her and adjusted his goggles.

She started the engine again. The blades of the gyrocopter started whirring furiously above them.

They waved to Patrice and Mrs. Hinges to stand back. Elle took hold of the controls and the gyrocopter rose up and into the air.

Marsh pointed southeast. "To the English Channel, and on to France!" he yelled over the noise and wind of the whirring blades.

CHAPTER 16

The girl and the Warlock had mastered the art of flying. They were so proud of themselves; so proud of their skills and the crafty machine that carried them through the air. They did not pay attention to those who were watching them.

For them, there were far more urgent matters to heed. The girl needed to go to Venice. She needed to follow this path. Much depended on it. Everything depended on it.

And so we flew across the fields. We flew over the heads of oak and birch and ash and on to the sea.

The flying machine was faster than anything the girl had ever flown. The Warlock proved to be a surprisingly resourceful copilot. Within the first hour they were working together, two bodies moving in unison with one another as if they were dancing.

The girl worried about the fact that they had no official flight papers. She pointed the nose of the machine well away from the well-flown air paths of other ships, to ensure that they passed unnoticed.

The Warlock worried about getting lost. He worried about the amounts of water in the tanks. But most of all, he worried about the girl. There were so many secrets he had to tell her.

Amid all the worry and concentration, the sea eventually made way for land, and more fields and trees.

From time to time the Warlock and the girl saw people on the ground. Most of them stopped what they were doing and pointed at the flying machine, which sped past over rooftops and trees. But somehow the people on the ground did not matter. They were on their way. And there was no time to waste.

The sun overhead signaled the arrival of lunchtime. Elle pointed at the dials and yelled, "I need to stop for a while . . . and we may as well fill up with water!"

Marsh pointed out a field with a canal running along it below them. With growing confidence, Elle set the gyrocopter near the water. A few floppy-eared cows eyed her warily as the 'copter settled down. Cows apparently had no business with flying machines, and with a few indignant moos, they sauntered off to opposite corners of the field.

"You get the picnic basket and I'll fill the gyrocopter." Marsh unrolled the hoses and walked over to the canal.

Elle took the basket and a blanket from the back of the 'copter and spread the latter out on a nice cowpat-free patch of meadow. A few late-summer flowers dotted the long grass. Lacy cow parsley heads bowed gently in the breeze.

Elle closed her eyes and inhaled the rich smell of grass baking in the sun. Insects buzzed around her, frantically making the best of what the end of summer had left to give.

Marsh dropped down onto the blanket next to her. She opened her eyes and smiled. To her surprise, the sight of him pleased her.

"What's for lunch? I am famished," he said. The skin around his eyes was faintly marked from his goggles.

Mrs. Hinges had packed cold ham and chicken sandwiches, a wedge of cheese, a few apples and a couple of flasks of cordial. Elle rooted around inside the basket and pulled out a brown paper parcel of strawberry jam tarts. She smiled at them with pleasure. They were her favorite.

"Would you like a sandwich, my lord?" She handed him the paper parcel. His fingers brushed her hand as he took it from her.

"I'm sure we can dispense with formalities now, don't you think? My name is Hugh."

"Very well, then. Hugh," she said, savoring his name. She bit into her sandwich and they enjoyed their food in companionable silence.

He finished his sandwich and stretched out. Next to her, she felt his large body extend across the blanket.

"It's lovely out here, isn't it?" she said after a while.

"Hmm. The sun is nice." His eyes were closed as he basked in the warmth. He had ridiculously long eyelashes for a man.

The lazy silence spread around them. Drowsy in the warmth she drifted off, almost asleep. A slow bead of sweat trickled down her rib cage.

Marsh sat up from the blanket. "If you'll excuse me for a moment, and if it won't offend your sensibilities, I think I would like to stretch my legs."

Elle suppressed an irrational urge to giggle. Well-bred gentlemen were rarely this open about the call of nature. Certainly not the ones she had met while chaperoned by her aunt. The boys in flight school were a different matter, of course, but it seemed strange coming from someone as uptight as Marsh.

She drifted off in the heat as he walked off to a clump of bushes near the canal. She sighed, happy to put aside the gnawing worry about her father that twisted and turned inside her for a little while. Here in this meadow, it was a lovely day—perfect for flying.

His shadow slid over her as he sat down on the blanket next to her. She kept her eyes half-closed as she watched him pick up an apple and bite into it. His jaw worked steadily as he chewed.

"Can I ask you something?" he said eventually.

"By all means," she said.

"Do you know what an Oracle is?"

She sat up, drowsy from the sun. "As in the oracles from classical Greek mythology?"

"Well, yes." He looked down at the exposed flesh of his apple.

"Then I know what an oracle is," she said.

"And do you about *the* Oracle?"

She snorted and rolled onto her side to face him. "What? Women with scarves on their heads who tell fortunes at parlor party séances?"

He looked away. "No." The conversation had suddenly turned awkward. "Is that a gun?" he asked, changing the topic.

Elle sat up and straightened her shirt. "Better safe than sorry. You never know who you might run into when you're in a foreign place."

"And I assume you know how to use it?"

"Of course. I bet you I'm a better shot than you are, my lord!"

He laughed. "I'll make that wager." He picked up the empty cordial bottles and walked across the field to the fence, where he carefully lined them up on the posts.

"One shot each. Loser sleeps in the gyrocopter tonight."

"You're on." She handed him the revolver.

Marsh took a stance and aimed.

She studied his face. A dark lock of his hair had fallen forward over his brow. Without really knowing why, she reached up and carefully traced it back behind his ear.

He closed his eyes as her finger moved over his sideburn and over his ear. "If you continue doing that, I can't be held responsible for what I might do next," he said.

"And what might you do next?" She laid the gentle challenge down between them.

He pulled the trigger. The bullet hit the post and the bottle toppled into the grass.

"Aha! That's not a direct hit," she said.

"It is if *you* miss," he answered as he handed her the revolver. "And besides, you cheated."

"A lady never cheats." Elle relaxed her shoulders and took aim. She took a deep breath and squeezed the trigger. A split second later, the remaining bottle exploded into a million bits.

She let out a whoop of excitement. "So it seems that you take the first watch then this evening," she said.

"Well done, madam." Marsh tipped his hat.

She curtsied. "Why, thank you."

They sat back down on the blanket. "I suppose we had better get a move on. Loser gets to pack up the picnic," Elle said.

"Oh no, you don't!" He leaned over and started tickling her. He smelled of apples and in that moment, she knew he was going to kiss her.

A sudden blast from a boat horn sliced through the warm air. They both jumped. A French narrow boat was slowly paddling up the river. The boatmen in their blue-and-white striped tops whistled and jeered as they came into view. One of them called out something particularly obnoxious and leery as they passed. Marsh rolled over her and shielded her from view with his body.

He collapsed onto the blanket, laughing as soon as the sailors were gone. Elle smiled and rolled over to the other side of the blanket.

"I'm sorry." His voice was suddenly formal again. "It was wrong of me to distract you like that."

"What do you mean?"

He didn't answer.

She picked a stalk of grass and started picking the seeds off it. The warm air around them was suddenly stifling.

"Tell me about your mother," he said suddenly.

She swiveled round in surprise. "Why on earth would you want to know that?"

He sat up and gently caught her face in his hands. "Elle, there are important things you need to know. And I'm not sure I know how to tell you or how much you already know." He let his hands drop away. "What do you remember from when you were a child?"

She frowned. "Well, there isn't much to tell, really. My mother died when I was a baby. My father raised me as best he could. My family has a good name, but he is the younger son, so we are not wealthy. My uncle's fortune and peerage is respectable, and my father lives mostly off his trust, but I have no money of my own." She picked away at the grass stalk as she spoke. "My father hired Mrs. Hinges to look after me. My aunt did her best to teach me all the things a young woman of class and breeding should know. I think my father had hoped to marry me well, but I think we all eventually agreed that I am never going to realize that dream." She threw away the stripped-down stalk and picked another one.

"I'm a bit of an odd duck, as you can see. With no inheritance or traditional accomplishments to speak of, I don't exactly possess the qualities that would make a model wife." She looked out over the field.

"I think you are capable of far more than you believe." He grew serious. "And I am not going to be the man who ruins things for you."

"Why would you say that?"

"Because you are special. Just like your mother was."

"My mother is dead because of her own selfishness. And I am nothing like her."

"That's not true."

She stared at him. "How would you know? You know nothing about my family. And what business is it of yours anyway?"

"I am a Warlock, and so you are every bit my business. The reason why that is so is what I am trying to explain to you."

"So that's what I am? A bit of business?" She felt her cheeks throb with the indignance. She threw away the second grass stalk and dusted off her lap. "I do not like to dredge up old stories about my family that have nothing to do with the present. And you, sir, have no right to pry into my personal matters."

"Elle, please listen to me for a moment."

"No. I don't want to talk about my mother. Nothing good ever comes out of doing so." She pulled away from him and stood up off the blanket. "Now, if you'll excuse me, we are wasting time and we have a long way ahead of us. The weather is not going to hold forever. I'd like to cover as much distance as I can before it rains." She started piling things into the picnic basket. The wicker creaked as she slid the buckle shut. She stood and hoisted the basket into the air. "Please bring the blanket with you when you are ready."

He didn't move. "Elle . . ."

Elle ignored him. With a flick of her wrist, she yanked the blanket out from under him and he rolled onto the grass. She bundled the blanket up with the basket and walked away.

How could she have been so foolish? There was no attraction between them, not on his side, anyway. All he cared about was the stupid key around her wrist. She stowed away the picnic things and got into her seat.

From the corner of her eye she watched him walk slowly toward the gyrocopter.

"We'll talk about this when you are ready," he said as he got into his seat next to her.

Elle did not reply. Instead, she cranked the starter lever and the engine hummed back to life. She did not want to think about her mother. She had some serious flying to do.

CHAPTER 17

Many miles away, a soot-blackened train belched steam from its flanks as it wound its way through the valleys that cleaved through the mountains of Carpathia. From beneath the sun-starved cover of pine trees, Shadow creatures watched on in hopeful silence. But the train had no intention of stopping: It was on its way to Constantinople.

The sun-fearers shrank back and bowed their heads in respect as one particular carriage passed. Its finely cut Lalique windows were covered with black sheets of India rubber, sealing out all light.

Inside the carriage, Eustace Abercrombie sat in a wingback chair. He moved his face out of the pool of lamplight as a waiter in a white jacket and gloves entered. Careful not to stare, the waiter placed a little silver tray bearing a telegram before Abercrombie. The waiter bowed and retreated as unobtrusively as he could manage.

Abercrombie opened the telegram, meticulously lifting the sealed edges of the envelope. As he scanned the contents, his face contorted with anger. Uttering a curse, he crumpled the paper and threw it at the wall. It bounced off the wallpaper and hit one of the lampshades, making the crystal teardrops tinkle.

His companion moved silently from the shadows beyond the lamplight. His inky hair was tied with a leather strip at the neck and hung down his back in a simple braid. Pale skin stretched over his aquiline features.

"What news, Eustace?" He spoke with a slight accent. Parisian, if one listened carefully.

"My lord Aleix. You are awake." Abercrombie took a sip of Arabic tea from a delicate tulip-shaped glass and pulled a face. "Feathers is dead."

"And the girl?"

"She lives. The Warlock is with her. They are on their way to Venice. They have managed to mobilize one of the professor's flying machines." Abercrombie looked at his companion. "They are outrunning us."

"The Council is in Venice."

Abercrombie slammed his hand down onto the table. "Damnation! Don't you think I know that?" His tea glass toppled over with a little tinkle.

Aleix stepped back and bared his fangs. "There is no need for anger now, Alchemist. Is there?" His stare grew very cold.

Abercrombie glared at him. "I sometimes don't know why we bother with your kind. I really don't."

"You bother because you need us. We are the princes who inherited the night and you are our keepers," he said, carefully avoiding the word *servant*.

"And best you do not forget who keeps you from turning to dust by the sun, princeling. Don't you forget."

Aleix flashed his fangs again. "It is because of our money that your Guild has thrived. So it may be best for *you* not to forget who feeds you, Alchemist."

Abercrombie picked up his empty glass and set it aside with some irritation. He reached out and pushed the brass service bell.

A man dressed in black hurried into the compartment.

"Mr. Chunk, I regret to inform you that Mr. Feathers

is dead. The Warlock has killed him. Please make arrangements to have him replaced by someone suitable."

A look of surprise crossed Mr. Chunk's broad face but he seemed to know better than to comment. He bowed. "Yes, master."

"How is the professor?" Abercrombie asked.

"He is fine, master. We checked on him a quarter of an hour ago. Sleeping like a baby. Them draughts you gave him work powerfully well."

"Good. But I want you to wake him now. See to it that his needs are met. I want him to start working immediately. We have no time to waste."

Aleix leaned forward. "Do you think that is wise? He may escape."

"And make sure he remains shackled. At all times," Abercrombie said through gritted teeth, his eyes not leaving Aleix's face.

"As you wish, master," said Mr. Chunk.

"Very well. Dismissed." Abercrombie waved his hand. "And tell the waiter to bring me another drink. I don't care what he brings, as long as it is not tea."

"Yes, master." Mr. Chunk bowed and left the room.

"I knew it was a bad idea to use the box as bait for the trap," Abercrombie said as soon as Mr. Chunk was gone.

Aleix shrugged. "Our plan almost worked, you know. If only they hadn't followed the cab, we would have had ourselves a fresh young Oracle by now."

"And for our efforts, Feathers is dead," Abercrombie said.

Aleix leaned over and helped himself to one of the blood-filled chocolate truffles in the box on the table. He bit into it and chewed for a second with his eyes closed. "Feathers was a fool."

Abercrombie grabbed his wrist. "He was my nephew," he hissed.

"Let . . . Go . . . Of . . . Me." Aleix bared his fangs again. They were covered with blood and chocolate.

Abercrombie released the Nightwalker and sat back in his seat. Aleix stood up gracefully and went to stand by the window. He closed his eyes. "Darkness approaches. If you'll excuse me, it is very late and I need to get some sleep before sunset." He straightened his smoking jacket and picked up another truffle. "These are very good. I think there is definitely a market for them," he said as he disappeared into the shadows.

The waiter came in with another glass of tea and set it down on the table.

"Here." Abercrombie picked up a pencil and started scribbling on the envelope of the telegram. He grabbed the waiter by the lapel, looked into the man's eyes with his dark stare. "See that this message is dispatched as soon as possible."

The waiter paled and started shaking. "Yes, sir, we have a mobile transmitter on the train."

It is a matter of life and death, Abercrombie said into his mind. *And get that tea out of my sight. I said, no more tea!*

The waiter bowed and ran from the compartment, tripping over the rug at the door on the way out.

Abercrombie rested his chin on his hands and brooded into the pool of lamplight before him. "Let's see how you like my next move, Warlock," he snarled out loud. "Your little expedition is about to be blown completely off course."

CHAPTER 18

The city of Nice came into view shortly before sunset. Elle took in the majestic curve of the *Promenade des Anglais,* which was tinged in shades of pink and lavender in the setting sun.

"See if you can spot a good place to land," she yelled at Marsh over the din of the 'copter blades.

People out on the promenade were looking up as the 'copter whizzed over them. Some were holding on to their hats and pointing at the spectacle above.

Elle turned the gyrocopter so she could survey the rooftops. She spotted a lead-gray roof on one of the buildings as they flew over it. It stood out quite starkly in contrast to the red tiles that covered the buildings further into the city, but more importantly, the roof looked new and it was flat. The trelliswork around the edge suggested a roof terrace, but it was now closed up—a signal that summer was at an end.

"Hold on, it's going to be tight!" She positioned the 'copter over the roof and started easing it down. The gyrocopter set down on the terrace with a slight thud. She opened the steam-release valves and powered down the reactor.

"Now, that's what I call making an entrance." Marsh pulled off his goggles. "I'll see if I can find a way off the roof. We may even have found our lodgings for tonight." He winked at her. "You hold the fort. This will only take a minute."

Elle sat back in her seat and listened to the hiss of the steam escaping from the engine. The enormity of what she had achieved today made her tremble. She had flown her father's machine, but he had missed seeing the moment of fruition of his life's work. The thought filled her with a sudden sense of sadness. She hoped he was alive and unhurt, wherever he was. Thinking about it made her chest ache.

The view was magnificent. From where she was sitting, she could see the whole of the escarpment, all the way to the rocky hill that sat to the side of the city. She watched the people on the promenade walk along, taking the air, while lazy seagulls circled through the rose-colored sky. Ladies with parasols and beautiful hats, on the arms of gentlemen in summer suits, walked along the rails and stared out over the sea.

Marsh arrived after a few minutes, with an open-mouthed hotel porter in tow. He opened the door and helped Elle out of the cockpit. "We are in luck. It is the end of the season and I have secured lodgings for us."

"Welcome, madame," the porter said, while doing his best not to gape at the flying machine.

Marsh opened the storage hatch and pulled out their bags. He handed them to the porter.

Elle pulled out the crank handle that started the engine and unhooked it. "Just in case," she said to Marsh.

"Good thinking. The hotel has instructions to allow no one onto the roof," Marsh said with a wry smile.

"Cheat," Elle mouthed at him as they followed the porter into the hotel. He led them down a few flights of stairs and into one of the corridors until they came to a set of doors. He pulled a key from his pocket and opened the doors for them.

The hotel room was decorated in the prettiest wallpaper of a delicate cornflower-blue and gold. Elle breathed in the smell of lavender furniture oil and fresh linen. Outside the French windows was a little balcony fringed by ornate trelliswork.

Marsh gave the porter a coin and he disappeared.

Elle turned to Marsh and raised her eyebrows at him. There was only one bed in the room.

"We are registered as Mr. and Mrs. Mason from London—for the sake of appearances," he said quickly. "This hotel is quite new, but they still have ladies' suites." He pointed at a wallpapered panel. "See, the maid's room is through there. The bed in there is quite serviceable and I will sleep there in adequate comfort without raising suspicion."

Elle snorted. "And you think landing on the roof in a flying machine hasn't attracted enough attention already?"

"The world is full of eccentrics and a hotel such as this one is quite accustomed to catering to the whims of their more colorful clientele. But suspicions aside, I can be here with you in a second, if you need me." He smiled at her.

Elle felt her heartbeat quicken, but she resisted the urge to respond. She wasn't going to flirt with him. Not after what had happened earlier.

Marsh, entirely unperturbed by her awkwardness, donned his hat. "Let's stretch our legs with a walk on the promenade before dinner, shall we? Would you care for some dinner, Mrs. Mason? I know a place that makes a bouillabaisse that is so delicious it will move you to tears."

Elle felt her stomach rumble at the thought of fresh seafood and she put her hand on his arm. "Thank you, Mr. Mason," she said, playing along with him. "If you'll allow me a moment to change into something more suitable before we go." She pushed him into the maid's room and shut the door. "You wait in there. I'll call for you when I am ready."

CHAPTER 19

That night Elle dreamed of burning men, and huge hands with thick fingers closing around her throat. Gray specters with black eyes searched for her as they passed overhead, spreading an eerie chant around them. Someone was out there. She could feel it. She tried to open her eyes, but darkness folded all around her.

"Who's there?" she whispered.

"It's me," Marsh spoke. She felt his presence next to her.

"What are you doing here?"

"This is a dream."

"But I am awake. And what are you doing in my bedroom?"

He laughed softly. "You are dreaming that you are awake and you are awake while you are dreaming. It's complicated. Everything here is a bit complicated."

She felt them float together in silence. "Where is here?"

"We are in the realm of Shadow," he said.

"The place mystics talk about? This is where the world of Shadow originates, isn't it?"

"The very same."

"I've always wondered about other places. Other realities. I always thought they were figments of the mind," she said.

"This place is as you would imagine it," he said.

"And why exactly are you here? I can manage my own

dreams, you know. I have done so for years. And if you ask me, this dream is rather dull. There doesn't seem to be anything here. Except those creepy things flying about over in the distance."

"How wrong you are. Everything is here. Shh. Listen."

Chanting sifted through the air, leaving luminescent tendrils of sound in the blackness overhead.

"What was that?"

"Alchemists. Those are scry-spells."

"Scrying? As in the parlor trick performed at séances?" she snorted. "Why can I see those sounds?"

"Everything is different here. We perceive things differently. Now be quiet or they'll see you."

Elle felt a shiver of scrutiny wash over her. "What are they doing?" she whispered.

"They're looking for you. I heard their howling in my dreams too. Which is why I'm here. I thought you might appreciate a little help."

Elle suddenly felt cold. The dark was turning menacing. She looked up. More silver tendrils unfurled above her. She felt strangely drawn to the patterns and she reached up to touch the silver lines with her fingers. She felt herself drift away from Marsh.

He grabbed her and dragged her back to him. "Stay close. Time and space work differently here. What looks like a few inches could end up being a universe away."

"Sorry," she mumbled. "But the shapes are so pretty," she murmured as another wave of luminescence passed over them. This one was purple.

"Pretty, and deadly. Now close your eyes and let it pass over you. Don't try to fight them. They can see you only if you draw attention to yourself. If you stay still for long enough they will give up and stop searching. You have to trust me. Here they come. Get down!"

The world tilted and moved. Elle felt the gaze of a

hundred prying eyes. She covered her face as the howls and cries drained her of all warmth. She felt Marsh tug at her. "This way."

She felt a slight shift.

"You can open your eyes now."

She looked about. The scenery had changed. They were drifting on the ice-still water of a pond. The ice was so cold that it was solid and liquid at the same time. It crackled and flickered as they moved over it. Around her everything was frozen and crusted with ice. Black trees clawed at the nothing above them. Their branches were shrouded in lace-fine crystals. She shivered and her teeth started chattering. The only thing alive was Marsh, next to her. Marsh and the shrieks of those searching for her that echoed far in the distance.

"This is what it must feel like to go mad."

"Some people do go mad from forays into the nether-worlds. Some find they can never fully leave, and they never wake up. Some become too afraid to sleep. If the body doesn't sleep, the mind descends into madness and dies."

"That's reassuring. But how did I get here? I definitely don't remember volunteering for the journey."

"People like us are drawn here naturally. Often it happens quite spontaneously."

"People like us?"

She felt him look down at her. "People with gifts."

"I don't have any gifts. And I would like to go home now. I don't like this place. It's eerie."

"We are both dreaming, Elle. The only way to find your way back is to take control of things from within you. We go where you take us."

This is not real. This is not real, she thought to herself.

They drifted along until the shrieks in the distance died down. The icy pond turned into a stream. The ice melted and trickled down the riverbank. Trees and vines in the most extraordinary shades of green, blue and purple burst forth from the sides of the river. Everything was shrouded in golden light and exotic color. Large white orchids wove into being and unfurled their fragrant petals. Bright hummingbirds fluttered between the blooms. A warm breeze wafted the rich perfume of the flowers over them.

"Oh, look." A blue butterfly landed on her arm. It flexed its wings and then fluttered off. She felt herself grow warm and she stretched as life returned to her limbs.

Marsh murmured something, but she was too drowsy to hear. She felt his arms tighten around her as the world tilted again and the river disappeared in a burst of luminescent shrieks.

She braced herself and buried her face in Marsh's shoulder. In contrast with their evanescent surroundings, he felt warm and real. The skin of his neck was deliciously silky. Unable to resist the temptation, she ran the tip of her nose against it, savoring the sandalwood scented closeness of him. "I'm scared," she said against his throat. "And you shouldn't be here. I don't trust you, Mr. Marsh. Not one bit." She shook her head slowly.

Marsh rested his chin in her hair. "We are safe here. I think they are searching for you in the wrong place. Look." He pointed off into the distance. The tendrils were squirming around in the black distance beyond. "They are looking for you inside your darkest fears."

"And where are we right now?"

He chuckled. "You have hidden us inside your deepest desires. And there's no denying that you are a woman with most ardent desires. Even though you hide it very well under that impervious exterior of yours. You should just let go and allow yourself to be. You would be so much happier, you know."

She leaned back a little to face him. "How dare you

poke around my most private thoughts without as much as a care for my honor and virtue? If you are to intrude like this, then you should be made to show me yours. It's only fair, don't you think?"

It was his turn to look embarrassed. "The inside of my soul is as black as night, Miss Chance. It's . . . it's been many years since I've allowed myself to desire anything." He spoke softly.

"I don't believe that for one moment," she said. "We are not progressing one bit further until you show me."

She felt the balls of his thumbs run across the edge of her jaw, caressing her chin. She could feel her resistance melting . . . along with all the reasons why she shouldn't be provoking him.

He smiled a slow smile. "There's no hiding what I really want in this place," he said. "I've wanted to do this since I laid eyes on you." With a gentle movement, he lifted her face to his and kissed her.

Oh, blast, he's right. And I do want him. How annoying. Those were the last few logical thoughts that fluttered out of her brain as a wave of desire took her.

The touch of his mouth sent a jolt of sensation through her. It was so intense that it struck deep into the marrow of her bones. Around them, the river turned into a copper-colored meadow and golden light washed over them.

She melted into him like flame-softened wax, until they were both no more than an abstract of lips and faces, skin and hands. Bodies touching, intertwined, they drifted weightlessly through the shimmering aether. She felt him trace the outline of her and she arched herself into him in response, aching to be one with him.

Clouds of tiny bright-colored flowers gathered round them. They filled the air with their musky perfume. Light refracted and wrapped around them like rich jeweled cloaks. Inside the pool of light they were all that existed. He moved against her with an urgency that could not be mistaken and she felt herself open up as she surrendered herself to him.

He hesitated. She felt him move away from her slightly, and they parted. The light dimmed to nothing.

"Not like this, not with them watching for us." His voice was strange, heavy-thick. She reached out for him, her burnt-umber hair draped over her slender-pale limbs. "I don't understand," she said.

"If I don't stop this now, I doubt that I will be able to," he murmured. His eyes were dark with wanting.

She tried to speak, but he placed his finger gently onto her lips. "Don't say it. I don't want you to get hurt. It wouldn't be right."

They held one another as they listened for noises in the silence for a while. "It sounds like they've gone," she said.

"I should go too." She felt herself float away from him in the dark-nothing. Suddenly she was very alone.

"Marsh . . ." Her whisper echoed in the dark.

"I am here," he said. "You must go back to your own dreams now. Think about where you came from. Who you are . . ." His voice echoed in the darkness . . . and then, only silence.

She drifted for a while, wondering what to do next. The dark-silence seemed very calm around her. She thought about her room and felt herself shift. Her bed appeared below her and she felt herself sink down into her body. The last thing she sensed was the weight of the bedcovers before ordinary sleep took her.

CHAPTER 20

The next morning, Marsh tapped on the panel door as Elle was putting the last pins into her hair.

"May I come in?" he asked. He was freshly shaved and his shirt collar looked crisp. "Did you sleep well?" She felt a ripple of energy surge through her as she caught the scent of sandalwood that rose up from his cheeks as he brushed by her.

"Like a log," she lied. "All that flying tires one out." She did her best to appear nonchalant. Last night's dream had felt so real, but it was still only a dream. And there was no way she was going to allow this man to think that she was infatuated with him. The mortification she would have to endure if he found out would be too much to bear. Fatigue and spending so much time in close quarters with this man was starting to do strange things to her. She needed to be careful, for nothing good would come of it. Of that at least, she was sure.

There was a knock at the door, and Marsh let in a waiter with a tray covered in silver cloches. The man set about serving up breakfast for them on the balcony.

Elle sat down in one of the wicker chairs and took in a deep breath of salty air. The view of the morning sea was breathtaking. She decided that Nice was definitely one of her favorite places. It was such a pity she wasn't visiting under more pleasant circumstances.

She studied Marsh from under her lashes, but he simply cracked open his boiled egg and dipped a piece of croissant into it seemingly oblivious to their nighttime adventure. "I think we should stick to the coastline. Head east," he said.

Elle took a sip of orange juice. It was freshly squeezed and tart on her tongue. She nodded. "That should make navigating easier. And we won't have to worry about mountain ranges that way. I have no idea how high the 'copter can go, and I'm not so sure I want to risk it."

"Do you think the machine could run on seawater?"

She chewed her croissant. "Hmm. Now, that's an idea, but no. I think the salt might build up in the chambers and cause the engine to malfunction. Perhaps not the best idea to test while in midair."

Below them, Nice came to life as tradesmen and shop-keepers set up for the day. In the harbor, the last few fishing boats were unloading the night's catch for the women who were waiting with sharp knives to scale and gut fish ready for market. Elle watched a group of seagulls squawk and fight for the best position to pick scraps, while a few scrawny harbor cats looked on. A church bell tolled and in some strange way the sound resonated within her. She closed her eyes. It was going to be a nice day . . . but a storm was brewing somewhere in the distance. She could feel the urgency of it in her bones.

"What is it?" Marsh said. He seemed concerned.

She turned her face to the sun and smiled. "Nothing. Everything." She shook her head. "Oh, I don't know. Everything feels wrong and right at the same time. I can't explain it."

He said nothing, but Elle noticed the slight look of worry that crossed his brow as he peered out over the sea, but she refrained from saying anything. Because sometimes it was better to just let the moment be.

After breakfast, they climbed the stairs up onto the roof. Curious hotel staff had gathered and they all stood gawping at the gyrocopter. The porter, suddenly elevated in status, proudly loaded their bags into the hold.

The concierge stepped forward and shook Marsh's hand. "Thank you for including our hotel in this historic flight," he said. "And we have something for your charming wife too." He handed Elle a posy made up of roses and lilacs.

Marsh took the concierge aside. "This is actually more of a test-flight." He tapped the side of his nose. "We would be grateful if you could keep the matter quiet, if you know what I mean. When we have the official launch, we shall make sure that we mention the test-flights and the people who generously helped us on our way."

Marsh handed the man a substantial tip. The concierge's eyes lit up. "Well, then we wish you *bon chance* till then."

Elle busied herself with checking the water tanks. She was rather grateful to note that the hotel staff had filled them up overnight in accordance with the instructions she had given them before she went to bed. She had been dreading the task of lugging water up onto the roof.

They boarded the gyrocopter amid cheers and waving handkerchiefs from the hotel staff. She started the reactor and after a few minutes, the engine shuddered to life.

Elle executed her newly invented lift-off maneuver and steered the 'copter off the roof. She hadn't bargained for the sudden drop though, and the machine dipped dangerously before taking flight.

Marsh went white as the 'copter dipped and then swooped through the fresh morning air, along the famous Bay of Angels that the city of Nice nestled against, before turning east to Monaco and Italy beyond.

They stopped somewhere around Genoa, near a farmhouse with a well. The farmer's wife stared at them somewhat suspiciously from her kitchen door as the 'copter descended upon the farmyard, sending chickens and geese running for cover. After a bit of charm from Marsh and a few coins, she agreed to let them use her well to fill the water tanks.

Marsh wandered up with a basket over his arm. *"Buona sera."* He gave her one of his little smiles.

"Why am I not surprised about the fact that you speak Italian," Elle said.

"Actually, I speak the universal language of point and hand over money, but the method has worked and I have managed to procure lunch."

Elle opened the basket and peered inside. The farmer's wife had given them a loaf of freshly baked bread, a crock of olives and some deliciously garlicky soft cheese in a jar.

"I think she said we could have these as long as we promised to be on our way as soon as possible. I don't think she's very impressed with our machine," he said drily.

Elle made tea with hot water from the little samovar attached to the engine. The gyrocopter had a smaller version of the one she had on board the *Water Lily*. No flight was complete without a cup of tea.

They sat on a low wall under an olive tree and looked out over the Genoese bay while they drank their tea and ate their lunch. The sea shimmered blue in the distance. White crests whipped up by the wind frosted the choppy surf.

"This is so beautiful." She turned her face into the fragrant brininess of the breeze.

"Hmm." Marsh looked out across the water, deep in thought.

"What's wrong?" Elle immediately felt foolish for asking.

He looked down at his hands. "Elle, we need to talk

about yesterday. But before we do, I need you to promise to try to listen to me and not to get angry."

"Speak away," she said. She had hoped that yesterday would blow over. That they had moved on. And she had no intention of showing him how much he had upset her.

"You need to tell me exactly what you know about your mother."

She went very still.

"I wouldn't be asking if it wasn't important," he said.

The suspicion that had been growing in the back of her mind reared up again. He knew something. Perhaps even more than her father did. And she would have to give him some answers if she wanted to know what it was. She sighed with resignation. "My mother ran off after I was born. I think I was about two years old when it happened, so I don't remember her. She left us to join a cult. And the cult killed her. They say she died in a zealot's frenzy. My father was disgraced and humiliated by the scandal. I don't think he's ever really recovered. And that is all there is to tell." She tossed an olive pip over the edge of the cliff.

Marsh was very still next to her.

She turned to him. "So now you know our terrible family secret. Is that shocking enough for you? Was it what you wanted to hear? Are you happy now?" She wiped at her face angrily where the wind was whipping her hair into her cheek.

"I knew your mother. And that is not how it happened."

"My mother died years ago. You must have been a child when she died."

He looked away. "I was not a child when it happened."

She had run out of olive stones, so she picked up a

pebble and threw it off the cliff. "How is that even possible?"

"I am a Warlock. I was younger than I am now, but once a Warlock comes into his power, he ages slowly. We live about ten times as long as ordinary men."

She looked at him with surprise, not sure what to say.

"I remember her. I remember your mother very well. Vivienne was an amazing woman. She was Pythia."

"Who on earth is Pythia?"

"Cybele, Pythia, the Oracle. All are manifestations of the same woman. Just like the larva, the pupa and the butterfly are the same. The Oracle is a woman of immense power and importance, but first you must become Cybele, then Pythia, and when the time is right, you will become the Oracle as is your destiny. There is much you must learn, before you will truly understand what it means to follow this path."

She turned to him. "So my mother's death does have something to do with all of this, doesn't it?"

"I think so. But there is more, which is why I need to meet with my Brothers of the Council. They will know what to do."

"So you *are* involved in my father's abduction. I knew it." Her voice was low with pent-up anger and bitterness.

"It's not like that. Not like you think. There is so much that you don't understand. Hopefully, you will in time."

She met his gaze. "Oh no, you don't. No more hints of mystery and half-truths. I told you my secret; now you are going to have to tell me yours. And I am not going to fly another foot unless you tell me what has happened to my father. And it's a long walk to Venice from here if the map is anything to go by." Elle folded her arms. "I have a right to know what this is all about, Marsh. Damn it, I am risking life and limb here too."

Marsh gripped the bridge of his nose with his thumb and forefinger and closed his eyes. "You are right. You do have the right to know."

She stared at him. "Well, out with it, then."

He sighed. "I strongly suspect that you have inherited your mother's gift. I felt it in you, in the motor on the first night we met. I think Patrice chose you to fly for us because he wanted me to meet you. I think he sensed that you were special, which is why he's kept an eye on you all these years. Your abilities and your father's disappearance are somehow linked to the carmot, but I don't know how or why."

She looked away. "I am nothing like my mother."

He took her hand. "I am sorry I've upset you, but there is a very strong chance that you might be the next Oracle. And you are untrained, and vulnerable to about a million things you don't even have the slightest notion about. It is the sworn duty of my Order to guard and train the Oracle. It has been for centuries."

"What utter nonsense." She pulled her hand away. "Don't you think I would have known if I possessed these special powers? And if you are right, then is it not your precious Council that took my mother away? Is it not because of Warlocks and the Shadow realm that she is dead?"

Marsh looked sad. "Elle, I am a Warlock. I cannot change who I am any more than you can. I'm sorry you feel that way, but you are wrong about me. I hope that you will come to see that I am only trying to help you. And I hope this happens before it's too late."

She stared at him for a long time before speaking. "Your Order destroyed my family and I can do nothing but despise that. Apart from finding my father, I want nothing to do with your cult. Your kind sows heartache and death wherever they go."

A mask of polite formality settled over his features.

He held out his hand and helped her up. "We need to get to Venice as soon as we can." He paused to dust off his hat. "Perhaps then I might convince you otherwise. But please promise me that you will leave some room to believe that I am on your side."

They walked across the dusty farmyard to the gyrocopter, each wrapped up in their thoughts.

The girl followed the Warlock back to the flying machine. I could feel the fear and confusion boiling inside her. Perhaps I should have reached out to her. Perhaps I should have spoken a soft word of kindness to ease her pain. But I was wary. I knew the fear and distrust she held in her heart for creatures of the old blood. It would not have helped to give her more cause to hate us. As it was, she thought that I was dead or that I had abandoned her. And so it was wiser to stay silent. To keep watch over her for what was to come.

Neither the girl nor the Warlock noticed the large shadow that drifted on the ground in the distance behind them. It slid by, silent as a cloud. From the sky, eyes watched and waited as a large fish waits to swallow a smaller one. For this was its hunting ground. Above the clouds, concealed from everyone except those who knew where to look, they had been waiting for some time for the girl and the Warlock to appear.

CHAPTER 21

Elle took off from the farmstead and steered the gyrocopter inland, east over the top of the Italian boot, toward Venice. The Tuscan countryside opened up before them in all its golden beauty, but she barely noticed the scenery. She stared grimly at the horizon ahead of her. The thought of Marsh knowing her mother was disturbing. It meant that he was at least as old as her father in normal years. No wonder he was so odd.

Her mother's esoteric past was something she had spent her life avoiding. The Chance family was good at pretending that everything was normal.

She remembered how sad her father was sometimes and how the scandal of her mother's death still haunted him—even after all these years. To drag up the past was only going to upset things all over again.

And yet, the Council looked to be the only way to find him.

She stole a glance at Marsh. He was studying the map on his lap, his face drawn and closed.

At that moment, a deep rumble shook the gyrocopter. A tree on the ground below them exploded as a flash of lightning hit it.

"What was that?" Startled, Marsh looked up from his map.

Then an oblong shadow shifted over them. It was so big that it blocked out the sun. Cold fear gripped Elle's chest. A giant airship.

"Sky pirates!" She banked the 'copter to the left. Another bolt of spark sailed past them and struck the ground with a crack. "And they have spark cannons!"

Marsh swore.

"Hold on!" Elle banked the 'copter to the right, where they could hover outside the firing range of the cannons.

The pirate ship loomed next to them. It was the biggest air cruiser Elle had ever seen. The pirates looked like little toy people as they moved about on the wooden deck suspended below the canvas patchwork balloon. The ship's fin-shaped rudders, designed for precision steering, creaked and angled toward them. Elle banked the gyrocopter away to avoid the updrafts of air that whooshed past them. She caught sight of the ship's figurehead. It was an iron skeleton holding two swords crossed over its chest. These were death raiders. Pirates who would do anything for money.

The spiked fording platform, complete with grappling hooks, was lowered. On the platform, a huge harpoon rested in front of a tangle of netting. The captain stepped forward. Even from this distance, Elle could see that he was dressed in a fine green brocade coat. He held on to the rigging and pointed as he shouted something to his crew.

"They're going to fire that harpoon!" Marsh shouted.

"Hold on!" She pointed the nose of the gyrocopter at the ground and did a nosedive. The little craft nimbly slipped underneath the hull of the cruiser and rose up the other side. Elle opened the throttle to gain as much distance as she could in the time it took for the cruiser to turn.

"Behind us!" Marsh shouted.

Elle looked over her shoulder and cursed. The pirates had swiveled the harpoon round. Again she banked and dipped underneath the large hull. But this time they were expecting her, and the larger ship dipped too, cutting off their escape route.

It took Elle only a few seconds to realize that they were trapped. There was no possibility that they would be able to get out of range of the cannons fast enough. They would only be able to hover close to the hull, so the harpoon could not be launched for as long as they had water in their boilers. After that, they would either be netted and hauled aboard, or they would crash-land.

"So it looks like it's capture by harpoon or death by spark cannon," Marsh shouted, echoing her thoughts.

"No, I am not giving up yet. If we can't go down, then we must go up." She gripped the controls and aimed the 'copter upwards. The din of the blades and the whine of the straining engine was deafening. Marsh nodded and gripped the straps of his seat harness.

The 'copter groaned and shot up into the sky. Elle leveled off above the cavernous balloon of the pirate ship. The downdraft of the little craft's blades made the patched balloon canvas billow.

"Look for something to throw out onto the balloon," Marsh said.

"It won't work. There is too much wind."

The pirate ship started rising, set on a collision course with the bottom of the 'copter. Elle banked to the side as the canvas rose up next to them. The 'copter spluttered and she urged it further.

"We don't have enough clearance. The machine won't go much higher than this." In answer, the engine spluttered again. Elle kicked the boiler unit under her feet and, to her relief, the steam that drove the propellers started humming through the pipes.

"We're not going to be able to hold off for much longer!" Marsh yelled.

"Don't worry, I have a plan," she yelled back.

"Are you crazy? Have you seen their net?"

"When I say the word, I want you to grab hold of this." She pointed at the steering mechanism. "Hold it steady. Can you do that?"

Marsh stared at her in horror.

"Trust me!" she said.

The 'copter shuddered again in the updraft and she eased off to the left, holding them steady.

With excruciating slowness, the pirate ship rose next to them, its terrifying hull dwarfing the gyrocopter. She gripped the controls as she watched the pirates aim the cannon and the harpoon at them. First they would fire a small blast of spark from the cannon thus neutralizing their engines. Then the harpoon. The giant net, once fired, would cover them, and the gyrocopter would be caught in it like a struggling fish. It was quite a common method used by airships to raid smaller vessels.

Motion slowed down. There was nowhere to run. Only the rhythmic sound of the gyrocopter blades drumming above her pressed into her eardrums. Elle pulled her revolver from its holster.

"Now!" she shouted as she let go of the steering. She slid the cockpit door open and took aim at the spark cannon just as the captain dropped his arm to signal fire.

Elle exhaled and squeezed the trigger. The bullets pinged off the iron hull just as the cannon fired. Tiny yellow sparks flew into the air like a striker to flint.

Wind rushed in and around them and then the spark ignited in a massive blue flame. The backdraft made the flames whoosh toward the cruiser, where it tore up the rigging and through the balloon, igniting the gas inside.

The last thing Elle saw was a flash of bright green as the captain and those pirates with a little sense abandoned ship in one of the few patched life balloons tethered to the deck. And then the entire pirate ship exploded with a gargantuan boom. Giant flames leaped out in all directions. The shockwave spread out and hit the side of the 'copter. It knocked them sideways, just as the pirate ship disintegrated in midair.

Inside the gyrocopter, the spark reactor blinked out. The steam engine spluttered, and before Elle could do anything, the gyrocopter fell to the ground like a stone.

Marsh yelled something, but the air was rushing by so fast that she couldn't hear what it was. In a futile gesture, Elle closed her eyes and thought of soft, bouncy, forgiving surfaces as she braced herself for impact. She felt a wave of energy tear through her and then, as suddenly as it had started falling, the gyrocopter stopped dead in midair. Elle was jarred out of her seat with tooth-rattling force. The machine hovered about a foot off the ground for a full second, and then dropped, hitting the ground with a crash. The wreck bounced once and landed with another thump, where it listed, creaked and came to a stop. Dust billowed and every part of the machine rattled and hissed.

Elle opened her eyes. Her ears were ringing and she tasted blood in her mouth. Glass from the shattered windscreen was all over her, and the metal frame around her was bent, but the 'copter was mostly intact. Carefully she moved her arms and legs, and they responded. With a growing sense of relief-induced hysteria, she realized that she was alive.

She shook her head to ease the painful ringing in her ears, but most of the sound was actually outside her head. It seemed to be coming from the boiler behind them. Steam was whining furiously from the bent release valves. She hit the purge valve to release the pressure, but it was stuck. Her efforts only made the valves whine louder. Elle coughed as she tried to breathe through the hot, damp air. All the pressure gauges were shattered and there was no way of telling how much pressure was still caught inside the engine.

She grabbed her safety strap and yanked at it. The

buckle was bent and the sliding mechanism wouldn't work. Her fingers trembled as she pulled her stiletto out of her bodice and shoved it into the buckle with all her strength. The buckle gave way and she fell out of the 'copter and onto the ground. She coughed and spat the dust out as she dragged herself onto her feet. On shaky legs, she stumbled around the 'copter wreck to get to Marsh.

He was lying back in his seat with his eyes closed. The straps of his harness were singed clean away.

"Marsh!" she yelled, shaking him.

His head rolled over onto his shoulder and a red trickle of blood escaped from his nose. She grabbed the front of his waistcoat and dragged him from the wreck. He was too heavy to lift, but she managed to stumble a few paces before falling to the ground. His heavy body rolled on top of her.

Elle looked up at the wreck. The valves were still whining away uninterrupted. That meant that the pressure was releasing. This was a good thing, but they were still too close to the wreck. She looked up and saw a gnarled pine in the distance. Summoning all of her strength, she stumble-dragged Marsh through the dust. The tree seemed a hundred miles away. Her boots scrabbled in the dry earth and with every haul she landed on her rump, but she managed to move him bit by excruciating bit, until she finally reached the tree. Exhausted, she fell onto the bed of needles, where she lay panting. Her knuckles were chafed where she had gripped his coat. Her throat felt raw and dry and she could taste the metal and blood on her tongue as she gasped for air.

She glanced over at the 'copter. The valves had stopped hissing. Only ominous creaks now emanated from the wreck.

Marsh lay completely still in her arms. The trickle of blood from his nose was stark against his pale skin.

With her fingers she traced the line to where it left a red stain on his collar.

No, she thought. "No. No. Hugh," she mumbled, and ran her hands over his chest. "No, please don't be dead. You can't be dead," she muttered. She slipped her hands into the front of his waistcoat and wormed her fingers into his shirt to find a place where she could feel his heart. She was shaking so much that it was almost impossible to tell if it was beating.

She put her cheek onto his chest and closed her eyes. Concentrating with all her might, she listened.

Please don't be dead. Please. Please. I can't feel his heart. I can't feel his breath, she thought frantically. *Please be alive.* She felt something shift inside her. It felt like that stomach-turning sensation after entering an air pressure pocket in midflight. Without really knowing why, she placed her lips over his and closed her eyes. Slowly she exhaled, pushing her breath into him. She willed him to breathe. Willed his heart to beat. A vacuum formed around her, encapsulating only her and Marsh. She felt a surge of power move through her, clear and blue as sea ice. It dragged and flowed, holding them together like two bits of debris caught in a current. Then, very softly, she felt the gentle thud of his heart against her fingers. She watched the color flow back into his face. The energy around them snapped out of existence.

Marsh coughed and opened his eyes. "Are we alive?" he croaked.

She let go of him and moved away, allowing him space to breathe. "Yes. I think we are."

It was suddenly completely and utterly silent around them. Small bits of what had once been the pirate ship were sifting down onto the ground around them like black flower petals.

As if annoyed that everyone was ignoring it, the gyrocopter chose that moment to explode with an almighty boom.

Marsh and Elle held on to one another for cover as bits of debris flew past them.

They lay like that for some time as the world settled around them. Marsh was the first to move. He sat them both up.

"You shot a pirate ship with a handgun. Are you insane?" he said.

She smiled. "Not bad for a few days' work. It's just a pity no one is ever going to believe a word of it told."

He started laughing. It was a silly shock-fueled laugh that started somewhere deep inside him, as if he couldn't help himself.

She started laughing too.

"You have soot on your nose." He wiped the mark off her skin, his fingers gentle.

"You have blood on yours," she said.

They looked at one another for a long moment. "I think you just saved my life," he murmured.

"Well, that makes us even, then."

"I suppose it does." He sat back against the tree and pulled a hip flask from his pocket. The metal was dented but it was still in one piece. He unscrewed the top and handed it to her.

She sniffed the top. "Absinthe," she said as the smell of anise hit the back of her throat.

"That's what us half-Shadow people prefer. There was no fairy in the bottle that I filled my hip flask from, so you won't have the visions if you drink it."

Something dropped onto the ground next to Marsh's boot in a little cloud of dust. It was a mangled fragment of black metal that had worked its way through the canopy of the tree. He picked it up and examined it. "Poor bastards. That was quite a blast."

"It's their own fault, to be fair. That balloon was filled with hydrogen."

Marsh looked at her in surprise. "But that's like flying a large bomb."

Elle nodded. "Passenger dirigibles must be filled with helium for that very reason. It's the law. But helium is expensive and hard to get hold of, so pirates and other rogue flyers use hydrogen, which works just as well but costs about a tenth of the price." She gestured at the sky. "And then accidents like this happen."

Marsh shook his head; he looked stunned. "I had no idea that the whole ship would explode."

Elle shrugged. "That's what you get when you mix with pirates. It's sad that men had to die for such foolishness."

He didn't answer for a while. Then he looked down at her. "Are we still friends? It would make me very happy if we could be."

Seeing Marsh so lifeless and pale had upset her more than she had expected. She could not deny that her dreams meant that she was attracted to him, even if he did not feel the same way. But she could be his friend without all the other complicated things in between. And that would have to be enough. Affectionate friends. The thought of it made her feel happy inside, as if a great weight had lifted from her heart. She took another swig from the flask and grimaced at the liquor. "Hugh, I do believe we are," she said.

He smiled and held her against him and they watched the last bits of pirate ship and ash drift to the ground.

"What shall we do now?" she said eventually.

He stretched and looked about. "Well, I suppose we need to procure some means of transport. Venice, I believe, is that way." He pointed off into the distance.

Elle swayed as she stood up. Her muscles had grown stiff and she ached all over. She cupped her hands over her brow and stared off into the distance. "I think I remember seeing a road running in that direction."

Marsh stood up and patted the pine needles off his trousers. "Then I move that we make for the road."

"Motion seconded," she said. "I saw some pirates abandoning ship just before the blast and I don't think I really want to run into any of them at this stage."

"You know, Miss Chance, for once I couldn't agree with you more."

There was nothing to salvage from the wreck, so they hiked across the fields until they found the lane that looked like it ran toward the east. The air was warm and heady with the scent of warm soil and a summer ended. Eventually, they came to a crossroad with a wooden sign in the middle of it. One of the arrows read *Venezia* in curly letters and that it was apparently five miles away.

Marsh leaned against the signpost and folded his arms. "And now we wait for someone to take pity on us," he said with a little smile.

CHAPTER 22

In a city far away, Sir Eustace Abercrombie sat in the antechamber of his hotel room. He stared out of the finely carved window screen at the tiled courtyard with its marble fountain in the middle. Bees droned in what remained of the year's jasmine still clinging to the trelliswork in the courtyard. The sun dipped toward evening. All was well with him on such a fine afternoon. His plans were going magnificently at the moment.

There was a discreet knock on the door.

"Enter!" said Abercrombie.

A servant in a red fez with a black tassel entered the room and bowed. He proffered a telegram on a small tray.

Abercrombie lifted the envelope and tore open the seal. As he scrutinized the message, his face grew like stone. He stalked across the room and yanked at the bell pull at least half a dozen times.

Mr. Chunk came running in. "You rang, master?" He was slightly out of breath.

"We need to speed up the experiments. I want the professor working through the night, if need be. See to it."

Mr. Chunk nodded.

"And wake the Nightwalker. I need to speak with him."

Mr. Chunk started. "But master, it is still too early in the afternoon."

"I don't care. His windows have been blacked out.

There is no reason why he cannot rise. We can meet in his sleeping crypt. See to it. Our guests are arriving and there is no time to lose."

"As you wish." Mr. Chunk nodded and retreated.

The runes on Abercrombie's face blurred as they whirred and moved while he brooded over the telegram. The news was not good.

A quarter of an hour later, Aleix stormed out of his dressing room, the folds of his velvet robe flying around him as he walked. His shiny hair fell around his shoulders in a dark, straight curtain. His skin was so pale that it was almost translucent in the lamplight and there were dark smudges under his eyes.

"Why, Aleix, you look terrible." Abercrombie waited in one of the red leather wingbacks that adorned the anteroom of the Nightwalker's crypt.

Faster than the human eye could see, the Nightwalker moved across the room and grabbed Abercrombie by the throat. "Why do you wake me at this hour?" he hissed. He bared his fangs at the Alchemist.

Abercrombie started laughing. "My, we are grumpy when we wake up first thing. You know you cannot harm me, Nightwalker. One shout and this crypt will be filled with sunlight. Now let go of me." To prove his point, Abercrombie pushed the wooden stake he had been holding up his sleeve against Aleix's chest. "You lot are like a pack of rabid dogs. I should put a collar on you." Abercrombie did not even bother to hide the contempt in his voice.

Aleix hissed at the insult, but let go of Abercrombie's throat. He turned away, shielding his expression from the other man. "Forgive me. I am indeed not at my best early in the evening. Pray, why have you woken me from my slumber before sunset?" The sarcasm bled through his voice like a stain.

Abercrombie's face grew serious. He handed over the opened telegram without a word.

Aleix grew even paler as he scanned the words on the page. "This is from the captain. Our pirate allies have failed us. The girl destroyed their ship in some huge explosion, it seems."

Abercrombie sighed and waved his hand in the air with contempt. "Hydrogen in the balloon. They didn't stand a chance. But no one really cares about a few pirates. What concerns me is the fact that the Warlock used his power to save himself and the girl."

Aleix swiveled round. "But destroying the ship would have taken an enormous amount of power. Why have we been thinking that he had none to use?"

"It would seem that our information has been incorrect."

"But I have not heard of Warlocks using their power in the open in more than a century," Aleix said.

"Well, the captain of the pirate ship would beg to differ."

Aleix shook his head in disbelief. "All they needed to do was grab one girl. How difficult can that be?"

Abercrombie gave a short laugh. "I almost feel sorry for them. Especially since it was one as powerful as Greychester. He must have forged a link with the girl. It's the only way he could have done it."

"Then she really must be the Oracle." A strange light filled Aleix's eyes. "I knew I sensed it in her when she walked into the café. But with all those cheap fairies floating about, it was hard to tell."

Abercrombie nodded slowly. "It seems we are on the right path, my friend."

Aleix closed his eyes. "The elders arrive. I can feel them approaching. Drastic steps are needed."

"Quite," said the Alchemist, studying his fingernails. "I think I have a plan that might just work."

"And that would be?"

"I think it is time to call in a favor from our friend in London, don't you?"

"Hmm. An interesting thought. And what do we do with the elders in the meantime?"

"They are your kin. Take them hunting. I'm sure there is enough blood in this city to keep them distracted for a while. A last good feed before you betray them would be quite romantic, don't you think?" Abercrombie smiled at the Nightwalker. It was quite extraordinary what Nightwalkers would do for money and power. Especially one who had fallen on hard times.

"Our friend will have to be discreet though. It is safe to assume that the Council knows about the girl. News of Greychester's actions will reach them soon," Aleix said, ignoring Abercrombie's jibe.

"Fear not, my night-walking master. Our plans will succeed. We simply need to trust in our allies," Abercrombie said.

The Alchemist and the Nightwalker stared at one another for a long moment. Then they both smiled.

CHAPTER 23

The farmer's cart that had eventually picked Elle and Marsh up from the crossroads trundled along the cobbled road that led to the dockside. They had reached Mestre, the dowdy sister-city of Venice and her anchor to the mainland. Elle and Marsh hopped off the back of the cart and waved a thank you to the farmer.

"I'll see if I can get us some tickets for the ferry," Marsh said. "You stay here." He motioned for her to sit down on the harbor wall. "And do try to stay out of trouble while my back is turned."

Elle pulled a face at his back. Try to stay out of trouble indeed. She busied herself with picking bits of straw and pine needles from her coat. It was a rather pointless task, given that her clothes were utterly ruined. After a few minutes, she gave up and watched the ferry crowd instead.

They were mostly day-laborers and tourists making their way back from Venice as evening drew in. A few automatons steamed their way through the crowds pushing luggage barrows. These automatons were made from shiny steel painted in places in ice cream shades of light blue, yellow or even red. Little puffs of steam escaped from their polished articulated legs as they ambled along. Elle loved Italian design. Automatons were very fashionable in Rome, mostly due to narrow alleyways and streets.

She caught a glimpse of gray in the crowds. She looked

again, but there was nothing. She could have sworn it was a gray cloak just like the one in her visions from the other night. Elle shook her head. She was still very edgy. Everyone looked suspicious all of a sudden. She squeezed the reassuring lump under her elbow. She had lost her stiletto in the wreck, but the Colt was still safely tucked away under her waistcoat.

Marsh made his way over to her. He fanned two ferry tickets. "Venice awaits, my lady."

A ferry horn sounded right next to them and Elle had to cover her ears. They felt raw and achy after the crash.

"Well, come along, then. The boat's not going to wait for us," Marsh said as soon as the noise had died down. Elle stood up from the wall and groaned. Every bone and muscle in her body ached, and it took a few steps before she was walking normally again. They shuffled along with the crowd and boarded the bright blue ferry.

On board, the crew started preparing to cast off. The gangplanks rose. Big clouds of steam started chugging from the chimney stack and the boat moved away from the quay.

"Come with me," Marsh said. "I want you to have the best spot for your first view of Venice." He took her elbow and led her to the railing at the bow. "Look!" He pointed out over the water. The great domes of Venice came into view against the backdrop of a salmon-colored sky as the ferry chugged across the water toward the Grand Canal.

"Oh my goodness, look at that!" Elle pressed her hands to her cheeks as she took in the curved domes and buildings. A few large passenger dirigibles floated lazily in the golden air above the city domes.

"Have you ever been to Venice? This city is far more beautiful than any picture or painting could ever capture."

She shook her head. "No. I've always wanted to come here though. Do they have an airfield?"

Marsh smiled at her. "No, I believe it's landing platforms and ladders here."

The ferry moored, and they jostled with the other passengers up the ancient stone stairs to emerge, breathless, onto the Piazza San Marco. The square was filled with people bustling about in the fading light of the early evening.

A few women were selling the last of the day's flowers from underneath large parasols, while shiny-winged pigeons fluttered and wheeled around the square in flocks as they came in to roost. Workmen shouted as they packed up for the day amid scaffolding and the rubble of what looked like an ancient building.

"That's where the Campanile—Tower of St. Marco used to be. It fell down last year. After hundreds of years, it just gave up and collapsed. Venice is like that though. It's the city that stays the same, despite the fact that it is always changing."

"Will they rebuild it?" she said, eyeing the scaffolding.

Marsh nodded. "Apparently they are rebuilding it exactly as it was."

She looked up at the façade of the basilica, which stood majestically next to the scaffolding. The buildings were tinged with soft light and she felt herself fill with excitement. "It's beautiful," she said.

"I'm glad you like it. Venice is one of my favorite cities. But first, my dear Miss Chance, I think we should find a place that will put us up for the night. And I think I know just the one. Let's go this way." He steered her off the busy square and into the labyrinth of alleys and footbridges beyond. Elle did her best to keep track of the route, but the close alleyways twisted and turned so frequently that she was soon lost.

Marsh suddenly stopped and looked behind him.

"What is it?"

He peered down the alley they had walked through. It was empty save for the growing shadows of the setting sun.

"Nothing," he said. "I thought I saw something. My nerves must still be on edge from the crash." He shook his head.

"I know what you mean. I keep seeing suspicious characters from the corner of my eye too. I thought I was going mad."

Marsh looked again, but the alley was empty. He shrugged. "If someone is following us, they're doing a fine job of it. Come. It's this way. We will be safe once we are indoors."

They rounded a corner and entered a small square. Bright light beamed through the lead-glass windows of an ancient building in front of them.

"I give you the Hotel Royale," Marsh said. "And I don't think I've ever been so happy to see it."

They stepped into the elegant foyer of the hotel, lavishly decorated with pink marble and Murano glass. Twisted pillars that looked more like they were made from sugar rather than stone reached up to meet arches that were so finely carved that they looked like lace. Everywhere you looked fine glass chandeliers that hung from the ceiling cast glimmering light. It was like standing in the middle of a giant confection shaped like a Gothic castle.

"Lord Greychester. We are very pleased to see you! It has been such a long time." The concierge greeted them with a broad smile. He seemed to be entirely unaware of their sooty faces and tattered clothes.

"Hello, Stefano. It is very nice to be here," Marsh said.

"This way, please. I will show you to your room. Would the blue room be adequate for the lady?"

"Do you like the color blue?" Marsh asked Elle.

"Um, I believe I do," she replied.

He turned to the concierge. "The blue room would be perfect."

Stefano clicked his heels together. "This way, please."

"How did he know we were coming?" Elle whispered to Marsh.

"He didn't. I have a standing reservation here. The Council regularly meets in Venice."

"No luggage?" the concierge asked as they climbed the stairs.

"It was destroyed in an accident on the way," Marsh said.

The concierge put his hand in front of his mouth in dismay. "Oh, how *terrible*!" He said the final word in Italian. "I will send word to your tailor to expect you immediately. And might I recommend a seamstress for the lady?" he said, nodding at Elle's singed coat.

"How very thoughtful," Marsh said.

The concierge led them into a suite and retreated unobtrusively, as only the very best trained staff in service could.

Elle looked about the elegant room with its wood-framed picture windows. "Are you sure this place is a good idea? It's terribly ostentatious."

Marsh shook his head and looked into her eyes. "This is a safe place, Elle. We will come to no harm here."

"And where would you be staying?" she asked, eyeing the ornate bed.

"I have my own suite. These rooms are for your exclusive use."

She cleared her throat and looked away. It felt strangely disappointing that she wouldn't have to fight with him about their accommodations. "Right now, I think I could do with a bath and a rest."

"That sounds like a capital idea. I need to go out for a

little while first. If your father is in Venice, we need to find him as soon as possible."

"And you are going out like that? You don't even have a hat."

"I must speak with the Council immediately and we have been greatly delayed by this afternoon's rather unfortunate crash landing." He ran his hand over his lapel. "Besides, this is an excellent disguise. No one would even give me a second glance in these clothes."

"Do you think the Council will help?"

He straightened his coat. "I am almost certain they will. In the meantime, stay here and keep the door locked. Open the door to no one but Stefano. He will bring the seamstress to you. Please choose whatever clothes and things you might need for the rest of the journey." He ran his gaze over her. "Perhaps something pretty to wear to dinner this evening, what do you think?"

She felt herself flush. "Thank you . . . but please remember to add the costs to my expense account."

He shrugged. "It's of no consequence. I will collect you when I return." With those words he stepped out of the room and was gone.

CHAPTER 24

A chill rose up from the dark canals and the dank air turned to fine mist that swirled like white fingers around the legs. Marsh shivered in his tattered coat. He lifted the lantern he had taken with him from the hotel to examine the carvings on the sweaty walls of buildings as he walked. Venice had been a place of Warlocks for centuries. Within the flaking stonework rested a myriad of markers. They revealed the way to wherever the Council met, for those who knew how to look.

He came to a narrow footbridge that led to a doorway. A glyph rendered faint by centuries of rain was carved into the stone next to the door. In the flickering light of his lantern, the triangle with an eye in the topmost point was the marker he sought. Marsh placed his palm over the glyph and closed his eyes. There was a faint vibration in the air around him and with a sigh the door creaked open.

He cast a quick glance over his shoulder and stepped inside. The door shut behind him with a gentle rumble. Before him, a steep staircase extended up to the rooms above. Marsh wasted no time in the narrow, damp hallway. At the top of the stairs he paused to gather himself.

"Enter." A voice spoke from the room that lay just beyond the stairs.

Marsh closed his eyes and walked through the protective veil that shrouded the entrance. He had found the Brotherhood, The Order of Sacred Warlocks.

Conrad De Montague, the Grand Master of the Council, sat at a large round wooden table, with eleven other men. He beckoned to Marsh. "We are pleased that you could join us. Please do come in." De Montague spoke in a soft, cultured voice that was almost too melodic.

The other Warlocks turned to look at Marsh. They were all dressed in black ceremonial cloaks with deep hoods. Each cloak had an elaborately wrought clasp of silver at the throat.

Marsh felt a frisson of power flow through him, and the torches against the wall flickered in reply. The Warlock masters of the thirteen dioceses that made up the civilized world were assembled. It had been many years since a full Council had sat. Warlocks were solitary creatures. Longevity and the quest for power made them wary of one another. The Council was one of grudging cooperation born of necessity, but none of its members particularly enjoyed their place on it.

"Gentlemen. My apologies for being late. We ran into trouble on the way." Marsh walked over to the Grand Master, bowed and rested his forehead against his leader's hand. It was a ceremonial gesture, but one that carried a very real message. Nothing other than complete obedience would be tolerated.

"So it would seem, Master Warlock." The Grand Master eyed Marsh's torn coat. "And our Cybele, how does she fare?"

"Miss Chance is safe and resting. I have made sure that she is well guarded at the hotel."

"That is good news. Please, sit. Make yourself comfortable. This is not an inquisition, you know."

Marsh pressed his lips together and sat down. "You will forgive my appearance. I thought it better that I attend without delay."

"Do not worry about that, Greychester. We are glad

to see that you are alive," said the Grand Master. "Now, please, tell us what news you bring."

Marsh did not answer immediately. He would have to lay the groundwork carefully. "My brothers, as you all might be aware by now, Eustace Abercrombie has found the carmot we liberated from the abbey a few months ago. He managed to intercept the box in Paris. I've had my men looking for him, but the trail has gone cold."

"And the key, it is safe? He has not succeeded in opening the box?" asked Master Obanwedya, his African-honey voice grave. He wore colorful robes of red and ochre under his cloak, signifying that he was a medicine man of his people.

"Yes. The key is with our new Cybele," Marsh said.

The Grand Master stroked his neat beard. His eyes were hard and black, like river pebbles. "It was a daring risk to take, pairing the key up with a creature so valuable and so vulnerable."

Marsh shook his head. "It was not what we had intended. My man, Patrice, made a slight error in judgment in that respect."

"The butterfly has not broken from its slumber, then? She has not ascended to being Pythia yet?" The Grand Master raised a shaggy eyebrow at him.

"No, she has not. I have also not yet managed to succeed in fully explaining to her the importance of who she is. She remains distracted by the mystery of the carmot and the disappearance of her father."

"But those are separate issues. We must not allow ourselves to become distracted by the Alchemists." The Grand Master paused. "But I sense some unease within you, Brother. What news do you bring?"

"As I said in my dispatch report, I am almost certain that Abercrombie thinks Professor Chance will be able to devise a plan to use the carmot. I don't know how they will manage it, but as long as they believe that they can do this, he will remain alive. My only concern is that no one knows what dark chores the Alchemists might dream up for someone with the professor's skills while he remains in their custody."

"But our Cybele and the key are here, in Venice, with you?" This time Master Chen spoke. "That seems like a big risk to take."

"I said, they are safe and under my protection," Marsh snapped. Of all his brothers, he disliked Chen the most. He was a greedy little man who made his money from selling opium. Marsh had little patience for men who brought such misery on the world.

"Gentlemen, please," the Grand Master said.

"There is another problem." Marsh rested his elbows on the table and looked at the assembly. "Miss Chance does not believe that she is the next Oracle. In fact, she remains completely resistant to the very thought of it."

They all started speaking at once.

"Silence!" the Grand Master said. He leaned over the table and fixed his gaze on Marsh. "Do you mean to tell us that the new Oracle that has arisen is unwilling to heed the call? This is Vivienne's daughter, is it not?"

Marsh nodded. "She is Vivienne's daughter undoubtedly."

"And she understands her importance?"

Marsh sighed. "I've tried to speak to her, but she refuses to listen. There is a lot of pain surrounding her mother's death. She has no faith in the Order. She blames us for what happened to her mother."

Another murmur of uncertainty rose up from the other Warlocks. They looked at one another, all speaking at once and shaking their heads in disbelief.

"But does she show her power?" Master Chen asked. His greedy little eyes twinkled.

"She dream-walks the Shadow realm and she sees the scry-spells the Alchemists cast, but she refuses to allow her mind to embrace the gift. She has buried these matters deeply within. It is going to take time and patience to coax them out."

The Grand Master spoke. "And what do you propose to do about the matter, Master Warlock?"

Marsh sighed. "I believe that she may be convinced with a little perseverance. But we cannot rule out the possibility that this one may never heed the call and that we may have to wait another generation for the Oracle to arise and take her place."

There was another outburst as all the Warlocks started speaking at once.

"I said, silence!" the Grand Master bellowed. They turned to look at him.

"We cannot allow a Cybele to roam free unguarded and untrained. You know how many there are that would wish to use her? And besides, hers is the sacred bloodline. Even if we waited for another generation, we may not have another woman who bears the gift. I also doubt we can wait that long, given the state of the core of Shadow." Master Lewis was grave as he spoke. Marsh had not seen the American for many years, not since the War of Independence.

"This Cybele is different from those who came before her. She has a mind of her own," Marsh said. "I don't think she will relent without a fight."

"Then we will have to make her yield," said the Grand Master. "This is not that unusual. The ancients used to do it all the time."

Everyone went silent.

"Surely you cannot be serious?" Marsh said.

The Grand Master looked at him and his eyes grew even colder. "Do I detect an emotional attachment to this woman? You do remember the rules, don't you?"

Marsh met his gaze with cool resolve. "I remember

them well. But dragging off a girl against her will is barbaric."

"How dare you show such disrespect to our Grand Master," said Master Chen. He hit the table with his chubby fist without much effect.

Marsh rose slightly from his seat, ready to confront Chen.

"Gentlemen. Please," the Grand Master spoke, waving his hand. "Let us not quarrel. These are trying times and this is not the time to be divided."

The other Warlocks grew silent again.

"Perhaps we should start at the beginning. Please tell us what happened. Why do you attend our Council dressed in rags?"

They listened in silence as Marsh told them of the pirates and their escape. Most of them grew interested when he told the part about how he and Elle had stopped the pirates.

"It has been many years since any of us has used that much power at once," the Grand Master said.

"It was necessary," Marsh said. He noticed that the other Warlocks were staring at him with open envy.

"Tell me, how was it?" The Grand Master's eyes were also lit up with desire. "It has been so long since any of us has touched the core."

"I struggled to draw from it. Having Elle—I mean, the Cybele—with me made it possible. I was amazed at her ability to channel the magic. I think she saved our lives."

The Grand Master sighed. "It is true, then. The Oracle will once again show us the way. We have been without one for so long. That old hag who has been pretending to hold the universe together since Vivienne died has been nothing short of useless."

"The old hag of whom you speak has devoted her life to service of this Order. It is not her fault that her powers were weak or that she was unable to perform the miracles you require. The world is still standing. We are all still here, are we not?" Marsh felt his voice rise. He was getting angry and this was not necessarily the best way to address the Council. He forced himself to calm down as he listened to murmurs of agreement around the table.

"Forgive me," the Grand Master apologized. "I spoke in haste. But even you have to admit that without this new Oracle we will continue to grow weaker, until there is nothing left of what we once were. We will lose our authority over those who stem from the Shadow. The wall that divides Light from Shadow will collapse, and we will be plunged into a new Dark Age of chaos and anarchy."

"I'm afraid that convincing Miss Chance is simply not going to be that easy," Marsh said softly.

"If you'll excuse me for butting in, I think it is even more important than ever that she be shown the way so she may help us," said Master Lewis.

"I agree that the need for an Oracle is grave, but Elle is different. She's like no woman I've ever met before. I do not think she will agree to this unless she fully believes in our cause. And taking her against her will would only make her more obstinate. In fact, I believe that it would kill her," Marsh said.

"So what would it take to make her agree?" said Master Chen. "Money? Jewels and furs?"

"Time." Marsh flexed his jaw. "Right now, all she knows is that her father has been abducted by villains and she will not rest until he is safe."

"Of course, the matter of the Alchemists," said the Grand Master. "So what do you propose we do?"

Marsh was suddenly reminded of why he hated attending these Council meetings so much. "Well, I was hoping you could tell me."

The Grand Master's eyes narrowed in thought. "And

you truly believe that we may be able to persuade this young lady to join us in service if we save her father, return him to her?"

Marsh nodded. "I believe we might, yes. If she sees that the work we do is for good, then maybe she will be persuaded to change her mind."

"Hmm, maybe," said the Grand Master. "But I don't think the Alchemists are going to succeed in whatever this new plan is. The Nightwalker elders will not allow their vassals to grow too powerful. They will step in to stop this before it's too late. So I do not believe that there is a need for us to interfere. And I think I speak for everyone here when I say that this Council has no desire to provoke a war with the Nightwalkers."

"But that is ridiculous," Marsh said. "The fate of the world depends upon it."

The Grand Master shrugged. "Welcome to the world of politics, my son." He folded his hands. "I think that the only way is to follow the tried and tested ways of our Order. Whether she cooperates or not is largely irrelevant. Bring us the girl so we may train her. Once she has been made to see her destiny and once she has helped us to grow strong, then we can think about fighting battles such as the one you are currently proposing. Who votes in favor of such a motion?"

There were murmurs of agreement around the table. Marsh went cold. The Grand Master's plan involved the ancient practice of dragging a young woman off to a cave and keeping her there until she relented and embraced her power. In truth, most never left the caves, living out their lives chained up in the damp darkness— a terrible fate if there ever was one. He felt a deep cold anger rise within him. "We will not do this!" He slammed his fist on the table. This time the wood did reverberate. "I have given this woman my word. We must take up arms and stop the Alchemists before they unleash whatever power they are planning to summon. With the carmot in their possession, they have every chance of succeeding. Do you not see that?"

"My dear boy, if we start a war with the Alchemists— or anyone else, for that matter—the fact that we have no power to speak of would be exposed. We would be ruined. We simply cannot risk being discovered. But with a new Cybele in our midst we would be invincible again. And we'll have time to do things our way. She is still young," the Grand Master said.

Heads were bobbing up and down around the table in agreement.

"Your Cybele's father is going to have to be collateral damage in the process, I'm afraid. Besides, the Chance family should be used to making sacrifices by now. They are the authors of their own fate. It is what happens when one interferes with the natural order of things." The Grand Master's hard eyes glittered as he spoke.

Marsh was seething inside. He took a few deep breaths before he spoke. "Do I take it that I do not have the Council's support?"

The Grand Master inclined his head. "Bring us the Oracle. That is the ruling of this Council."

"And what of the Alchemists? What if they manage to create the carmot stone? Every supernatural creature that dwells in Shadow or that has the old blood in its veins will flock to this new source of power. There will be utter chaos, and we will be as powerless as you propose."

"Lord Greychester, the Alchemists have been trying to invoke the power of the carmot stone since the dawn of alchemy and they have never succeeded. Betting that they will fail again is a risk I am willing to take. The death of one scientist is regrettable but understandable. Now, tell us; are you going to bring this young woman to us, or do we have to take her?"

Marsh rose from the table. "I see this meeting is over," he said. "I have sworn an oath of loyalty to this Council and so I will obey. I will bring you the Oracle, but not if it is against her will. You will give me time to persuade her. Or else I will hide her where you will never find her. And believe me, I am very good at hiding. She will disappear without a trace."

The Grand Master pressed his lips together. Long seconds ticked by while he considered the ultimatum. "Very well, then, you have three full moons to try. But if you fail, we will come for her." His voice was soft, but like steel.

Marsh gritted his teeth and bowed stiffly. "As you wish, my lord. Now, if you'll excuse me, please, gentlemen. I have important business that I need to attend to."

"Oh, and Greychester . . ."

Marsh turned to face the Grand Master at the top of the stairs.

"If you betray us, the penalty will be death for both you and the girl."

Marsh met the Grand Master's gaze. "I will pretend that you never said that to me. Don't think I won't challenge you over the insult."

There was a sharp intake of breath from the others. There had not been a duel between Warlocks for many years. The Grand Master started laughing. "You may try, insolent pup. I would very much enjoy teaching you a few lessons."

"Till we meet again, old man," Marsh said as he left the room.

Back on the street, he paused to take a few deep breaths of cold night air. His hands were shaking inside his gloves. He had won the battle, but he was very far from winning the war.

CHAPTER 25

Elle stared out of the lead-glass window at the canal below. The color of the water had changed from the strange almost-the-color-of-spark-blue to a thick black, like velvet. Light refracted in flecks of gold from the windows and shimmered off the surface as the water moved. She had bathed and dressed. The seamstress had come and gone. Stefano had brought her tea and so there was nothing left to do but to wait.

It had been a strange day and she still could not believe that they had survived the crash. She had never seen magic of that magnitude in action. She shivered and rubbed her arms where the skin showed between her sleeves and the tops of her fine new satin gloves. Marsh was obviously a very powerful man and the thought made her a little afraid of him.

The door handle rattled. She stiffened and turned to meet Marsh as he entered the room.

He turned up the spark lights. "Oh, hello. Why are you sitting in the dark?" He looked slightly concerned as he crossed the room to join her at the window.

"I like looking at the canal and it's prettier if the light inside is low."

"The seamstress came as promised, I see," he said.

"I was lucky because she had this in my size. She said something about a previous order that was canceled. Personally, I think it's a bit too flouncy for my taste, but do you think it will do?" She spoke a little faster than she meant to and her cheeks grew warm as she felt his gaze flick over her, taking in the layers of pale pink organza and satin that draped around her slim figure like flower petals. She was not used to men staring at her like that.

"Eleanor, you look lovely." Ever so lightly, he touched the matching ribbon she had tied around her neck to hide the fading bruises at her throat. "And I'm glad you are healing."

"Thank you," she said, somewhat awkwardly. "You've changed too, I see." He was dressed in a new dinner jacket. The edges of his collar were freshly starched. But the fine tailoring and starched linen could not hide the dark shadows under his eyes.

"Yes, I stopped off at my tailor on the way back. He always keeps a few things in my size for when I am in Venice." He gestured at his new white silk waistcoat. "They should deliver the rest of my new things tomorrow. Did the seamstress have everything else you needed? If not, we can call someone else." He spoke quickly, as if he wished to please her.

"Thank you, you are too generous. I think I have all I need. But enough talk about luggage. Tell me, did you find any news about my father?"

He was still staring at her.

"Well? Did you?" she asked again.

He rubbed a hand through his hair, mussing up the careful combing. "Nothing. I'm afraid the Council knows no more than I do about the Alchemists or the whereabouts of your father. Elle, I'm sorry. I really thought they would be of more assistance."

Hope crumbled inside her. "Do you mean to tell me that we came all this way for nothing? So what now?"

He sighed. "I really thought they would be more helpful."

"I'm sorry, but I'm not really surprised. I had the feeling that they weren't going to help. I say we go to the consulate tomorrow. If they don't know anything that might help, I will ask them to send out a wire to all the other consulates with my father's description. Surely someone in this world must have seen him."

Marsh sighed. "That could take months."

"Well then, I must go home and hire an investigator. Surely there must be people who specialize in finding missing persons?"

"Those people will only take your money and leave you with nothing," he said.

"Well what other option do I have?" she said. "You said yourself that the police are not much help." She knew Marsh had a point, but giving up just seemed so senseless. "I am not giving up, Hugh. I can't." She could be stubborn too.

He pressed his lips together. "Shall we discuss our plans over dinner?" He patted his stomach. "I don't know about you, but defying death always makes me ravenous."

She did not feel like eating. In fact, she was feeling decidedly queasy. She wanted to rush outside and scream out her father's name at the top of her lungs, but instead she rose and picked up her new satin reticule.

"Dinner sounds like a fine idea," she said, forcing a smile. Marsh was right. Their simple luncheon looking out over the ocean near Genoa seemed like a lifetime ago. Perhaps a hot meal would bring a new perspective to the search for her father.

Dinner at the restaurant inside the Hotel Royale was a glittering, opulent affair. The restaurant's patrons sat at tables covered in starched linen and arranged in neat rows. Refracted and mirrored from every angle in silver and fine-cut crystal were well-groomed faces and gleaming jewels.

The dinner seating was in full swing when Elle and Marsh entered the room. More than a few people glanced up and nodded at Marsh as they were shown to a table.

"Why are they staring at us?" Elle said out of the corner of her mouth.

"Because I am Viscount Greychester and I am about to have dinner with a breathtakingly beautiful woman."

"What happened to the dowdy and eccentric Mr. and Mrs. Mason from London?"

He smiled. "You and I make far too striking a couple for that disguise."

"You are so vain," she scoffed.

"Look," he said softly, pointing at a mirror on one of the walls. Elle started at their reflection. Marsh was darkly handsome behind her. Her new dress was low cut and showed off more of her curves than she normally put on display. Bruises aside, the pink of the gown made her skin look soft and luminous.

"You are like peaches and cream tonight," he murmured behind her. Her whole body filled with languid electricity as his words passed over her. He was difficult to resist when he behaved like this. And it was dangerous. They were affectionate friends and she would have to take care not to let any of her fanciful thoughts show.

The maître d'hôtel led them to a table in the middle of the room. Elle took her seat in the chair proffered by the steward; back straight, gloved hands folded on her lap as she had been taught.

A string quartet started up, filling the room with soft baroque sounds—the unofficial music of Venice.

"So tell me of the Council?" she said as soon as the waiter walked away.

Marsh opened the red leather-bound wine card and flicked over the gold tassel that hung from its spine.

"Politics. The Council is tied up in diplomatic conundrums. They are of no use to us right now."

"What does that mean? You are a member, could you not make them help us?"

He looked up from the menu and his eyes softened. "The Council of Warlocks is an ancient one, Elle. They tend to think about matters in the long term. It's a common affliction amongst the long-lived and the immortal."

Elle sighed. "Marsh, what does that *mean*?"

"It means that they view your father as an incidental loss. It means that you and I are on our own in this endeavor."

"How can they say that? My father is one of the great scientific minds of our age. His work is invaluable."

"You have to remember that the Council does not care about science and progress. It is the very work that your father does that causes the Shadow to shrink and diminish. For each new miraculous modern invention that sees the light of day, a creature of magic in the Shadow loses its place in this world and disappears. At the rate we are going, the world will swing into an irreparable state of unbalance sooner than we think. In fact, come to think of it, the Council may even see the loss of a scientist as advantageous."

"Perhaps I should address them. Maybe I could appeal to them," she said.

His expression hardened. For a moment Elle could have sworn she saw fear in his eyes. He shook his head. "That is a very bad idea. Truly, we are better off on our own. Please trust me on this."

Elle looked down at the words on her inscrutable Italian menu as she fought the rising sense of despair that was threatening to overwhelm her.

"I'm sorry, Elle. They would not be moved on the point." He reached out to take her hand.

"It's hardly surprising," she snapped. "I should have expected nothing less from Warlocks."

Marsh looked at his menu for a long time without answering. "The oysters look good," he said eventually.

"So does the smoked fish," she said sarcastically. Suddenly her traitorous stomach rumbled, despite the fact that it was tightly laced up inside the boning of a long evening corset.

As if in answer to her rumbling stomach, the waiter appeared.

"Wine?" Marsh said.

Elle nodded. "Yes, please." She was going to need a stiff drink.

He ordered a bottle of white burgundy. In ordinary circumstances, she would have been impressed.

"I suppose we should celebrate the fact that the Council won't help us, if anything," she said once the waiter had poured their wine. She lifted her glass. "Good riddance to them. I would rather die than accept their help anyway."

"You will never know how wise your words are," he muttered.

"I'm sorry?"

"Nothing. Never mind." He smiled as if to reassure her. "So tell me, are you partial to Italian food?"

She looked at the menu, somewhat perplexed. Conversations with Marsh took such giddy turns sometimes. There was definitely something he wasn't telling her. And she needed to find out what that was. Preferably before the evening was over.

"Yes," she said. "There is a little place that I go to whenever I fly the Rome route. I am rather fond of their linguine. But then again, I suppose that I am less afraid of eating street food than most women I know. Mrs. Hinges would have an apoplexy if she found out. She is irrationally afraid of all foreign food."

Marsh laughed. "Street food? Is that what you call it?"

"Well, it's hardly fine dining."

The waiter appeared with an expensive-looking bottle and refilled their glasses.

Marsh handled his like a man quite accustomed to tasting wine. He smiled at her. "For now, let's celebrate the fact that we are both still alive, shall we?"

Elle sipped her wine. It was woody on her tongue. "I had almost forgotten that we nearly died today."

Marsh stared at her in surprise. "You are a fascinating woman, did you know that?"

"Thank you. You are not so bad yourself, when you remember your manners." The wine was warming her insides, loosening the tightly laced anxiety that had held her together thus far.

The waiter reappeared and Marsh ordered for them.

"We will find your father. I gave you my word on that," he said once the waiter had retreated.

"And how do you propose we achieve this?"

"I have many contacts here in Venice. We'll start with them." He took another sip from his glass. "The Alchemists will go where the Council has no influence. If my theory is correct, then they will seek out a place that has significance, but which is out of reach politically."

The waiter placed a plate of finely sliced smoked salmon in front of Elle and a platter of oysters for Marsh.

Elle picked up her fork and pushed it into the wedge of lemon. "And who are these contacts?" The sharp citrus smell rose up and settled between them, like a conspiracy.

"I think we should start at the Venetian archives. I know the chief scribe there. He is an old friend. If we narrow down the search to a list of places where a carmot stone might be wrought, then perhaps we will be able to deduce the location from the other clues. There are a few other possibilities, but I'd rather not talk about them tonight."

"I still say we should go back to England, but I've read some Greek and Latin, so I suppose it couldn't hurt to have a look," she said.

Marsh gulped down an oyster. "I know you don't believe me, but the answers are here in Venice," he said as he set down the shell.

Elle wasn't so sure. She had the distinct feeling that there was more to the matter than her affectionate friend was letting on. The trick was to get him to tell her. And Marsh was not the type of man who was easily tricked. She would have to employ her wiles to make him let his guard down.

She smiled sweetly at him and they finished their meal companionably enough. Despite the fact that she was feigning, Elle found herself enjoying dinner far more than she should, and on more than one occasion, he made her laugh louder than was strictly appropriate. She was in high spirits and a bit giddy from the wine when she finally put down her spoon. Her mouth was sweet with the taste of cinnamon-stewed pears.

"It's quite late, and I think I'd rather retire. It has been a terribly long day."

Marsh signed the bill of fare and placed it on the corner of the table.

"The unstoppable Miss Chance wants to go to bed? Whatever will they say if the news gets out?" He smiled at her. "Come on, I have a surprise for you. It won't take long. I promise."

He offered her his hand to help her up. She wobbled a little as she stood. Burgundy and tiredness were a lethal combination. "Oh, very well. Come along then," she grumbled.

* * *

Outside the crisp night air made them gasp as they stepped out of the hotel vestibule. Elle felt her head clear as she took in the night air.

Marsh said something to the concierge and then turned to her. Even in the dark, she could feel the intensity of his gaze. "I know it's not much, but I wanted to say thank you for saving my life today. Look!" He pointed at the canal as a gondola glided up beside the hotel jetty.

"A gondola ride!" Elle felt excited despite herself.

"I give you the most beautiful city of Venezia," Marsh spoke into her hair, sending little shivers up and down her neck that had nothing to do with the cold.

She held on to her skirts as the boatman helped her into the gondola. He handed her a blanket to wrap around herself. Marsh settled in the seat next to her. He rested his arm casually along the back of the bench behind her.

"How very proprietary of you," she said, looking at his arm.

She saw the side of his face lift slightly as he smiled. "We wouldn't want you falling into the canal now, would we? The water might look pretty under the stars, but I would strongly recommend against a swim in it."

"I think I believe you." She studied the undulating black surface next to the boat.

"You should smell it in the heat of summer. Now, there's something that would make a stone troll move."

She laughed despite herself.

As soon as they were in the middle of the canal, the gondolier burst into song. It was a sad aria about lost love and a lady who threw herself into the river Arno.

"The boats are all painted black, you know," Marsh said, once the boatman's aria had ended.

"Really?"

"They are—although there are many theories as to why. Some say it is out of respect for those who succumbed in the great plague. Others say it is in mourning for the fall of the Venetian state a few hundred years ago."

The gondolier nodded in approval and launched into a lively tune, ducking his head as they passed under a stone bridge.

Elle rested her head on Marsh's arm and watched the lime-stained bridge stones in the flickering lantern light make way for night and stars as the boatman's song washed over her. Had things been different, this would have been the most perfect and romantic evening of her life. It was so easy to believe all the lies—so easy and so very dangerous. She pushed her thoughts aside. The clever thing to do was to play the game. Marsh was more likely to give away whatever he was hiding if he let his guard down, and so the best plan was to lay low and play her part, for now. She took another sobering breath of evening air. There would be ample time for battles later.

CHAPTER 26

Achoo! Elle sneezed and the ladder under her wobbled. They were in the back archives of the Venetian library of St. Mark. The morning sun was streaming in dusty shafts through the high windows above them.

"Careful," Marsh said. He reached out and grabbed hold of the rungs. Elle steadied herself against the polished beam of the dark-wood shelf and reached up again.

"I just about have it." She balanced on her toes, but the volume was beyond her fingers. "Damnation," she swore as she tilted back on the ladder, nearly tipping over.

"Here, allow me." In two steps, Marsh climbed onto the ladder next to her. She felt the length of his big body stretch up against hers as he reached up past her to grip the book. They stood like that, coddled by vellum and wood panels, alone in a universe of books. Her body came alive with the electric sensation that coursed through her whenever he was near. Despite herself, she looked up at him and smiled. He looked like he was going to smile back at her, but then he looked away instead. Her heart contracted with disappointment when he cleared his throat, turned and stepped onto the ground.

Dust puffed up from under Elle's boots as she landed on the floor next to him. She watched him lay the volume down on the table and take a seat. Gently he eased open the pages.

"So what exactly are we looking for?" She rested her chin in her hands.

"Any reference to places with mystical or magical properties where Alchemists might forge a carmot stone." He spoke without looking up.

"That doesn't exactly narrow it down, does it?" She turned to the shelves and scaled the ladder again. Dusty sunbeams from the high windows above bathed the room in soft light. The entire library was bedecked in rich frescoes held up by marble columns.

Elle dragged another volume down. She stepped off the ladder and opened it. *"The Pythia Scrolls,"* she read. She turned a page and peered at the text.

"Here follows the chronology of the first Pythia and those Pythias that followed . . ." She read the words slowly, translating from the page.

She has found it. A small voice whispered in the back of her head. Elle closed the book and stepped back. She felt slightly dizzy for a moment.

Marsh looked up from the volume he was studying. "Go on," he said. There was a strange intensity in his voice as he spoke.

"The translation of this text needs quite advanced Latin, so I might have it wrong." She walked over to the table and laid the book down on the polished wood. They both studied the page in silence.

"Looks like vellum. It must be a medieval copy. Quite a magnificent document. Rare, too, by the looks of it. Not many occult works were copied during those times. Fewer survived the purges. It's a miracle any actually escaped the clutches of the inquisitions," Marsh said.

Elle read further. She rested her chin on her hands as she translated.

". . . and since the earliest days, the Earth goddess Gaia dwelled in the place they called Delphi . . . and so Gaia took as her guardian, sorry, a hero . . ." She stumbled over the words. ". . . the snake-god Python to be her lord and protector." Elle sat back in her chair. "I thought that Delphi was supposed to have been built in honor of the Greek gods."

"The Greeks came later. The mythologies were written down by those who had little knowledge of the world of Shadow before it was split from the Light after the Dark Ages, and so it can be a bit misleading. My Order teaches that it was in Delphi where the power of the Brotherhood was first discovered. The gift of healing. The power of the sun. The first Warlocks worshipped Apollo. But that was long after the first Pythia."

Elle rolled her eyes. "You make it sound almost noble when you say it that way." This conversation was becoming very odd indeed.

"The Oracles were the ones who showed us the way." He leaned forward, his eyes suddenly bright. "Don't you understand? The Warlock Orders would not have risen to power had it not been for a woman named Pythia and all her daughters of the same name."

She sighed. "These tales are all very charming, but they are not helping us find my father, now, are they?"

"Maybe they are." He turned the pages of the book. "Look. Here." He pointed at a row of illustrations. "The Oracles influenced almost every important event in the ancient world, until the Romans came."

"And then they disappeared. Logic and reason triumphed. And thank you to the Romans, I say."

"Not entirely. The Oracles may have left Delphi, but their gift lived on. When they scattered across the world, they spread the knowledge and our Order flourished." He stared at her fiercely. "Elle, they endured."

Elle closed the book with a thump. "Don't start with all that preposterous Oracle nonsense again. My mother might have been taken in by these lies, but I am *not* Pythia or Cybele or the Oracle or whatever it is that you call these women." She prodded the cover of the book with her finger. "For goodness' sake, I can't even predict what I'm going to have for breakfast, let alone prophesize to an army of sorcerers!"

Marsh looked at her intently. "Have you ever tried?"

"Tried what? Gaze into a crystal ball? Hold a séance? Don't be ridiculous."

He shook his head. "Those things are all parlor tricks. Have you ever tried to use your gift?"

"How many times do I need to say this? I. Don't. Have. A. Gift."

"I think you do." She was making him angry, judging by the lines next to his mouth.

"Oh, please, Marsh. You might be taken in by these occult lies, but I have half a brain, and I know it's all nonsense. And besides, how would you know if I had magical powers?"

"I met you in the dream plane, Elle. I was quite enlightened by what I experienced there. Surely you must remember the golden meadow where we met?"

She felt herself flush with embarrassment. "How dare you?" she snapped. "Even if what you are saying is true—and I'm not saying it is—how unbelievably caddish of you to mention it. If I recall, you invited yourself into my innermost thoughts without a care for what that might do to me and then abandoned me in the dark. I had to find my own way home. What a gentleman you are, Marsh." It was not often that she allowed herself to lose her temper like that, but this thing had been brewing between them for a while.

It was his turn to blush. Color played across his cheekbones before he looked away. "You are quite right. It was impertinent of me to speak of it. But you are making it so very difficult for me to help you." He ran his hands through his hair. "Elle, I don't know what else to say to convince you. You have the gift. You are capable of so much more than you allow yourself to believe. I just wish you would stop being so stubborn and listen to me!"

"I think our work is done here." She closed the book with a thump. "Sitting in a dusty library is not going to help find my father." She picked up a few volumes from the table and shoved them back onto the shelf.

"You know, *you* could find your father, if only you tried," he said.

Her hands stilled. "And how would I do that?"

Marsh sat forward with his head held between his hands. "I know of a place close by where we could try to invoke your gift." He spoke softly.

She sighed. It was the kind of sigh that made her whole body heave. "Marsh, let it go. It won't work. And besides, why can't you do a spell like the Alchemists did?" She put her hands on her hips. "Surely you must know a seeing spell or something that would find him. You are a powerful Warlock after all."

He ran his hand over his forehead. "I can't." His voice was barely audible.

She frowned. "Why on earth not?"

He looked away.

"There are reasons, I . . . I—" He closed his eyes. "Can I trust you to keep a secret?"

She nodded. "Yes, always."

"You may never reveal this to another living soul. Our lives depend on it."

"Marsh, I give you my word. Besides, who would I tell?" She sat down in the seat next to him.

"For many years now, the Council has forbidden Warlocks to use their power, except in the tiniest of amounts and only in emergencies."

"Why would they do that?"

"Because our magic has all but run out."

"What do you mean your magic has run out?" she said.

He sighed. "As everyone knows, the Romans were the first powerful empire to choose science and logic over magic. Until they rose to power, the worlds of Shadow and Light were one, and creatures of both sides lived in relative harmony. The Greek epics tell the tales of these things. But the Romans caused great suffering and the creatures of Shadow eventually rose up against them. The balance between Light and Shadow is like a set of scales. If one side grows heavier than the other, the balance is upset and the world is thrown into chaos. After Rome fell, the Shadow grew so large and powerful that it threatened to extinguish the Light. Terrible wars were fought. Blood flowed like rivers until the most powerful of the Shadow entities were vanquished and the balance was restored. In order to ensure that this balance was maintained, the first Council of Warlocks split the world into Light and Shadow. Those with no magic chose the Light while the others remained in Shadow. For centuries the division has maintained the balance. But now, as the world's knowledge of science and biology grows, so the ancient ways disappear to make space for this growth. The divide prevents the world from tipping into chaos, but as the Light grows, so those of us who still belong to the Shadow lose our powers and slowly drift to our doom. If things carry on this way, we will eventually be swallowed up by the Light and there will be no more magic left in the world."

"So it's true, then? If I were to say that I don't believe in fair—"

He held up his hand to silence her. "Yes. As soon as you say the words, one of the small people blinks out of existence and dies."

She stared at him. "But the Council of Warlocks is one of the most powerful organizations in the world."

"That may have been so in years gone by, but for a long time we have been maintaining appearances, all the while conserving what little power we have left. Without a proper Oracle to help us, our power will disappear altogether. When that happens, the divide between Light and Shadow will collapse. The peace and order we have maintained for so long will be no more. There is no telling if anyone would survive such a catastrophe." His eyes grew cloudy.

"I don't understand. There is so much spark out there. And the Alchemists seem to have enough magic, so why not use some of theirs?" she said.

Marsh shook his head. "As the Shadow retreats, we all fight for the same few pockets of magic that are left in this world. The Alchemists are deeply irresponsible in their use of this magic." He clenched his jaw at the thought. "The only exception is Spark. The electromancers chose the path of Light when the world divided. Their magic is blended with scientific process. It is no longer organic and so to use electromancer magic will surely kill us."

"You must have used magic before. You are a Warlock," she said.

"Perhaps in years gone by. But it has been years since I yielded any proper power." He looked despondent as he spoke.

"But there must be some way of stopping the world from plunging into chaos?"

"There is," he said. "You."

She blinked. "Me?"

"Yes, you."

"But how?"

"An Oracle is the guide. She navigates the layers of the universe and with this knowledge comes the gift of channeling and foresight. If you would imagine the world as multiple layers, like the pages in a book—the Oracle is the binding that holds it all together. There can be many Cybeles. Each generation, a few of them will ascend to the second stage of Pythia. But there can be only one Oracle in existence at a time. And she is a creature of immense power and importance. This is what the first Pythia did for the Warlocks. And in return they swore to care for and protect her and her daughters in all time to come."

"Hmm. All that still sounds rather dodgy to me," Elle said. "Who is the Oracle at the moment?"

"The Oracle who ascended after your mother died twenty years ago was no true Pythia. She has done her best to maintain the balance, but her attempts have been barely effective."

"And what sort of life would an Oracle have, once she becomes this person?"

"Oracles were revered and cherished by our Order. Temples and sanctuaries were built in their honor, for their safety and comfort."

"But the Warlocks failed in their task. Delphi was abandoned and the women were killed or taken as slaves, scattered across the world. You said so yourself."

"Yes. We lost Delphi, but we have always cared for women we find who have the gift. Your mother was very gifted, but unfortunately she was murdered by those who would see us obliterated." Marsh took her hand before she could say anything. "Abercrombie and his Alchemists are but the tip of the dragon's tail. The situation is far more complicated and perilous than you could ever imagine. We are hanging on by the thinnest of threads. You must take up your gift and use it. You must."

"And what if I don't?"

"If you ascend, you will be in control of your abilities. You will be able to control what happens. If you do not . . . well, there are many out there who would seek to get hold of an untrained Cybele before she has had the chance to complete the metamorphosis to Pythia.

These are desperate times. The Council will not hesitate to do what is necessary to get what it wants." He looked into her eyes. "Elle, convincing you to complete the metamorphosis on your own terms is the only way I know to keep you safe."

A slow-ticking clock at the end of the room punctuated the silence that stretched between them like an ellipsis.

"Marsh, you don't honestly think that I am going to swallow all this wibble about magical women who rule the world? In fact, I seem to recall you being rather against the whole idea of women's suffrage. So why should I believe you?"

"Elle, this is different. This runs so much deeper than a few well-meaning ladies waving placards. Surely you can sense within you something of the legacy the women in your bloodline have left from within?"

She shook her head. "I'm sorry, but it's simply not rational."

"Are you honestly telling me that you feel nothing?"

Elle rubbed the back of her neck wearily. He wasn't going to let the matter go and she was not about to start admitting to all the odd things that had been happening. There was no way she was going to do that.

She sighed. "Very well, you win. But only by erosion. What would I have to do? To be a Pythia, I mean?"

He squeezed her hand again. "Come with me. I'll show you."

She straightened her shoulders. "I will go with you. But only to prove that you are wrong about me." She picked up her new floor-length cloak with the hood from the coat stand.

"Oh, I think you might surprise yourself."

"Don't be so sure," she said, as he led the way.

CHAPTER 27

"Where are we going?" Elle asked under her breath.

"Cemetery Island," he murmured. "Look grief-stricken. I told the boatman that you wanted to visit the grave of your long-lost relatives."

"Oh," she said, bowing her head.

Outside, the sky had turned gray. The air smelled damp and salty in the midday gloom. Elle looked up at the clouds. It looked like rain.

The boatman watched them from the corner of his eye as he stoked the coal furnace and boiler that powered the boat. It started puttering more vigorously, and with a lurch, it started ploughing through the choppy water.

"He doesn't look happy," Elle whispered.

"The Venetians don't like strangers poking around their dead. Now, keep your head down and pretend you're grieving."

She sat with her head bowed for the rest of the journey. Marsh handed her his handkerchief and she held it to her face. Inside the hood of her cloak she closed her eyes and inhaled his sandalwood smell. Her mind was reeling with all he had told her in the library. It was almost too much to take in at once. Even though he knew about the dream, he clearly didn't care. His only interest was the Oracle and the Shadow. The little bit of hope inside her evaporated and she cursed herself for being so shallow. She should be worrying about her father and about the world coming to an end instead of gawping at this man like a mooncalf.

She felt the boatman's gaze fixed on her and she stared back. He averted his eyes. The dull ache inside her hurt like grief. Perhaps it showed.

After what felt like ages, they neared a stone jetty that jutted out into the sea. The boat bumped against it with a gentle thud, and the boatman doused the engine. He muttered something in guttural Italian and gestured for them to disembark.

Marsh had a word with the man and after a few more coins were exchanged, the fellow seemed content to wait. He drew his hat down over his face and settled down on the seat.

Marsh helped Elle out of the boat. He put his arm around her as they stepped out onto the jetty.

"I can manage, you know," she said.

"I know, but you are supposed to be grief-stricken, remember?" He started walking up the gravel path that led to the cemetery. In the distance, the cloisters of the church and monastery on the island came into view.

"The monks here are allies of the Council." They passed a group of novices on the gravel path.

"I thought the Shadow and the Church were enemies."

He laughed. "We are. But we also have a mutual understanding."

She studied the crumbling edifice of the monastery. These buildings were ancient. The pink stone was veined with gray damp, like a wedge of old cheese.

"The monks have protected our sanctuary here, along with their own, for a very long time."

"This used to be a Warlock sanctuary?"

He nodded. "And a monastery. The place only became a cemetery because Emperor Napoleon ordered it during the wars." Another group of brown-robed monks approached them on the path. A few of them inclined their heads at Marsh as they passed.

"Let me guess, Venice was founded by Warlocks."

"The Phoenicians actually, but there were Warlocks among them." They stepped through a pink-tinged archway and the stone cloisters rose up around them.

Elle looked around. "Won't they mind?"

Marsh shook his head. "They are used to us visiting here from time to time."

"But how do they know you are a Warlock?"

"Only a select group know of this place. And the monks control who enters and leaves. Look around you. It's a small island. There is nowhere to run, and nowhere to hide."

"Hmm," Elle said. The corridor became progressively less opulent as they walked. She noticed that the stone walls and floor were worn shiny with age.

They reached a set of steps. Marsh lifted a spark lantern off one of the walls and lit it. He turned and placed his hand on the smooth stones that framed a small wooden door. The wall rumbled softly as he opened the door.

"In here. Whenever you are ready." He bent down to avoid hitting his head on the low doorpost and disappeared into the dark room. She could see the light from the lantern fight with the shadows inside.

She looked at the door and her breath quickened. A gentle pressure settled inside her chest. Something beyond the door radiated out at her like tendrils. They curled around her, drawing her into it.

She took a deep breath. If this was the only way to find her father, then this was what she would have to do. Saving the world could come later.

She stepped through the door and blinked in the gloom. She was standing in a small circular room. The walls were built from rough-hewn stone that had later been carved in places in intricate detail. A row of little windows circled the roof, allowing for light to shine in. But it was the floor that made Elle stop and stare. Under her feet was the most exquisite mosaic she had ever seen. Thousands of precious stones, gold and silver were laid to form the image of a woman and a large snake in an elaborate embrace.

"Beautiful, isn't it?" Marsh said softly.

"It is," she breathed. "Those look like real rubies and sapphires." Her fingers strayed to the bracelet still stuck around her wrist. "The picture—what does it mean?"

"It is the legend of Pythia."

"The same as the text we found?"

He nodded. "The very same. At your feet is the first Cybele. She is the daughter of Gaia—Mother of all. Gaia is the one to the right."

Elle looked at the figures at her feet. They were dressed in classic Grecian robes.

"The story continues in the pictures around the edge. Look there. One day Gaia met Python, the snake-god. She was very beautiful and Python fell in love with her. As a token of his love, he gave her the gift of sight and the gift to reach into the layers of the universe to bring harmony and peace. Out of their love, a daughter was born. But Gaia was jealous of her daughter and fought with Python. The arguments became so violent that Gaia left Python, taking her daughter Cybele with her. But Cybele loved her father and she was angry with her mother for taking her away from him. So, when Cybele grew into a woman, she changed her name to Pythia to spite her mother. Pythia means 'of Python.' She did it so she could remember her father's name until she joined him in the afterworld one day. And Python, in recognition of his daughter's loyalty to him, gave her the same gift of sight as her mother. He also gave her the ability to hold the universe together." He paused. "That is the Oracle's greatest gift: wisdom and the ability to hold the world and everything in it together."

Elle shrugged. "Strange story. I'm still confused though. What's the difference between Cybele and Pythia?"

"A woman with the gift is called Cybele until she undergoes the transformation. Once this happens, she forgoes all of her other names to become Pythia. Pythia is the Oracle until the day she departs for the underworld."

They studied the mosaic in silence. The women in it had long hair that flowed over their shoulders and down past their waists.

"So what do I do?"

"I'm not sure, to be honest. I've not had the privilege to witness Pythia speaking in situ in my lifetime. I was an apprentice when your mother left to be with your father." He gestured at the floor. "I think perhaps you should stand in the middle of this floor and see what happens."

"Very well, but I had better take my boots off. The floor looks so delicate. I'd hate to damage it." She bent over and pulled off her boots and stockings.

CHAPTER 28

Marsh watched Elle step onto the mosaic. They stared at one another for a few tense moments. Nothing happened.

Elle spread out her arms and let them drop to her sides. "See. Nothing," she said. "I told you, I wasn't your girl." She looked up at the ceiling. "I knew nothing would happe—"

Her eyes rolled back in her head, her knees buckled and she sank to the floor.

Marsh started. "Elle!" He stepped forward to help her, but a wall of pure energy met him. Fearing that he might harm her, he drew back.

"Elle," he said. "Elle, can you hear me?"

She stirred and sat up. It was a strange type of sitting up, almost as if her spine moved her into an upright position all on its own, without help from her arms and legs. She opened her eyes.

Marsh gasped. The whites of her eyes had gone very white and the irises were dark, almost black. They reminded him of the eyes he had seen on the murals and vases of ancient Greece.

"Who seeks the counsel of Pythia?" Her voice sounded different. It resonated against the walls.

"I do, honorable one," Marsh said, frantically trying to recall the ritual words.

"And what is it which you seek to know, Warlock?"

Fear gripped him. He needed to ask the question carefully. Oracles were notorious for their cryptic and strange answers. They also had the tendency to stop answering whenever they felt like it. He decided to start with the most important question first.

"We seek the whereabouts of the man known as Professor Charles Chance. We need to know where to find him."

Elle's head rolled back. The hood of her cloak had slipped and her hair had worked its way loose. The auburn waves spilled down over her shoulders. She remained like that, with her head tilted back, for a few long moments.

Suddenly her head jerked back up and she stared straight at him. Marsh felt a tremor of awe laced with fear shoot through him. Legends of how frightening Oracles could be were not far wrong. He felt as if he was looking into the eyes of the wisdom of ages itself. And he was terrified.

"The man you seek is in the city of Constantine. The tracks that the iron beast follows to the City are fraught with shadow. You will find him among the lords of the dead of the forests."

"And will our endeavors be successful?" he asked.

The Oracle looked straight at him.

"You will find more than you bargained for, Warlock. Beware of those you trust when the moon is almost full." She closed her eyes and dropped back onto the floor, where she lay very still. Marsh reached out. The energy that had surrounded her was gone. He bent over her.

"Elle. Elle, wake up." He touched her face.

CHAPTER 29

The coolness of mosaic tiles seeped through the fabric of her clothes. Elle opened her eyes and slowly sat up. Her hair fell in a curtain around her. It had come loose from its knot somehow. She looked about. "What happened? Did I faint?"

"You did, in a manner of speaking. How are you feeling?"

"I'm fine. Yes, I'm fine." Marsh was staring at her with great concern.

She rose to her knees and gave her hips a pat. "See, I told you that this was a waste of time. No prophesy." She pulled her hair back and started tying it into its knot.

Marsh was staring at her as if she had sprouted another set of arms. "You truly have no idea what just happened, do you?" The expression on his face was very odd.

She smiled at him. "Of course not, silly. How would I remember if I fainted?"

"How extraordinary."

"Extraordinary? I think it's more a case of I shouldn't wear my underwear laced so tightly." She patted her midriff. "What is wrong with you? You look like you've seen a ghost."

"And you honestly don't remember anything?"

"No, I've already told you so. You are acting very strangely. What is it?"

Marsh crouched down next to her and gripped her

shoulder. "Constantinople," he said. "Your father is in Constantinople. The city of Constantine. It has to be."

"Excuse me?" Elle said.

He let out an incredulous laugh. "The most important event in two generations and no one to confirm what I just witnessed," he muttered, running his hand through his hair.

"Marsh, have you completely lost your mind?"

He recovered himself and stepped away from her. "Elle, you spoke as the Pythia. Pure and clear, just as was done in the legends of old. The volume of power you accessed and channeled a few moments ago was astonishing. I've never seen anything like it. You told me where your father is."

Elle felt herself grow excited. It felt like some part of her—the part that had always felt wrong—had clicked into place inside her. And it felt right. "Do you honestly believe that?" She eyed him.

"I do." He grew serious.

"Well, then we need to go to Constantinople as soon as possible."

He sighed. "There is one more thing you need to know."

She frowned at him "What?"

"It is said that Pythia should live out her days in silent contemplation and devotion," he said.

Elle dropped her arms. "You have got to be joking," she said.

"The Pythias of old lived in chastity in the temples, learning and meditating. Now that we know you are the Oracle, you must devote your life to your calling. We can stay at the hotel until the Council has prepared a place for you."

"But my mother lived with us. I was born after all."

"Vivienne ran away from the sanctuary to be with your father. And away from our protection, she went to her doom." A look of sorrow crossed his face. "Elle, you are too important. We cannot afford to take any risks. You have to come with me so the Council can take you into their protection."

A terrible feeling of dread filled her. "Let me make sure I understand this correctly: I am to be locked away like a nun in a cloister, to live out my days in isolation so a council of old men can ask me things in order that they may further their political power?"

"Not if I have any say in the matter," he said. "I will make sure that you have every luxury and comfort you desire."

"So it's to be a gilded cage with velvet draperies then?"

"Your life will be no different to the lives of other women. But instead of devotion to your husband you will be devoted to the Council. And they will revere you like a goddess. We should go. There is no time to waste."

Elle felt like the floor had given out from under her. She had to fight the urge to scream and hit him. "You!" she said, prodding his shoulder. "You have been plotting to bring me to this place all along, haven't you?"

He looked away. "Elle, it's complicated. I needed to make sure that I was correct about you being the Oracle before I took any further steps," he said.

She shook her head. "Patrice was right. This has all been a conspiracy to drag me here. To this place. I bet my father's abduction was just a ruse to get me here. Wasn't it?"

He looked shocked. "No, it's not like that."

She folded her arms. "Then what *is* it like, Hugh? Tell me. Tell me that you haven't been working toward recruiting me for your precious Council all along. Tell me you haven't been plotting to get me here so they can use me as they wish."

He remained silent.

"Elle, you don't understand." He shook his head.

She snorted. "I understand enough, it seems. And I'm not moving from this spot until you tell me the truth."

He sighed with exasperation. "Yes. The Council knows you are the Oracle. I notified them from Oxford."

"And how long have you known?"

"Since the night we drove up from London. And our shared dream confirmed it. But many can walk the Shadow realm. I wanted to make sure, so I brought you here."

"So you have been stringing me along, cleverly leading me into your trap, haven't you? And now I suppose I'm to be handed over like some prize to a life of slavery and servitude."

"I'm trying to find a way that will satisfy everyone. And you're not making it easy for me."

"Easy for you?" She felt her anger rise. "And what if I don't want to go?"

"What you want is irrelevant. Don't you understand? You alone have the power to ensure that order in our world is kept in balance. This is an awesome responsibility. You have a duty. A calling. You need to be trained. And I am here to help. And the Council will help too."

"And what about what I want," she said softly.

His expression grew gentler. "You need to think of the greater good, Elle. It's not only about you anymore."

"But I would have to give up flying. My studies in physics. My father . . . Mrs. Hinges, Patrice. Everyone I love. This is my whole life you are talking about."

"I know this is a lot to take in, but in time you will see that I am right. You will be safe and cared for. I am sure that you will find contentment over time. You just have to give your new life a chance."

Elle folded her arms. "I am *not* going with you," she said.

He started. "Why on earth not?"

"Why? You have to ask that?"

He frowned. "You should be overjoyed. This is the

biggest honor that there is for a woman. Even in these modern times," he said.

She felt herself grow angry. "'For a woman.' Is that what you think?"

"You are making it sound all wrong."

She lifted her chin. "I won't do it then. Only two people in the world know what I have just done. If you push me any further, I shall scream blue murder. I shall deny all knowledge of this business. You can't make me."

He stared at her. "Elle, the Council *can* make you do this. I have fought hard with them to allow me to bring you to them of your own free will. The alternative does not bear thinking about."

She stepped away from him. "Don't you dare. And if you do, then you will find that you have some careful explaining to do to the police as to why you lured a young woman unaccompanied into a room, with utterly improper intentions. I am sure the London papers would love a story about Viscount Greychester and his lascivious occult activities."

Marsh's face grew still, his eyes hard with anger.

Her insides trembled, but she held his gaze. She was bluffing of course, but right now bluffing was her only weapon. She was not going to allow herself to be dragged off to this new life without a fight.

"I should remind you, Miss Chance, that you are a thousand miles from England and entirely at my mercy for your survival."

Elle felt little waves of fear break inside her. This situation was becoming dangerous. Underneath her cloak, she reached for her Colt and took it into her hand. Carefully, she slipped the safety catch loose. The mechanism that loaded the bullets into the firing chamber clicked.

Marsh frowned at the tiny sound.

"I must say that it is nice to finally see your true colors, Mr. Marsh. Now that we both know what it is that you want." Elle raised her arm and pointed the gun at him.

"Take one step closer to me and I will shoot you where you stand. I am not bluffing."

He didn't move. He didn't even blink.

"Now take me back to the hotel. I wish to move to other accommodations. Without you."

She didn't think it was possible, but his face grew even stonier and angrier. The silence stretched between them and Elle felt her bravado evaporate. He was bigger and stronger than her. And there were many monks about, prepared to protect the Warlock among them. About a hundred other fearful thoughts flashed through her mind as the tense seconds ticked by.

After what seemed like an eternity, he broke their standoff. "Very well, then," he said. "What are your demands?" A deep sense of pain in his eyes accompanied his words.

"I want to know where my father is. When I know he is safe, I wish for safe passage back to England."

"And if I don't agree?"

"A dispatch will be written and sent to *The Times* in London. If you or any Warlock comes anywhere near me, the paper will receive instructions to publish a full exposé about the truth behind the Council, the lies they are telling. For added measure, there will also be information about Viscount Greychester and his lascivious occult fetish for forcing young women to do things against their will."

"As you wish." All the friendliness and familiarity they had built up since Paris was gone. "I shall accede to your demands. But the Council of Warlocks does not have your father. The Alchemists have him and he is in Constantinople. I also cannot bind the Council in respect of your demands. The current Oracle is old and frail. She grows weaker every day. If you do not rise up and take the position, the Council must wait for you to die so a new Pythia may complete the process. And I cannot promise that they will wait for nature to take its course."

Elle shook with fear, but she forced herself to stay still. She needed to get out of this place, and the only way to achieve this was to remain in control. She would worry about the rest of the things he'd said as soon as it was safer. Right now, all she wanted to do was get off this island.

"Let's go. You first." She motioned with the gun barrel.

"There is one more thing you need to know about being the Oracle," Marsh said.

"No, there is not. I don't want to learn anything more about this. It is over."

He pressed his lips together. "Very well. May it be on your head then, Pythia who will be Oracle."

"And stop calling me that. My name is Eleanor."

CHAPTER 30

The journey back to Venice on the boat felt much longer than it had on the way there. Elle's fingers ached from gripping the revolver, but she kept it trained on Marsh under the folds of her cloak. He sat beside her in stony silence, looking deeply troubled, and he maintained his brooding presence all the way to the hotel.

With her new portmanteau packed, she found a quiet little hotel with wrought-iron trelliswork in front of every window and large iron locks on every door. She paid for the room with the emergency money she carried tucked away inside her corset. It took a little while to convince them to accept sterling, but in the end, they relented.

Safely inside her room, Elle sagged against the door, exhausted. The tiredness left a deep chill that seeped right into the marrow of her bones and she shivered at the profound strangeness of the sensation. As if in answer to her thoughts, the sun broke through the clouds and reached with watery light through the window casements. The sensation of warmth on her skin made her groan with delight. Sunshine and rest were what she needed. She raised her hand and studied the light as it fell over her, bathing everything inside the room in shadows and light. Everything except her.

Elle stared at her arm with growing horror. She stood up and looked behind her. The chair cast a dark shape beside it. So did the little dresser and the washstand, but behind her was no familiar outline. The sunlight seemed to pass straight through her. It was almost as if she was no longer anchored to anything. As if her presence no longer made an impression, no matter how much she waved her arms or jumped up and down. She no longer cast a shadow.

Elle felt the chill inside her return. Marsh had taken her threats seriously, which was unexpected, and she had bought herself a little time, but she was in big trouble. She needed to find a way to fix things, and there was no time to waste.

Her stomach rumbled. She glanced at the clock, and she realized that she had missed lunch. Lost shadow or not, at least she was fairly sure she was still alive.

She rang the bell for service and ordered a tray of tea and a plate of little balls of deep-fried rice that the Venetians favored. She also asked that stationery be brought to her room.

She was writing furiously when her meal arrived. An hour and several cups of tea later, she bound the dispatch with string and sealed it with wax.

With the papers in hand and with the revolver in place, she donned her cloak and locked the door behind her.

Outside on the canal, she hailed a boat. Glancing over her shoulder to make sure that no one was following her, she told the man to take her to the British Consulate. No one seemed to notice that her small, cloaked figure cast no shadow as she strode into the building.

With her letter safely dispatched and a telegram sent to her uncle, she stopped off in a bookshop opposite the consulate. She found a convenient corner where she watched the street to make sure that no one intercepted her dispatch.

She stood by the window until the owner politely

coughed and asked if she needed assistance. Compelled to keep up appearances, she purchased a notebook and a novel. Satisfied that nobody was following her, she made her way back through the winding streets and little bridges, taking care to walk in the places where the buildings cast their shadows, so no one would notice her predicament.

As she walked, she relaxed a little and her anxiety was replaced with a sense of sadness. Venice was achingly beautiful and she would have loved to visit this place under different circumstances.

After the bookshop, she caught another boat to the shopping district. It took a little while, but she managed to find a jeweler who would give her a decent price on the earrings. She sold them for less than they were worth, but needs must. Not for the first time, she lamented the fact that the diamond bracelet was still stuck around her wrist. The jeweler tried to wedge the clasp open with one of his sharp little pliers, but to no avail. She would probably have to wear the dastardly thing for the rest of her life at this rate.

Back at her hotel, she ordered a hot bath and more tea. She sipped the brew as she soaked in the hot water. What to do next? She watched the water trickle off her fingers. She was certainly in a fine mess—there was no mistaking that.

A soft knock at the door interrupted her fretful thoughts. She got out of the tub and she stepped into her new dressing gown.

"Signora." It was one of the hotel maids. "A message has arrived for you." She curtsied and proffered an envelope on a small tray. Elle thanked the maid and bolted the door again.

She tore open the seal on the envelope and pulled out a thick sheet of paper. It was addressed to her, written in a masculine hand.

Elle,

Words cannot convey how sorry I am about the manner in which we parted ways this afternoon. I hope you can accept my firmest assurances that I never intended to deceive you and that my intentions, while veiled, were honorable. I can only hope that in time you will forgive me for presuming too much.

I accept that I can do nothing to change your mind, but hopefully the enclosed will assist you in your endeavors to find your father. Please accept it as a token of my apology. The train departs at 10 o'clock tomorrow morning. Please stay in your hotel until then. It is not safe in the city at night.

Your servant, HM.

She picked up the ticket that had fallen from the letter onto the floor. It was a return ticket to Constantinople. First class. What was Marsh playing at? She studied the gilt-edged ticket. It presented a tantalizing opportunity. A berth on the Orient Express would take her directly to Constantinople within three days. Even with the money she had got for the earrings, she would only be able to afford third class, and that would take her an extra day. A dirigible flight was even more expensive. She would have to wait for her uncle to wire money to her. Even if he agreed to help her, she would be delayed in Venice for a week. It was a perfect conundrum.

Take the ticket. You must hurry. There is no time to lose . . . do not tarry here in this place. It is not safe. She shivered as she felt voices whisper to her.

"All right, I'll take the train, but only if you promise to keep quiet!" she said to the voices. She needed to find her father so she could return to her old life as soon as possible, before she completely lost her mind.

The girl who casts no shadow did not sleep at all well that night. Over and over she woke from muddled dreams, unsure of where she was, afraid of crossing over to the realm of Shadows again. I could sense that she searched for the Warlock in the dark. But all that met her was silence. The girl believed that she was completely alone and abandoned. She hugged her pillow and sighed in the dark. She did not know we were there, ghosts and fairies watching over her. But humans are often ungrateful.

Eventually she gave up on sleep and went to sit at the window, where the dawn light gently eased the gloomy gray into day. She looked across the canal and I felt her blood turn to ice. For in the shadows someone was waiting. He was wrapped in a gray cloak that covered his head and face. The watcher must have spotted her at the window, because he melted back into the shadows.

With a sigh, she got up from her seat and started dressing. She fiddled with the bracelet around her arm. It was a gesture that was becoming a familiar part of her mannerisms.

I could have shown myself at that stage, but I did not. I was angry with the girl. I was angry that she denied who she was. And I was sad, because her petulant denial made yet more of the Shadow retreat. No matter how much I willed her to say yes, she didn't.

I sensed that others were sad too, so I stayed hidden within the diamonds, where it was safe. For no one could touch me while I rested there. Not even the sharp bite of the jeweler's pliers.

The girl would need my help soon, but the time for these things was yet to come. And so I let her be. Perhaps, if she suffered a little, she would come to her senses. Sometimes a little harshness helps to focus the mind.

By seven o'clock, she rang the bell for coffee. A tray with pastries and the morning paper was brought and the girl flicked through the pages to distract herself while she ate. There was an article on the front page about a large pirate ship that had exploded in midair near Genoa, and the girl scrutinized the words, trying to discern what they said with the little Italian she knew.

By half past eight, the girl had been ready for ages. Unable to wait any longer, she summoned the porters to take her portmanteau downstairs. She was ready to go to the station.

CHAPTER 31

In contrast to the medieval splendor of old Venice, the station was a squat building propped up by cast cast-iron pillars. It clung to the side of the Grand Canal as a crass insult to the gentle architecture around it. Porters jostled for tips as people embarked and disembarked from the boats and gondolas. Gypsies sold trinkets spread on blankets on the drizzle-laced steps that led up from the water, while their children stood watch.

Elle made her way through the bustle and into the station with her portmanteau. The smell of coal smoke, coffee and unwashed bodies assailed her from all sides. She glanced round, but there was no one behind her.

"Departure from platform one. It's that way," the station official said to her when she showed him her ticket.

Elle stopped and stared in open admiration at the magnificent machine before her. The Orient Express sat at the platform like a dowager in mourning dress. Veils of gray steam laced with incandescent spark particles escaped from pressure valves that were situated just under the footplates. Every inch of her polished black flanks gleamed in the dull morning light.

She walked along the platform until she found her carriage. She handed her ticket to a conductor dressed in dark green and gold livery. He studied it, took her bag and then stood aside so she could board.

Elle needed both hands to hoist herself into the carriage. Moving about was not as easy as it looked when dressed in a long corset and skirts. She was already regretting the fact that her jodhpurs were packed away at the bottom of her portmanteau, along with the revolver.

"First class is this way, madam," the conductor said behind her. He shuffled off down the carriage, gesturing for her to follow. As she turned, Elle caught a glimpse of a gray shadow as it slipped behind a pillar. It looked suspiciously like the cloaked figure that had been outside her window earlier that morning.

She peered out the window to get a better look, but the figure was gone, replaced by a newspaper boy, checking his stack of news sheets.

She shrugged. Her nerves were getting the better of her and she was hearing voices and seeing cloaked monsters everywhere she looked.

"Compartment three-oh-three," the conductor said. At that moment, a whistle sounded outside and someone on the platform shouted in Italian. Unperturbed, the conductor waited for the noise to pass, before continuing. "For the lady on the left and the gentleman on the right. Will you have any staff attending?"

"No, thank you. And I am travelling alone. There should be no gentleman in this compartment," she said.

"But madam, the gentleman is already here . . ." The conductor looked confused and pointed to a man seated in the opposite side of the compartment, engrossed in his newspaper.

"Thank you, my good man. We will let you know if we need anything further." Marsh lowered his newspaper. He seemed amused.

"You!" Elle said.

"A good morning to you too, Miss Chance."

"You!" she repeated. "I should have known you were up to something!"

Great billows of steam rose up outside the windows.

"I was starting to think that I was going to Constantinople on my own." He gave her one of his electric smiles.

"*Mr.* Marsh. Of all the arrogant men in this world, you are possibly the worst. And if you think I am going to Constantinople with you, you are sorely mistaken. Now, if you'll excuse me, I am leaving." She picked up her portmanteau.

At that moment, the train shuddered and started moving. Elle stumbled and had to grab onto the brass rail to stop herself from falling over. The Orient Express bound for Constantinople had left the station. Its steam engines propelled the machine forward with impressive acceleration.

"The next stop is in Austria, so you might as well sit down," Marsh said.

Elle wrenched the compartment door open. A blast of cold air grabbed at her petticoats. The train was now over the long cast-iron railway bridge that connected Venice with the mainland. Slate-gray lagoon water whooshed past below her at a speed that was altogether too frightening for her liking. If she jumped, she would most likely drown.

Defeated, she slammed the door shut and sat down heavily on the brocade seat. She clutched her portmanteau to her chest with grim resignation. She was stuck in a confined space with Marsh. Again.

"Told you so," he said from behind his paper. From her seat she could see that he was watching her with a rather amused expression on his face. In that moment, she hated him with all her might.

"Fine. But only until the next stop. And then I never want to see you again."

He rolled his eyes. "Don't you sometimes get a little tired of being so constantly outraged?" he said. "If I had wanted to harm or abduct you, I would have done so hours ago. Elle, you are as safe with me as you always were."

She glared at him. "And while we're on the subject, where is my shadow? It disappeared yesterday and I haven't managed to find it."

He sighed. "The divide between Light and Shadow is like a membrane. It separates every aspect of the two realms. But, as we move about, we leave our mark on the universe and a person's shadow is that imprint on the barrier between the two realms. You are Pythia. You do not leave an imprint because you are the very force that holds Shadow and Light together."

"Oh," she said.

"I promised your uncle I would take care of you, and so, against my better judgment, here I am." He bowed his head. "At your service, madam."

"My uncle?" She felt herself grow cold.

"Actually, I received a long-distance message from my good friend Lord Geoffrey Chance late last night. He said that he'd received a very concerning cablegram from his niece yesterday. Something about her going off to the East to rescue her father and that she was sending him an important dispatch and that he was to go to the papers if there was no further news. He was most perturbed by the message, but he knew I would be in Venice to meet the Council so he contacted me."

She felt her cheeks blaze. "And so you took it upon yourself to book two tickets?"

"Well, your uncle was most concerned about you. I assured him that all was well, but that you felt he needed to hold certain important information in case something happened to you, which is why you sent the dispatch. He accepted that but begged me to keep an eye on you. For your father's sake. Apparently, you can be quite a handful sometimes."

"So you *were* spying on me! I knew it," she said.

"I did no such thing. But I did promise you that I would help you find your father, and I did promise your uncle to be your chaperone for this trip, and so I am settling my entire debt to the Chance family in one go."

"I don't need your help," she said.

He snorted. "Tell that to the two men in gray I dispatched from outside your hotel this morning. One of them got away, but I think I saw him lurking about the station a little while ago."

"You are a devious man, Mr. Marsh," she said in a low voice.

He shook his head. "You don't know the meaning of the word. But, as a token of good faith, I told your uncle that he should expect your dispatch and that he should deal with the matter as per your instructions. So your little insurance policy is in place. If I take one wrong step, the whole world will know."

She raised her chin. "Why are you doing this?"

He pressed his lips into a thin line. "Regardless of what you might think of me, I swore an oath to protect the Oracle. It is one of the most sacred vows of my Brotherhood. Constantinople is a dangerous place. The Alchemists are a treacherous lot. And if hanging a sword of Damocles over myself is what it will take for you to trust me, then that is what I must do." He pulled a sealed telegram from his pocket and handed it to her. "Your uncle sent me this to give to you."

She sat down on the brocade seat and took off her gloves. Her fingers trembled slightly when she opened the telegram. It was from her uncle, begging her to be careful. The telegram went on to instruct her in the strongest possible terms to defer to Lord Greychester on all matters and that she was in good hands as long as she followed his advice. He also said that if she needed anything, she should ask Marsh with her uncle's blessing.

Elle sighed and set her portmanteau down. "And what

guarantees do I have that you won't try to drag me off to your Council the moment I fall asleep?"

"Elle, you have made your position perfectly clear. And I will not stoop so low as to make you do something that is against your will. In this, I have disobeyed the Council. They do not know where we are, nor do I intend to tell them. I give you my word as a gentleman that I will not speak of the matter again." His expression grew serious. "But we will eventually have to face the consequences of your decision together, you and I."

Elle was silent as she took in what he was saying. Was he telling the truth? She felt little slivers of guilt and regret wriggle around inside her. Her uncle was a good judge of character and she was unlikely to get any further help from Lord Geoffrey now. Marsh was right. She was a woman on her own, in a strange country, with limited resources, and as much as it pained her to admit it, she really was going to struggle to find her father by herself. She needed help, and at present Mr. Marsh seemed to be the only help on offer—whether she liked it or not.

She sighed. There was no way around it. She needed to swallow her pride and make what had happened between them right.

"I'm sorry about yesterday at the sanctuary." She bit her lip. "It's just that I felt so ambushed; and I didn't really stop to consider what I was saying and . . ." Her voice trailed and she took a deep breath. "What I mean to say is that I am prepared to call a truce, if you promise to do the same."

He nodded stiffly. "I was in the wrong too. I shouldn't have presumed so much with you," he said. "I was at fault for allowing my feelings to get the better of my judgment. For that, I apologize."

"Apology accepted. We have a truce. But if you try any of your tricks or if you say a word about me being the Oracle, then our agreement will be null and void. Understand?"

"Understood." He picked up his newspaper and opened it again.

Elle took off her coat and hung it on the hook below the hat rack behind her.

"That dress is very fetching. You look lovely," he said quietly.

Elle felt a fresh blush explode across her face. She had chosen a cream embroidered lawn dress with small silk buttons on the sleeves for the journey. The seamstress had convinced her to add a little straw travelling hat with a black ribbon to match the outfit. The little hat was now perched on top of her hair, which she had pinned up in a braided knot.

"Thank you." She studied the compartment to distract herself. The polished wood paneling that lined the compartment was set against the green of the upholstery. Crystal teardrop lamp shades covered the spark lights. They tinkled softly as the train moved along over the tracks. Even the windowpanes were engraved cut glass.

"We are certainly travelling in style. Thank you for the ticket, by the way," she added.

He smiled. "This is not the Orient Express proper. We will only be joined up with it once we get to Vienna."

"That's good to know," she said. "And we will be sleeping here, both of us?"

"Allow me to show you." Marsh put his newspaper aside and stood up to pull the lever situated next to the window. "The beds are underneath these benches." The bench swiveled round to reveal linen sheets and soft wool blankets, all ready and made up. "Pillows in here." He opened one of the wooden overhead cupboards.

Elle leaned over and looked at the mechanism. It consisted of a series of gears and a coiled spring. "Hmm. Clever," she mused.

Marsh pulled the lever for a second time and the bench swiveled round to reveal the brocade seat. "Also, there is a screen divider that splits the compartment in two. To ensure propriety and privacy at all times." He pointed at the folded screen, cleverly tucked away behind a curtain. Elle nodded, feeling quite relieved that she would not have to share sleeping quarters with him. They might be on speaking terms again, but that did not mean they were back to being affectionate friends.

The morning lumbered along in stilted silence. Elle did her best to concentrate on the book she had bought from the bookshop opposite the consulate yesterday, but she struggled to concentrate. A dull headache throbbed at her temples and the air around her felt heavy—as if a terrible storm was brewing. She set the book aside and settled down to watch the day roll by. The train left Italy behind. Houses and farms became sparser and the hills more wooded as the tracks wound into the Austrian mountains.

She studied the gray clouds looming low over the mountaintops. "Looks like we might be in for some bad weather."

He looked up sharply from the folder of papers he was working on. "I beg your pardon?"

She frowned. "I said that based on my observations of the low-lying clouds and the fact that autumn is soon to be upon us, that we might have some adverse weather and precipitation on the way."

He leaned forward and looked out of the window. For the first time since their argument yesterday, the tension that hung in the air between them abated. "I suspect that you might be right," he said and then promptly went back to his papers.

A trolley with refreshments rolled by. The waiter knocked on the door and asked if they wanted something.

"Oh, look!" Elle cried out in delight when the waiter

rolled the trolley into their compartment. Perched on the side of the trolley was a spark-powered steam-driven coffee unit. The steel and brass pipes gleamed and she could hear the boiling water gurgle somewhere inside the machine.

"What can I offer for the lovely lady?" the waiter asked, delighting in Elle's interest.

"Ooh, could I have a cappuccino?" she asked.

The waiter's face fell.

"Only if it wouldn't be too much trouble; I would so very much like to see how the machine works."

The waiter pulled out his pocket watch and looked at it. He shook his head. "In Italy, no one drinks cappuccino after ten o'clock and it is now half past eleven."

"Oh, I beg your pardon," Elle said. "The machine looks so interesting and I wanted to see how you do the milk. Does it heat up using this nozzle?" She pointed at a brass spout at the side.

The waiter's scowl lifted. "Yes, that is the steam outlet valve. We fill the filter with water here." He seemed to change his mind and pulled out a porcelain cup and saucer. "As we are no longer *in* Italy, and for a beautiful lady like yourself, I will make the exception. Watch and be amazed." He pulled out jars of coffee and milk and started preparing the coffee by measuring the dark grinds into the pan attachment. After pulling and tweaking a series of levers, a jet of thick brown liquid poured into the cup. The compartment filled with the smell of fresh coffee. "Now for the milk." He started blasting steam through the jug.

A few minutes later Elle had a magnificent cappuccino sitting on the foldout table before her, accompanied by a featherlight almond pastry.

The waiter looked at Marsh. "And something for you, sir?" he inquired. Marsh had been watching the cappuccino operation in amused silence from over the top of his newspaper. He gave another one of his half smiles. "A small coffee for me, please. I am not getting involved in the cappuccino debate."

The waiter gave him a knowing nod. "A very sensible decision, sir."

With another sequence of tweaked knobs and a hiss of hot water, the waiter placed a tiny cup of strong black coffee before Marsh.

"See." He pointed at the cup. "The secret is in the *crema*. That is what we call the golden foam that sits on the top. If that is rich and good, then the coffee will be excellent. In Italy we call this the tails of the rats because the coffee coming out of the machine should look like two tails of a rat. Otherwise," he gestured with his hands, "it is no good."

Elle laughed with delight. "Thank you, sir, for the education."

The waiter made a theatrical bow. "Always a pleasure to assist a beautiful lady." He wheeled his coffee contraption from their compartment, whistling.

Elle took a sip from her cappuccino, savoring the taste. "You know, I think they might be on to something with this invention. If I could get a better look at the plans, I'm sure we could build such machines. We could open coffee shops and people could stop by on their way to town for a cup of coffee and something sweet. We could ask Mrs. Hinges to make cakes."

"I think you might have a difficult time convincing people to give up their tea though."

"We could serve tea or coffee." Elle made a note to give the matter some more thought.

CHAPTER 32

They reached Vienna shortly after lunchtime. Elle watched passengers embark amidst much offloading and loading of luggage. The compartment shuddered as the carriages of the Venice train were shunted to join up with the rest of the Orient Express.

Marsh flagged down an elderly conductor. "Excuse me, how long will the train be stopping?"

"We will be departing from Vienna in about two hours, sir." The conductor nodded and shuffled on.

"Where are you going?" Elle watched Marsh shrug into his carriage cloak.

"I thought I might go for a little walk. Say hello to an old friend. Get some fresh air." He pulled on his gloves and lifted his hat off the rack. "I would ask you to join me, but you might find my destination objectionable. And we have an agreement about you-know-what, so I won't."

He was up to something. She could tell by the slight way in which his mouth curled up with amusement.

"Actually, I think I might join you," she said.

"Are you sure?" he asked.

She nodded. She didn't want to admit it, but for at least half an hour the strange whispering voices had been telling her to go with the Warlock. Right now they were all talking together, urging her to get up and put on her coat. She rubbed her ear in an attempt to silence them. She did not like the thought of hearing whispers no one else could hear. It meant that she was either going stark raving mad or this was some strange Oracle-related side effect like the loss of her shadow. Neither of these explanations was particularly attractive.

"I don't think it's wise. My friend is a sensitive creature. I fear that she might be frightened by your strong opinions."

He was going to visit a woman. Elle felt a strange sense of unease creep up her insides. She needed to know what he was up to now.

"I would have thought that a nice cup of tea would be an excellent diversion from the monotony of the train." She did her best to sound nonchalant.

"But you have to promise that you won't make a scene."

Elle nodded solemnly. "I promise." Elle picked up her reticule and followed him out of the compartment. "Where are we going?"

Marsh just smiled and offered her his arm as she stepped off the train. He was playing her. That much was certain. And she would have to play along if she was to have any hope of finding out what he was up to. She smiled back at him as they set off across the station concourse.

"I haven't been to Vienna since I was very young," she said as they walked. "My father was invited to give a lecture at the university here years ago and he brought me with him. I don't remember much, except that he took me to a café and bought me the biggest slice of chocolate cake I'd ever seen. I thought I had died and gone to heaven." She shivered as the wind rushed at them when they turned a corner. "Goodness, it is definitely getting colder."

Marsh smiled politely, but said little. Outside the station, they hailed a horse-drawn carriage to take them into the city center. Steam had not quite settled in Vienna as it had in the rest of Europe.

"I thought we agreed that there would be no more games, Mr. Marsh. Where are we going?" she said as soon as they were inside the carriage.

"There is someone I would like you to meet," Marsh said as the cab turned down the cobbled *Ringstrasse*, fringed with its elegant slim-windowed buildings.

"Who is it?"

He sighed. "Perhaps this is a bad idea. We should forget about it." He leaned forward to signal the driver.

Elle reached out and put her hand on his arm. "Don't. I promise I'll keep an open mind. Now, where are we going?"

"You'll see." Marsh tapped the driver hatch and gave the man an address. After a few minutes, the carriage pulled up outside a baroque town house. Marsh told the driver to wait for them when they got out.

At the top of the little steps, they came to a faded door with a heavy iron knocker. It was shaped like the head of a small horned godling. The brass was tarnished and gray, but the eyes were inlaid with bits of green glass.

Marsh lifted the knocker and tapped on the door. A few chips of peeling paint flaked off the door and landed at their feet.

The house was silent. Elle was about to turn back to the cab when an elderly butler opened the door. "You!" he said rudely. The wrinkles around his eyes receded as they widened in surprise. "It has been so many years since we've seen you," he said.

"Hello, Heinrich. Is your mistress home?"

The butler seemed to remember his place. "Do come in, my lord." He shuffled ahead of them into the front parlor. "Please. Let me take your coats. Madam." He held out his gnarled hands to take hold of Elle's coat. Elle gave Marsh a withering look. He ignored her and handed his own to the old man. She followed suit, not sure if she'd ever see the garment again.

"I'll go tell her that you are here." Heinrich shuffled off into the darker recesses of the house with their coats bundled up under his arm.

The parlor looked old and smelled of must and camphor, the scent of old people. Elle judged that the antique table and faded seats dated back to at least a hundred years ago. Thick dust sat in the corners and the curtains were drawn. It had the cold feel of a room that was not often used. She put the toe of her shoe over a patch on the carpet where the thread had worn through. Marsh stood by the window. He was peering out through the gap in the curtains, with his hands folded behind his back.

From the shadows, a clock broke the silence with the slow deep rhythmic beats of its clockwork heart. It was the only sound between them and the predatory quiet of the house.

Heinrich reappeared. "Please, come this way," he said, as he herded them out of the front room and up a flight of stairs. At the top of the stairs they came to what looked like another parlor.

Heinrich pushed open the door and ushered them inside. Coals glowed among the thick ash in the fireplace. The walls of the parlor were lined with dark wood paneling and shelves. There was every indication that this room might have been a gentleman's study at some point, but the shelves had since been cluttered up with all manner of strange paraphernalia. Jars of unidentified objects suspended in yellow-brown liquid stood nestled alongside books and bunches of dried herbs. Something moved next to Elle's foot and she realized with a start that she had almost stepped on a cat. Two more were staring at her from the backs of sofas. The smell of old people and damp fur was almost overpowering.

A small noise emanated from the corner. It was something between a cackle and a sniffle. "Hugh!" the brittle voice said.

"Hello, Rosamund," Marsh said. There was a softness in his voice that Elle found surprising.

The brittle voice belonged to a tiny old lady. She looked so old that she was shrunk to the size of a child. She sat in a fraying armchair trussed up in a collection of crocheted blankets. At the sight of the visitors, two more cats hopped off the old woman's lap and sauntered into the shadows.

"Oh, I never thought I'd see you again. Not before . . . before . . ." She trailed off into a wheeze. Elle watched in amazement as the woman's wrinkled face puckered up and her eyes filled with tears.

Marsh moved forward and kneeled down next to her. He put his hand on her lap. "No, please don't. I didn't come here for that."

She touched her gnarled old hand to the side of his face and peered at him. "Just look at you. Still so handsome."

Elle felt another shudder of unease work its way up her spine. She gently cleared her throat.

Marsh remembered himself and looked at Elle.

"Roz, I have brought someone to meet you," he said. "This is my friend, Eleanor Chance."

The old lady looked up at Elle and her face hardened as she composed herself. "Oh, I wish you had told me you were coming. I would have made myself ready." She beckoned at Elle. "Do come closer, dear, so I can see you."

Elle moved forward and kneeled on the footstool next to the chair.

Rosamund peered at Elle with age-bleary eyes. "Oh, Hugh, she is lovely. I do wish you the best." Her eyes filled with tears again.

The old crone was jealous, Elle realized. It was very creepy to behold.

"Miss Chance is an associate. I have brought her here to talk about your gift."

The old lady's gaze swiveled back to Elle. "She has it? One has finally manifested?"

"Yes."

Rosamund sat back in her chair and a look of immense relief spread across her wrinkled face. "Oh, that is such good news. Such good news indeed. It's been so long and I am so very tired. Heinrich will be so pleased. Respite at long last."

She flicked her watery gaze at Marsh and a look of pure cunning crossed her wrinkled face.

"Do you think she might give me a little . . . ? Not much, just enough to ease the pain in my joints. The winters are never easy. And especially now when I will be allowed to let go . . ."

Marsh sighed. "This is not the reason why we are here. She has yet to fully complete the metamorphosis."

The old lady's eyes widened. "An unschooled Cybele? Oh my. Is . . . this . . . Vivienne's daughter?"

At that moment, Elle's unease reached saturation point. "Excuse me, could someone please tell me what is going on here?"

Rosamund reached over and took Elle's hand in her own. She closed her eyes. "Oh, yes, the power in this one runs strong. Strong and pure. I've not felt that in many years. I should have sensed it sooner."

Elle pulled her hand away and stood up. The sudden movement set another cat running. "Marsh, I demand to know what is going on here?"

"Why, the power of the Pythias. The power that holds the universe together . . ." Rosamund said.

Marsh folded his arms. "Rosamund has been the Oracle since your mother died."

"They call me the paper Oracle. I have abilities, but they are not enough for true power." She shook her head. "Thin like paper and never enough . . . just enough to know it was there . . . enough to act when no one else alive could . . . but not enough to use." Her voice thinned and trailed off as if she had fallen asleep. She started and gestured around the room. "I turned to witchcraft in the end. It wasn't much consolation, but it helped."

Elle bit her bottom lip.

"Have you felt it in your dreams?" Rosamund asked.

Elle nodded. "Yes."

"And they've spoken to you, haven't they?"

"They have," she whispered.

The old lady clapped her hands with glee. "Oh yes, that's exactly it." She leaned forward. "Do me a favor, dear. Pass me that bag on the shelf. The blue one."

Elle did her best to ignore the specimen jars with their contents floating silently in their yellow liquid.

"That's the one," Rosamund said. Elle handed her the bundle of balding velvet.

With great care, Rosamund unwrapped the bundle. With unsteady hands, she lifted a crystal sphere from the folds of fabric and held it up to the light.

"The Oracle stone."

Elle peered at the crystal in its brass setting. It was the size of a walnut and yellowed with age.

The old lady prodded her. "Look into it. Concentrate. Tell me what you see."

Elle suppressed a sigh. She didn't need any special powers to know that she was going to murder Marsh as soon as they left this place. She frowned and focused on the crystal. It would only take a moment to humor them.

Bright light flashed before her eyes. She saw a train. It was dark. The moon hid behind trees. A carriage with a horse stood in the dark. Wolves howled. Blood trickled against the railings. "You must heed the warning. You must listen to us. There is no time to waste." The whispering voices insisted.

She gave a cry and sat back.

Marsh put his hand on her arm. "Elle, what is it?"

Rosamund cackled with childlike delight. "She saw something. Yes, yes, she did."

Elle stood up. She needed to leave this horrible little room as soon as possible. Marsh stood up too and put his hand out to steady her. "It's all right. No need to be alarmed. Roz is an old friend. I was hoping she could help you."

Elle shook her head. "I would like to go now. Our train is leaving soon and we don't want to be late." Her mouth was suddenly dry and she felt dizzy.

"I'm sorry. Coming here was a mistake. We should go," Marsh said. The old woman was still grinning with glee.

"Thank you for seeing us. I am very sorry for arriving unannounced and disturbing you."

The old lady's face fell. "Oh no, must you go so soon?"

"I'm afraid so. We are only stopping in Vienna for the briefest of time. Our train is departing within the hour." He went down on one knee and took Rosamund's hand in his. Gently he raised it up to his lips and kissed it. The gesture was intimate, intense, the touch of a lover. It was the touch of many things left unsaid, and it made Elle blush.

Rosamund's face softened and she looked very sad. Then she looked up at Elle. "Come here, my dear. It's all right. You don't have to be afraid."

Elle went up to her and sat back down on the footstool. She watched as Rosamund carefully took the crystal on its chain and put it around Elle's neck. "I want you to have this. The gift you carry is a terrible burden. Just look at what it has done to me." There was a gentle twinkle in her eyes. "Please take it. It belongs to the

Oracle. Your mother wore it once and now you will too. So it must be."

"My mother wore this?" She suddenly felt herself fill with a strange longing for the woman she had never known.

Rosamund nodded. "The stone will bring you wisdom."

"Thank you," Elle whispered. Their fingers touched. She felt the old woman move her gnarled hands over hers, gripping her wrists very firmly for someone so frail. "Now this won't hurt a bit," she whispered. "Just let me have a little."

A sudden jolt of energy shot through Elle's body. She tried to pull away, but it was as if she had been welded to the old woman. It felt like all the air was being pushed out of her. She gasped as she sank to the floor.

"Roz!" Marsh roared. He grabbed the old woman by the shoulders and shook her. The connection broke and Elle fell backwards off the footstool.

"I said no!" Marsh said. His face was drawn and angry.

Rosamund was glowing, but there was fear in her eyes. "Please, Hugh, don't be angry. Will you deny an old woman a small comfort? She has so much to spare. I gave her the crystal. The debt was paid."

"All this time and you haven't changed. Still only thinking about yourself." There was a bitterness in his voice. "I can see that coming here was a mistake. Let's go." He helped Elle to her feet.

Elle glanced behind her as they left the room. The old lady was rocking backwards and forwards in her chair and she could have sworn that the old woman's wrinkles had lessened and she was sitting taller.

"What on earth was that all about?" Elle said as they got back into the carriage. "Who *was* that woman?"

"Rosamund is the Oracle. But she does not have the same abilities you do. She used to be a friend. Years ago." His lips were still tight and he looked angry. "I thought she might have gained at least an inkling of wisdom in all these years." He shook his head. "I should have known better."

"What a strange lady. What was all that hand-holding about?"

Marsh did not answer. He just stared in front of him as the cab trundled along over the cobbles. "I'm sorry for subjecting you to that, but I fear for you, Elle. An untrained Cybele is an open invitation for trouble. I thought Rosamund might be able to tell you how to complete the metamorphosis on your own. So you could at least protect yourself, but I have failed." He looked utterly miserable.

Elle lifted the crystal over her head and held it in her hand. "My mother wore this once."

Marsh looked at the stone in her hand. "She did. As did every Oracle before her for the last five thousand years."

He ran a hand through his hair. "There is so much you still don't know. Promise me one thing, will you?"

"And what would that be?"

"Promise me that you will never allow another being to draw energy from you like Rosamund just did. Every time it happens, a bit of what you are disappears. You must promise me."

"Is that what she was doing? Why you were so angry?"

"Yes. If I hadn't stopped her, she would have drained you dry like a husk. She would have assumed your life force and become young again. You would have ended up as a pile of dust on the floor."

She was silent. "Well then, I suppose I should thank you for saving me. Even though you were the one that took me to see that awful woman in the first place." She folded her hands in her lap.

"There are many out there who will seek to use you in the same way. A Cybele is an empty receptacle for power. The Shadow will seek to fill that receptacle and those who hunger for power will seek to drain it. Every time that happens, a bit of you will disappear. One of the skills of the Oracle is to ensure that this does not happen when magic is channeled. You have to learn how to protect yourself. Do you understand what I am telling you?"

Elle nodded slowly. "Perhaps you are right." She dropped the crystal into her reticule and closed it.

"And do you see now what you might become if you don't learn how to use your gift properly?"

Elle felt herself grow angry. "I am nothing like that woman. And I will never be like her. Even after a thousand years, I will not."

Marsh stared at her for a long moment. "You know what? I think you might be right." And for the first time that day he looked slightly less unhappy.

CHAPTER 33

The station was crowded when they stepped from the carriage. Soldiers in bright uniforms stood about along the platform. The brass buttons on their uniforms glinted as they moved. Most of them seemed to be congregating around the third-class seats at the back of the train. Ladies in smart travelling dresses and furs stepped ahead of porters with large trolleys of luggage.

Marsh helped Elle onto the train step. His hand remained on her waist when he hopped up onto the step behind her. She smiled at him.

"You know, you are rather pretty when you smile, Miss Chance. You should try to do it more often." He spoke close to her ear.

Elle rolled her eyes. "Mr. Marsh, if I didn't know you better, I would say that you were flirting with me."

Marsh gave her an enigmatic look. "Oh, but there is much you don't know about me."

She edged past him and into their compartment. Whatever it was, their little visit to the old woman seemed to have lifted something inside him. It was as if a dark cloud had shifted away. Elle stopped at the door of their compartment. The air inside felt thick and unpleasant. She reached out before her.

"Elle, what is it?" Marsh said behind her.

"Can you not smell that? It smells like something died in here."

He gently moved her out of the way. "Wait. Let me

have a look." He stepped past her and into the carriage. Elle peered into the compartment. Everything looked as it had before.

Marsh reached down and pulled out their trunks. They appeared locked and untouched. He checked the bunks and on top of the racks too.

"Seems to be all right," he said. "I can't sense anything."

She stepped into the compartment and opened one of the windows. "I don't know, maybe it was my imagination, but it was the strangest sensation. Like someone had disturbed the air."

"Perhaps." Marsh took off his hat and gloves and sat down on his bunk. "It has been quite an afternoon so far, hasn't it?"

"You can say that again. I do hope that lovely waiter with the coffee machine will be round again. A nice hot drink is precisely what I need right now."

"Leave it to me." He disappeared from the compartment.

She pulled the crystal pendant out of her reticule and studied it. She was starting to build up quite a collection of jewelry of dubious origin. The crystal sphere was held in place by a cage of intricately worked brass filaments.

She rubbed the yellowing dome with her sleeve. A light flashed before her again. . . . *Soldiers in brown uniforms, moving like clockwork. Dead eyes staring ahead of them. Trains. People. Explosions. Suffering. Dead. So many dead.*

She cried out and let go of the pendant.

Marsh came into the compartment. "What's wrong?"

"I don't know. One moment I was looking at the stone and the next thing there were these visions. Marsh, there is so much evil in the world. Bad things are going to happen."

He sat down next to her. "You saw something?"

"I can't remember exactly, but they were terrifying things. There will be much suffering in times to come."

"I know you don't believe me, but you should use your gift to help others. To warn them so they don't make those mistakes." He gripped her shoulders gently and pulled her to his broad chest. "It is our duty."

He was still holding her when the whistle sounded and the train started moving.

"Someone called for a hot drink?" A waiter poked his head into the compartment. He spoke with a heavy Austrian accent. "Oh, excuse me," he said.

At the sight of the coffee machine, Elle brightened up and disentangled herself from Marsh's embrace. "What have you got?" she asked.

The waiter smiled. "Could I interest you in a lovely cup of Viennese chocolate, madam?"

CHAPTER 34

Eustace Abercrombie was feeling particularly pleased with life. He settled down in a comfortable chair, put his feet up on the ottoman and lit a cigar. The caliph of Constantinople might be a complete bore, but he was an excellent host, and the elaborate luncheon he had just enjoyed was the reason for his current state of contentment.

Abercrombie half closed his eyes and allowed himself to drift off into the beginning stages of a nice nap. He loved the quietness of the afternoon, before the Nightwalkers woke.

Nightwalkers. The mere thought of them turned his digestion sour. But, they were a necessary evil, born of an alliance so ancient that only the very oldest of the Nightwalkers remembered its origins. The ancient truce between those who were immortal and those that could step into the sun. The children of the night would rule the dark hours and the Alchemists, with their study of the planets, would guard the Nightwalkers by day. In return, those of the night paid handsomely for the service. And there were few things in the world Alchemists loved more than gold.

But the world was changing. Change was so close he could feel it. He knew about the secret experiments and tests conducted by the elders in dark cellars and dungeons. The day when Nightwalkers could walk in the light and no longer needed protection from zealots and the superstitious was nearly upon them. And when that happened, the Alchemists would no longer be needed. Their alliance was coming to an end and Abercrombie knew it was up to him to ensure that it ended in their favor.

He would make sure that Alchemists would stand free from the Night Lords and with all the power and the money they could hope for. Yes, that day would come very soon. He reached over and pulled the wooden box with the brass edges and the inlay out from its hiding place inside the ottoman at his feet. He held it up to the light and examined it. He could almost feel the power of the carmot inside radiating out at him.

"Very soon." He moved the box from side to side feeling its weight. "Very soon indeed."

CHAPTER 35

The Orient Express steamed into Budapest shortly after sunset. The generous curves of the River Danube swept through the twin cities of Buda and Pest, dark against the plum-colored sky. Lights twinkled on the bridges that married the cities on either side of the banks into one.

The locomotive trundled into the station, embracing the passengers waiting on the platform with clouds of incandescent spark-laced steam. Station workers and porters bustled up and down on the platform, helping people embark and disembark from the carriages.

Marsh carefully placed his papers back into their leather folder and consulted his train schedule. "Not a long stop. Only fifteen minutes." He looked at Elle. "Shall we go for a drink before dinner? We should be moving again soon."

Elle sat back and stretched her back slightly. "I think that would be nice," she said. Elle couldn't really say why the misery she felt had lifted after her visit to the strange old lady, but she was grateful for it.

"Then I shall leave you to change." He pulled the brass handle that closed the screen divider between them. "I for one would like to shave while the train is not moving. Razors and moving trains are not really companions."

The divider slid into place, leaving her alone in her half of the compartment. She drew down the window blind to shield herself from prying eyes on the platform and set about unbuttoning rows of small buttons. She stepped out of her dress and petticoat and laid them on her bunk. Next to the screen divider, there was a lever that said *"Toilette"* on its brass and porcelain handle. She pulled it and one of the panels slid round, converting the compartment corner into the loveliest little washbasin and toilette cubical. She leaned over to study the pipes behind the basin. "These pipes must run to the spark reactors in the main engine. That must be the way they heat the water."

"What was that?"

"I said the hot water must be coming from the train's spark reactors. It's like the samovar on my ship."

"Must be." Marsh was humming a tune to himself.

Elle stepped up to the screen. The polished wood panels were held together with brass hinges. One of the hinges had worn and bent slightly with use, leaving a gap between the panels. Unable to stop herself, she put her eye up to the gap.

Marsh was standing over his basin with his back to her. His face was covered in white shaving soap. A long razor with an ivory handle rested in his hand. He had stripped down to his trousers and his body swayed gently as he ran the blade over his cheek.

Elle's gaze wandered over the muscles in his back and she felt her breath catch in her throat. He was magnificent. Not that she had seen many half-naked men in her life, but still. It was rather a mystery why he wasn't married. Or at least engaged, but he was rather closed on the subject. She watched him raise his chin to shave his throat.

There must be something wrong with him, she decided. Or maybe there was a secret code amongst Warlocks never to marry. Or maybe he preferred the company of gentlemen. She somehow doubted that. Perhaps it was because he was so closed. Maybe most right-thinking women sensed how dangerous he was.

She checked her thoughts. With a flush of embarrassment, she realized that she was behaving worse than a thirteen-year-old debutante hiding behind a curtain at a ball.

A whistle sounded and the train lurched into motion. Elle fell forward and grabbed on to the handrail to stop herself from crashing into the screen. The divider shuddered as the spring mechanism engaged. To her horror, the divider drew back. She had grabbed the wrong lever by mistake.

Marsh turned round in surprise and his eyes lit up with amusement at the sight of her in her pantaloons and corset. He made no attempt to avert his gaze.

Elle put her hands to her chest to cover herself. "Sorry. Wrong lever," she mumbled sheepishly.

"If you say so." His gaze slipped over her curves.

She grabbed the lever and pulled it, but it jammed. She yanked it again, but the spring was stuck.

Marsh chuckled and stepped forward. Suddenly they were very close to one another. She could smell the fresh shaving soap on his skin. He leaned closer and unhitched the corner of the divider, which had become hooked on one of the luggage straps in the overhead luggage rack. "There you go," he said with a slow smile before the divider slid back into place.

Mortified, Elle pulled one of her new evening dresses out of her portmanteau. It was made of the softest opal-colored silk. She shook it out and finished dressing as fast as was possible within the confines of the compartment. She tidied her hair in the mirror and dabbed freesia oil behind her ears. The smell of flowers filled the air around her.

For the first time, she was glad that the bracelet was still stuck around her wrist. At least the diamonds meant that she would not have to stand back for the beautiful and well-heeled ladies she was about to encounter. She picked up her stole and knocked on the screen. "Marsh?"

He pulled the screen back and looked down at her. "I think I preferred the last outfit." His mouth quirked up into another slow smile, but this time there was something soft in his expression. "Ready?"

She smiled up at him. "Ready and famished."

CHAPTER 36

The dining cart was filled with elegant people all dressed for dinner. Feathers, diamonds and furs abounded as fine ladies in fashionable narrow-cut rail-carriage dresses sipped their drinks. Their companions, dressed in dark dinner suits, stood about, talking. The confines of the train created a strangely intimate atmosphere for what was a fairly formal occasion.

A dark-haired woman sat on her own, perched on one of the high chairs at the bar. She looked up and smiled as Elle and Marsh sat down at one of the tables.

Elle glanced at the woman's dress. It was unusual, black like midnight, against the pale skin of her exposed décolletage. The hem and sleeves were drawn up with satin ribbons. She looked like a dark angel perched on the chair.

"Loisa!" Marsh said. He smiled at the woman warmly. "What a lovely surprise."

"Hugh!" The woman held out an elegant gloved hand.

"Delightful to see you." He bowed over her satin-covered hand.

The woman lifted her chin. "And the same to you, darling." Her lips curled into a slow smile.

Elle felt an acute stab of jealousy at their familiarity. Perhaps it wasn't so much that there were no women in the man's life. Perhaps it was because there were so many that any mention of them would give rise to indiscretion. That would explain things. How disappointing.

"Elle, I'd like to introduce you to a dear friend of mine. May I present the Baroness Belododia. Loisa, may I present Miss Eleanor Chance."

The lady smiled, revealing a row of perfect white teeth. Her skin was so fine that it was at the point of being translucent. Despite the powder and rouge, two faint blue crescents rested below the woman's exquisite eyes, which gave her a slightly haunted look. Elle felt a little shudder run up her spine. The baroness was a Nightwalker. She bowed her head. "Your ladyship."

"Miss Chance, how do you do. I am always pleased to meet a friend of Hugh's." She drawled in perfect English, her accent slightly heavy on the "r"s.

Elle wasn't sure she liked the way the woman used the word friend, but before she could respond, the baroness had moved and was sitting next to her.

"Please, do join us," Hugh said drily.

"Thank you, darling," the baroness drawled. "Now, would you be a dear and bring us some drinks, yes?" She cocked a perfectly arched eyebrow at Marsh.

"I am at your service, my lady."

Elle folded her hands. Even the ancient and the undead were not immune to Marsh's charms, it seemed.

The baroness smiled at her again in what must have been a warm smile while she was still alive, as if she were expecting Elle to say something.

"So are you travelling all the way to Constantinople?" She didn't know many Nightwalkers, especially not highborn ones, and so she wasn't quite sure what to say.

The baroness laughed. "Good heavens, no, I am only going as far as Bucharest. I always spend the winter at my uncle's estate in the Carpathians. You might have heard of my uncle, the count?"

Elle's eyes grew wide. "You mean?"

The baroness's smile widened. "Ah yes, I see you have heard of him, then. My uncle Vlad is quite well known in England, I think, no?" She folded her gloved hands primly. "At least since all that terrible business with that lawyer's wife in Whitby." She shook her head and her perfect dark curls bounced. "I don't know what he was thinking, but then again, men are so predictable, aren't they?"

Elle felt herself warming to the baroness. "I suppose they are," she said.

Marsh arrived with a bottle of champagne in an ice bucket. He popped open the cork and poured out three glasses for them. This was much to the consternation of the waiter, who hovered behind him with a tray. Marsh sat down at the table and smiled at them.

"Ladies," he said.

The baroness reached out and tickled Marsh's chin. "Such a handsome butler you would make, my darling," she pouted. "You should come to the estate for the winter. We Nightwalkers do so love to ski."

"Oh, you couldn't afford me," he said.

The baroness picked up a tiny jug of blood that the waiter had discreetly placed on the table next to her. She tipped a drop into the glass and watched the red curl to the bottom, staining her drink pink. She raised her glass and inclined her head. "To friends," she said.

"To friends," Marsh echoed. "And a truly lovely friend you are."

"Oh, darling, you are too kind." Loisa fluttered her eyelashes gently. On a lesser woman the gesture would have been coquettish, but not on her.

Elle watched the baroness sip from her glass. "Please don't think me rude, but do you mind me asking? Can Nightwalkers drink champagne?"

The baroness laughed again. "She is so adorable, this one. So fresh and lovely." She stared at Elle with her glittering dark eyes.

Elle felt the hairs on her arms rise. "I'm sorry. I didn't mean to offend by asking." She started to offer an apology, but the baroness put her hand on Elle's arm. She could feel the coolness through the gloves.

"Of course I don't mind you asking, my dear. It is sometimes so nice to find frankness among all these rules of protocol, don't you think, Hugh?"

Hugh gave Loisa a pained smile and took a swig of his champagne.

"Yes, my darling," the baroness said, turning to Elle. "We can eat and drink. Our bodies are exactly like they were when we were human. But food gives us no nourishment." She wrinkled her nose. "It tastes like eating cardboard and there is simply no point to it. What we need is the essence. The energy. The pulsing life force that lives in blood." Elle saw something predatory flicker in Loisa's eyes. "Alcohol, on the other hand, we can taste. And most of us like it, especially if it is flavored," she said, tilting her glass and the red blob at the bottom moved. Elle wondered what kind of blood it was.

"But how does the blood work?"

The baroness took another sip of her champagne and smiled. "And clever too. Hugh, I *am* impressed. Your standards are improving." She spoke without taking her eyes off Elle. "Unfortunately, sweet one, I am an old Nightwalker. I was born long before our elders became involved in politics and all of the scientists started analyzing why things work the way they do. So in answer to your question, I honestly don't know. I never get involved with such matters. They just make me sad." She laughed, and the sound was like breaking glass.

There was a gentle tinkle of brass bells at the other side of the carriage, announcing that dinner was served.

"Ladies, speaking of sustenance, will you do me the honor of joining me for dinner?" Marsh said. "I for one am curious to see what miracles of gastronomy are about to be served up in the dining cart."

"But of course, darling. I would love to. How lovely of you to ask."

The three of them were shepherded into the dining cart and shown to a table.

Marsh seated himself opposite Elle and the baroness who had somehow appeared in the seat next to her. She watched the waiter discreetly remove the silver from the table and replace the knives and forks with ivory-handled steel cutlery. The Orient Express catered to the needs of their Shadow passengers in every way, it seemed.

Dinner involved five courses for Elle and Marsh. The baroness's meal consisted of five matching liquid courses, served up in crystal goblets. Elle was amazed at how interesting and elaborate the dishes were, considering that they were on a moving train. The kitchen rather quaintly matched the solid and liquid menus for the convenience of guests.

Elle took a bite of her roast breast of pheasant while watching the baroness take a sip of pheasant blood from the gold-rimmed goblet before her.

"Hmm," Loisa murmured, and pursed her red lips. "Delicious. I do adore pheasant, don't you?" she said. "Especially this time of year."

Elle nodded and smiled. To her surprise, the baroness was turning out to be most agreeable company, when she wasn't flirting with Marsh. Knowing that the baroness was well fed made her seem much less scary.

The baroness, in turn, spent most of the time chatting with Marsh about people and past events that Elle knew nothing about. Marsh flirted back with consummate expertise and it was not long before he had the elegant baroness giggling into her goblet, almost spluttering her dinner over herself and the tablecloth.

How does he do that? Elle wondered with no small

measure of annoyance. She found herself feeling annoyed about the fact that she was annoyed. The man was driving her to the brink of insanity.

The corners of his mouth curled up into a little smile and she felt something inside her quicken. It would be so easy to fall in love with a man like him. He was absolutely mesmerizing. But he was a liar and a manipulator too. She pushed the thought firmly out of her mind and concentrated on the baroness's convoluted tale of how they used to go sledding downhill at night a hundred years ago.

Desserts were tiny slices of dense chocolate cake with cream for her and Marsh and a cup of sweetened mulled pork blood for Loisa, followed by cheese on a board.

Marsh put down his spoon and sat back. He patted his waistcoat and signaled for a cigar. "That was a most excellent dinner. But, ladies, if you would excuse me; I am in dire need of a good cigar, a snifter of brandy and some male banter in the saloon. Loisa, could I perhaps impose on you to amuse my lovely companion while I excuse myself?"

The baroness's face brightened. "It would be my pleasure. There are many hours till dawn and the train at night can be so dull sometimes. I know Eleanor and I are going to be great friends." Loisa gave a little moue. Marsh smiled and left the carriage.

Then she turned to Elle and focused her sharp dark gaze on her. "Shall we play some cards?"

Elle felt a small frisson of fear run over her. She didn't think she could ever become accustomed to the stare of Nightwalkers. Even the nonthreatening kind.

"Let's," she agreed.

Loisa held up her arm and signaled a waiter. "May we have some playing cards, please?"

The waiter returned with a deck of cards on a small wooden tray. The baroness had taken off her gloves. She curled her white fingers, slightly blue at the nails, around the deck and started shuffling the cards, faster than the eye could follow. She cut the deck expertly and placed the cards face down on the table.

She looked at Elle with a conspiratorial smile. "Finally, we are alone. I have been *dying* for him to go for a brandy."

Elle looked at her with some surprise. She had thought that quite the opposite was true.

"So tell me, darling, what have you done to capture my poor Hughby's heart like that?"

Elle blinked. "Excuse me?"

"Ah, you don't know it, do you?" She gave Elle a sly look.

Elle suddenly felt like a mouse watched by a sleek cat. "Um, Viscount Greychester and I are merely good friends. We are travelling on business."

The baroness snorted and gave her a knowing smile. "Viscount Greychester never does anything unless it is for his pleasure." She drew a wooden case from her reticule and pulled out a cigarillo.

"You don't mind, do you?"

Elle did not smoke herself. She failed to see the point and it was a rather smelly habit, but Loisa Belododia made even smoking, the most unladylike of activities, look elegant and sophisticated. She had to admire the woman for that.

Loisa lit the cigarillo and deeply inhaled the smoke. "Most of us smoke, you know. It reminds us of what it felt like to breathe. Some say that cigars poison the lungs." She shrugged. "Who knows if that is true? Who cares. We are dead anyway." There was a touch of sadness in her voice. She picked up the deck and started dealing the cards. "Gin rummy?"

Elle nodded. Why not? How many people could claim

to have played gin rummy with a highborn Nightwalker—on a train?

Loisa brightened as she looked at her cards. She pulled one out of her hand and placed it on the table before her and picked a card from the deck. She slipped it into the fan of cards in her hand.

"So how long have you known the viscount?" Elle said, trying to sound casual.

Loisa stared at Elle. "Long enough. I am one of the few who has stuck with him regardless of what others were saying at the time. But you are so very young. Too young to know about the gossip," she said.

"Gossip?" Elle said.

The baroness let out an elaborate sigh and fanned out her cards. "Oh, I am not sure I should tell. It's never good to drag up old ghosts."

Elle leaned forward. This sounded important.

The baroness put her fan of cards face down on the table. "Oh, very well, I'll tell you," she said. "But you have to promise not to say anything."

"You have my word," Elle said.

"You must know by now that Hugh is a high-ranking Warlock, yes?" She arched her carefully shaped eyebrows at Elle.

Elle nodded. "He has mentioned it."

"But do you know that he is one of the youngest Warlocks ever to be elected to the Council? The Council, as I'm sure you also know, guards and controls the use of Shadow force across the world. Statesmen and kings rely on them to keep the balance in the natural order of the world. It's their role to keep the Shadow in check so the balance is maintained."

Elle nodded again. "So I have been told."

The baroness sat forward, her gaze intense. "Without the Council of Warlocks, the world would be in chaos. Creatures like me would be hunted down and killed by the religious and those who have no tolerance for the Shadow. The world would turn to chaos just as it did in the Dark Ages when the first Council in Rome collapsed. And not only for Nightwalkers, but for all creatures of Shadow."

She shuddered. "The Dark Ages was a terrible time. Not many of my kind survived. They came after us, armed with iron and fervor, seeking our destruction, no matter what the cost. We were hunted. Then came the inquisitions and the burnings." She picked up her cards and spread them in front of her face. She gazed at her cards. "We lived in secret, like animals. Always hiding."

"I'm so sorry," Elle said, not wanting to offend. "I'm sure that must have been awful for you."

"We, the immortal ones, have to put our faith in such fragile creatures. And all for the simple fact that they can venture into the sun. I will never understand why some of my kin made pacts with day-dwellers in the way that they did."

"The system seems to have worked though. Everyone seems to be living in relative peace nowadays. There is much tolerance," Elle said.

The baroness narrowed her eyes. "Warlocks are not immortal. Like all who live in Shadow, they have their weaknesses. And there are some who say that the Council grows weaker every day. They say that there are others who would be more suitable to the task of Guardians. Some say that the Shadow should have more power than the Light."

Elle looked at her cards. "I must confess that I don't know much about the topic," she said as tactfully as she could. She put a card down and picked one up from the deck. She smiled. "Gin," she said, and fanned her cards on the table.

The baroness laughed and clapped her hands.

"Well done. Let's play again!" She picked up all the

cards and in a whirr of movement she started dealing another hand.

"So you were busy telling me something about Hugh," Elle said, steering the topic away from the political debate.

"Ah yes! Hugh, how could I forget such a delicious boy?"

Elle smiled. "I don't think he could be called a boy. I mean, how old is he? Or at least, how long do Warlocks live?"

The baroness pouted again and laid down two cards. "To me, he will always be a boy, but I would say that they live about ten times as long as normal humans, maybe more. When Hugh and I met two or three human lifetimes ago, he was barely a man. Oh, you should have seen him then. He was so awkward and gangly, with the floppy dark hair and those long black eyelashes. He was adorable." The baroness licked her lips. "But the boy grew to be a man with much sadness within him."

"What happened?" Elle found that she had quite forgotten about her cards.

"Hugh had just come into his powers when he met a girl. I don't know, it must have been about a hundred and fifty years ago now. Time goes so fast, you know. The woman's name was Rosamund. She was very beautiful. All blond curls, if you like that kind of thing."

Elle started. "Did you say 'Rosamund'?"

"Yes, I know, it is such a frivolous name, but it was fashionable back then, I believe."

Elle nodded. "Do go on," she said.

"Well, Rosamund fell madly in love with Hugh. But Hugh was too busy studying and learning about being a Warlock. He was largely oblivious to her until her family started hinting to his about marriage proposals. His family thought it a good match, but Hugh balked at the idea. He refused to propose." The baroness rolled her eyes. "Rosamund was furious. You see, she had told all her friends that she had bagged herself the handsome son of an earl and so she ended up being utterly humiliated when Hugh didn't do as she had planned.

"Gin!" The baroness put her cards down on the table.

"Good heavens," was all that Elle could say. She picked up the cards and dealt another hand.

The baroness leaned forward and said in a low voice, "But that was not the worst of it. In retaliation, Rosamund started spreading scandalous rumors about Hugh. All of which were completely untrue, of course. Hugh would never do such things to anyone." She placed a card onto the deck. Elle picked it up. It was the Jack of Hearts.

"What happened then?" Elle shifted the card in her hand.

"Ah," the baroness patted the air with her dainty hand. "There was a huge scandal. Rosamund's family were saying that Hugh had seduced their daughter against her will and that he had unnatural occult proclivities involving young maidens and rituals. The rumors tore through society. Rosamund's family wanted to involve a judge. There was a lot of negotiation behind closed doors and the matter was brought to a close quietly, with no charges proven. But in a way this was worse than a public trial. Hugh was ruined."

"That's awful." Elle felt her insides clench with mortification.

"Yes, it was," the baroness said. "In the end, I heard that Rosamund ran off with a soldier. He was killed in battle and the last I heard was that she had turned her hand to witchcraft to survive. Some say she took to using magic to suck the youth out of young women to feed her own unnatural immortality. No one knows where she is now. But I hear she is still alive."

"Witchcraft?" Elle thought about the crystal in her luggage.

"Yes, the low-class kind. She showed a lot of promise to begin with, but in the end it turned out she never had any real abilities. The poor thing. Just enough to deceive people. You know, fortune-telling, calling up spirits, potions and such things." The baroness shuddered. "Peasant tricks. Terribly *voyant.*"

She discarded another card and studied her hand. "All that would have been fine, but Hugh's reputation was in tatters. No one wanted him anywhere near their daughters after what had happened. He was shunned from social occasions for being licentious and a libertine. Ostracized in a time when being seen in society was everything. And I can tell you that the accusations of such dishonorable deeds broke his young heart. I watched him turn bitter because of it." She looked up at Elle. "And for what? For the whims of a spoiled girl."

The baroness paused to take a last drag from her cigarillo. "Hugh developed a very deep distrust of women after Rosamund. Especially ones who had the power to hurt him. I remember how he became utterly ruthless for a while. Took his pleasure when and where he wished. But in the end, he simply got bored and gave up. He devoted himself to his study of the Craft and the business of the Council. Being a Warlock is everything to him. He believes in no greater cause."

Elle stared at her cards. It felt like her stomach had fallen out of her body and in its place a big lump of mortification and guilt had formed. Had she really threatened to cry rape if Marsh did not do what she demanded? No wonder he had been so angry. She suddenly felt like weeping.

"So you would imagine my surprise to see him here with you, on this train. Sharing a compartment. It's all so very *intimate.*" The baroness put her cards down.

Elle cleared her throat. "I can assure you that there is nothing between us. We are merely travelling on business. It was safer to arrange matters in this way."

The baroness stared at Elle. Her eyes were suddenly serious. "Whatever you are up to, please promise me that you won't hurt him. He is a good boy, and anyone who trifles with his affections again will have me to deal with."

Elle swallowed. She wasn't sure, but she could have sworn that she had seen the briefest flash of fang when the baroness spoke.

"I won't do anything to hurt him," she said solemnly, and not just because of the threat the baroness had made.

She also made a mental note to start carrying some garlic on her person as a precaution. The baroness nodded and a small smile crept onto her lips. "Ah, I can see it now. You love him too. This is so wonderful."

Elle felt herself grow warm. She smiled at the baroness. "We are just friends. Nothing more. But enough of such serious talk. Shall we order some coffee? You should see the machine they have that makes it. I do hope it's still running this late."

"Let's," Loisa said slowly as if she was making up her mind about something. She signaled to the waiter. "And brandy." Then she took both of Elle's hands in hers. "My dear Miss Chance. I think you and I are going to be firm friends."

They played a few more rounds of cards. Elle felt like she had passed some unspoken test and she found herself relaxing.

Loisa was warm and funny once you got past the fact that she was a deadly Nightwalker. After her second brandy, Elle felt her eyes grow heavy. She was doing her best to stay awake, but the cards grew blurry before her eyes. She stifled a big yawn behind her hand.

"Time for bed," Loisa announced. "Good night, my darling. Tonight was a wonderful evening and we must meet again soon. I am going to sit on the roof to watch the moon for a while." They kissed one another on the cheeks warmly and bade each other farewell.

CHAPTER 37

Back in their carriage, Elle closed the compartment door firmly behind her. She rested against the door, her mind reeling with snippets of earlier conversation.

She started undressing, and took a few deep, liberating breaths as soon as the laces of her stays gave way. Her new nightdress was made of soft cotton and it was slightly too big for her. The fabric slipped off her shoulders as she pulled it over her head.

She gazed off into the distance as she ran her hairbrush through her hair. She stopped combing and studied the hairbrush. It was fine bristle with silver on the handle. All of her luggage had been replaced, quickly and discreetly. Her mind was so full of other thoughts that she had hardly noticed it happen. And Marsh had attended to all of it, without mentioning it.

Marsh.

She had the nagging feeling that she had been completely wrong about him. Could he have forsaken his Brotherhood to keep her safe? Was the baroness right? Did Marsh have feelings for her? Did she have feelings for him? She thought about the baroness tickling Hugh's chin and how annoyed it had made her. Was she jealous?

She slammed her hairbrush down. Damn. She did have feelings for him. How inconvenient.

She slipped into her bunk. Being in love with Hugh Marsh was utter madness. There was no future with him. The image of Rosamund's wrinkled old face sprang to mind. The same Rosamund? It had to be. She had seen how he'd kissed her hand.

Would Hugh watch her grow old slowly while he remained the same? Would she also end up a wrinkled, mad old lady in a house while he visited with a new, younger woman? She didn't think she could stand that. No, it was best that she left the whole matter well alone. As soon as her father was safe, she would go back to her old life. Flying was her passion, though somehow flying freight seemed so dull now, but what were her alternatives? She definitely did not want to belong to the Council of Warlocks, though. She shuddered at the thought.

The door slid open and Marsh entered their compartment. Their eyes met and he looked away. "I'm sorry, I did not know you were in," he said.

She sat up halfway in her bunk. "It's all right. I'm sorry, I should have closed the screen," she said.

"I hope Loisa didn't drive you completely mad with her chattering," Marsh said.

"The baroness is a very interesting woman. I didn't realize she was related to such famous Nightwalkers."

Marsh nodded. "Ah, yes, her uncle, the count. Terrible business that was back in its day."

Elle laughed. "Why, were you there?"

He looked at her with slight surprise. "Actually, I was," he said.

"Tell me, Hugh. How old are you?"

His eyebrows arched up at the question. "Loisa has been busy, I see." He started removing his waistcoat. He stopped at the second button.

Elle realized that she was staring at him.

"I'll close the screen, if you don't mind."

"Yes, I think that might be best." She swallowed.

He drew the divider across and she lay in the half-dark listening to him shuffle about.

The train thump-di-thumped along on the tracks below her.

"If I were an ordinary mortal, I suppose I would be about thirty right now. In real time, I am two hundred and eleven," he said.

"So you are a real Warlock then?" she said.

"Yes, I suppose you could say so, depending on what you mean by real Warlock." She heard fabric rustle as he undressed.

There was a soft thump. He growled.

She got out of bed and stood by the screen to see what the cause of the noise was. She was about to peer through the gap in the panel when Hugh yanked the barrier aside. They stood in front of one another, swaying gently in time to the moving train. "This cravat," he mumbled.

Her hands went gently to the offending necktie. "Let me help." Deftly, she lifted the fine silk fabric and started working at the knot he had drawn tight. As she worked, she inhaled his now familiar sandalwood smell. It was mixed with tobacco and there was a slight hint of brandy on his breath. It was strange how she could discern such fine details. It was as if she had known him for all her life.

The knot gave way under her fingers and, transfixed, she found herself caressing the top button that held his collar until it came free.

His breath quickened at her touch and his hands held hers, his elegant fingers caressing hers.

Her fingers stilled at the square of skin at the base of his neck.

"Elle, I . . ." His eyes were luminous as he looked at her.

"Shh . . ." In an act of utter bravery or madness, she stood on her toes and kissed him.

Their mouths met. The touch of his lips sparked an

energy that plunged to the very depths of her. In that moment, she knew that this was the one kiss of her life. It was the touch of him she would remember forever. The kiss she would dream of when she was lonely. It was the kiss she would relive when she was alone. It would transcend the physical, the realms of Shadow and Light. All other kisses that followed, if there ever were to be any, would not compare.

He groaned and pulled her tightly against him, his lips claiming hers. She felt his body against hers, hard and powerful, aroused. His hands slid down the length of her with an intensity of desire she did not anticipate. She gave herself over to it and arched herself into him, willing him to feel her passion.

Light started flickering behind her eyelids. She fought it, for she wanted to stay in the here and now, holding on to his shirt, urging him closer in the moment, but the pull of the Shadow was too strong and she was hurled violently into the vortex.

It was summer . . . The golden evening sun caressed the garden like a lover with perfume of freesias and lilacs . . . Hugh stood on the terrace. His hair was graying slightly at the temples . . . He held out his hand . . . A woman in a strange dress walked up to him, her hair and face obscured by a wide-brimmed hat. Children ran and played on the grass, their tinkling laughter around them.

She opened her eyes with a start. Marsh had pulled away from her. There was a look of utter confusion in his eyes.

"You saw something. I felt it. I mean, I think I saw it too." He frowned and touched his forehead. He was breathing heavily.

She swallowed. There was too much to say. She couldn't even begin to find the words.

"It can't. You are the Oracle. You . . . this is interfering with everything." He turned away from her, his hands clenched tightly at his sides. "Touching you is like drinking from a cool clean fountain after suffering from a great thirst. It is . . . perfection." She saw the tension in his shoulders. "But I know what that will do in time. We cannot. *Must* not."

"Um . . . I . . . " she said.

He turned and put his hand on the screen and his eyes filled with sadness. "Elle, I think I had better close this screen. Best if you went to bed now." He could not look at her.

She closed her eyes and looked away. He did not want her, and there was nothing she could say to change that. Like an obedient child, she stumbled into her bunk. The light on his side of the compartment went out. She could hear him shifting about in the dark and eventually it went quiet. In the darkness, she swallowed down the burning lump of disappointment and rejection that had lodged in her throat. How could she have been so stupid to let down her guard like that?

The train thump-da-thumped in sympathy, jiggling them in their bunks, as if it wanted them to get up and do something, but there was nothing either of them could say.

As usual he was right; she had seen what was to be. Perhaps it was for the best. Somewhere in the future there would be a happy Viscount and Viscountess Greychester. They would live with their children in a house filled with sunshine and laugher. What hurt the most was the fact that she was almost certain that she would not be that woman.

CHAPTER 38

The train had stopped moving. Elle sat up in her bunk. "Marsh?" she whispered in the dark. There was only silence. She slipped out of her bunk and drew the divider aside. A shaft of metallic light from outside fell across his empty bunk. She peered out the window. They were in the middle of nowhere. Only the darker looming shapes of mountains interrupted the cloud-streaked night sky. The moon fought to make itself seen through the trees.

Something was wrong. She felt the wrongness scrabble inside her with its tiny claws, like a trapped bird.

There was a soft noise outside the compartment. Without a sound, Elle lifted the lid of her trunk and drew the Colt out of its holster. She slipped the safety catch off with a quiet click. With the revolver resting in her hand, she went to the door and opened it slightly.

"Hugh?" she whispered.

Two dark figures crashed into the compartment. One grabbed her and pinned her to the wall. Elle felt her nightdress rip as one intruder stepped on the hem.

She twisted round and kicked one of them in the knee, but she was barefoot and he was so much stronger than her.

"Let go of me, you bastards!" she said between gritted teeth. She felt a sudden surge of energy pulse through her and it crackled over her skin like static.

"Ooh, they said the little kitty would put up a fight."

One of the men grabbed her by the hair. And shook his hand as if touching her had stung him. "Now, be a good girl and come with Uncle Chunk. There are people who have business with you."

"I am not your kitty and I am going nowhere," Elle said. She wrestled her arms up from beside her and pulled the trigger. The discharge of the round in such close quarters was deafening.

One of her attackers loosened his hold on her and dropped to the floor like a sack of spuds, but the other held firm. She tried to aim at him, but he grabbed her wrist and twisted it back painfully. The Colt dropped to the floor and skittered away.

"Now hold still. I've orders not to hurt you too much," he said as he shoved a piece of cloth over her face. An acrid smell filled her nose and mouth. Chloroform, she thought in a panic. She couldn't breathe. The cloth was suffocating her. She wrestled her face away and took a breath so she could scream, but the world started swimming around her. "Let go of me," she gasped, and tried to scratch at the strong hands holding her, but the world tilted . . . and everything disappeared into darkness.

Marsh walked down the corridor of the train. He had gone to investigate the reason for the train stopping. Something was wrong. He could feel it in his bones.

"Problems on the track, sir," a sleepy concierge had told him. "We have sent two engineers to clear it away. It's probably just a fallen tree. Nothing unusual for these parts. It would be better if you went back to bed. We will have this sorted out in a few minutes and we'll be on our way before you know it."

Marsh looked about in frustration. There were no other inquiries that he could make. With a growing sense of unease, he turned back to the compartment.

He looked at his pocket watch. It was four o'clock in

the morning. Hopefully this stop wouldn't detain them for too long a time. He cursed himself for not choosing to travel by airship. But the next flight to Constantinople from Venice departed in two days' time. It would have taken them longer to get there. And the thought of being stuck on an airship after the incident with the pirates made him quiver. The train was more anonymous. And he had been hoping to see Rosamund. That had been a disaster. The woman never failed to disappoint. And then he had allowed himself to kiss Elle. He had tried to resist, but she was so beautiful standing before him in her nightdress. She made his insides melt when she looked at him like that. No woman had ever made him feel that way.

They would have to speak about it in the morning. He needed time. Time to woo her, to do things properly. She deserved that. He ran his hand through his hair to clear his thoughts.

The thwack of gunpowder igniting on steel reverberated through the train. Every nerve in Marsh's body stood on end as his finely tuned senses felt the vibrations in the ether. That was the sound of gunfire. He started running.

He skidded to a halt outside the door of their compartment. The door was open.

"Elle?" he called. There was only silence. He was sure he had closed the door on his way out.

The tinny smell of gunpowder filled his nostrils. He summoned up a ball of light from the lamp in the corridor and flung it into the darkness ahead of him. It was a handy trick he had learned in the military, but one he had not needed to use in years. The compartment was empty but there was a metallic tang in the close space that made his blood run cold.

Elle's sheets and bedclothes hung off the bunk. He ran his hand over them. The linen was still warm from her body and the faint smell of freesias drifted from them. He felt his chest constrict. *Please no,* he thought. The rug before the bed felt wet and sticky. He examined his fingers in the dwindling light with a growing sense of unease. His suspicions were correct. His fingers were covered in blood.

He peered out of the carriage window into the darkness. Nothing but silence and ominous forest spread out before him. He rushed to the other side of the carriage and flung the door open. The moon struggled its way out from between the clouds and trees. A horse snorted and shook its head. A carriage harness jingled. He heard the sharp crack of a whip and the dark shape of a carriage rumbled into motion.

Without meaning to, he shouted. They were getting away.

Marsh launched himself at the carriage. He managed to grab the back railing. The carriage was covered in something dark and sticky that smelled like tar. With all of his strength, he dragged himself up onto the roof of the carriage.

The coachman turned round and aimed a yellow blast of alchemy at Marsh. He blocked the deathblow but the eddy of energy hit him in the ribs and knocked him sideways, off the carriage. He landed with a thump on the gravel next to the tracks. Stunned, he could only watch as the carriage sped away into the dark.

He lay alone in the dark for long seconds, unable to move. Slowly, the feeling ebbed back into his body. He could feel the large chunks of gravel that lined the tracks dig into his back. He struggled to sit up, but his limbs would not respond

Up ahead, the train whistled. The locomotive let out a great huff of steam and the carriages creaked. The train started moving. He was going to be left behind.

With all of his strength Marsh tried to push himself up

off the ground, but his arms gave way. He slumped back down as the last of his strength slipped from his body.

Above him, a dark shadow moved. Quiet as a whisper, it landed beside him. Marsh felt soft lace sleeves on his face as cool hands traveled over him.

The train was moving faster now. Not long before it would be gone.

Arms that were inhumanly strong dragged him upwards. He groaned as his knees hit hard metal steps. A pale face with dark eyes looked down at him.

"Loisa," he whispered.

"Stay still, you're bleeding," she said. His head rolled to the side, and with odd detachment, he watched the ground move below him.

"Sir, are you all right?" The voice sounded far away. He looked up. The conductor's face swam in and out of his field of vision. Hands lifted him and a searing pain ripped through his side. He looked at his hands. They were red. There was blood on the railing and on the floor around him. Not his blood, was it? The faces of a few startled passengers peered out from their compartments. People were asking questions about what had happened. Their faces floated about in front of him, the words sounded like noises under water. They disappeared before he could answer.

Somewhere in the distance, a woman screamed belatedly. Was she screaming because of him? He closed his eyes for a moment. . . .

"Hugh . . . Hugh, can you hear me?"

He opened his eyes. "Loisa," he tried to say, but his lips wouldn't move enough to let the words out.

"Hugh. Wake up." He felt someone patting his cheek. It was really irritating. He moaned in protest.

"Damn you, Warlock. Wake up. I'm not letting you die on this train."

Marsh felt himself teeter on the edge of the encroaching darkness. There seemed no point in fighting it any-more. He had failed everyone. What point was there in living in a world without her? Elle was gone and there was nothing he could do about it, was the last thing he thought as the oily darkness slipped over him, slick and black.

Slowly, Elle drifted into consciousness. It was dark and she could smell a familiar musty scent of leather and sweat. Her eyes felt heavy, crusted with sleep, and her tongue felt too big for her mouth. It was hard to move.

She sucked in a lungful of the metallic air and a wave of nausea swept through her. Fighting against the en-croaching darkness, she opened her eyes again. The world tilted into focus. Her wrists ached when she moved and her calves were cramping. Someone whistled outside. A spark reactor hummed.

She forced herself to focus. Seats . . . wood panel-ing . . . the curve of a hull . . . silence outside . . . the absence of the smell of horses.

She was on an airship.

Slowly, painfully, she tried to drag herself upright. She needed to find a porthole to see where they were, but every joint and muscle screamed in agony as she moved. Another wave of nausea swept over her. She fought it, but once more everything went dark.

CHAPTER 39

Marsh sat in the dining cart, his coffee and breakfast untouched on the table in front of him. Hunched over and brooding, he watched the station and the platform slide into view.

Bucharest. And Elle was gone.

He took a determined sip of his cooled coffee. It was bitter and set his teeth on edge.

He shifted to find a more comfortable position, but his tightly bandaged rib cage made him think better of it. The blast of alchemy and the fall last night had caused more damage than he cared to admit. He felt empty and hollow, like something had been ripped from his insides. He was almost sure he knew what that missing thing was. The power that rested within him was almost all gone. The glowing node that made him a Warlock had diminished to a few glowing grains, deep inside him. And for the first time in his life, he was properly afraid.

A slight commotion on the platform caught his attention. A group of liveried attendants were dragging a clutch of black-lacquered sarcophagi from the train onto a trolley. He recognized the gilded red family crest of a dragon on one of the smaller coffins. It was Loisa Belododia's travelling coffin. She was on her way to her family's winter palace in the Carpathians. It was an ideal place for her kind this time of year because the days were short and overcast. Nightwalkers thrived in the cold.

Loisa had saved him last night. In the compartment, when no one was about, she had dripped a few drops of her ancient blood onto his wounds. It was not enough to heal him, but she dared not give him more. The mixing of Warlock and Nightwalker magic was too dangerous. The blending had been known to turn the recipient into a grotesque and raging monster. The drops of black blood, thick like molasses, knitted the broken bones and sealed up his ruptured organs. He survived.

Loisa had sat with him for a long time, with her cool fingers resting on his arm. Shortly before sunrise she had leaned over and kissed his brow. She had whispered a prayer in the old language that he would be well, before the first rays of sunlight had sent her rushing back to her compartment in a cloud of black lace that trailed behind her.

He watched the trolley of coffins move off the platform. Loisa could be no further help until sunset. But by then, she would be safely ensconced at the winter palace for the season.

What did Loisa say to Elle last night? Loisa was one of the old ones and, as was the case with most creatures blessed with immortality, she thrived on gossip and discord. Not that it really mattered now. There was no way of knowing what Abercrombie would do with Elle. The mere thought of it made him queasy. He stared darkly into his cup. He had made a complete mess of things. He was a failure.

He sighed at the stillness of the carriages. The train had better hurry up. He needed to get to Constantinople without delay.

The conductor walked past with his pocket watch in his hand. Marsh signaled the man over to his table. "Excuse me, when are we departing?"

The conductor looked at him apologetically. "We will have a three-hour wait here, my lord. They need to stock and realign the carriages." He cleared his throat. "Also, there is the matter of reporting what happened last night to the police."

Marsh felt the distance between him and Elle grow. Three hours. A lot could happen in three hours.

"I have already given my statement," he said. "I don't have anything to add. The disappearance of Miss Chance is a matter for the British High Commission and I have already sent a man with a dispatch. There is nothing more to be done until I get to Constantinople."

"Yes, of course, my lord." The conductor cleared his throat. "Perhaps it might assist in passing the time to take in some of the sights of the city. Bucharest is very beautiful. Some fresh air perhaps?"

Marsh resisted the urge to shake the man. Instead he simply nodded. "Yes, I think you might be right." He rose and picked up his hat and gloves. With a determined tug, he pulled his new black carriage coat over his shoulders and stepped off the train.

He walked slowly. The pain in his side felt unwholesome and corrupt and it worried him. He needed help.

On the street, he stopped to focus. Bucharest, he thought cynically. Another city that was doing its best to be Paris. Filigree spark-lamps lined wide boulevards. Everywhere buildings were going up in the New-Baroque Parisian style. He hunched himself up inside his coat against the cold wind that tugged at his clothes. The new Bucharest would be of no assistance to him. What he needed would be in the back streets.

He turned off the boulevard and walked down one of the cobbled lanes. The face of the city changed instantly. Hollow-eyed children stared at him from the porches of traditional adobe houses. Here and there a brightly painted onion dome poked out from between the rooftops. Horses with red woolen tassels on their harnesses ambled by, their haunches steaming in the morning cold as they pulled wooden carts loaded with everyday things. Wisps of smoke from cooking fires stole around corners.

It took him about half an hour to find the first marker. They were not that hard to find if you knew what you were looking for, but in this strange place, even he struggled. This marking was on a drain cover. The Warlock triangle with the eye in its apex was cleverly worked into the grooves of the metal. He stood on the cover and closed his eyes. The tiny flecks of power left inside him flickered faintly, and he shook his head in frustration. It was not enough to find the next pointer.

He shivered and closed his eyes, concentrating energy inside him. This time, he felt another flicker, showing him the direction.

Two streets down, he found the small shop. The faded Warlock symbol of the triangle was on the sign jutting out above the door, inside a winding pattern of leaves. Warlocks had not always been allowed to conduct their business in the open. Many of his kind had met their death quite brutally in centuries past. Here in the more remote countries, where superstition ran deep, creatures of Shadow were still treated with suspicion and so the evidence of the otherworldliness was often disguised.

He peered in through the dirty glass panes of the shop. Dusty bunches of herbs hung from the ceiling and the shop was lined with cabinets containing many little drawers. He had found what he was looking for. He was outside the doors of a Warlock apothecary. Every city had one, although many had taken to the road in recent years, selling their jars and potions from horse-drawn wagons. Snake oil was apparently a big seller for many of his commercially minded brethren. A grubby sign in Cyrillic script in the glass pane of the door hinted that the shop was open.

Had his noble order come to this? He knew the answer to his question, and the emptiness inside him ached in reply.

He pushed the door and stepped inside. The astringent smell of tinctures and herbs hit him as the door closed behind him. A man with a long beard looked up from behind the counter and nodded. Marsh wanted to laugh. His Warlock brother looked like something out of a children's book. He wore a gray smock that matched his beard. On his head was a pointed cap that flopped over to the side.

The man said something in Wallachian that Marsh could not follow. When he did not respond, the man shrugged. "Yes, how may we help?" he tried again in French.

Marsh walked up to the counter. "Good morning, Brother. I wonder if you could . . ." He used the old language and made the sacred sign.

The man's eyes widened.

"My lord. Forgive me, but we were not expecting anyone from the Council to visit." He bowed.

Marsh shook his head. "I am not here on official business. I am just a travelling Warlock in a strange city seeking out a friendly face."

The man's beard separated into a smile, but his eyes remained wary. "Then welcome, Brother. My name is Vasili." He took off his cap and gray smock. He was wearing a respectably clean waistcoat underneath.

"It's been years since I've seen any of us in traditional medieval dress."

"Oh, I wear that for the street customers and for tourists. The novelty gives my wares some authenticity," Vasili said as he stowed the bundle under the counter and gestured to the back. "Come, will you take some tea?"

Marsh nodded. "Thank you, that would be most agreeable. And perhaps we could talk. You see, I might be in need of a favor."

"Hmm." Vasili sniffed and looked at him with some concern. "Forgive me, I am not trying to be rude, but is that Alchemist and perhaps Nightwalker I smell?"

Marsh nodded. The man was more competent than he had hoped. "It is a very long story, but you are quite correct, Brother. I've run into a few rather unfriendly people of late. Except the Nightwalker. She is a friend."

Vasili nodded and his beard jiggled. "Well, then I suppose you are fortunate to have found the right place. Let me close the shop and we can talk." He walked to the front door and locked it. He turned the sign over to show CLOSED.

"This way." He led Marsh to the back. In the narrow hallway, he called out something in Wallachian. A small woman in an apron appeared from the back. She assessed Marsh with her sharp black eyes and then disappeared.

"My fifth wife." Vasili winked at Marsh. "She cooks nothing but cabbage. Come, let us go to my study." He led Marsh to a room off the corridor. Away from the herbs in the shop, the house did indeed bear the distinct smell of slow-cooking cabbage.

Vasili's study was a revelation. Every conceivable space was filled with glass jars and other bits of apparatus. Plants in terra-cotta pots spilled out from everywhere.

"I specialize in herbology," he said in answer to Marsh's curious glances. "I have been trying for years to extract the minute particles of magic held in plants into making cures. Some I have been successful with, others not so much."

He moved a glass jar with a withered-looking plant inside onto another counter and gestured for Marsh to sit. Mrs. Vasili bustled in with a tray, which she set down without a word. She gave Marsh another sharp look before shuffling out again.

Vasili poured them each a cup of the strong black tea from a metal pot. He dropped a sugar lump into the bottom of each before handing one to Marsh.

"So, how has the Craft been in these parts?" Marsh asked as he took a sip of the tea. It was strong and sweet, made in the way that most of the Eastern peoples preferred. It was drunk from the saucer after it had cooled rather than the cup, a practice he had never quite managed to become comfortable with.

Vasili rolled his eyes. "Ah, don't talk to me about the Craft. We've not seen any proper power flow of the Shadow realm in these parts for years. Not since I was a boy. But we make do with what we have. A dash of inferior spark here, a sliver of essence distilled from plants there." He paused to slurp his tea from his saucer. "Mostly we do only enough to reassure the people. As the Council decrees."

Marsh nodded and raised his cup. "As the Council decrees."

"So what brings you to my doorstep, Brother, if I might be so bold to ask?"

"I've had a few . . . shall we say . . . unfortunate accidents in the last few days."

Vasili merely stroked his beard. "My eyes and ears are closed. Many come to me because they don't want the world to know about whatever proclivities they might have and I speak of it to no one."

Marsh cleared his throat at the thought. "Quite." He took another sip of tea. "Last night, I literally had the Warlock knocked clean out of me. I was hoping you might have something restorative. To keep me going until I am healed and my own levels can be replenished. I barely managed to find the markers to your place."

Vasili looked at Marsh in alarm. "But the markers are in plain sight."

"I know."

"Well, I suppose I could have a look, but I have so little power myself. I may not be able to do much." He regarded Marsh. "What we need is another Oracle. That's what we need. Someone to open the pathways for us again. These are dark days for our kind, my lord. Dark days indeed. Pretty soon there will be nothing left of our Craft and we will become ordinary mortals, like everyone else. Who knows how the Shadow will react to the shift in balance."

Marsh nodded. "Who knows?"

"Would you mind if I had a look?" Vasili asked. He gestured at Marsh.

"Ah, yes. It's this pain here, in my ribs." Carefully, he unbuttoned his waistcoat and opened his shirt. Vasili gasped in surprise as the bandage came away in his hand. "Oh my." He leaned in to have a closer look.

Marsh looked down at his side. An angry raised scab ran across his rib cage. Dark blue, purple and yellow bruises spread across his side in a mottled blotch. In a few places where the Nightwalker blood had touched him, the dark blue skin was raised and blistering.

"Oh my," Vasili said again. "Look at the reaction. I haven't seen an injury like this since the wars." Marsh winced as the apothecary touched the tender skin. "Too many different types of power in one place. You will be lucky if this ever heals, I'm afraid. What kind of alchemy was it? And be sure to tell me the truth. Your recovery depends on it, you know."

Marsh nodded. "It was yellow with a strong sense of sulfur. It packed quite a blast. Nothing like it was in Napoleon's wars, but the composition felt sophisticated and it was strong."

"Good heavens, they could have killed you!" Vasili

exclaimed. "I thought we had a nonaggression pact with the Alchemists."

"We do. This is different, though. They took something—someone—important away from me."

"Lift up for me, please."

Marsh gasped as he raised his arms. "I'm sure it looks worse than it is." He winced as Vasili poked a particularly painful bit of skin with his finger.

"Hold still, I might have something that will help." Vasili bustled off down the narrow passageway that led to the shop and came back with a tub of grayish-looking ointment. He opened it and dug his fingers into the pot. "This will tingle." He slopped the ointment onto the wound.

The astringent smell of herbs filled the air. "What is that?" Marsh asked. His rib cage felt like it was on fire.

"Witch hazel and hemlock. And a few other ingredients you might not know. It's made with my own method. You see, I think I have found a way to extract the Shadow forces from these plants. They are their own healing spell."

Marsh winced again. It felt like an army of ants were crawling over his skin.

"Does it tingle?" Vasili asked.

"Yes," Marsh responded with a little hiss of air.

Vasili nodded, pleased. "That means it's working." He stopped applying ointment and studied Marsh's rib cage. "Hmm . . . might not be strong enough to heal the wound completely, but you'll live. And it will certainly hurt a lot less. That wound was about to start dissolving you alive, Brother."

"I had feared that," Marsh said quietly.

Vasili started wrapping strips of cotton bandages around Marsh's chest. "Now, keep these bandages on. I'll give you a tub of the ointment to take with you. You need to put it onto the area twice a day until the bruising is completely gone." He looked at Marsh. "But know that it is going to take a long time to get better."

"I understand."

Vasili tied off the wrappings with an expert knot. "You are lucky you found me when you did." He patted his own chest. "I was a medic in the war. Saved many a soldier with my skills, I did. Now, remember, another blast like that and you will be dead for sure. Your body won't be able to survive another. Do you understand?"

Marsh nodded. "I'll do my best."

The older man returned to his seat and poured himself another cup of tea. Carefully he picked up a sugar lump and dropped it into his cup. They both watched the lump disintegrate, the slick of sugar settling at the bottom of his glass. "I am sorry if I'm speaking out of turn, and you'll forgive me for saying so, but it is an interesting situation, you know. And it's not often someone like me gets to speak to someone from the Council." He eyed Marsh.

Marsh looked at him in surprise. "How so?"

"Well," Vasili nodded. "Far be it from me to tell a Council member how to practice his craft, but surely you would know that you are on the cusp?"

"The cusp?"

"Yes, my boy. The cusp. All writings about the bleeding-off of power were banned many centuries ago. Probably before your time, I'd guess. Normally if a Warlock is drained of his power, he dies. But if done correctly, the magic leaves the body and an ordinary man remains. In the old days, when a Warlock became tired of living, he would slowly allow his power to drain away so he could live out his days in peace as a mortal. They say it takes a very fine control to get to that point." He chuckled. "Or in your case, the right dose of fighting." The older man looked at Marsh for a long moment. "Please forgive the blasphemy for saying so, but have you ever thought of just letting it all go?"

"Let it go?" Marsh looked at him.

"Yes!" Vasili nodded. "Let go of the Craft. Become an ordinary man with no powers. Marry, have children and grow old gracefully. Die. All the things a man should do." He grew nostalgic. "I have had many years to think about my mortality. Living a long life is not all it is made out to be, I can tell you. I have now outlived four wives, and the fifth, as you can see, is on her way. My children are all dead, so are their children. The family tree I started now barely knows me—so far are the shoots from the trunk these days. There is no one in my line who carries my ability to take up the Craft. And so I will die alone one day." Vasili sighed. "It is a lonely path, the one we take in the end."

"Indeed it is," Marsh said.

Vasili gave him a friendly pat on the arm and without a word he wandered off into the shadows of the hallway. Marsh had started buttoning his shirt and waistcoat when the old man reappeared. He held out a parcel wrapped up in brown paper. "More ointment. And this." He handed Marsh a little bundle of leather.

Marsh untied it. "Mandrake root?"

"Do the ritual. You know which one. Your power will seep into the root. Bury it under an oak tree. And as the root rots and returns to the earth, so your power will disintegrate and return to the realm of Shadow. You will be free of this terrible burden. But only if you want to. Or not. I don't care either way."

"Thank you. What do I owe you for the ointment?"

Vasili shrugged. "No charge. Look after yourself, my boy. The world is a dangerous place."

Outside the shop, Marsh carefully stowed the parcel inside his cloak. The wind had picked up and he felt cold. He could smell snow, even though it was still early in the year for it. He tightened his cloak around him and started walking in the direction of the station. The old man's ointment seemed to be working and as he walked, his constricted chest opened up a little.

He let his thoughts wander. Give it all up? He knew the ritual the old man had spoken of. It was a suicide ritual. Once used by the Brotherhood in cases of extreme dishonor. He had never thought of using mandrake root with it though. The solution seemed so simple it was inspired.

And Elle? It always seemed to come back to her. He quickened his pace as he reached one of the fancy French-looking boulevards. He needed more time to think. And time was the one thing he didn't have right now. He had an important train to catch.

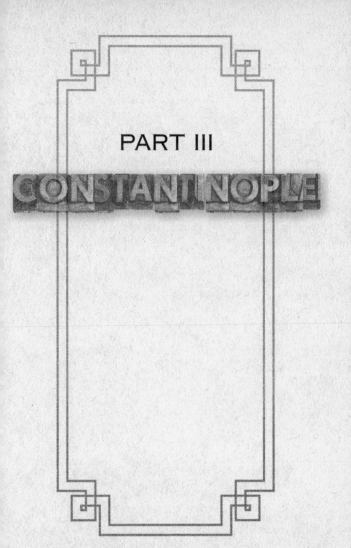

PART III

CONSTANTINOPLE

CHAPTER 40

The girl with no shadow was in trouble and it was my fault. I should have shown myself to help defend her. I should have come forth to help her escape, but we were bound so tightly as we were carried away into the night that there was nothing I could do. I had left Paris because the girl had given me a way of escaping that terrible iron staircase that had held me prisoner for so long. I had never dreamed that this quest for freedom would become so large.

And I was afraid, for fairies are cowards more often than not. The temptation to spirit away and hide is far stronger than the need to stand and fight. When I finally crept from my diamond-hard fortress, I found the girl on her side with her hands shackled. Her long hair was loose, streaming over her awkwardly turned shoulders.

We were in a place of darkness. I could smell evil seeping from the dust and stone around us. There were others in this place; I could taste the rage and anguish of their captivity and desperation in the air around me. This was a place beyond the Shadow. We were on the verge of darkness.

I stole across the floor. I felt myself tremble slightly as I moved. The lack of absinthe had made me weak and feeble, unable to defend us. I reached for the door but drew back. The door was banded with pure iron and there would be no escape through it. The terrible realization that I had tarried in the safety of the diamonds for too long enveloped me. They were coming. They were coming for the girl.

Although I had failed and almost all hope was lost, I

would protect her from these monsters somehow. There was little point in mindless bravery though, for sometimes victories were won by small increments. As the mighty pine rises up from one tiny seed, so our escape plan would grow.

I sensed that there was still time. And so I slipped back into the diamonds and waited for the moment to come to pass.

It was the pain in her shoulders that finally made Elle drift up from the deep slumber that held her. Everything felt heavy and swollen. She opened her eyes and the world shifted into focus. She was lying on her side with her cheek against cool stone. Her arms were tied behind her back. She struggled to sit up, but a thick wave of dizziness flooded her.

She leaned over and retched, but her stomach was empty. Her throat felt swollen and raw. She slumped against the wall and whimpered.

Someone cleared their throat and she looked up. A large man with his face hidden in a gray cloak was standing by a wooden door.

"Welcome to Constantinople, little one. I am so glad to see you."

She tried to say something, but her tongue was too swollen in her mouth to speak.

He lifted the cowl off his head and a slow smile spread over his whiskered face.

More nausea filled her and she retched again. "Patrice? What are you doing here?" she croaked.

"Dear Eleanor," he tutted, and shook his head. "Not feeling so well, are we?"

Another wave of dizziness washed over her. "Help get me out of these things. Before someone comes."

He gave her an oily smile. "Silly girl. I am the someone who might come. But not to worry, pretty, you will find that you feel much better once the powder they gave you wears off in a few hours."

A sob escaped from her throat. "Untie me, would you?"

"It's taken so much time and effort to finally get you here. It would be a travesty to let you go. But I can't bear to see a lady in so much distress, so I'll untie you just a little bit. And besides, we need you alive." He reached over and unlocked the shackles on her wrists.

Elle cried out as the hot blood rushed into her fingers. Every nerve in her arms tingled. She straightened up and flexed her shoulders. Her arms felt dead and heavy, like lead. She leaned forward and took a few deep breaths to calm the panic that was rising up in her chest. Blood and air coursed through her, the fog lifted and her mind slid into gear.

She looked up. "Patrice?" Her voice was rough and hoarse in her throat.

"Yes, the brain is working now, isn't it?"

"What? I don't understand."

"You know, I am very cross with you. You shot one of our best men. He died on the way here."

Elle started shaking. "Patrice, how could you? Marsh trusted you."

"Ah, good old Mr. Marsh. And how fares my former business associate? The last I heard, he was lying on the side of the railway tracks somewhere in Transylvania." He looked at his fingers. "The wolves or one of the forest creatures must have got him by now." He pursed his lips in a mocking pout.

She stared at him. "I don't believe you. You were supposed to look after Mrs. Hinges. What have you done with her?"

Patrice chuckled again and shrugged his shoulders. "Believe what you want, it is of no consequence to me. But I must say how very noble it is of you to show such concern, given your current plight." He flicked an invisible fleck of lint from his cloak. "Although the role of damsel in distress does not become you, my dear. You are looking rather peaky, if I might say so."

Elle just stared at him with naked hatred.

"Oh, all right, then," he said with some irritation. "The old lady is fine. She'll wake up with a headache, but no serious harm has been done." His hand went up to his head where Mrs. Hinges had hit him with the frying pan. "*Quid pro quo,* as they say. I'm not a complete monster, you know."

"What is this place?"

"You are exactly where you need to be," he said. "Especially given the trouble you have caused us. We were most disappointed in the service our pirate friends provided."

Elle let her head roll onto her chest. She was tired and very thirsty, but she could not give in quite yet. She needed to get more information from Patrice.

"That was you? How did you get here?"

"Always so stubborn. It's almost painful to watch. You did make things rather difficult for us in Paris. You should have just let Chunk drive you to the sanctuary in the cab. It would have been so much easier. And setting poor Feathers alight like that . . . how awful." He tutted and folded his hands behind his back.

"Oh well, I suppose I might as well tell you, seeing as there won't be anyone else to tell. While you and our friend Marsh were conferring with the Council of Warlocks in Venice and canoodling down the canals, I took a flight across the Channel and caught the Orient Express in Paris. You were kind enough to join me in Vienna." His gaze flicked over her. "He was all over you right from the start, you know. I knew he wouldn't be able to resist you. My plan worked so beautifully. It was like watching a play. But none of that matters now."

She had never noticed how cold his eyes were.

"So all this time you have been pretending to be my

friend? Pretending to be close to me so you could steal this ability you say I have? I thought we were friends," she said between clenched teeth.

Patrice laughed. "I am an opportunist. And you presented an opportunity too good to let pass. I'm sorry you have to get hurt. I truly am. You are a sweet girl, but business is business, I'm afraid." He looked up at the vents above. "The moon will be full soon. We have been planning this for a very long time, you know. Waiting and watching you grow into the new Oracle. Just like your dear mama."

Elle glared at him. "You do not talk about my mother."

He laughed again. "Ah, but I do. The Warlocks are so spineless, don't you think? All tied up in politics and diplomacy. Stealing your mother away from them was almost as easy as it was to steal you. She died fighting to protect you, the poor thing." He looked up to the sky. "The irony of it all is so beautiful, don't you think? The whole Chance family, sacrificed for our cause. And soon, oh, very soon, it will all come to fruition. You wait and see."

Elle felt her whole body flood with heat as anger filled her, blocking out the tiredness. "Where is my father?" she said.

Patrice started laughing. "Your father has proven to be a most useful asset. His knowledge of the fusion of Shadow magic and electricity has been so informative. It would have taken us years to get there, were it not for him."

"I demand to see my father. Right now," she said. Her voice wavered as another wave of dizziness flooded over her.

Patrice laughed again. "You are not going to be demanding anything, my dear. In fact, it is only because I am somewhat fond of you that you have the luxury of this accommodation. They were going to throw you into the old well."

Elle clenched her teeth and concentrated on staying upright. She was not going to give this man the satisfaction of seeing her crumble.

Patrice picked up a jug of water and a plate of flatbread that had been left by the door. "Here." He shoved it down in front of her. "Eat. As I said, they want you alive."

He reached over and picked up a chain from the floor. In one deft movement he looped and locked the chain into the shackle that was around her ankle. Checking to make sure that it was secure, he put his hand on her cheek. "I'll be back for you later. Now, behave yourself while I'm gone."

Once the key turned in the lock, Elle counted to a hundred and fifty before she leaned over and grabbed hold of the jug. She raised it to her cracked lips and drank deeply. The first few swallows made her choke and she had to stop and cough. "Slow sips," she said to herself.

She drank almost half of the water at once. Then, careful not to spill any, she set the jug down and slumped against the wall. She closed her eyes and felt herself drift back into the darkness.

The melodic sound of chanting filtered through the blackness. Elle opened her eyes and groaned. While she had been sleeping, life had returned to her limbs and now it felt like every bit of her body was filled with pins and needles. She pushed herself up against the wall, but she was shaking so much that she only managed to sit. Gingerly, she checked herself for broken bones and dislocated joints. Her muscles were stiff and she felt bruised, but she seemed to be in one piece. She did the same with her legs. There was a large shackle around her left ankle. She followed the chain to the point where it was tethered to an iron ring in the wall. She let the heavy chain drop and sat with her back against the wall again. There was no possibility that she would be able to break it.

Elle took in her surroundings. The bare room around her was vaguely circular. The rough walls looked dusty and old. She ran her hand over the flagstones of the floor next to her. They were smooth and waxy with age and a dry chill rose up from them. There were no windows save for a row of vents high above her. Sunlight pooled in a dusty shaft in the center of the floor.

What day was it? She wondered. Was it morning or afternoon? She had no way of knowing.

She thought back to when Patrice had woken her. It had been light then too. It could be later in the after-noon or early the next morning, but she could not tell how long she had been sleeping. The singing stopped. She looked up. There must be people about. That meant someone might be able to hear her.

"Help! Somebody help me, please!" Her throat was so raw that all she managed was a hoarse croak. The thick walls swallowed up the sound.

She felt a wave of despair rise up into her throat, but she could not allow herself the luxury of panic.

Instead, she measured the length of the chain attached to her ankle. It was about twice as long as her arm. She crawled across the floor to see how far the chain would reach. Her legs felt like they were made of rubber.

The chain reached as far as the pool of light in the middle of the floor, but it was not long enough to reach the heavy wooden door on the other side of the cell. There was a drain in the middle of the floor, but the grate was stuck. She tugged at it a few times, but it would not budge. She realized with growing horror that she would have to use that drain to relieve herself. She peered down into the darkness of the grate. There was no telling how deep it was or how narrow. She wasn't sure, but she could almost make out a strip of blue sky in the vent above her, but even without the shackle around her ankle, she doubted that she could climb to the top. She returned to her place by the metal ring in the wall and sat down as calmly as she could. She was trapped with no hope of escape.

Carefully she lifted the jug and drank more water. Her stomach felt hollow and soapy inside.

She did not know how long it was since she had eaten. The last meal she remembered was on the train, with the baroness and Marsh. The feeling of despair rose again. Marsh. What if he really was dead?

"No, I am not going to believe that you are dead, Mr. Marsh. You are far too annoying for that." The silent room swallowed her voice. She thought of his eyes and his messy hair, and it filled her with a physical ache.

Quite abruptly, her stomach rumbled. She picked up one of the flatbreads and started chewing on it. The bread was dry and the edges were very tough, but edible. She ate a little more and then finished most of the rest of the water. She wiped down her face and hands with the torn hem of her nightdress dipped in the remaining water at the bottom of the jug.

The food and having a clean face revived her a little and she sat back looking at the grate above her head. The patch of blue was gradually turning a golden color. It would be dark soon. She was still dressed in her nightdress and there were no blankets, or anything to lie on. She would be cold tonight.

The enormity of her predicament overwhelmed her like a dark, boiling mist. She wrapped her arms around her knees and buried her head in her lap. No one was coming for her. And in that stone cell, for the first time in what seemed like forever, she finally allowed herself to cry.

CHAPTER 41

Elle woke to the sound of keys rattling in the lock. She struggled to sit up, her body stiff and sore from the night spent on the cold flagstones. The door creaked open and she braced herself for another encounter with Patrice. Instead, a young man in a gray habit entered the room. He set a tray of food down in the middle of the floor. Steam rose up from one of the bowls.

"Please. You must help me," she said. The young man shook his head and muttered something in a language she did not understand. He retreated hastily and she was left alone in silence.

She crept up to the tray. On it was a steaming bowl of what looked like porridge, and another jug of water. The tray was resting on top of a gray woolen blanket. She took the blanket and wrapped it around herself before picking up the bowl. She couldn't identify the porridge, but it smelled faintly of cinnamon. There was no spoon on the tray, so she slurped the gruel straight from the bowl with her fingers. It was warm and creamy and possibly the most delicious thing she'd ever tasted.

She drank more water and then settled down with the blanket wrapped around her. The clasp of the diamond bracelet caught on the blanket. She stared at it. The stones looked so very out of place here. She moved the bracelet with her thumb to ease it out of the wool.

As she rubbed it, she felt her skin tingle. The diamonds glowed with a greenish light. The light intensified and then, without much ceremony, a crumpled absinthe fairy appeared before her.

Elle started with surprise. "My goodness, have you been in there all this time? I thought you had escaped a long time ago."

The fairy shook her wings and shrugged. Elle stared at the creature's blue-green skin. Fairies didn't often let people get so close to them, but judging by the frayed edges of her wings, this one was definitely a bit worse for wear.

The fairy surveyed the cell. She twittered with dismay as she took in the stone floor and the bare walls.

"I know. It is bad, isn't it?" Elle said.

The fairy nodded.

"Do you think you might be able to undo this lock?" Elle raised her ankle. "If I can get free from this chain, then maybe we can work out a plan of escape."

The fairy examined the shackles. She put her hands on the keyhole and peered into the lock. She looked up at Elle and nodded.

Elle moved her leg so the fairy had more space to work. The fairy closed her eyes and strained until a small puff of green magic escaped from the keyhole . . . but the shackle remained fast. The fairy looked up at her and raised her shoulders. She gestured at Elle, miming the act of unlocking the lock.

"I'm sorry, but they took me from my bed. I don't have anything to pick the lock with. Not even a hairpin."

The fairy tried again. Her face scrunched up with concentration as she strained against the metal. There was another puff of green and the fairy slumped down next to Elle. She made a small, frustrated noise.

It was hopeless. The lock was too heavy and there was no way of knowing whether the shackle had been hexed beforehand.

"Here, have some water." Elle held the water jug up for

the fairy to drink. The fairy scooped some water from the jug and took a few sips. She wrinkled her face in disgust.

"I know, not quite what you are accustomed to, but that's all there is."

The fairy shrugged and settled down next to Elle. They sat in silence for a while.

Elle looked up at the vent. The sky was turning a rich blue. It was perhaps about midmorning right now. In the distance, she heard noises. Carts rumbled. Horses neighed. There were definitely people about. The fairy sat on the flagstones with her legs crossed. Her chin rested on her fists.

"Do you think you can fly up to the grate?" Elle pointed upwards at the vents.

The fairy looked up at the grate and nodded. Then she smiled.

Elle was suddenly filled with elation. They had a plan.

"Fly and go find help. Please. Find help. Find people who are able to get us out of here."

The fairy stood up and shook her wings. She straightened her shoulders and, with a soft flutter, she flew up to the vent.

"Be careful," Elle murmured as she watched the fairy disappear through the grate.

She slumped down again and closed her eyes. A wave of loneliness flooded through her. Was it her fate to follow this path? If she got out of here alive, should she give herself over in service to the Council? Surely, working for the good of all was a noble and honorable thing to do. But her chest constricted at the thought.

And what about Marsh? They were incompatible on so many levels. She was not in his social class. Then there was the whole matter of living until you are nine hundred years old. How would she deal with growing old alone while he stayed more or less the same?

But she loved him. That was the awful truth of it. He

had made her fall in love with him, and then he'd rejected her. And there was nothing on earth she could do about it. The thought made her insides ache and her eyes sting.

She leaned back against the coolness of the wall. She didn't think it was possible to feel so much despair. Then the light started flickering. This time she did not bother to fight it. Images raced through her mind and she clutched at her temples and gritted her teeth as the vision passed.

... *alchemists. Great flashes of fire. Confusion. Night-walkers with bared fangs. A blood moon rising in the sky. Dark shadows moving across the countryside. People running and screaming in the streets. She needed to warn someone that something terrible was about to happen, but she was too tired to move. Everything blurred to gray.*

Elle opened her eyes. Trouble was on the way.

CHAPTER 42

No one noticed me as I slipped out through the tallest window of the old stone tower, for I was barely a flicker of light
that glided down to the street from above. I landed on the
bare branch of a Judas tree and breathed in the air. For the
first time in years, I was outside. I felt the spirit of the tree
reach for me in greeting as I touched it. It was glad of my
presence, for not many of my kind were ever allowed in this
place.

The tree stood watch over a little square. Below, people
were going about their business on the Byzantine-cobbled
street. Not one of them looked up or paid me even the
slightest heed. I was a very long way from Paris. The thought
filled me with so much fear that I wrapped my arms around
myself to stop the shivers that overtook me. I was tired, for
the vent was a lot higher than it had looked, and my need
for wormwood was growing stronger. I would not last very
long out here on my own. And this was a place that did not
tolerate fairies.

I sat there for a little while to soak up the rays of sun. It
wasn't exactly warm this early in the morning, but it was
better than the stone cell below where the girl lay.

The girl. Something had to be done. Desperate for an answer, I peered through the branches and looked up and
down the cobbled street. I needed to find someone who
could speak Fairy, but this was a large city and I could not
fly that far.

I waited for a while, until an old man in a turban slowly

walked by. His waistcoat was worn and saggy at the pockets and his short beard was graying. On his head he carried a very large wooden tray piled high with ring-shaped bread. The tray was supported by a frame that rested on his shoulders.

People eat bread. People speak Fairy. If I followed the bread, perhaps I could find someone who would help.

Like a leaf in the wind, I fluttered down from the branch and landed on the tray as it passed by below the tree. Careful to not make a sound, I stowed between the red-brown rings of bread. The shiny sesame-studded crusts felt slightly warm under my fingers. I picked a sesame seed off one of the rings and nibbled at it. Wormwood it was not, but it tasted lovely. So I ate it, and another. In fact, I ate until I could eat no more. Sated, I settled down at the bottom of the bread pile. The platter bobbed and swayed as it made its way through the streets. The warm bread against my back made me feel very sleepy. And so I closed my eyes for just a moment.

The train whistled and discharged a final blast of steam. The *Orient Express* had arrived at the end of a journey that crossed almost all of Europe.

Marsh stepped onto the platform.

Constantinople. The locals called it *Istanbul*, which simply meant "City" in Turkish. He preferred the old name.

He secured the services of a porter and trolley for the luggage, and together they strode through the multi-colored crowds, dodging sellers and slow-moving women dressed in layers of veils. Outside the station, he hailed a cab. He watched them load the luggage onto the trap. Two portmanteaus. One of them a lady's.

His hotel was in the old quarter, near the Sultan's palace. It was an elaborate building, wood-carved in the old Ottoman style. The walls were brightly painted in whites, gold and turquoise. Two rooms were reserved, only one occupied.

He did not tarry at the hotel, but set out almost as soon as his luggage was delivered, pushing past startled porters in the corridor.

Downstairs, at the desk, he ordered a cable telegram. With a little pencil tied to the desk with a piece of string, he addressed the envelope to Patrice in Oxford.

ALCHEMISTS HAVE SUCCEEDED STOP ELLE TAKEN STOP BRING REINFORCEMENTS TO CONSTANTINOPLE STOP MATTER OF UTMOST URGENCY STOP.

He handed the communication to the hotel telegrapher and strode out into the street with grim determination. It was time to look up an old friend.

The road rose steeply up toward the Topkapi palace. The marble home of the caliph of Constantinople sat on top of the hill like an ornate brooch on a woman's shoulder.

At the great white carved gates of the palace he stopped and had a word with the guards. It took some head nodding and explanation, but eventually he was led along the winding garden paths and through the royal gardens to the inner palace. The open arched walkways were adorned with painted birds and flowers. He remembered the patter of silk slippers and the rustle of harem silks from his last visit to this place, as a boy, two centuries ago.

He was shown to a fine white summer house that overlooked the bay. The view of the famous Golden Horn spread out before him. Hundreds of low narrow banana-shaped fishing boats floated in the harbor below. At a distance, they looked like logs rising and falling in the water.

This morning the sky was gray, and no sun glittered

on the blue waters of the strait. He sniffed the cool briny air that wafted toward him.

"Viscount Greychester! What a lovely surprise to see you." The caliph of Constantinople was behind him.

Hastily, he lifted his hat and bowed deeply. "Your majesty, forgive me. I did not hear you approach."

The caliph smiled and shrugged. "I see you have been seduced by the beauty of my city." He glided toward the stone seats that lined the summer house. "I fear you may have missed the best weather."

He gestured to seats covered in opulent blue-and-gold fabric. "Come. Please sit. Let us talk for a while."

Marsh sat down on one of the pillowed seats so that the caliph's head was higher than his own. It was prudent to observe protocol when one could. The caliph was a man of about sixty. His white beard and moustache were carefully groomed and he wore an elaborately folded linen turban. He had the face of someone loved and feared in equal measure.

"Thank you for seeing me," Marsh said.

The caliph waved his hand. "Think nothing of it, Mr. Marsh. You are an old friend of the family. Legend has it that you used to run through the palace and tease the harem girls terribly when you were a boy." He chuckled.

"The old caliph was a most excellent friend. I missed him when he passed."

A silent servant stepped forward and put down a gold tray, upon which were two exquisite brass kettles, the smaller stacked on top of the larger, delicate tea glasses and a selection of delicious-looking pastries. With deft hands, he lifted the small brass teapot and poured them each a cup.

"Please, have some baklava. My pastry chef tells me he makes the best in the kingdom. This is why I employ him."

Marsh helped himself to a square of the syrup-soaked

pastry. "Thank you." He washed the intensely sweet little square down with some tea.

"So tell me, what brings you to my kingdom, Master Warlock? I am sure you are not purely here for a taste of the caliph's pastries. Excellent as they might be."

Marsh inclined his head. "Indeed, I am not."

"You are, I am sure, aware that we have disavowed ourselves of all involvement in matters involving the Shadow realm. This is a city of Light, and Creatures of the Shadow are not welcome here. My kingdom claims neutrality on all other issues."

"I am here on a matter of a more personal nature. I have come to you as a friend, and not as a Warlock. My Council has nothing to do with my visit."

The caliph considered his words. "Please continue."

Marsh told the caliph about Elle and their search for the professor, carefully leaving out the part about her being an Oracle.

The caliph played with his beard before he spoke. "And I take it that you feel affection for this woman?"

"I love her." A strange warmth filled his chest. He loved her.

"Then I commend you on your quest. There can be no more noble a quest than a man seeking to rescue his beloved." The caliph smiled and leaned forward. He looked Marsh in the eye. "Don't tell anyone, but I am a hopeless romantic. Personally, I have sixty wives and concubines and I try to romance each one of them. Sometimes I hardly have time for anything else, I tell you."

Marsh nodded. He felt a grudging admiration for the caliph. He was struggling to keep up with one woman, never mind sixty of them. "I must find her before it is too late. Can you help me?"

"We do not know for sure that they are in my kingdom though. My vizier has reported no sightings of the Shadow. Nothing strange has happened."

"Your majesty, I know she is here."

The caliph nodded and stood. "For you, my friend, I will ask my informants to sweep the city to see if there are any unusual visitors. But I will not be seen to support the Shadow. If there is even a single hint of my involvement in this matter, then my assistance will cease immediately. Is that clear?"

"Your majesty, I am deeply indebted to you. I shall give the details of my hotel to your vizier. If you hear anything, please let me know."

A liveried servant had sidled up to the entrance of the pavilion. Marsh caught the discreet signal from the corner of his eye. "The visitors have arrived, your majesty," the servant said with a reverent bow.

"Ah, so be it, then. You are going to have to excuse me. Duty calls." The caliph rose and took his leave. At the door, he paused. "Remember, this is a favor to an old family friend. We will do nothing that could be seen as taking the side of the Council. If I see even a hint of spellcraft, I will have no option but to have you executed for breaking my laws. Is that clear?"

Marsh bowed. "Of course, your majesty. As you wish."

The caliph left, followed by his entourage, who had materialized as soon as he had stepped out of the summer house. A few stayed behind to help escort Marsh back to the gates. He noticed that a few lingered, watching him for just that little bit longer than was necessary.

Outside the palace, Marsh hailed a rickshaw to take him to the harbor. His ribs were still very tender and he had no desire to reopen the wound. He regretted his decision almost immediately. The rickshaw driver was a sinewy man in baggy white trousers and sandals. He skidded and skittered the rickshaw down the hill, narrowly dodging other carts and people. Marsh got out at the bottom of the hill, dazed, but relieved that he wasn't dead.

"What have we here, then?"

I woke with a start and looked around in confusion. The towers of bread were gone, but I was still on the wooden platter, now surrounded by a circle of faces. Staring at me from all sides were dark-haired and dark-eyed men who wore red hats with black tassels on them.

"Eh, Serdat. Looks like you have a stowaway in your simit bread," said the voice. I tried to crawl backwards, away from the one who spoke, but a finger came out from behind and poked me in the back. I looked around, and shrieked in fright. The face of a boy was peering at me. He grinned at me with a row of very white, very menacing teeth.

"What is it?" one of the other men said.

"Not sure," said the first, stroking his chin. A thin layer of silver stubble made a scratchy noise under his hand. "It's either some sort of Shadow creature or a very large insect. If it's an insect, I am going to ask for my money back on that bread!"

"Hush, Ashim. I'll not have you insult my bread like that." It was the old simit seller who spoke.

Another finger reached out, and tried to touch my wings. I managed to move away, but I was too slow. A shimmer of blue-green fairy dust drifted off one of my wings and settled onto the breadboard like sorrow.

I folded my stinging wings up against my back as tightly as I could, but it was difficult, because the shivering had started again.

"Careful, you are hurting it!" said the man with the beard. "Look how frightened it is. It might be worth something, and I'll not have you kill it before I can make a profit."

The other men laughed and called out in protest.

"Come, friends. Let us not hurt Serdat's pet," one of the men said. He gave the man with the beard a rough shake. "But be careful. Small things can sometimes be vicious. It might curse you and make your balls fall off." He hacked out another laugh. I could feel the mist of his garlic-laced breath settle over us.

Still grinning, he reached into the folds of his white cotton tunic and drew out a packet of thickly rolled cigarettes. He pulled one out and lit it. Acrid smoke curled around us and I started to cough.

"It doesn't like the smoke." The one called Serdat peered at me. Then, without warning, he lifted a glass preserve jar and plopped it over me. All sound was extinguished. I watched them laugh and pat one another on the shoulder, pleased at my capture, their bodies grotesquely distorted through the curved glass.

The simit seller lifted the jar and screwed the lid on. Panicked, I flew up and hit the lid with all of my strength. Without the power of wormwood, I could not change to spirit form. In fairy form, I needed air to breathe. The air in the jar was stale and hot. It smelled like vinegar and pickles. The smell stuck in my throat. I slipped down to the cool sides of the jar, leaving a soft streak of blue-green behind.

Through the mottled glass I saw that the man had produced a large dagger from his baggy trousers. The tip of the knife pierced the lid as he punched a few holes into it. Air streamed into the jar and I gasped with relief.

Rage returned and filled me as the air flooded back into my lungs, but without the power that absinthe gives, there was little I could do. I folded my arms and glared at the men, powerless against their brutishness.

They were still smiling, and staring at me through the glass, when the simit seller lifted the jar. Through the distortion of the glass I saw something open up below me. The jar tilted as he slipped it inside his satchel, and then things went very dark.

The harbor was busy. Fishermen dragged large woven baskets filled with fish onto the bare-wooden planks.

Passengers clambered out of boats of all shapes and sizes from their crossing of the straits that split Constantinople into east and west. It was a thronging, vibrant mix of noise and smells.

Marsh pushed through the crowd, asking questions as he went along. Has anyone seen an English woman with red hair? A woman in the company of unsavory men?

After about an hour he sat down on a bench and rested his head in his hands. Nothing except blank stares.

It was nearing lunchtime and the sun was breaking through the clouds. He put his notebook away and walked back up the hill and into the city. He wasn't going to risk another ride in one of the rickshaws.

Halfway up the steep street, he spotted a water seller with a barrel strapped to his back. The man was speaking behind his hand to a man in an apron. They both looked at Marsh and nodded. He was being watched.

At the top of the hill, he caught a tram in the direction of the Grand Bazaar. As he stepped onto the street, he noticed a man in a dark blue tunic stepping off the tram behind him. Their eyes locked for the briefest of moments. The man nodded and crossed the road. He was being followed, by the looks of things.

Outside one of the entrances to the Bazaar, he found a kebab shop with a proprietor who spoke French. The shop was small and dark inside. He ordered grilled lamb and a glass of watermelon juice, then chose an inconspicuous corner to sit. The patrons in the shop stopped eating to stare at him. Marsh ignored them and dipped his hot flatbread into the bowl of garlicky yoghurt that came with the meat. The restaurant slowly turned back to its business, but he felt the stares and the hushed conversation around him.

A man sidled up to him and sat down at his table. Marsh looked up, but carried on eating.

"You are the Englishman asking questions down at the docks." He smiled at Marsh, displaying a row of crooked teeth.

Marsh looked at him. "I might be. What business is it of yours, friend?"

"I hear that you pay money for information."

Marsh bit into a piece of lamb. It tasted of herbs and wood smoke. "I might. What business is it of yours?"

"I might know something."

"And what might that be?" Marsh said in measured tones.

"I might know of some newcomers to our beautiful city. They arrived on an airship not so long ago."

Marsh looked at him sharply. "What newcomers?"

"A group of painted men and a woman with red hair." His face cracked into a fine sneer.

"And how do I know you are not lying?"

"You don't. But my cousin works as a ground attendant at the airfield. He saw them with his own eyes."

"Who did he see?"

"A group of men and one of *them*."

"Them?"

The man made a gesture. It was a symbol for the warding off of evil. "One of the dark ones. The cursed ones. I cannot say its name." He spat on the ground.

"I'm sorry, what do you mean by dark ones?"

The man glanced over his shoulder to make sure no one was listening. "One of the undead. The ones who drink the blood of the living."

Marsh started. A Nightwalker? What would they be doing in Constantinople?

"They had a woman with them. My cousin says that he did not see her properly, but she had long red hair and she was dressed in a white dress. They carried her like she was dead, or under a spell or something. My cousin says that he thought she might even have been bitten. It was dark, so it's hard to tell for sure. Serves her right for being a blood-whore."

Marsh grabbed the man by the throat. "What do you mean, bitten?"

The man sputtered under his grip. "Please, you are choking me," he wheezed.

Carefully Marsh loosened his grip, but held on to the man's throat. "Speak, damn you."

The man's eyes watered as he struggled to breathe. "All right. My cousin says that the woman looked like she was sleeping. They hailed a carriage and rode off into the night."

"Where did they go?" He released his grip a little.

"I don't know, but if you gave my cousin a few coins, he might remember who the driver was and which way they said they were going."

Marsh let go of his throat. The man sat back in his chair and coughed. "That is no way to treat a friend," he croaked.

"You are lucky that I didn't kill you. Friend."

The man rubbed his neck and looked at Marsh with reproach.

Marsh ignored the look. "So where is your cousin now?"

"He is at work. His shift ends at six o'clock tonight, and then I will meet him for a glass of tea before we go home for dinner."

"Where are you meeting him?" Marsh was in no mood for games.

"At one of the tea houses near the Hagia Sophia."

"Which tea house?"

"I will write it down. But first you must agree on a price."

Marsh glared at the man.

"Four hundred," the man said. "My cousin won't talk without the money."

"Hundred and fifty."

The man rolled his eyes. "Are you crazy? My cousin is risking his life by speaking to you. Would you say a man's life was worth that? Three hundred and fifty."

"I would say that your skinny life was worth less than that. I could kill you right here as you sit and find out for myself," said Marsh. "One hundred and seventy-five, and don't try me for more."

The man nodded. "You are taking advantage of an injured man. But I see your point," he added before Marsh could do anything else. "Two hundred, and that is my final offer."

"Two hundred it is, then." Marsh slapped his hand on the table and then shook the man's hand.

He pulled out his notebook and pencil. "Now give me the address of the tea house."

The man rattled off the street name and a few directions. "You bring the money with you when we see you?"

"I will. And remember, I am under the caliph's protection, so no funny business. I want your cousin and the driver there, or there will be no bargain. Don't try to cheat me. I am in no mood to be trifled with."

The man put his hand on his chest in mock outrage. "I would not dream of it, sir."

"Very well, then, I shall see you and your cousin later."

The man stumbled away from the table. Marsh finished his meal in silence. There was nothing he could do until after six.

After lunch, he decided to take a walk around the bazaar to pass the time. The great market of Constantinople was heaving with people going about their shopping. Marsh wandered along the avenues, past the myriad of wares on sale. Under the great blue domes one could buy almost anything. A carpet seller yelled, proclaiming the quality of his wares. Two stalls down, someone was selling finely crafted lanterns. Farther along was a shop selling brass goods built from old clock gears and springs. A tailor wearing magnifying combobulator goggles sat cross-legged on a table, sewing.

As he walked, he caught glimpses of royal gold and blue tunics. The caliph's men were close.

He turned off the main walkway into the sanctuary of one of the hans. A lone tree grew out of the cobbles that lined the courtyard. The walls of the workshops glowed softly despite the lack of afternoon sun. He surveyed the han. These open-air courtyards never ceased to amaze him. They dated back to the days when they had been used as lodgings for travelers and traders. From the shop-fronts he could tell that the han specialized in making jewelry. There was a little shisha café to the side filled with locals. He sat down at a table and ordered a pot of tea. When it came, he poured himself a cup and took a sip.

Was Elle alive? Had she merely been asleep, as the man had said? The thought of her bitten and drained by Nightwalkers made his breath catch in his throat with distress. Let them try. He would hunt down and stake every last one of them. He felt the Shadow shudder and contort around him as the vehemence of his thoughts radiated around him.

Surely the Alchemists wanted her alive? There was no other logical reason why they would have bothered transporting her all the way to Constantinople if they didn't need her alive. Did they know that she was the Oracle? Was her father part of the conspiracy? He didn't believe that. From what he had gathered, the professor was an honorable man.

A faint shadow fell over the table in front of him and Marsh looked up.

"Could you please come with us, my lord." It was one of the caliph's men.

Marsh stood and pulled a few coins out of his pocket to pay for the tea. "Of course. Do you have any news?"

"This way, please." Two more guards joined him as they walked.

"What's going on?" Marsh said.

"It would be best if you come with us quietly." One of them parted his tunic and touched the hilt of a large dagger in his belt.

Marsh did not argue.

They stepped out onto the street from one of the gates of the bazaar. Outside was an official-looking carriage. The guards helped him into the back and closed the door. He heard the door lock behind him as he sat down. The guard on the bench opposite sat upright, with his rifle by his side, eyes sternly trained on the seat in front of him. So this was not to be a social call, after all.

CHAPTER 43

I sat in the vinegary darkness for a long time and worried about what the man was planning to do with me. There were horrible stories about people boiling fairies alive to extract their essence. I wished with all my heart that I had stayed in Paris.

The rest of the day passed in a dark blur, punctuated by the sudden bursts of light when the man pulled the jar out of his satchel to show someone what he had found. Each time, I would shrink away from yet another series of distorted faces peering through the glass.

Eventually, after what seemed like an age, the man pulled the jar out of his bag. He set it down onto a table. It was hard to tell, but from the colors and lights, it looked like we were in a restaurant of sorts. The muffled noises of people talking thrummed against the glass.

The simit seller was talking to another man. I could see the white of his apron through the glass. They gestured as they spoke, haggling over something. It did not take much to work out that the something was me.

The simit seller threw up his hands and made to pick up the jar. The other grabbed his arm and shook his head. They continued to talk.

Then the other man pulled out a wad of notes. He handed the money to the simit seller. He took his time to count the notes, and with each leaf of paper, I felt my fate slip away a little further.

Satisfied, he shoved the money into a pocket inside his sagging waistcoat. The two men patted each other on the shoulder. Then the simit seller lifted up his satchel and, without so much as a glance, walked off, leaving the jar on the table.

My new owner came up to the jar and peered at me through the glass. "Please don't boil me. I promise that you will get no power that way," I whispered. But it was no use. He did not understand Fairy.

The man's eyes were kinder than those of the simit seller. In a moment of weakness, I stood up and placed my hand on the glass, near where his cheek was.

The man stood away from the jar and disappeared. I slumped against the glass without a care for my wings. These things mattered little, for I would be dead soon, of that I was sure.

The man came back after a little while. He lifted the jar and studied me for a few long moments. His eyes looked huge compared to the rest of his face through the glass. With a jolt, I fell forwards, almost into the jagged edges of the air holes. I closed my eyes and waited for the end that was surely set to come.

There was a soft rumble above me as he unscrewed the lid. I felt a gush of cool air. The jar moved and tilted slightly and I slid. I scrambled to keep my foothold on the slippery surface, but it was no use. The jar shook a little more, and with a last tilt, I plopped onto something soft.

I was sitting on a clean piece of folded cloth. I was inside a birdcage made of brass and bamboo—the type used for canaries and finches. I shivered at the irony of it; certain birds ate fairies.

The cloth under me was clean and soft. To the side of the cage was a bowl of water, and next to it, two sugar cubes.

While it could not sustain me indefinitely, there were few things in life that fairies love more than sugar. Especially tired, hungry, distressed fairies. Without a care for manners or decorum, I crawled over to the sugar and started gnawing on the edge of one of the cubes.

"That's right, little one. Eat and rest. You are safe now." The man spoke softly so as not to frighten me. I looked up at him. Without the distortion of the glass, he no longer looked like a monster.

Carefully, he picked up the cage and walked with it to an ornate wrought-iron hook in the wall. The cage jiggled as he hung it from the hook.

"Tonight, when we go home, I will give you to my daughter."

The sugar in my mouth turned to dust and I started shivering. When they were naughty or wouldn't go to bed, fairy children were told terrible stories about being sold to human children. Children pulled the wings off fairies, and squashed them while playing. They were monsters.

Outside my little cage, the chairs and tables of the market shisha house spread all around. A few more men in red conical hats sat about, drinking tea and smoking from tall glass jars. The water inside the glass bubbled as they sucked on the little pipes that led off them. The sweet smell of tobacco smoke assailed me again. Someone laughed. It sounded like my new owner, but then again, most humans sound the same.

The only way I could escape would be to find some absinthe to spirit into. At a push, any other bottle of strong liquor would do. I glanced around the room. There were only men here and they were all drinking tea. I briefly considered spiriting into tea, but decided against it almost immediately. It would be very hot and I would only succeed in boiling myself alive.

The man returned and lifted the cage off the hook and threw a cloth over it. I swung from side to side as we moved through the crowds in the street.

The sounds of many people surrounded the cage. I could smell cinnamon bark and turmeric root, the whisper of plants long dead, as we walked.

Eventually, the cage stilled and the man pulled the cloth away.

"This, little one, is my stall." He gestured about him. Great mounds of ground spices were piled up all around. The smells and colors were overwhelming.

"Allow me to introduce myself," he said. "I am Mustapha al Mehet, spice merchant, at your service." He bowed before the cage.

Out of habit, I bowed back.

The man smiled. "Seeing as I saved you from that dog, the bread seller Serdat, I am sure that you will return the favor by seeing to it that my shop is blessed by good fortune?"

With a sinking feeling, I realized that this was an order, not a request.

I nodded; anything to preserve me for a little while longer. I closed my eyes and summoned up some fairy dust. With an exaggerated swoop, I scattered it about. The green and gold luminous particles glittered as the slight breath of air that wafted through the market picked them up.

The fairy dust was an illusion, but it looked impressive. And all that mattered right now was that the man should believe me.

He smiled with delight as he watched the fairy dust shimmer across his shop. Satisfied, he tied an apron around his waist and set about the business of selling his wares.

Suddenly there was shouting. Men in blue tunics trimmed with gold came into the stall and pointed at my new owner. He shook his head and spoke to them in loud tones.

They shook their heads and gestured at him.

He shook his head and raised his shoulders.

The men came up to my cage. They stared at me with stern eyes, but I could not tell what they wanted.

One of them picked up the cloth and covered me. My cage shuddered as it was lifted from its place, and so I was borne away to yet another fate.

I reached up and held on to the bars. The door of the cage was locked with a small brass padlock, but that did not matter. I would have to bide my time carefully, for they would grow careless at some point. Men always did. And so I did what I do best. I watched and waited, for I had vowed to see sunshine and trees again.

Marsh felt the carriage jolt as it pulled up inside the walled gates of the palace. The guards opened the door. "This way, please." A guard in formal attire and white gloves directed him through the doors. The feather in his turban quivered as he kept himself rigidly at attention as Marsh walked past. They led him down one of the palace corridors.

Marsh did his best to map the layout in his head, but the building had been designed to confuse intruders, and he gave up after about half a dozen turns.

As they walked, his hand strayed to the side of his waistcoat. Elle's Colt revolver was safely nestled inside. He had found it on the floor next to her bunk on the train while packing their things. From the missing round in the chamber, he determined that she had managed to shoot one of the blighters. At least he hoped that she had. He prayed silently that the blood he had found did not belong to her. It was not the first time he had uttered such a prayer.

They marched down a flight of steps and entered through an archway. Marsh noted the ornate wrought-iron gate, which was cleverly disguised by a screen as he passed through the archway. Pure iron. The one thing that completely neutralized magic. If he were to hazard a guess, the walls would be reinforced with iron bars as well. As a general rule, he could handle iron fairly well in his daily comings and goings, but given his weakened state, he could end up paralyzed and helpless if he tried anything.

The caliph's vizier waited inside. "Viscount Greychester. How soon we see each other again."

"Vizier."

"So, I have been told that you have been busy in the streets of our city today."

Marsh inclined his head. "Depends on what you define as busy, I suppose."

The vizier lifted his chin. "Ah, yes. This brings us neatly to the point. You see, my men questioned your informant in the café where you had your lunch."

"Did your men manage to find out anything more from him?"

"Well, you will imagine my surprise when I learned that the woman you seek was carried off into our city, unconscious, and by a group of men and that they were accompanied by Nightwalkers. Leaving aside the fact that our city appears to have been sullied by the filthy undead, do you know of any Order where its members deliberately scar and desecrate their faces?"

Marsh didn't answer. He was not going to play the vizier's silly little game.

"No? Well, I will answer that for you. And then you can tell me why the Alchemists are planning a sacrificial ceremony in Constantinople? And, more importantly, why the Council of Warlocks sent one of their members at the same time."

A death ceremony? The man in the café would not have known that. Marsh suddenly felt sick. Clearly, the caliph was not his ally.

"It is true that the Alchemists have captured the lady I seek. But I do not know why they have taken her, and I can assure you that the Council has nothing to do with the matter. I am here on my own."

The vizier's eyes flashed. He reached over and grabbed the lapel of Marsh's cloak. "You lie . . . my lord."

"As do you, lord Vizier. And I should let go of me if I were you."

The vizier let go of his lapel and started chuckling. "Do you think me a fool, sir?" he said. "Do you honestly think I am merely going to let you walk out of here, to start another war with the Alchemists?" He shook his head.

Marsh kept his gaze steady. "I can assure you that the last thing I need right now is to start a war. All I want is to find Miss Chance and to go home to England. That is my only motive."

The vizier stared at him. "His majesty is fond of you and so I am to be deprived of the pleasure of putting you to death. You will remain here, in the palace, until arrangements can be made for your immediate deportation."

Marsh stared at the man. "I think you are gravely mistaken."

The vizier looked mildly offended. "Oh, I think not." He straightened his elaborately embroidered brocade tunic. "This audience is over. The caliph's wishes are to be carried out without further debate. Good day to you, sir."

At the archway the vizier paused. "Oh, and one last thing. I almost forgot." He gestured to one of the guards. "We found this in the spice market. You may as well take whatever else you brought from the Shadows with you too."

The guard set what looked like a birdcage covered in a dark blue cloth on the floor. Then the gate clanged shut, and the lock ground as the key turned.

Marsh stood in the middle of the room. He stared at

the gate in disbelief. The caliph couldn't be serious, could he?

He walked over to the gate and gave it a rattle. It was firmly locked. Two guards armed with rifles stood guard on either side of the arch. They looked at him suspiciously. One gripped the hilt of his rifle more tightly. "We have orders to shoot you if you try to escape. Please step away from the gate." Those appeared to be the only words he was going to say.

Marsh let go of the gate and sank down onto one of the red and orange sofas. He thought about Elle's Colt in his pocket, but the pistol was no match for two rifles. He needed another plan.

Something rattled under the cloth. At the sound, he leaned over and tugged at the edge of the fabric. The cloth slipped to the floor, and Marsh stared in surprise. Under the cloth was a brass and bamboo birdcage, and inside was a Parisian absinthe fairy.

He stared at her through the bars. He was no expert, but even he could see that she wasn't looking very well. Her wings were ragged and she gripped the bars of the cage as she stared up at him.

"Good heavens. How on earth did you get here?" he said.

The fairy spoke, but her speech was like the crackle of dry leaves and he had too little power to decipher and amplify what she was saying. He rubbed his eyes in exasperation. The fairy stopped speaking and buried her face in her hands. She looked like she was crying.

Marsh looked away. Watching a fairy weep was a terrible thing to see. It upset even the hardest of men.

"There now," he said, feeling decidedly large and clumsy. Then he had an idea. He reached into his coat and pulled out his hip flask. "Here. There isn't much left, but it should help." He unscrewed the top and held the rim of the bottle near the cage.

The smell of absinthe reached the fairy. With a flash of green, she turned to spirit form and disappeared into the flask. Marsh slowly turned the lid back onto the flask and put it back into his coat. He sighed. At least one of them was safe for the time being.

CHAPTER 44

Elle rested her head against the cool wall. She had tried to amuse herself by counting the stone blocks in the wall, but a dull headache was nibbling around the edges of her brain and the counting was making it worse. It felt like the air was pressing against her as it did just before a thunderstorm.

We are with you. A voice spoke.

A shiver ran through Elle. "Who's there?"

We are.

"Who are you?"

We are the voices of Oracles past. We are with you.

"Mother?" Elle whispered.

We are not one person, Cybele. We are Pythia. We are a small part of every woman who has worn the crystal. When you die, a small part of you will remain here too. It is your duty to keep us.

She shook her head. The sensation of voices speaking from within was making her dizzy. "That's all very interesting, but you might have noticed that I am in a bit of a pickle right now. A little help might be good?"

We can help. We can share what we know with you.

"I am in a dungeon somewhere. Perhaps some advice on how to escape might be more useful?"

There was a flutter of soft laughter. The voices had a sense of humor, it seemed.

The Alchemists have always served their own purposes. Beware the alliance with the dark ones.

Elle sighed and ran her hand through her hair. She noticed that it was starting to grow greasy. She wished again that she had a ribbon to tie it up. "That's true, but do you think you could contact someone and ask them to rescue me?"

All we can do is teach you our secrets so you may save yourself.

Elle closed her eyes. She was definitely going mad.

You must learn to use the energy that is channeling through you. You must complete the metamorphosis.

Elle's mind was reeling. "How do I do this? And what is all this about people touching me and draining me?"

This is the way that the Oracle is used. If you give yourself over to the Warlocks, they will use you to channel the power they need for their rituals. They will see the paths that lie before them. Each Oracle is different. Some are stronger than others. Some wear out quickly. Others last for centuries. Every time someone draws power through you, your life essence is damaged. This is why the Warlocks have forbidden anyone to draw power from others.

Elle shuddered. "Yes, I know." She thought of Marsh and how he stopped Rosamund from doing just that.

The Warlock fears that he will lose your trust in him.

"You can read my thoughts?" That was disturbing.

You don't know how to shield your thoughts to those who can see. Your mind is like a painting for all to view. Not only us.

"Marsh did say that there was one more thing that I should know, but I was too angry to listen to him."

If the Alchemists tried to use you right now, they would most certainly kill you.

"So how do I protect myself? I mean, from these people who would hurt me?"

It takes a long time to learn control. Most Oracles start their learning when they are girls. But the world is so different today. Everything happens so fast, so we do not know.

"Very well, then. I suppose it wouldn't hurt to know a few tricks." She closed her eyes. "I'm ready."

Then let us begin.

CHAPTER 45

A soft, incessant buzz from the inside of his pocket roused Marsh. He was stretched out on the sofa, thinking. Carefully he unscrewed the top of his hip flask and let the fairy out.

She was looking much better. Rest and the alcohol must have done her some good.

The fairy spoke and gestured at the window. Marsh frowned. Fairy was one of the most difficult of the known languages. Not only was it a very fast language with many words difficult to pronounce, it took special skills to decipher the quick-fire communication.

"I'm sorry, what was that?"

The fairy flapped her arms in frustration and started speaking again. Marsh considered using the last of his power to amplify and slow down what she was saying, but decided against it. It would tip him over the edge and he wasn't quite sure what would happen once his power was all gone. He might turn into a heap of dust. There was no way of predicting the outcome.

He also wasn't sure that going to the effort would be worth it either. Fairies were generally only interested in trivial quandaries, such as sleeping and finding sugar.

"I'm sorry, little fairy, but I can't hear you," he started saying.

The fairy threw her head back in frustration. She looked about the room and spotted the polished desk by the window. The guards had brought Marsh an early dinner. On the tray was a pot of granulated sugar. She flew up to the sugar and pointed at it.

"Please help yourself."

The fairy shook her head. She pointed at the lid.

"Very well." He walked over to the desk and lifted the lid off the pot for her.

The fairy flew to the pot and started scooping sugar over the edge of the bowl.

"Careful. You are making a mess," Marsh said.

The fairy ignored him and carried on scooping handfuls of sugar onto the table. When a respectable heap of sugar lay on the table, she stopped and dusted the granules off her wings. Then she fluttered onto the desk. Looking about, she found a matchstick wedged into the side of the leather inlay. She wrestled the matchstick out and carried it over to the sugar. She gave Marsh a reproachful look and started raking the sugar across the table.

Marsh watched in amazement as she scraped the shape of a letter into the sugar.

"*L?*"

The fairy nodded and started jumping up and down.

"You are trying to give me a message, aren't you?"

The fairy raised her shoulders in exasperation and nodded again.

Clearly she thought Marsh was being exceedingly slow.

"Hold on, I have a better idea." He pulled his notebook and pencil out of his pocket. "I will go through the letters and when I hit the right one, you let me know."

The fairy heaved her shoulders in a gesture that seemed to say *Finally!*

"Right, let's see. *A?* no? *B, C, D?*"

The fairy nodded.

Marsh wrote *D* in his notebook.

"*E, F? G? H? I?*"

The fairy nodded again.

They carried on for a while longer until Marsh had scrawled down the following message.

L
DANGER
DUNGEON
PARIS
MUST HELP

The fairy slumped down on the desk.

Marsh looked at the message. He puzzled over the words and then looked at the fairy with growing amazement.

"Are you trying to tell me that you know Elle? That she picked you up at Aleix's in Paris?"

The fairy nodded.

"And you were with her when they took her?"

The fairy nodded again and turned her wrist from side to side as if she was wearing a bracelet.

"Where is she?"

The fairy pointed at the notepad and they sounded out the words.

TOWER
FLEW UP

"Where? Where is the tower?"

The fairy looked around the room and hoisted up her shoulders. She pointed at the cage and shook her head apologetically.

"You don't know, do you?" Marsh said with growing disappointment. "They caught you once you were on the streets and now you don't know where you are?"

The fairy nodded. Then she started gesturing.

"The tower is big?"

The fairy nodded.

"And there is a tree?"

The fairy nodded again.

"So you would be able to recognize the tower if we were to walk past it?"

The fairy nodded again.

Marsh drew his flask out of his pocket and opened it. She pointed at the flask, motioning for Marsh to drink.

"I know you can make me see things if I'm drunk enough, but it won't work. There isn't enough wormwood in the flask. And besides, you'd have nowhere to sleep."

The fairy dropped her head in disappointment. She pointed at his notebook.

"Yes, we will look for her, as soon as we manage to get out of here," he said.

The fairy nodded and spirited into the flask.

"Rest now, I need to think of a plan," Marsh said, closing the flask and carefully putting it back in his pocket.

CHAPTER 46

Elle slumped forward so violently that the shackle around her ankle drew taut. She was exhausted and her head was pounding. "This is so difficult," she said.

It is. You are the force that holds Shadow and Light together. There are very few who can reach up and grasp what lies in the universe above and below us. It is within the natural order of things that the ones who can wield such extraordinary powers are few. There are the lesser Shadow creatures and those who were created from a blend of power with this world, like the Nightwalkers and the wolves. Their magic is not pure though. It corrupts those it touches.

Elle frowned. "Nightwalkers are *lesser* creatures?" Blimey, she wouldn't ever want to say that to one in person.

With such ability comes great responsibility. The existence of the world as we know it depends on maintaining the balance.

Elle nodded. "I appreciate that, but I need to rest, if you don't mind."

Of course.

Elle pulled her blanket up around her. She needed to close her eyes for just a moment.

"How long have I been sleeping?"

Too long.

"You are lucky that I am chained to this wall," she

said. "I can think of the bottom of a few lovely wells for you to visit."

A fact we are well aware of. Now let us try again.

Elle sighed and lowered her eyelids. She waited for what she decided to call the rush. The nauseating sensation as if she was speeding through the air rose up inside her. She gritted her teeth. Her head felt like it was about to explode. Images flew past her eyes, some too fast to recognize. She opened her eyes and swooned.

"I can't," she panted.

Well done. Now rest.

Elle slumped back against the wall. She couldn't ever remember being this tired. The voice started speaking softly.

While you rest, we will tell you a story. When the world was younger and people believed, those who practiced the Craft were in harmony with one another and the world. But then greed and the lust for power intervened, growing over the old ways. Ceremonies and festivals were forgotten. People no longer honored the forces that kept them safe. Practice of the Craft was torn apart, split between those who walked in the Light and those who walked in Shadow. But the Alchemists went one step further. They chose the path of darkness. In their quest for gold, they became slaves to those who would use them. Their souls turned black with hate, and thoughts of revenge filled their minds. They planned and schemed and waited.

Elle opened her eyes. "And what will happen now?"

The clouds are gathering.

"What does *that* mean?"

It means that for the first time in centuries, now that the energies are low, the barrier that was placed between Light and Shadow could fall. The outcome will change the world.

"But that is madness," Elle said. "Would they kill one

another over such power? Scientific principles suggest that Shadow power is energy and energy is infinite. Energy doesn't disappear, it just goes somewhere else."

You are correct. The challenge lies in finding where that next place is.

A rattle in the lock made Elle jump. She crawled backwards until she felt the wall against her back. One of the gray-cloaked guards stalked into the room and dumped another tray down. He glared at her and then stomped out again.

She slumped against the wall in despair. Where was Marsh right now? Was he even looking for her? Would he keep his promise to find her father? Surely there was no good reason for him to continue the rescue now that the Alchemists had her. The thought made her sad.

She was lost. The Warlocks would simply seek out another Oracle to train. No one was indispensable in this world, and she would disappear and it would be as if she had never existed.

She looked up at the grate and wondered about the fairy. The delicate hope that she had been cultivating was withering. She pushed the pool of self-pity forming inside her aside. If she was going to get out of this place alive, she was going to have to jolly well do something about it herself.

She picked up the spoon from the tray. It wasn't much, but it would have to do. She started rubbing the spoon against the bit of chain where it joined with the shackle. If she worked hard at it, she might wear the metal out. And once she was no longer chained to the wall, the options of escape would be far more varied.

CHAPTER 47

Marsh studied the ground below his window. It was a very long way down, too far to jump even if he could loosen the iron bars enough to escape. Something told him that the caliph knew how to keep prisoners.

He checked his pocket. The fairy was sleeping soundly in the flask. He hoped she could actually find the tower. He also hoped it wasn't already too late. He peered at the guards. They both stared into space with looks of serene boredom on their faces.

Marsh reached into his cloak and pulled out the pistol. He held it in his palm, felt the weight of it. It was not enough to shoot his way out of here, but he had a plan. All he needed was a distraction.

The Colt made him think of Elle. But then again, everything made him think of her. No matter what he did, she never seemed to leave his thoughts. She had the most adorable dimples in her cheeks when she smiled. His thoughts turned to a few of her other curves that were also appealing, and he felt himself grow uncomfortable in places that were not entirely convenient at that moment. With some effort he cleared his mind. Now was not the time; he needed to concentrate.

After what felt like an eternity, there was a commotion at the gate, and not long after, the vizier glided into the room with a guard on either side of him.

"Lord Greychester. I hope that you have enjoyed your

stay here at the palace," the vizier said. "I trust that all your needs were met?"

"Lord Vizier, how nice of you to drop by."

The vizier gave him a cold smile and inclined his head. He gestured to one of the guards, who produced a leather folder. He handed it to Marsh.

"A first-class ticket to Paris, by dirigible. The flight leaves this evening. My men will escort you to the airfield. Their orders are to make sure that you don't get lost and miss your flight. The streets of Constantinople can be so confusing to foreigners."

"Of course. How very gracious of his majesty. But, unfortunately I must respectfully decline his offer." In one swift movement, Marsh grabbed the vizier's bony arm and twisted him around. He braced the man against his chest, lifted the Colt and cocked it. "Not a move or he dies."

"Well played, my lord," said the vizier. "But I doubt if this act of bravery is going to do you any favors."

Marsh ignored him and started moving toward the gate. "Open it."

The guards looked at the vizier. He gave them a curt nod and they complied.

"Put down your weapons while you're at it."

The guards hesitated.

"I said, drop your guns." He tightened his grip on the vizier. He was dangerously close to losing his temper. The little man whimpered and squirmed.

The guards set their rifles down on the marble floor.

"Now show me the way out of here."

The guards looked at the vizier. The man nodded again. "Do as he says. He won't get very far once he is outside the palace and his majesty finds out that his hospitality has been abused."

"Move! Take me to a side gate. Not the main entrance," Marsh said.

The walk out of the palace was torturous. The vizier refused to walk and Marsh had to drag him along. The effort made his ribs hurt with each step, but he held out. After what felt like hours, they rounded a corner and exited a small courtyard. On the other side of the courtyard was a wooden door.

"Open it."

The guard knocked on the gate and a key rattled in the lock. Another guard opened the door from the other side and peered at them in surprise.

"It's all right," said the vizier. "Do as he says."

"Stand by the wall," Marsh said to the guards. "And count to one thousand."

The guards looked at him. "Count, I said!"

The guards started counting.

Marsh took the gate key from the guard and stepped through the door. Quickly he locked it.

"You can let me go now," said the vizier.

"Not quite," said Marsh. "Let's walk to the end of the lane, shall we?" They took one of the cobbled lanes that led to one of the bigger streets. At the intersection, Marsh stopped and looked at the vizier. "I must thank you for being such a good sport, old chap. I apologize for taking you hostage, but I have urgent business elsewhere."

"You won't get far, you know. The caliph will have his entire guard comb the city for you as soon as you let me go. You stick out like a sore thumb. There will be no hiding. My men will find you. Be sure of that. And if they do, you will be a dead man."

"That's good to know. We might need the caliph's guards once I find Miss Chance." He hoisted the vizier up by his tunic. "Please tell the caliph that I thank him for his hospitality and that I apologize for any inconvenience caused. As soon as I have rescued my friend, we will depart from this place as promptly as we are able."

He shook him for good measure. "Do I make myself clear?"

"I will be sure to do so."

As soon as Marsh loosened his hold on the man, the vizier's hand darted to his waistband. Quick as a fish he dragged a dagger from the folds of his tunic. With a vicious move, he tried to stab Marsh in the stomach.

Marsh swerved as the dagger flew past his abdomen. Marsh let go of the vizier with one hand and with his other he landed a punch to the man's jaw. The vizier dropped to the ground like a sack of turnips.

Then Marsh did what no self-respecting gentleman of breeding should ever do. He ran for his life.

Marsh wove through the evening crowds that thronged in the streets. A brightly painted tram-omnibus nearly ran him over as he sidestepped the traffic. As he walked, he kept looking for blue and gold livery in the crowds. He couldn't go back to the hotel to collect his luggage, for the place would be watched and he needed to disappear. There was also no way of collecting Patrice's reply to his telegram. Marsh shrugged his shoulders with irritation. He would try to send a message to the hotel later, but right now there was nothing he could do. He just hoped Patrice would have the sense to follow his trail without getting caught.

The city grew poorer and the wooden houses more dilapidated as he walked. It took some effort, but eventually he found a little guesthouse. Carved into the eaves of the building was the Warlock triangle. It was cleverly disguised by the decorations, but to Marsh it was unmistakable.

The owner of the guesthouse looked up from behind the counter. His curved horns were neatly hidden under a close-fitting hat, but there was no mistaking the fact that the owner of the guesthouse was one of the children of Pan.

"I need a room for a few days."

The faun nodded.

"A quiet room." He paused and looked the faun in the eye. "And you never saw me."

The faun shrugged, picking up the notes. "I ask no questions, Warlock. These are dark times and one good turn deserves another."

Without taking his eyes off Marsh, the faun said something to the back. A woman with large hips and a face that was fading in its beauty came out from behind a curtain. She was carrying a large bunch of keys. She motioned to Marsh, who followed her up the stairs.

"We don't want any trouble here," she said.

"Then we want the same thing," Marsh replied.

"My son will help. He will be with you in a minute," the woman said before going downstairs. A small boy appeared at the door, and while he was somewhat odd-looking with his mother's dark eyes and his father's pointy face and curly brown hair at least he appeared to have escaped the burden of having horns like his father.

A few quiet words, and a few more notes handed to the boy, procured a white linen shirt and trousers, a baggy waistcoat and a red fez.

Marsh dressed quickly. He stowed the Colt inside his coat and patted his pocket. Money was the currency of secrecy in this world. He had enough cash with him to tide him over until Patrice got to Constantinople. If Patrice managed to track him down, that is.

The boy reappeared and eyed Marsh in his disguise. He stifled a giggle. Marsh smiled back.

"What is your name?" he said.

The boy grew shy. "My name is Inut," he said solemnly.

Marsh extended his hand and shook the boy's. "How

do you do, Inut? I am Mr. Marsh, and I need to find a certain tower as soon as possible," Marsh explained. "An old stone tower with a tree growing outside in the courtyard. Do you think you can help me find one like that?"

"There are many old stone towers in the city," the boy said. "We could spend weeks visiting each one. But I will help."

"Splendid. Let's try the area near the airfield first."

Hours later, in a dusty alley, Marsh kicked an abandoned wooden crate in frustration. It set a series of dogs barking across the silent city. The almost-full moon simmered above them. Marsh looked up at the white disk in the sky and despaired.

"Damn it to the underworld and to damnation." They had been wandering around for hours.

The half-faun boy sat down on a doorstep. He rested his head on his knees. The fairy was hanging her arms out of Marsh's pocket, her head drooping down. It was almost midnight.

"Why didn't you tell me Constantinople was so full of old stone towers?" Marsh said.

Inut stifled a yawn and rubbed his eyes. "I did," he said. "You didn't believe me."

Marsh couldn't argue with that.

Inut yawned. "The city is old. Many wars. Many towers, even after earthquakes."

"Fair enough, but where is the next one?"

Inut dragged himself up and stumbled.

Marsh looked at his pocket. The fairy was now curled up in the bottom and was fast asleep. He rubbed his face. He felt like he had sand in his eyes.

"Maybe we try the one by the money lenders," Inut mumbled. He started walking down the road, swaggering like a drunkard. The sight of the faun-boy asleep on his feet brought Marsh to his senses.

Marsh walked up to him and stopped him. "I'm sorry, Inut. This is not fair. It is very late and—right now I think we could be looking straight at the tower and not see it," he said. "Perhaps we should try again tomorrow."

Inut eyed him gratefully. "We look again tomorrow."

"Yes, we look again tomorrow. But first, let's go home. Your mother must be worried about you."

He lifted the half-asleep boy in his arms and headed back to the guesthouse.

The next morning he woke as the sun came up. He washed and dressed quickly, pausing to check his injury. The apothecary's salve had worked and the wound was nearly knitted up, but yesterday's scuffle with the vizier and carrying Inut home had taken its toll. He examined the blue-black bruising with a grimace. Whatever those Alchemists had used, it was nasty.

He started dressing. Thoughts of Elle's hands on his collar flooded his mind. He shouldn't have played that game with her, but the liberal after-dinner brandies had made him bold, and she was the one who started it. He would have to apologize to her about turning away from her like that when all this was over. He only hoped he got the chance, and that it wasn't too late. He pulled on his waistcoat and put his flask into his pocket. The fairy had not stirred yet.

He was busy working through the contents of his bag, which Inut's father had collected for him, when there was a soft knock on his door. Inut entered timidly. "Excuse me, sir, but my mother says to tell you that breakfast is ready," he said.

"Oh, splendid."

"Can we go hunting for towers again, sir?"

"As soon as we've had our breakfast."

Inut sped out of the room and down the stairs as fast as he could.

Marsh followed him downstairs. He felt his stomach rumble as the smell of strong Turkish coffee met him halfway down the stairs. He found Inut's mother in the dining room, clearing a few dishes away from the table.

"Good morning . . . again," Marsh greeted her.

"Good morning," she said politely.

"Many guests?"

"Not so many," she replied, putting a plate of bread in front of Marsh. "Most are peddlers come to the city to find remedies to sell." She shrugged.

"I see." Marsh helped himself to a fresh fig from a wooden bowl on the table. He bit into the fruit, tasting the sweetness.

Inut's mother watched Marsh from the corner of her eye. Marsh carefully put his knife down.

"I must apologize again for keeping your son out so late last night."

She nodded. "Inut is a good boy. We don't want any trouble."

"There is no trouble, but I need to find this tower. It is a matter of life and death."

Inut came into the dining room with what looked like a rolled-up piece of paper. "My father says we should use this." He handed it to Marsh.

Marsh carefully unrolled it, and smiled. It was a map of Constantinople—carefully drawn, with illustrations to show the landmarks. He felt his hopes rise. Some of the illustrations looked like towers.

"Tell your father I say thank you. Thank you very much indeed."

"I will." Inut also smiled.

Marsh pointed at the map. "Now show me the towers we found yesterday."

An hour later, armed with the faun's map and dressed in his traditional disguise, Marsh took to the streets, this time without Inut.

He paused to straighten his fez and checked the map. The streets were filling up with traders and people going about their business of the morning. Not many paid attention to the tall man walking down the road and looking up at the buildings.

Shortly before the noon hour, Marsh stepped into a square. A fountain that trickled grayish-looking water greeted him. An old man was at the fountain, watering his mule.

Marsh stopped under the branches of a Judas tree. They were a common sight in Constantinople. The trees mostly looked like they were dead, with their black leafless limbs reaching up into the sky. Then, as soon as spring arrived, they would burst into blossom, covering the city in soft pink petals before their leaves sprang forth. Marsh looked up at the branches. There were no pink flowers and the leaves were turning brown and dying. They crunched underfoot.

He pulled his flask out of his pocket and opened it. The fairy morphed into fairy form and fluttered her wings. She looked at Marsh with annoyance.

"My apologies for waking you again, but is this the tower?"

The fairy shook her head, her eyes downcast, and folded her arms as she hovered before him.

"Look, I am sorry you are tired, and I am even sorrier for bothering you every time I find a tower, but the sooner we find it, the sooner we can go home." Marsh sighed and pointed at the stone building behind the fairy. "Please tell me, for the love of all that is good in this world, is that the confounded tower?"

The fairy spun round and looked at the building. Then

she looked up at the branches of the tree. Marsh watched on in amazement as she started humming and buzzing with excitement like an oversized bumblebee.

"Is this it?" he said, almost unwilling to believe it.

The fairy nodded so vigorously, her whole body bobbed up and down. She pointed at the tower.

Marsh had to suppress a whoop of delight. "Oh, if you weren't so little I would hug you right now," he said.

He surveyed the building, and his joy evaporated. The tower looked like it had ten-foot-thick walls. The buttresses were heavily fortified. Steel bars covered the windows.

He walked across the square to take a closer look. As he turned a corner, his eye caught a flash of dark blue uniform and he ducked down into the alley, just in time to see two soldiers of the caliph's guard walk by. Both of them had swords and dangerous-looking pistols at their sides. They sat down on the stone bench opposite the fountain and opened their lunch boxes.

Marsh cursed under his breath. He was trapped in the alley. The guards seemed happily distracted by their lunch, but he couldn't risk being seen. Not when Elle was so close.

He motioned for the fairy to go back into the flask. He needed to rethink his strategy.

Carefully he backed away and started walking in the opposite direction, away from the tower. He walked with muscle-bunched tension. Finally, he rounded the corner. Sagging with relief, he rested inside a doorway.

"That was close," he whispered.

The fairy buzzed from inside of the hip flask in agreement.

"At least we know where she is now. Let's go back to the guesthouse."

Silently he stole down the alley, passing two more guards

who were on the other side of the road. They were chatting. Marsh kept his head down and managed to pass without them noticing him. Then, as he reached the end of the street, one of them called out.

"Oi," one of them yelled, and then said something in rough street Turkish.

Marsh froze. Slowly he turned around. The guards walked toward him. They were talking to one another. He made himself stand still as he waited for them.

One of the guards smiled and pulled out a metal cigarette box. He said something, but the rough Turkish spoken on the streets was vastly different from the fine Arabic- and Persian-laced Ottoman Turkish he knew. He recognized one word though; the guard was asking for a match to light his cigarette.

Marsh put his hand in his pockets and felt around. He was about to raise his shoulders to indicate that he could not help, hoping they wouldn't notice his lack of language, when something appeared in the palm of his hand. To his own amazement, he pulled a box of matches out of his pocket. He handed the matches to the guard, who took them and lit his cigarette. He handed the box back to Marsh with a smile. Marsh stood completely still as the guards walked away.

He waited until they had disappeared round the corner before he started walking. When they reached the end of the alley, the fairy flew out of the flask.

"Did you do that?"

The fairy nodded.

"Then I have to thank you, little fairy. For saving my life." The fairy smiled and pushed her chest out.

Marsh smiled as they walked, silently thanking Inut's father for the clothes. He would be back this evening for Elle. Nothing would stop him now.

* * *

Back at the guesthouse, Marsh paced the length of his room, from one end to the other. The floorboards creaked under his weight as he walked. He had all of his things laid out, ready to go.

Inut had been a good assistant. Marsh had sent him out to collect a list of rather unusual things, and the boy had returned with the goods, without looking ruffled. He had even used some initiative. Marsh had asked him to find a bottle of absinthe, but as none could be found, he had returned with a bottle of Turkish raki—the vicious aniseed-flavored drink favored in these regions. The fairy had pulled a face when presented with the option, but eventually she relented. Fresh raki was better than stale absinthe. The bottle of raki now stood on the shelf, glowing a soft green color as the fairy slept. He smiled. She deserved a rest after all she had done.

Frustrated, he ran his hand through his hair. The plan was a simple one, because simple was all he could manage at this stage. He had to find Elle. If it was the last thing he did.

When this was all over, he was going to take her away somewhere. Far away, where they would live out their lives. Somewhere quiet, away from all the politics of Light and Shadow. The thought eased his anxiety and he smiled. Yes, it would definitely be worth it. If she'd have him, but he was going to need to do an awful lot of explaining first.

CHAPTER 48

The afternoon shadows were long on the walls when they came for her. This time there were many of them. Elle stood with her back against the wall. She watched them through the fronds of her hair as they filed into the cell. Their faces were shrouded in gray hoods.

One of them—the leader, it seemed—stepped forward. He let his hood fall back so she could see his face. His head was shaved smooth, and lurid runes moved under his skin. It was one of the faces from her nightmares.

He gripped her chin and turned her head from side to side to examine her face. "Hmm, such a pretty thing. I am pleased," he said.

Elle tried to draw away, but he held her firmly.

He wrinkled his nose as he took in her greasy hair and dirty nightdress. "Why has she not been allowed to wash?" he barked. A few of his followers jumped at the tone of his voice. "I said, why has she not been attended to?" No one answered.

He let go of Elle's chin and his head snapped around. He stared at the others. "She must be prepared. Everything must be perfect. Do I make myself clear?"

"Yes, master," they murmured.

He clapped his hands. "Attend to the preparations. Call Patrice. I must speak with him at once!"

They bowed and scuttled out of the room. The Alchemist turned and stared at Elle. "You are ready. I am sure of it now. And our plan will work so much better now that you are." He let go of the crystal and it dropped back into its now familiar place. Then he turned and left the cell.

Elle wrapped the blanket about herself and stared at the locked door with growing frustration. There was no telling what these men were up to, but whatever it was, it wasn't good. She closed her eyes and focused her new seeing skills at the door, feeling for anything she could use, but the rebound from the magic that surrounded the door was too strong, and the images were just a blur.

She opened her eyes in frustration and let out a small sob. What use was having special powers if you couldn't use them in an emergency? She wanted to go home.

Work on scraping through the shackle was slow going, but she had managed to wear away some of the metal. They took the spoon when they collected the tray, but the diamonds in the bracelet around her wrist were not going anywhere. And they were harder than anything she could lay her hands on. She rubbed and rubbed against the shackle. Tiny shavings of metal fell to the floor. If she kept at it, she might be able to wear the link thin enough to break it. She hoped there was enough time though. Judging by her last visitor, she feared it might be too late.

Suddenly there was a commotion at the door. It flung open and a group of acolytes and servants entered. Elle cowered under her blanket.

The acolytes were directing the servants, who carried an ornate copper bath. They set it down in the middle of the floor, in the sunny patch. Next to it they put a wooden table. One of the servants set about arranging an assortment of soaps, oils and brushes on it. Another set up a polished metal oval standing mirror next to the table, while the last servant carried a chair. Elle watched in amazement as her cell was transformed.

Two servants left, and returned wrestling a day bed, complete with linen, and set it down against the wall. One servant even plumped the pillows and arranged them neatly, while another brought folded towels.

More minions were carrying buckets of steaming water down the stairs. The water was dumped into the bath. The cell filled with the smell of attar of roses.

"Why are you doing this?" she said to one of the acolytes.

He ignored her, but she tugged at his sleeve. "Please, you have to answer me," she said.

The acolyte just looked down at his feet.

"Hello, my lovely. And how are we today?" Patrice was standing at the door with his hands in his pockets. He tutted. "Now, don't you go upsetting the acolytes. Life is hard enough for them as it is."

"Patrice, you are lucky I am chained to this wall. Or else you would be a very seriously injured man right now."

He laughed. "Ah, the famous Chance temper. How charming. Now, my dove, there is no need for such animosity. You should be grateful that I am doing you a favor." He gestured at the new furniture. "You will find your circumstances much improved." He smiled at her. "You should learn to be more gracious when someone does something nice for you."

"Let me out of these chains and I'll show you grace."

"All in good time, little one. All in good time."

"Don't you call me that. You have no right to speak as if I am your friend."

Patrice held up a hand in mock apology. "Fair enough. I shall leave the terms of endearment for your Warlock. Although I doubt that you will ever see the sop again."

"Marsh is not a sop. He's more of a man than you are."

Patrice laughed. "Oh, I think we both know he is a

coward and a cad. He's not coming for you, you know. A little bird told me that he got off the train in Bucharest. He's home safely, in his drawing room in London by now. His little Chance-dalliance long forgotten."

One of the servants emptied the last bucket of hot water into the bath. Patrice ran his hand through the water. "Perfect," he said.

Elle glared at him. "Who was that man? The one who was here earlier?" It was all she could do to hide her disappointment over the news about Marsh. Surely he wouldn't abandon her. The hope she felt inside evaporated and made way for a deep sense of anguish. He was not coming for her.

"Sir Eustace is exactly who he says he is. And right now he is the master. And if that is what he says you should know, then that is all you need to know. Now, you be a good girl and have a nice hot bath. Then, have some lunch. It will do you good." He motioned to one of the servants who put a platter of food on the table. Elle's mouth watered when she saw there was fresh bread, cheese and fruit.

The servant placed a jug of water next to the platter. Another placed a paper box onto the chair.

"Once you've finished bathing, you are to put that on." Patrice nodded at the box. Then he turned and picked up a lock of Elle's hair on her shoulder. He lifted it and turned it between his fingers. "Also, be sure to do something nice with your hair. Something classic, to go with the dress, hmm?" Then he leaned over and sniffed the lock.

She jerked her head back to free her hair, but Patrice held on to it, pulling it. She winced. "You need to work on your attitude, Eleanor. Your temper does nothing but make life more difficult for yourself, you know. It did not help your father and it's not going to help you either."

"Where is my father?" she said in a low voice.

Patrice raised his eyebrows in mock surprise. "Did they not tell you?" He tutted again. "Your dear *old papa* is dead."

Elle felt her knees buckle and she leaned against the wall for support. "Patrice, so help me. As soon as I am out of these chains, you are a dead man."

"You are way past help now, my dear. I am your only salvation," he said softly. He stood back and clapped his hands. "Leave us," he commanded. The last of the servants and acolytes bowed and left the cell.

Once they were gone, he turned to her. "Be sure to obey these orders. You are to be washed, dressed and fed. You are to wait in readiness until you are called upon. Nothing more."

"And what if I do not?"

"If you do not, then I shall drag you out of here naked and kicking. We don't need all this fragrance and frippery. But the master thought it would be a nice touch. I, for one, have no qualms with handing you over a little used."

She felt the blood drain from her face. The expression in Patrice's eyes was blank. He looked like a man who meant what he said, with no reservation.

He motioned to the bath and the chair. "Contrary to what some might say, the Alchemists are a civilized order. They agree that there is no need for barbarism in this day and age." His eyes grew cold. "But if you shun their gift, then there is no problem with proceeding as they did in the days of old." His eyes flicked over her. "You are a beautiful woman, Elle. I've always thought so. But you were always too ambitious, too selfish and wrapped up in your own little world, to notice my regard. I really am quite looking forward to you defying me."

Elle shuddered with revulsion. "Patrice, you are mad. Did you know that?"

He laughed again. "Mad? No, I am not mad. I am an opportunist."

"And what exactly am I preparing for?"

He gave her a look that was steeped in pure evil. "Oh, I am not going to ruin the surprise for you. Just know that you are to be honored greatly." With those words, Patrice left the cell. The door closed behind him with a solid thud.

Elle stayed where she had slumped to the floor. She watched the steam curl slowly up off the surface of the perfumed water in the bath.

Patrice is a liar. The voices spoke.

"I agree." He was playing games with her. She was sure of it. Her father could not be dead. She refused to believe it. And Marsh?

You must have faith.

She rattled the crystal in frustration. "Why can't you just give me a straightforward answer for once!"

The answers are for you to find, Pythia. We are merely your compass.

Elle sighed. Marsh had been so cold. He had turned her away. It was hopeless.

The power of salvation lies within you. It has always been within you.

The voices were right. It was time to take matters into her own hands. She wasn't sure how many days had passed, but she knew her body was dirty. The thought of complying with Patrice's orders somehow made her feel even more sullied. But he did seem deadly serious about the alternative. And she would not let him do that. Ever. She shuddered again. She could not believe he was the same man she met in Paris not so long ago.

She crept over to the table and opened the paper box.

Inside was a piece of wispy blue material wrapped in tissue paper. Nestled next to the fabric was pair of copper brooches, a golden, braided belt and a pair of fine leather sandals. She held the fabric up to the light. It had a definite shape to it, even though it was rather flimsy. It looked like something she'd seen draped over women in classical paintings. She held the fabric up against her and looked into the mirror. Her hair was messy and hung over the fabric, but the purpose was clear.

It was a dress cut in the classical Greek style.

So she was going to be the Oracle, whether she liked it or not.

That has always been your destiny.

Elle rolled her eyes. The voices were going to take some getting used to. She dropped the fabric back into the box, and looked down at her feet. They were covered in gray streaks of dirt, and the soles were black.

Remember, you have the power to control men. It is through you, because of you, that they gain power. It lies within your gift to take that power away too. Remember that your responsibility lies with ensuring that power is used for good.

She felt herself fill with a deep sense of pragmatism. She would think about Marsh and her father later. The voices were right. There were more important factors at play here. It was ultimately up to her. And no matter what happened, she was not about to allow these men to take what was not theirs. Abercrombie and Patrice wanted her to make herself ready. Well, she would be ready for them indeed.

With quiet resolution, she pulled off her nightdress and stepped into the warm, fragrant water. If she was going to die, then she may as well look her best for it. And if she managed to escape, then at least she would be dressed enough to get out to the street to find help. Either way, being clean and dressed seemed to be the preferable option at this stage. There was no time left for sentiment.

The chain attached to her shackle clanked against the metal bath as she moved in the water, but she hardly noticed it. Elle was devising a plan.

CHAPTER 49

In the guesthouse, Marsh slipped his carriage cloak over his shoulders and buttoned it up. He pulled on his gloves and put on his hat. It was time to go and he was more than ready.

Inut was loitering by the door with a broom in his hand, pretending to sweep the floor. Marsh turned to the boy and handed him an envelope. "Give this to your father. If I do not return by the end of tomorrow, he is to post it without delay. It is very important. Can you do that?" The boy took the envelope with some reverence and nodded. "Well, then I bid you a good evening, young Inut." Marsh touched the rim of his hat. "You have been most kind and helpful. I will always be grateful for that." He felt a sense of eeriness as he spoke.

Constantinople was settling into the rhythm of early evening as the sun cast its last weak reddish glow along the skyline. The air was filled with the smell of wood smoke and a thousand spicy dinners cooking. Marsh set out at a brisk pace. Even without his abilities, he was good at being inconspicuous. To the world, he looked like any other gentleman tourist seeking out the forbidden pleasures that the city of Constantinople had to offer. Opium dens and houses of ill repute were not hard to find. Apart from the odd surreptitious glance, no one paid him much attention.

He reached one of the many wooden bridges that connected the city. Two royal guards were looking out at the river. He held his breath and willed himself to stroll casually past them. At the other side of the bridge he looked back briefly. The soldiers hadn't looked at him, but he wasn't going to tempt fate by loitering. Instead, he turned into a side street and disappeared into the half-light.

Thanks to the faun's map, he managed to find the square again without too much difficulty. The Judas tree stood lonely and bare in the blue-gray light that filled the space between sunset and complete darkness. Its black branches reached for the sky. The square was deserted, but Marsh decided not to tarry. If his calculations were correct, a full moon would soon be rising tonight. Whatever the Alchemists were planning, it was going to happen tonight. Of this he was sure.

He hoped Elle was all right. A tiny ember of hope glowed inside him.

Quiet as a shadow he stole round the square and ducked into a deserted doorway. The fairy had told him that she had flown out of a grate on top of the tower. He could see the crumbling structure looming up from the middle of the cluster of buildings. The tower must have grown into this villa as buildings were added onto it over the years.

At the other end of the alley, the yellow light of a lantern marked an entrance. A guard in a gray cloak slouched against the doorway. He was no more than a boy, his face still clear and unmarked by runes. An acolyte yet to undergo the ultimate initiation that earned them the scars of their Guild.

This was definitely the right place, then. They could not have advertised it better if they had made posters and pasted them on the walls. He would have to go round the other way to avoid the boy raising the alarm.

Silently, he backtracked to the square and slipped into the alley that ran alongside the building.

He rounded the building in the opposite direction, but it took him a good few minutes to walk all the way. The building was much bigger than it looked.

Quietly Marsh crept up on the boy. Judging from his dejected stance, he must have misbehaved for them to make him stand guard instead of attending what would probably be the biggest ceremony this Order had conducted in centuries. He didn't want to think about the reason for the ceremony tonight. Instead, he reached into his pocket and pulled out a small bottle. Carefully he poured some of the liquid onto his handkerchief. It was a tincture of mandrake root, chloroform and a few other secret ingredients purchased—with the help of Inut—earlier today.

Marsh reached up and grabbed the boy from behind. His eyes widened as Marsh clapped the cloth over his nose and mouth. A few seconds later, the boy slumped against him, limp and unconscious.

Marsh carefully let him down against the doorway. The mixture would leave him out cold for at least six hours, perhaps more. With quick fingers, Marsh felt inside the boy's robes until he found the keys. He unlocked the door. Then he jammed the key into the lock and pushed against it with all of his strength. The key snapped off in the lock. The door would not be locked again in a hurry. With his exit secured, he slipped into the building.

Inside was a narrow passageway that led downhill. It was quiet and empty. Marsh drew a stick of chalk out of his pocket and made a mark on the wall, indicating the direction he was taking. Judging from what he had seen of other Turkish buildings, this one was likely to be like a maze inside. He made another mark on the wall a few paces further on. It was going to be easy to get lost.

He walked down the passage and into another, all the time looking and listening for anything that could lead him to Elle.

Suddenly the sound of voices reached him. Marsh ducked into a dark alcove. He stood very still as an acolyte and a guard walked by. The guard was carrying a tray with an empty bowl and a jug on it.

Marking the wall with his chalk, Marsh walked in the direction they had come from.

He walked until he reached a wooden door with a padlock on it. It was the only door in the corridor that was locked like that. Carefully, he lifted the padlock and examined it. It rattled against the door as he maneuvered it.

There was a shuffling noise, and Marsh froze.

"Who's there?" A man spoke from the other side of the door.

"A friend. Now be quiet."

Marsh pulled the ring of keys out of his pocket and examined them. He selected one and pushed it into the lock. It didn't fit. He tried two more before he felt the click of metal biting into metal. With a swift twist of his wrist, the lock sprang open and he slid the bolt back.

The door creaked open and Marsh took two steps back. He gasped for air and covered his face as a rancid wave of heat and stench assailed him.

The man grabbed him by the arm and pulled him into the cell. He closed the door and slid the bolt into place. "Quick, before they see you."

The man inside the cell had dark red hair, like Elle's, except that it was graying at the temples. He was dressed in a long linen smock that was covered in an array of gory-looking brown and red stains. The smock was held in place by a leather harness around his chest and shoulders. The man also had a contraption that involved a magnifying glass strapped to his head. It made one of his eyes seem grotesquely large compared to the other. Eyes the same color as Elle's.

"Professor Chance, I presume?" Marsh said as soon as he caught his breath. Inside the cell, the stench was even worse.

"Who wants to know?" the man said somewhat nervously.

"Marsh, Hugh Marsh—Viscount of Greychester." Marsh shook the professor's hand. "And I have come from England to rescue you."

The professor shook Marsh's hand. He turned his head and squinted, almost as if he did not believe Marsh was real, and the magnifying glass on his head rattled.

"What on earth have they done to you?" Marsh said as he took in the surroundings. If he breathed through his mouth, he could just about handle the smell . . . but only just.

The professor's cell had been converted into a laboratory. A series of long wooden benches took up most of the space. On top and to the side of the tables was a collection of copper kettles of varying sizes. A network of rubber tubes connected these to one another. Glass iambics and retours filled with spark glowed ominously as they sat clipped onto metal stands.

To one side of the room, Marsh spotted the source of the heat; a large furnace glowed behind a grate, locked with another large padlock. To the side of the furnace, an unmade cot with dirty sheets sat sourly against the wall.

Then he spotted the source of the smell. It was a heap of dead chickens and other small animals, and he did his best not to gag.

"I'm terribly sorry about the ghastly pong in here, old chap, but they made me do it. Those dastardly Alchemists."

Marsh surveyed the carcasses.

"Normally they come to take them away," the professor said, "but no one has been yet this afternoon, so I do apologize. They do look rather horrible, don't they?"

Marsh nodded.

"They were already dead when they brought them to me, you know. I am supposed to fill them with spark, to get them going again. The study of re-animation alchemy, they call it. Lazarus electro-biology and thaumaturgy. Not my field of expertise, as you can see."

He pulled the magnifying glass back over his eye. "I think I've done it though. Look here, if you wire up the animation candidate with wires to the center point—..."

"Professor!"

The professor looked up from his experiments. "Yes?"

"How long have you been here, sir?"

The professor shook his head. "I'm not entirely sure. It was night. There was a train involved. We traveled due east, I think." He shook his head again. "I haven't seen the sun, so I don't know how long. Days, I think probably. I don't—I can't remember, but I think I made a note." He muttered and rifled through the notes and bits of paper that were strewn in between the apparatus.

"Let's take a moment, shall we." Marsh led the professor to the cot and sat him down. "I am a friend of your daughter."

The professor looked at Marsh sharply. "Eleanor?"

Marsh took a step back. The professor's magnified eye, so close to him, was somewhat disconcerting.

"Oh, sorry." The professor pulled the headpiece off and put it onto the bench.

"Yes, Eleanor."

The professor looked suspicious. "How do you know her? You look familiar. Do I know you?"

"She and I traveled here to look for you."

"Then where is she?" he asked, looking around.

"Professor," Marsh said, as gently as he could. "These

people, the Alchemists, they have Eleanor. I am sorry, but they managed to intercept us on the way here and they have taken her prisoner."

The professor stared at him in horror. "But Ellie's at home in England. She was due back for a week off from her flight duties. We were going to work on the flying machine." His voice wavered. Suddenly he looked up at Marsh. "Mrs. Hinges." He grabbed Marsh by the arm. "Is Mrs. Hinges all right? Please tell me these monsters have left her unharmed."

Marsh gripped the professor's hand. "Mrs. Hinges is fine. I've left her in the care of my most trusted man. And from what I can tell, she is a woman who is quite capable of caring for herself."

The professor nodded. "Yes, I suppose that she is."

The older man seemed fragile, like his mind wasn't entirely whole. There was no way of telling what the Alchemists had inflicted on him, but for now Marsh hoped his absentmindedness was not permanent.

"Professor, you need to understand something. I believe that they have taken Elle for an altogether more sinister reason. Your daughter is a very special woman. You do know she is the . . . well, the Oracle?"

The professor's eyes widened. "How do you know about that?"

"It is a long story. I am a Warlock."

The professor stared at him. "So you've finally found us."

"I fear that they are planning to use Elle to rip open a hole in our reality. They want the world to flood with power, so they can wield it for their own dark needs."

"Oh, I know all about that plan. Frankly, I think it's quite insane." The professor's eyes grew misty. "Vivienne and I tried so hard to keep Elle away from all of this. My wife would have been so terribly upset if she were alive to see this." He covered his face in his hands.

Marsh patted his shoulder. "I'm sorry."

"It has happened then, hasn't it? Elle has received her gift."

Marsh nodded. "She has."

"We tried to shield her in the hope that it might skip a generation, you know?" his voice trailed off.

Marsh gripped the man's arm. "Sometimes we cannot get away from who and what we are. But right now, she needs our help. And we have to see if we can find her before it's too late." Marsh considered briefly if it might be better to leave the professor locked in the cell while he continued his search.

"Well, what are you waiting for, then, man?" The professor gave Marsh a nudge. "And while we're at it, let's find a way to get this thing off me." He pulled at the shackle around his ankle.

Marsh looked up in surprise.

"Smartly, now, we don't have all day," the professor said. "We're not going to get very far with that glum attitude."

Marsh pulled out the ring of keys and tried them one by one. None of them fitted.

"Blast," said Marsh, as he yanked the last key out of the lock.

"I have a better idea," the professor said. He motioned at the workbench. "Do you know how to use spark?"

"I do indeed." Marsh picked up one of the cylinders and held it up to the light. Getting an accurate blast of spark without electrocuting the professor was going to take all of his concentration. He held the cylinder up, ready to smash it.

"Good grief man, not like that. You'll kill me for sure." The professor looked horrified. "Hand me that machine on the desk and I'll show you my invention."

On the table was a contraption that looked like a cross

between a concertina and a small bellows with a pipe attached to it. Marsh picked it up and studied it.

The professor smiled. "One of my first experiments . . . It caused the original subject to incinerate, so they weren't interested in it, but I've thought of a few new applications since. I haven't been able to think of a way of doing this on my own, or else I would have liberated myself by now." The professor grabbed hold of the contraption and slid the glass cylinder of spark into the back of the bellows. "You hold it like so." He demonstrated. "Then you aim the nozzle at whatever it is that you wish to blast and then, with a bit of concentration . . . *Kazam!*" He pushed the bellows and a beam of spark shot out of the nozzle. It burned a hole in the floor. "The trigger mechanism could do with some refining, but on the whole, it works."

Marsh stepped back. The professor smiled triumphantly and handed the contraption to Marsh.

"Try aiming at the chain first, I'm not sure I want you to aim this thing at my foot just yet."

"Couldn't agree with you more." Marsh held on to the machine. Feeling his center, he focused on the spark in the tube. The energy felt rough and scratchy compared to his own Warlock power, but it would do. He pressed the bellows.

A pure blue line of spark shot out of the nozzle and melted right through the chain. Blobs of molten iron sizzled on the flagstones.

"By golly, that was impressive. With the right amount of tweaking, think of what the army could do with this. We could build a pistol that shoots rays of spark instead of bullets. Think of the possibilities," the professor said as he unraveled the chain from the loop in the shackle.

Marsh put the machine aside. "Indeed, but I don't think we should leave that lying around for the Alchemists to find and use."

The professor's face fell. "You are quite right. We'll take it with us!"

Marsh started laughing. "You know what? I think that is just about the best idea I've heard all day." He hoisted the spark blaster up and onto his shoulder. The spark glugged up and down in the tube and Marsh put out a hand to still it.

"Hmm. I must remember to make a note to think of a better carrying harness or strap," the professor said.

With the spark blaster in place, Marsh opened the door and peeked out into the passage. He stepped out into the quiet passage. "Professor!" He called after a few tense moments. The professor appeared at the doorway, without his smock. Marsh watched him as he carefully locked the door.

"What on earth are you doing?" Marsh said.

"Now they will never know our secret." The professor tapped the side of his head.

"Quite."

"They always go this way when they leave. I've watched them. We must hurry. There are only about two hours left."

Marsh was not entirely sure what the professor was on about, but there was no time to wonder. They needed to find Elle.

CHAPTER 50

The moon was rising. Silver light ran like mercury down the walls of the cell. They were coming for her. Elle heard them chanting in a low hum as they walked slowly down the stairs. Every nerve in her body was on edge.

A key turned in the lock.

She stood and straightened the blue dress. Not good for running in, she thought as she looked down. The wispy fabric draped over her curves and pooled in soft folds at her feet. In ordinary circumstances she would almost have been impressed by the effect, but right now she was too terrified.

The door opened slowly.

An Alchemist with his hood pulled low over his face stepped forward. The others formed a circle and bowed their heads in reverence. This time they were all dressed in gray robes, the hems embroidered with runes in fine silver thread. She recognized the leader as he stepped forward. Abercrombie.

Abercrombie lifted his hood and his smile made her shudder.

"Cybele. You are ready. It is indeed an honor to be escorting you."

She held her head high and tried to look down her nose at him, but he was taller than her.

"You will forgive me, but I prefer not to speak to strangers without the proper introduction," she said.

"Oh, there is no need to be haughty. You and I are old friends in the Shadow plane." He leered at her.

"You are no friend of mine."

"Very well. Allow me to introduce myself, then. Sir Eustace Abercrombie, at your service." He took her hand and bowed formally over it.

Elle pulled her hand away and held it in a fist tightly at her side. For a split second, she contemplated punching the man in the nose, but he was bigger than her and she was outnumbered. She was not going to give them an excuse to hurt her any more than was necessary.

Abercrombie stood back and ran his gaze up and down over her. "So majestic, don't you think?" He spoke to someone behind him without taking his eyes off her.

Another hooded figure stepped forward. His pale skin was luminous in the lamplight. "Indeed, she is magnificent." He spoke with a French accent—Parisian, if her ears did not deceive her. He turned his head and a lock of long silky black hair escaped from the side of the hood. Her eyes widened with surprise.

"Aleix? Is that you?"

He inclined his head slightly. She could see his eyes glimmer in the shadow of his hood.

She noticed Patrice standing next to Aleix. His hood was pulled over his forehead, but there was no mistaking the moustache. "Eleanor. In the French Foreign Legion they have a saying: There are no friends in the desert. And you would agree that we Shadow-dwellers find ourselves in a rather savage desert, in a manner of speaking. In fact, we are in the desert and you are the oasis. An oasis of power that we all thirst to drink from." A few of the others murmured in agreement.

Abercrombie chuckled. "Oh, my dear, don't look so hurt. What is a little conspiracy amongst friends when there is so much to gain?" There was another murmur of agreement. She could almost touch their eagerness.

Abercrombie continued. "I had you pictured as being more plucky. And yet, here you are, all meek and mild."

Elle looked at Patrice. "I will never forgive you for this. And you will not take what you want from me. I will resist to the end."

Abercrombie's laugh filled the cell. "That would be absolutely fine with us. If this is how you choose it to be, then so be it. I would like to mention though, that you do have another option. It would be terribly unsporting for us to misinform you in this regard."

"And what might that be?"

Abercrombie met her gaze. "Join forces with us. Join us and we will make you our queen. You will have more power and riches than you ever dreamt of. We will make you like the majestic high Oracles of the days of old. And in return, you will grant us the power we need to finally be free."

"You mean you would put me on a pedestal and pamper me like some prize cow while you drain me dry until I outlive my usefulness? I think not." She felt herself grow angry despite her fear.

He laughed again. "There is no need to be so cynical. You would receive no different treatment from your precious Warlocks." He grew serious. "So what is it going to be? Are you to join us, or are we going to have to do this the hard way? The choice is entirely yours, dear girl. Either way, you will give us what we want before the sun rises tomorrow."

She knew they were lying to her about the proposal, but where the truth ended and where the lies began in all this was anybody's guess. It was all so confusing. She closed her eyes and thought about Marsh. How she would never be able to tell him how sorry she was for the things she had said. She thought about her dear sweet eccentric father. Who would talk to him about mathematics and flight theory? And Mrs. Hinges? Who would make sure she was taken care of?

They can all manage by themselves.

The voices were right. The world would manage without her. But before it did, she would have to rid the world of these evil men and whatever it was that they were planning. She was not about to let them succeed, even if it was the last thing she did.

Suddenly an awesome sense of power filled her and when she spoke her voice had a resonance that was not her own. "Alchemist, you will not take from me what you have no permission to take. By the power that my mothers before me command, all you do shall be returned to you threefold." A sudden gust of air whirled around the cell. A few of the cloaked figures shifted slightly and looked at one another.

Abercrombie started laughing. "How magnificent you are. You look like a goddess in that dress, with your hair all around you. But alas, I must call a halt to matters now. Enough of the brave games. The moon is rising and we have important business to attend to."

He reached over and touched his fingers to the center of Elle's forehead. Hot alchemy flashed against her skin. She resisted for an instant, but her feeble barriers didn't hold. Suddenly she was far away from her own body. She watched her knees buckle under her.

Hands caught her and lifted her up onto the flower-adorned litter they had ready and waiting outside the door. A wreath of flowers was pushed into her hair. She was borne away in time to the deep-toned death chant of Alchemists. Then everything went black.

CHAPTER 51

Marsh and the professor found themselves walking down a narrow alcove-lined passageway. The corridor sloped steadily downhill and it became darker and closer as they walked.

"What is this place?"

"It is an avenue of meditation," Marsh said. His voice bounced off the walls.

"But why the alcoves?"

"Blood rituals. The Alchemists believe that pain and blood brings them closer to the power their rituals give them. These spaces in the walls are for that. Apparently, an act of bloodletting in each one of these alcoves completes the path to enlightenment. They say blood binds Nightwalker and Alchemist together."

"Extraordinary." The professor peered at the dark walls.

Suddenly, the deep sound of chanting reverberated through the passageway. Marsh stopped and dragged the professor into one of the alcoves. He signaled for them to be silent.

The professor nodded. They both listened for a moment, but the chant echoed off the alcoves and the stone of the walls, making it impossible to pinpoint the direction it came from. Suddenly the chanting stopped.

"What was that?" said the professor.

"The ceremony is about to begin," Marsh murmured. A bubble of worry was starting to form in his chest. He knew enough Alchemistic to know a death-chant when he heard one.

Checking that the coast was clear, they stepped out of the alcove and into the passageway. Marsh glanced over his shoulder. They were horribly exposed here in the corridor, with nowhere to hide but the creepy alcoves that flanked them. Anyone passing would immediately recognize them, despite the fact that the professor had taken off his horrible smock and magnifying glass.

"We need to find cover. Let's go this way." Marsh motioned for the professor to follow. Their footfall clop-clopped loudly on the flagstones.

They kept walking until they found another passage that led off the main corridor they were following. Marsh made another mark on the wall with his chalk, but his plan to use the white marks to navigate was proving to be useless.

"This place is worse than a maze. How on earth do these people find their way about?" The professor's voice echoed off the walls.

Marsh gave him a harsh look and put his finger to his lips.

"Oh, yes, of course. Sorry. How quickly one forgets." He lowered his voice to a whisper.

"It is very quiet. I suspect that they are all gathered for whatever secret ceremony they have planned. No Alchemist would want to miss whatever they are doing to-night."

"I think you might be right. Normally there are many more of them. I heard them walking up and down the passageways at night."

Marsh unhitched the blaster and put it down on the ground. The spark in the cylinder made a galumphing sound as the blaster settled on the ground. He flexed his shoulder. The thing was turning out to be rather heavy and uncomfortable and his ribs were starting to hurt again.

"So which way should we be going?" the professor asked.

Marsh looked up and down the tunnel. "Elle is being held in the tower in the center of the building. That would be due east, which I believe is that way. But I can't be sure. This place is very odd." He pulled the brass compass Elle had lent him out of his pocket and held it up in the gloom to take a bearing. The needle swiveled round and round as if it was wound by clockwork. "Well, that's no use, is it?"

"I say, is that my compass?" the professor said.

Marsh blushed. "I do believe it is. Elle lent it to me. But the tunnels must be guarded by some sort of hex."

"Or magnetic field." The professor peered over Marsh's elbow at the compass. "Which way were we heading when we started?"

Marsh closed the compass and put it back in his pocket. "I thought it was east, but now I'm not so sure. Looks like we are going to have to survive on our wits for the time being, professor."

Professor Chance peered down the dark passage. "Let me see. We are walking down the passage, which appears to be straight, but we keep ending up in the perpendicular direction."

"Must be some sort of trick to stop people from escaping."

The professor walked a few paces down the passage, turned around and then walked back. "I have it," he said.

Marsh looked at him, not comprehending.

"It's a circular labyrinth!" He bent down and drew a line in the dust on the floor. "I think the passageways are wound up on themselves. We appear to be walking round and round, each time turning back on ourselves. It is one continuous spiral, with intersecting shortcuts.

We could walk here for an eternity and never know it."
He pointed at the passage they had taken. "Unless we
know a shortcut, like that one."

"And how did you work that out?"

The professor smiled. "Simple. The ones who brought
me food and the dead animals kept on complaining about
the labyrinth and how tedious it was to walk the whole
route."

"Professor, has anyone ever told you that you are a
genius?"

"Oh, I wouldn't go that far." The professor smiled in
triumph.

Suddenly the passageway echoed with voices. Marsh
grabbed the spark-blaster and the professor and took
the side passage.

"Look, a doorway," the professor said.

Marsh tried the handle and the door slipped open and
they stepped into the darkness. The voices grew louder
and a group of young Alchemists in robes walked by.
Marsh and the professor held their breaths as they listened to the voices echo in the passageway. Holding the
door open slightly, Marsh watched the swirl of robes as
they went by. "We need to follow them."

He felt the professor tug at his sleeve.

"What is it?"

"Look," said the professor. He pointed off into the
dark.

Marsh turned and went very still. They were not
alone.

Two red eyes glowed at them from the darkness. He
could feel the dark power swirling around them, thick
and viscous.

"What are you doing in my lair, Warlock?" a croaky
voice said. He felt the professor step behind him.

"My apologies. I did not know that this place was
yours," Marsh said formally. It was always a good idea

to address the Shadow formally. At least until one knew who, or what, one was addressing.

"But now you have found out, Warlock."

A ball of light appeared in the middle of the room. It radiated out and cast shadows on the walls.

The professor peered out from behind Marsh and gasped. "Look at that."

Marsh removed his hat and bowed deeply. "Again, might I offer my apologies, changeling. We did not know that this was your abode. With your leave, we shall be on our way now."

The changeling's eyes flickered. It was a spindly creature with skinny arms and legs. Its greenish skin glowed pale in the light. As it moved, its distended abdomen shifted. It looked like an ancient baby with the body of a spider.

"What on earth is that?" the professor whispered.

The changeling peered at them with its slanted eyes. Slightly pointed ears poked out through its black hair. Marsh did his best to hide the revulsion that was forming and creeping up the base of his spine. "It's a changeling."

"Why is it called a changeling?"

Marsh sighed. "Changelings are the punishment the universe metes out for trifling with the Shadow. They were called baby-stealers in old folktales. Now please be quiet so I can get us out of here."

"Not so fast, Warlock. I demand tribute," the changeling interrupted them.

Marsh held his breath. "I am sorry, but we have none to give."

The changeling sneered, revealing a row of sharp and rather horrible-looking little teeth. "Well, how very unfortunate for you. I would think that a handsome Warlock like yourself would have been more . . . resourceful. I am quite fond of hearts." A sly smile crossed its face.

Marsh realized with no small measure of unease that

the changeling was female. And female changelings ate their mates after they were done with them.

"I am sorry, my lady, but my heart is promised to another. It is no longer mine to give."

The professor looked at him. "Is that true?"

"Not now," Marsh said out of the corner of his mouth.

"Hmm . . . the true love of a war sorcerer. How delicious," the changeling said. She shuffled forward and stuck her tongue out, tasting the air around them. She seemed to be paying particular attention to the air around Marsh.

Marsh held very still, but angled his face away from her. She smelled like rotting strawberries.

"Hmm." She smacked her black lips. "The Warlock speaks the truth. Strong love. Very strong," she muttered to herself and shuffled back to the nest of rags she had been sitting in. The professor peered out from behind Marsh.

The changeling settled among the rags and folded her arms. "Now, why should I release you when it would give me so much pleasure to detain you here?" She rubbed her belly with her spiny fingers. "My belly aches with loneliness, Warlock. What am I to do?"

"It would bring you no pleasure keeping us here," Marsh said.

"Oh, but I disagree . . . if only to see you suffer."

"What do we do now?" the professor said. He was rattling on the door but the latch seemed to be stuck.

"You don't, by any chance, have an egg or an acorn in any of your pockets, do you?" Marsh asked the professor.

The professor patted his waistcoat. "I'm sorry, but I'm afraid I do not."

"Well then, I fear we are in for a rather unpleasant wait." Marsh was only slightly amused at the fact that the professor had actually checked his pockets before answering. "I was hoping we could make it vanish."

"And how would we do that?"

"Well, we could brew beer in an acorn or an eggshell. If legend is to be believed, the creature would say 'Well, I've never seen the likes of that,' and disappear. Or we could shove it into an oven."

The professor considered the matter. "Neither plan seems executable at this point."

"Quite." Marsh kept an eye on the creature. Changelings could move very fast if they wanted to. This one looked as if it was poised for action.

Suddenly he felt a massive surge of power. It pulsed through the building.

The changeling shrieked and shrank back into the shadows.

"Elle. That has to be her," Marsh said.

"What? How do you know that?" the professor said.

Marsh grabbed his arm. "Professor, you need to trust me. On the count of three, shove the door open as forcefully as you can, all right?"

The professor nodded.

The changeling was still cowering in her nest. He lifted the spark-blaster, balanced it on his shoulder and pushed the bellows.

"Open the door and tell me how to get out of this labyrinth, changeling, and I will let you live."

The changeling stopped cowering. "Why should I say?"

A stream of spark-light hit the ledge the changeling was sitting on. She screamed in pain.

"Tell me," Marsh said.

"Follow the black stones. The ones in the walls, they lead the way," the changeling wheezed. "Make it stop, war sorcerer. Make it stop!" The changeling squirmed out of the light.

"Three. Run!"

And for the second time in so many days, Marsh and the professor ran for their lives.

At the end of the corridor, they stopped for breath.

"Do you think that creature will follow us?" said the professor, looking back over his shoulder.

"I doubt it. They tend to be territorial. Let's hope that if she does survive the spark-blaster, we won't be worth the effort. But I for one am not in favor of waiting about to see what else might be living in these tunnels."

"Agreed. Look, a black stone. And there is another one."

As they walked, the professor looked at the blaster. The spark cylinder was two-thirds empty. "Well, at least we know we can get at least three clear shots from a machine of this size. I must remember to make a note of that."

The low hum of chant suddenly resumed. Marsh stood very still and listened.

"Come, professor, there is no time to lose."

They followed the black stones and the sound of the chanting. The long winding passage seemed to stretch ahead for miles. The professor looked up and pointed at the fine roots that were pushing through the stone in the roof. "I gather that we are underground. Possibly underwater too, by the looks of things." Water was dripping from the tunnel roof, making the floor slippery underfoot.

"And we also seem to be heading away from the tower." Marsh felt a sense of growing unease.

The floor in the tunnel was rising again. The air smelled fresher.

Suddenly, Marsh stopped and sank onto his haunches. He motioned for the professor to be quiet and pointed at the flickering shadows that could only be torchlight playing on the walls. The professor narrowed his eyes and nodded.

Slowly, they crawled ahead.

A blast of fresh air met them as they reached the end

of the stone passage. Marsh paused and motioned to the professor to crawl up beside him. They looked over the ledge. Marsh swore softly as he took in the sight before him.

"Oh, my word," the professor breathed.

Below them, a row of narrow stairs led down into a crumbling amphitheater. In places, the sandstone had been chopped away to reveal a circle of black stones. They stood out like rotting teeth in a gaping mouth.

The deep rhythm of the Alchemists' chant filled the air. The procession of robed figures was coming from the tunnel on the other side. Half of them were dressed in gray, the other half in black. They filled the bottom rows of stone seats as more and more of them entered in double file.

And in the center of the amphitheater, where the old Greek stage used to be, was a circular stone altar. It was covered in strange symbols and decorated with flowers. Marsh did not have to think hard on its purpose.

The chanting rose up again. Another group of robed figures appeared. They were carrying a litter. Marsh caught a glimpse of pale skin and blue silk nestled between the flowers on the litter and his heart leapt into his throat.

He had found Elle.

The litter halted and they lowered her onto the stone. Her eyes were closed and she wasn't moving.

She moved her head when they touched her. With a wave of relief, Marsh realized that she was alive. He rested his head against the wall and thanked the gods for that.

The chanting stopped abruptly. One of the Alchemists signaled. Six others approached, wheeling a large object covered in gold cloth into the stone circle.

The fabric slithered away to reveal a machine made of brass and glass tubes. Its insides glowed and the whole thing puffed and thrummed. Two assistants set about connecting large rubber tubes that encircled the altar. Billows of steam escaped as the pipes slid into place. When the last tube was in place, spark started crackling in blue circles around the bottom of the altar. The room grew hushed and silent with expectation.

"What on earth are they doing?" the professor muttered.

"They are waiting for the appointed time."

Marsh felt the professor lurch forwards as he spotted Elle, and he gripped his arm, motioning for him to keep still.

"We have to stop this madness! We must stop it now, before it's too late."

The chanting resumed in a low hum as the last three of the figures at the very end of the entourage stepped forward. They took up their places next to the altar.

The chanting stopped. In the silence, the three threw their hoods back to reveal their faces in the wavering light.

Patrice! Marsh felt his blood boil as he looked down at the figures next to the altar. "I am going to kill him with my bare hands."

The professor looked at him. "What was that?"

"Nothing. Nothing at all." Then he recognized the man next to Patrice and his blood ran cold. It was Aleix, the Nightwalker from Paris.

"Nightwalkers," the professor breathed. "How extraordinary. And who is that next to him?"

"You don't want to know," Marsh said.

"Who *is* that man?" The professor pointed at the third figure. "Look at the markings on his face. It's extraordinary."

Marsh ground his teeth. "That, professor, is Eustace Abercrombie, Overlord of the Alchemists."

CHAPTER 52

The chanting ceased and Elle opened her eyes. She felt like she was floating in midair and the flickering light of the torches made her dizzy. Cold stone pressed against her back as they lowered the litter onto the altar. Heavy, humid air pressed down on her, making her skin slick with moisture. The energy of so many Shadow creatures in one space swirled and pressed heavily against her.

Her teeth started chattering with fear. She clenched them together as hard as she could.

The chanting reverberated through her bones.

Cold metal shackles clamped round her wrists and ankles, biting into her skin as she was pinned to the stone. She wrestled down a fresh wave of claustrophobia. This was not the time for panicking.

Three cloaked figures stepped forward. Aleix, Patrice and Abercrombie lifted their hoods to reveal their faces to the crowd.

Abercrombie took another step forward. His raised arms looked absurdly thin and pale as they poked out from under the folds of his robes.

"My brother Alchemists." His voice boomed through the amphitheater. "Tonight we stand at the doorway of a new beginning. For centuries, our people have been persecuted and abused. The power that was once ours alone has been stolen, leaving us weak. For too long, we have been treated no better than slaves. Slaves to masters who were completely oblivious to our true power."

A murmur passed through the crowd. The black-robed attendees turned to one another and shook their heads. This was no way for day-keepers to speak.

Abercrombie spoke again. This time, his voice rose and filled the amphitheater. "Tonight, I stand before the Nightwalkers with an ultimatum. In a gesture of respect for the centuries we have spent together, I am now offering you the opportunity to make amends. I now ask you to throw aside the pact of servitude that has bound us together for too long and make restitution." He gestured at Aleix. "I ask you to do this as your brother has done. From this night on we are no longer master and servant, but equals."

A murmur of uncertainty rippled through the assembly. One of the robed figures stood and pointed at Aleix. "He has betrayed us. He must be made to see the sun. Get him!"

Abercrombie stretched out his arms. "I command you to make the choice now. Choose or face the consequences!"

"There are no consequences. If you breach the pact, we will retaliate," another robed figure spoke.

Abercrombie laughed. It was a breathless sound. "With the help of modern science we, the Hermetic Order of the Celestial Alchemists, will seize the power that the Shadow realm holds and then we will blend it with the Light. We will unlock and take back what was taken from us. And with it, we will destroy those who would see us destroyed. We will take what is ours by birthright. Behold the Machine!"

Patrice pulled a lever and the machine lit up, its parts expanding behind him until the thing was monstrous and tall as a church organ, an ominous column of brass and riveted glory.

The robed figures roared. The Alchemists in gray resumed their chanting. The Nightwalkers sneered and bared their fangs. A scuffle broke out between a few of the Nightwalkers and Alchemists who were seated near each other. The Alchemists drew stakes from their robes and started stabbing at their neighbors.

Aleix turned to Abercrombie. "This is not what was agreed. You said they would be spared."

In the front row, a group of Nightwalkers stood up. Their faces were contorted with anger. Elle watched Abercrombie signal his guards.

"Your elders are trapped, Nightwalker. There is nothing they can do to stop us now." He turned to the crowd. "My Brothers, let the Reclamation begin!" With a great flourish, he produced the wooden brass-edged box from the folds in his robes and held it aloft. It was the same box Patrice had given to Elle in Paris.

"Behold!" Abercrombie held the box aloft and the drumming and chanting ceased. The brawlers stopped and looked at him.

"In my hands, I hold the most sacred item known to our Order." Some of the scuffling ceased as the crowd stopped to stare at the box.

Patrice stepped forward and grabbed Elle's arm. His lips moved in a silent incantation and with a gentle click, the clasp of the bracelet sprang open.

"You've been able to do that all this time?" she croaked.

Patrice ignored her as he pulled the bracelet off her arm. He handed it to Abercrombie, reverently, with both hands.

Abercrombie carefully laid the row of diamonds onto the top of the box, aligning them with the brass edges. There was a soft click and the lid of the box slipped open. Abercrombie held the box aloft.

"In my hands I hold pure carmot. And with its power, we will rule this world as masters. Our time as slaves has ended."

The Alchemists cheered.

Abercrombie signaled and Patrice stepped forward. "After years of searching, we have found a Cybele strong enough to withstand the challenge that lies before her. She will be the one from which our newfound power is birthed."

Again the crowd roared with approval. Some of the Nightwalkers had started fighting their way out of the stands, but guards met them, waiting at the entrances. One or two tried to break free, but were restrained and wrestled to the ground.

Abercrombie started chanting a series of strange words. The incantation grew in volume as he spoke, amplified by the energy that swirled around them. Carefully, he opened the glass-fronted door at the top of the machine. Gently, as if they were bird eggs, he placed the chunks of carmot into the little chamber and closed the door. For all the fuss, they were just gray, nondescript lumps.

Abercrombie gave Patrice a nod.

Patrice pulled the other levers on the side of the machine with a flourish and the machine hummed to life. Bright blue spark ran up the tubes that stuck out of its sides and collected in the crystal dome at the top. The insides of the machine started whirring, while small plumes of steam leaked from its flanks.

Elle felt the energy of two realms swirl through her, blending together into something that was black and sinister. She felt like she was caught in a rush of water. It stung, threatening to tear straight through her.

She gritted her teeth. She was not about to give these men the satisfaction of seeing her suffer.

The energy filled her, rising up inside her chest. Pressure built up and expanded, straining against muscle and bone. It grew, threatening to explode out of her, and waves of pain ripped through her. Something wet trickled out of her nose and she tasted salt and copper in her mouth.

I must stop this. I must not let them take hold of this power. They are not worthy of such.

Abercrombie raised his arms again. "My Brothers, the Oracle speaks!" The crowd cheered.

Elle suddenly realized that she had uttered her thoughts, but that no one seemed to understand what she had said. Words were forming in her head and with detached fascination she realized that she did not know the language either. The words were sitting inside her, tightly packed like seeds in a pod, just waiting to burst free.

She braced herself as she felt another wave of energy. It pulsed through her with excruciating intensity.

The entire amphitheater started trembling. She looked up. A dark shadow had formed over the altar. Slowly it gained momentum until it became a swirling vortex directly above her. Blue bolts of energy crackled around the edges. Through the haze, the dark shapes of unspeakable creatures swirled around in its depths. They were the specters of malevolence that languished in the darkest parts of the Shadow realm.

Elle felt something incorporeal inside her tear. This thing was stretching her so that she felt as if she was about to disintegrate.

She clenched her fists and closed her eyes. She needed to stop these things from entering the world if it was the last thing she did. And it was going to take every bit of her resolve to do it.

CHAPTER 53

Marsh stared at Elle on the altar below like a man in a trance. This could not be happening. He would not let it happen. Not to her. Not now.

A terrible sound reverberated through the amphitheater. It was as if someone had torn through the fragile membrane of reality that separated this world from the other. Shadow magic and dark energy poured through the vortex. It spilled into the amphitheater and pooled around the altar. He cast another look around the amphitheater. The Alchemists and Nightwalkers stared at the vortex, some of them open-mouthed.

There were hundreds of them. Even with the massive distraction playing out before them, Marsh and the professor were outnumbered many times over.

If he managed to draw from the power swirling about to fight them, it would mean that his enemies would do so too. There was no way he could wield enough power to attack and defeat all of the Alchemists assembled before him.

Elle screamed and his blood curdled as he watched on, helpless.

"We have to stop them, Mr. Marsh. We have to," the professor said.

"I know." A plan was growing in his mind.

Abercrombie suddenly turned his gaze away from the vortex and looked up to where Marsh and the professor were crouching.

"I know you are there, Warlock. You know you can do nothing to stop us now." He started laughing.

A number of Alchemists turned away from the ceremony and looked up at the stairs. Their eyes were hollow and empty, their bodies mesmerized by the power swirling around them.

"I wouldn't be so sure of myself if I were you, Abercrombie!" He stood up from behind the little wall and straightened his shoulders. He had lived a long time, but none of those years seemed to matter now. A strange calm settled upon him. He would die right here if it meant he could save Eleanor.

He closed his eyes, focused on finding his center. He needed to draw up whatever power he could in one go. There would be no second chances today.

"What are you doing?" The professor grabbed his leg. "Get down, for goodness sake."

"Stand well back, professor. The dark energy the Alchemists are calling forth will most likely cause me to burst into flames when I draw on it. I don't want you to get hurt."

"Good heavens, man. Have you gone quite mad?"

Marsh didn't answer. Light and Shadow energy always flowed together. They were like two sides of a coin, the one unable to exist without the other. Hopefully he could draw out enough of the one to stop the other before it was too late. His face twisted in a wry smile. "We need to shut that machine off somehow. And I think a flaming Warlock might just be what the situation demands, professor."

"Now, hold on for just a minute," the professor said. He grabbed Marsh by the arm and pulled him down to the ground, next to him.

"What are you doing?" he hissed at the professor.

Abercrombie started laughing again. "What's wrong,

Warlock? Have you lost your nerve? Your kind always were cowards."

"Don't do that." Marsh took off his hat and ran his hand through his hair. It was slick with sweat.

"Perhaps you should try this, before you needlessly cause yourself to combust."

"What is it?"

"As the inventor of the machine that these villains are currently using, I must insist that I might be of assistance."

Marsh shook his head. "You built that thing?"

"I did. Why do you think I am here? I told you that electro-biology was not my field. They gave me that work to keep me busy."

"And what does it do?"

"Oh, it is an ephemeral multidimensional energy amplifier and necromantic reanimator."

"A what?"

"A machine that rips open the different planes of reality and reanimates dead things and other spirit-type beasties," the professor said. "The dead-things bit being an accidental but surprisingly appealing by-product of the energy process," he said.

"And why do they need Elle if they have a machine?"

"According to my calculations, the Oracle acts as a magical lightning rod for the machine. Too much power is flowing out of the Shadow realm into the Light. Something to control and channel the overflow is needed. Without her, the machine will overload and explode."

"Why didn't you say something sooner?" Marsh hissed.

"My dear boy, you will forgive me for being somewhat shocked at the spectacle that is playing out before us. For heaven's sake, that's my daughter down there. And besides, you never asked."

Marsh sighed. "So how do we turn the machine off?"

"Take this. I'm so glad I went back to collect it when

we left my rather unpleasant little laboratory." He handed Marsh a metal prong that looked like a piano tuning fork.

"And?"

"Oh yes, of course, you haven't seen the plans, now, have you. It is a safety switch. Hence the reason why I named the machine an *ephemeral* energy amplifier. You see, the machine kept overheating during my trials and so I needed a way to shut if off quickly, before it exploded. There is one problem though . . ." The professor went quiet.

"And what is . . . the problem?"

"You need to be close enough to insert it into the slot next to the big lever. Now, hurry, and get down there. We have no time to lose." The professor glanced over his shoulder and down the corridor.

Marsh lifted the spark-blaster. "Do you know what the range on this thing is?"

The professor looked at the blaster. "Well, I've only tested it in the cell, but I think it could safely cover about ten yards. I'm not sure how accurate it would be if one were to aim any further."

Marsh pulled the Colt out of its holster under his coat and cocked it. The professor peered over his shoulder and his face lit up with recognition. "Why, that is Elle's. I got it for her when she started flying. To keep her safe." He looked at Marsh. "Is it loaded?"

Marsh nodded. "It is loaded, but there are only four rounds left. Elle used one to defend herself. You had better hang on to both. Cover me as best you can. And if they come for you, shoot them to the underworld, all right? And run. Whatever you do, do not let them take you alive. Do you understand?"

The professor nodded. "I'll do my best."

The professor gripped the spark-blaster. He glanced over at the altar. "Do you think they have hurt her?"

"I'm not sure." Marsh was doing his best not to give in to the rage and panic he was feeling.

There was a whooshing sound as the storm gained momentum. Elle cried out again. This time her voice was weaker.

"Hold my hat," Marsh said. "I'll be right back."

The professor nodded.

Marsh shook the professor's hand. He pulled out a card and handed it to the older man. "This is the address of a guesthouse in the old quarter. There, you will find money and a passage back to London. If I do not make it out alive, I want you to go. Go there and tell them I sent you."

The professor gripped his hand. "Good luck, old chap. It was an honor to have fought with you. Now go and liberate my daughter, before it's too late!"

Marsh stood up from behind the wall. He gathered up some of the black power that was pouring out of the vortex, and which was now sloshing halfway up the amphitheater. It burned his insides like acid, but he held firm.

Abercrombie laughed again as he spotted Marsh. "You are too late, Warlock!"

"It is never too late." Marsh started running down the stairs. He needed to get to the machine before it was too late.

Abercrombie looked at Patrice, who was standing next to the machine. He pointed to Marsh. "Kill him!" he bellowed.

CHAPTER 54

"Kill him!" Abercrombie shouted over the din of the machine. Elle turned her head and looked in the direction in which the Alchemist pointed. Through the fractured light she recognized Marsh. He was running down the stairs, toward her. Patrice stormed round the altar and collided with Marsh in a bone-crunching tackle. Both men rolled down the stairs as they fought each other.

Elle tried to move, but the force engulfing her was like fast-flowing water. She was completely pinned down.

I must be dying, she thought. The guiding voices of the Pythia were silent. There was no one to turn to.

The sound of a thousand worlds ripping apart filled the air. A thick wailing shriek sounded from far away. It was the sound of pure evil. The specs of a thousand malicious creatures hovered above her in the vortex. They shrieked and clawed their way toward her. The rush of energy lifted her off the altar so she was suspended in the air. The black energy spilling out of the vortex rippled through her, down the chains and into the ground, where it shimmered with sinister blackness. Her only anchors to the world were the shackles that held her to the altar. She felt evil clawing and hissing at her. Whatever happened, she had to stop them.

Time and movement slowed down. She felt a violent rush of energy pulse through her. She turned her head in its direction. Abercrombie was standing under her, his arms stretched wide, head thrown back as if in ecstasy.

Runes and symbols crawled under his skin like black spindly insects. A giant ball of raw magic was forming in the space above his outstretched hands. She felt another surge rip through her, leaving her insides raw, on fire.

He's using me to channel this. I am the conduit. I am his source. I am his power.

She focused on the energy around her. It roared in a torrent that ripped through everything. She took a deep breath and poked at it with her will. At her touch, the torrent slowed and cooled. She could control it. It listened to her.

Elle spread her thoughts wide. She wrapped her will around the altar and Abercrombie. She encircled the giant ball of power. Then, with every bit of strength she possessed, she gripped it. The energy contracted. It wound around itself so tightly that it became a black ball. The cloud above Abercrombie's head disappeared. Elle gritted her teeth as the pressure built up inside her. Her insides stretched and bulged like an overfilled water bag. She glanced over at Abercrombie. He was frowning and looking at his hands as if they were the cause for the sudden loss of magic.

Elle felt something inside her give way. The energy was starting to leak out all over. She had to get rid of it. She aimed all of her anger and frustration at the black ball inside her. *This is for my mother. And my father, and for everything you've done to me since Paris!* Then, summoning all her fury, Elle hurled the black ball into the vortex.

The blast of raw energy that issued from her was so intense it turned the air white. The rebound spun out at them and hit Abercrombie square in the chest. Before he could even react, he hurtled straight into the machine. Glass smashed and metal groaned. Spark leaked from the shattered dome and streamed into the vortex. The hum of the machine amplified to a deafening din. Night-walkers and Alchemists were grabbing their ears, screeching in pain.

Then, quite abruptly, the machine cut out.

The glow of spark vanished from the glass dome. The air went still as if in a vacuum. The vortex started collapsing in on itself.

Chaos broke out. Alchemist and Nightwalker alike ran for the exits. The machine shook violently. The impending implosion turned the vortex to a deep pit of blackness from which no light could ever escape. Panicked Alchemists and Nightwalkers trampled one another as they fought to save themselves.

A massive ball of energy ripped through the amphitheater. The vortex started spinning, creating a maelstrom that sucked up everything in its wake. Giant blocks of stone tore out of the walls and disappeared. The machine broke loose from its tethers and flew into the maelstrom. There was a bright flash of light as it exploded.

Marsh dove for the altar. He grabbed hold of Elle. Air rushed by as they looked into one another's faces. "Hold on to me! The shackles will hold us," Elle whispered.

Marsh wrapped his arms around her and they held one another close. The whole amphitheater started shaking. One of the chains that held them popped out of the stone. They hung perilously suspended in midair between the ground and the vortex.

Elle looked at Marsh. "I won't let go! I'll never let you go!" Several of the slower members of the hooded audience flew past the altar as they were sucked screaming into the swirling mass.

She had to stop it before it dragged everything into the dark. Elle threw her head back and let out a cry. It was a primal sound that rippled through everything.

A terrible crash of thunder tore through everything as

the vortex finally imploded. The floor shook and, with a mighty rumble, the amphitheater split in two.

A few more large blocks of stone flew past them into the maelstrom. Air whistled as the vortex sucked itself out of existence, leaving behind nothing but complete and utter silence.

Elle and Marsh fell back down onto the altar. Blood ran from Elle's face. Marsh felt the hot trickle of blood against his hand as it ran out of her ears. She made a little sighing sound and very gently her head rolled back against his chest. Marsh held on to her with a growing sense of horror. Elle was pale and deathly still. He laid his head on her chest. "Please, my brave darling. Please don't be dead," he whispered as he listened for her heart.

A deep booming sound resonated around them and what remained of the amphitheater shook. More stones fell out of the walls and crashed into the middle of the arena.

"Earthquake! We need to vacate the area. This whole structure is going to collapse," the professor yelled. He tugged at Marsh.

"I thought I told you to get out!"

Another stone crashed onto the ground next to him. Gently he let Elle's body slip onto the stone.

"She's gone." He was oblivious to the rocks that rained down around him.

"We need to let her go, lad." The professor spoke softly, as if his heart would break. He wiped his hand across his face, leaving dust-streaked tear marks on his cheeks.

Marsh shook his head. "No. I am not leaving her here." He grabbed hold of a rock and smashed the chains that held her to the stone. They were brittle from all the energy that had coursed through them and they shattered on impact.

A large standing stone toppled and hit a carved pillar. Rocks rained down around them in earnest. Marsh gathered Elle into his arms and they ran for the passageway.

"Professor, you go first. Blast anyone in our way!" he yelled over the noise of falling rubble.

They ran. They ran until the passage turned into a tunnel. They ran until the tunnel ended in a gateway. And in a choked plume of dust, they ran into the small square with the Judas tree to the side of it. Under the tree they stopped, coughing and gasping the cool night air.

Around them the city was in chaos. The smell of burning buildings and broken earth assailed them as the people of Constantinople sought to deal with the earthquake that shook their city.

As gently as he could, Marsh laid Elle down on the cobbles under the tree. Her skin was like the palest ivory in the dusty moonlight around them. Her hair fanned out in the dried leaves. Gently he stroked her cheek. And then, with the slightest of movement, her eyelids flickered open.

"Professor, she's alive!"

The professor crouched down and put his hand on the side of her face. "Oh, Ellie. Stay with us. We will get you some help."

Elle smiled and closed her eyes.

"We need to get off the streets. I know where we can go for the time being," Marsh said. He summoned all of his strength and lifted Elle up into his arms. Together, they stumbled their way down a rubble-strewn alley. At the end of it, they paused to catch their breaths.

Marsh looked down at Elle. Her breathing was shallow and fast, but she was still alive.

"Mister. Marsh! Mister. Marsh. This way!" Marsh looked up. Inut was running toward him. "Mister. Marsh.

I got a little wagon for you. Come, bring the lady. Let's take her to my mother."

"Inut, what are you doing here?"

The boy grinned. "I knew you would be needing some help later. So I fetched my father's barrow. Come. It's this way. Bring the lady. She looks heavy."

And so they carried the greatest Oracle in living memory back to the guesthouse in a barrow borrowed from Inut's father.

CHAPTER 55

Elle floated deep in the soft darkness. She wasn't sure where, but it felt nice. It was a place of perfect silence. In the darkness she was safe. No one could touch her here. She had no name. No body. Nothing mattered. All she needed to do was be. Complete. Weightless. Bliss.

She lay back in the velvety blackness, suddenly aware of a sense of up and down. Something was trying to catch her attention. She did her best to ignore it, but a strange and vague awareness kept tugging at her. She felt her hair floating around her. She became aware of her arms, then her legs. And all the while the something kept tugging at her mind.

Please come back to me. The words wormed their way into her head. They nagged at her.

I shouldn't be here, she thought. *But I like it here. Here I don't have to worry about anything.* She felt her limbs grow heavy. Lifting them seemed like such an effort. She rebelled. *I want to go back to floating,* she protested.

The time is not right yet. It is too soon for you to join us here. The voices spoke, jarring images and memories into her consciousness.

One image in particular flickered in her mind. It was very faint. It was a man smiling. They were in a summer garden and the late evening sun touched everything golden. She heard herself laughing as she felt the man's arms fold around her.

A strange longing filled her. *I want to go back,* she thought.

She started struggling and swimming through the darkness. The darkness fought back, sticking to her and dragging her down like a moth drowning in oil. She struggled and fought and suddenly she felt herself caught up in a strong current. The current dragged and pushed her up, away from the blackness. Everything became bright. Sounds crashed into her consciousness.

She took a big gasp of air and opened her eyes. Above her, the unfamiliar wooden boards of a ceiling came into focus. She stared at the wood grain, confused. Slowly she became aware of the softness of a mattress beneath her. She was covered in sheets and clean-smelling blankets. She tried to move, but there was something heavy on top of her pinning her arms down under the blanket.

Too weak to struggle, she lifted her head. She found herself face-to-face with a shock of dark, wavy hair. It smelled of sandalwood. Marsh lay on the outside of the blankets. The weight of him pinned her down as he held her.

What ridiculously thick hair he had, she thought absently. He made a strange sobbing sound. She felt his breath catch before he wrapped his arms around her more tightly.

"Would you mind letting go of me? I can't breathe," she croaked.

His head shot up and he stared at her. He looked tired. There were dark circles under his eyes and his eyelashes looked damp.

"You came back for me," she murmured.

"I never left you." He smiled at her, but she was too tired to think about it, so she closed her eyes and drifted off. She slept without the blackness.

* * *

The next time she woke, the sun was shining through the window to the side of her bed.

She groaned. Her whole body felt like a thousand wooden mallets had pummeled it. Everything ached. She tried to sit up, but it hurt too much.

"Easy now, my darling. You need to do this slowly." Marsh was in a chair next to the bed.

She lifted her arm out from under the covers to push herself up. She noticed that it was bandaged. She frowned. What was it about her wrist? The image of a shackle and a diamond bracelet popped into her head. Images of crashing stones followed. Then everything that had happened flooded back into her mind.

She looked about in a panic. "The Alchemists. Where am I?"

Marsh held her hand. "You are safe now. They were all killed in the earthquake. Sucked into the void. Buried in the rubble. We went back to the site to look for survivors, but there was no way that anyone could have survived the collapse. Except us, that is. You stopped them. You stopped the Alchemists." There was something strange in the way he said it.

"Hugh, I'm so sorry about what I said. Before." She looked in his eyes. "I'm so ashamed of what I said, but I didn't know. And later, on the train, Loisa told me. She told me everything about Rosamund and what happened. I should have listened to you . . ."

"Never mind that. I promised myself that I would do this, the moment you opened your eyes." Then he kissed her with such intensity that it reached right into her soul.

"Ahem." Someone coughed.

They both looked up. Elle saw her father standing at the door. "My lord, if you wouldn't mind—a word with my daughter, if you please."

Gently, Marsh let go of Elle. His eyes held hers as he walked to the door.

Elle smiled at her father. "You are alive."

The professor nodded. He sat down on the bed next to her and held her hand. "Ellie, my darling. I am so glad you are better. You gave us such a terrible scare. We've been so worried about you." He placed his hand on the side of her face. He was never a man for great shows of public affection, but his eyes were shiny as he spoke. There was a scratch on the side of her father's face. Elle kissed his hand. "What happened to you?"

He ran his hand over the healing scar. "Oh, that is nothing. I think it makes me look rather dashing. Do you think Mrs. Hinges would like it?"

"I think she'll tell you that you look like a pirate."

Her father laughed. "Well, that will certainly get a rise out of her."

Elle suddenly remembered something. "Oh, I almost forgot. We did it. We flew the gyrocopter."

The professor blanched.

"You did what?"

"The gyrocopter. We found it in the workshop. And the key with the message. You know?"

The professor shook his head. "And it flew?"

"Yes. All the way from Oxford to Italy. Until we ran into some sky pirates. We'll have to make the next model a little more blast-proof though. And we need to work on an onboard communication device. It is ever so windy and noisy in the cockpit."

The professor rubbed his chin. "I've been meaning to ask how you got to the train so quickly. But, my dear, I don't know how to tell you this, but the flying machine was a failure. I couldn't get the reactor to work. It was a complete disaster. I left the key to the workshop for you to let the scrap metal collector take what he could salvage."

"But it flew. We flew," Elle said.

Marsh smiled as he stood in the doorway. "And your daughter is a spectacular pilot. I have no doubt that if you put a pair of wings on a bucket, she could fly that too."

The professor shook his head in amazement.

Elle looked around the room. "Where exactly are we?"

"In a small guesthouse in the old quarter in Constantinople." Marsh stepped away from the door. "We are safe and amongst friends for now, but we will need to start making our way home soon." He looked pointedly at the professor.

"Ah yes, the matter of the caliph. Inut told me this morning that the Royal Guard is still busy helping with the aftermath of the earthquake. But I suspect that it won't be long until they discover the reason for the phenomenon," the professor said.

"I, for one, would be far happier if we put some distance between ourselves and this place before that happens. I was deeply saddened to discover that the caliph had allied himself with the Alchemists. He will probably want someone to blame. And someone will probably have to pay for all the damage caused as soon as the dust settles." Marsh paused. "I may be many things, but I am definitely not noble enough for that."

"The Alchemists," Elle said. "They were on the train and there was this cell. And then there were the voices. They tried to teach me things. I think what they taught me may have helped with stopping the Alchemists."

Marsh sat down on the bed and hugged her. "Shh, my darling. It's not important anymore. We can sort through all of that in time. And there will be all the time in the world for that, once you are better."

She shook her head. "And Patrice! Oh, Marsh, you need to know about him. He cannot be trusted."

"I know. Patrice is dead, Elle. There is no way anyone could have survived the collapse. I very much doubt anyone got out of there alive after us."

"No one?"

"Well, half of them got sucked into the vortex they created. A few of them ran away, but that was about it."

They were all quiet for a moment.

"I think it will be a long time before anyone tinkers with the Shadow realm again. The primal chaos that makes up the universe is not something to be trifled with."

She looked up at him. "I know how that works! I learnt it in the dungeon. The voices taught me."

Marsh frowned. "What voices?"

"The Oracles. I know their secrets now."

The professor cleared his throat. "I'll leave you for a moment, shall I?"

Elle could have sworn that her father winked at Marsh as he closed the door.

"What was all that about?" she said.

Marsh smiled at her. "Your father and I had quite an adventure before we found you being served up to the powers of darkness. He's a brave and resourceful man."

Elle frowned and rubbed her forehead. "Exactly how long have I been unconscious?"

"Almost two days. We thought you were dead, but I couldn't leave you behind. So we carried you out. The falling stone blocks nearly killed us."

She shook her head. "And the fairy! Oh my goodness, what happened to the fairy? She must be out there in the streets, all by herself. The poor thing. We have to find her."

Marsh smiled. "It's a long story, but we crossed paths courtesy of the caliph's guard." He pointed at a bottle standing on the shelf. It glowed with a slight green light. "She says the local moonshine is not quite what it is in

Paris, but it will do. She has requested that we wake her when we are home. Her name is Adele, by the way. You should make a point of asking." He paused. "But, tell me, if you can remember, what happened after the train?"

"I don't remember much. They drugged me or did something to my forehead that made me pass out. I remember a dirigible and then I woke up in the dungeon. And there were these voices in the stone . . . Oh, Marsh, I am the Oracle, aren't I?"

Marsh took her hand and looked into her eyes. "You are. And I am sorry that I ever dragged you into this terrible mess. I know I had no right to and I will always blame myself for what happened. For the way Patrice used us both." He looked very sad and his gaze was distant for a moment. "When I think about how you almost died . . ." He shook his head. "And that is why I intend to take you away from all of it. You were right. You were right about all of it. The Council. The Order. Organized occult in general." His face grew stern. "There is nothing sacred about it anymore." He slid onto his knee next to the bed and took her hand in his. "My love, as soon as you are better, we are going as far away from all of this madness as possible. This I promise."

Elle looked at him. "What did you just call me?" she said.

Marsh smiled one of his devilish, lopsided smiles. "Elle, I never thought I would do this, but I've had a word with your father and he has given me his blessing." He cleared his throat. "Eleanor Chance. I love you more than I ever thought any person could love another. I am a complicated man and my life has always been full of twists and turns, but right now, here before you, things cannot be simpler." His voice wavered slightly.

"Will you be my wife? I promise that I will try to be the best husband I can. If you'll have me. Will you?"

Elle's heart was so full that all she could do was nod. She reached over and pulled him to her. "Of course I'll have you." And then she kissed him.

EPILOGUE

The café off the Boulevard Saint-Michel was never the same after its former owner disappeared. Without the Nightwalker to watch over them, the absinthe fairies had been sold off in their bottles, one by one. Without the absinthe, the artists and poets cleared off, leaving only hard sailors and a mix of riffraff from the underworld that drank in brooding silence as the red paint flaked from the walls.

A woman now worked behind the bar. Her black hair was always wet against her pale-blue skin and she looked ill at ease in the tight dress they made her wear. But the dress was still better than being stuck in equine form and being harnessed before a carriage and so she held her tongue. Every so often, her hand would creep to the nape of her neck, where freshly healed scars evidenced the cruelty of her former master—something she would rather forget.

The midnight shift was their busiest time and so she remained behind the counter. She sulked and poured rounds of cheap cognac and coffee for grubby gaslight trolls who stopped by after their shifts. They spent most of their time smoking cigarettes and grumbling about how the spark-light companies were stealing their work.

Outside, the cold gray rain slithered down the blacked-out windows of the café. A short man in a long carriage cloak with the collar pulled up around his face strode through the rain and opened the door. He walked over to the counter, leaving a trail of wet footprints in the thinning sawdust on the floor. The sylph shied away as she felt the power that surrounded him. Putting a safe distance between herself and the man, she lifted her chin in order to inquire after business.

He said nothing, but placed a coin onto the counter. "I have an appointment," he said.

"Upstairs." The sylph shrugged and inclined her head toward a set of molting red velvet curtains that led to the back.

The man touched his hat in thanks and ducked behind the fraying edges of the curtain. He climbed the iron stairs up to the dimly lit back room.

Patrice waited for him at one of the low tables. He was much thinner and paler than he had been, but he still smoked a small cigar that filled the room with its cheap, foul-smelling smoke.

"Glad to see that you made it out alive, Patrice."

"Warlock Master De Montague. How do you do," Patrice said. He did not stand or extend a hand to greet the Warlock. In the dim light, the grubby edges of a crutch were just visible above the edge of the table. "I see my offer was too good to resist."

"So was mine."

Patrice inclined his head in response.

"And how is your . . . injury?" asked De Montague with a slight hint of sarcasm. Patrice looked down at his leg. Black otherworldly burns flickered and played under the skin. He had dragged himself from the edge of the vortex, but not before it had seared his living skin to blackness. The specter of what remained of his bottom half hovered in the space between Shadow and Light.

The effect left the bone and muscle in a state that was half-real, half-not-real and incredibly painful.

Patrice shrugged and shifted in his chair. "I have good days and bad. Did you bring the money?"

"Yes, I did." De Montague produced a pouch from the inside of his cloak. He placed it onto the table. It made an expensive-sounding thunk on the stained wood.

"Open it," said Patrice.

De Montague knocked the bag over and a heap of gold coins spilled out.

His companion gripped his cigar between his teeth and slid a coin onto his palm. He examined it in the light before dropping it back onto the heap on the table.

"It's in the bag under the table," he said.

The Warlock reached down and pulled out a wooden box. The box was smooth and polished, with slightly battered brass edging. A row of exquisite blue diamonds were inlaid into the lid.

"The carmot. Safely returned to you, as requested," he said. "They never knew I took some of it. I left them with just enough to make the experiment look authentic." He shook his head. "Who knows what the Alchemists might have done if they'd actually had the whole lot?"

"Who knows indeed." De Montague tucked the box into his cloak.

Patrice scraped the coins into the pouch and tucked them into his waistcoat. "It was a pleasure conducting business with you, sir."

"He's gone, you know," said De Montague.

"Who?"

"Marsh. He's left the Council. Given up the path of Shadow for good. And I believe that he's marrying the girl over Christmas. A winter wedding—or so the London society papers say."

Patrice shrugged. "How lovely for them. But it's none of my business. You got what you wanted. The Alchemists are all but destroyed and we have a shiny new Oracle who has blasted loads of lovely power into the world without even knowing it. The rest, I don't care about."

De Montague put his hand out to stop him. "Not so fast," he said. "I may have a few little matters that might interest you."

Patrice shrugged and sat back. "I'm listening."

"I need someone to do a collection for me. You see, Marsh made us a little promise and he has unfortunately failed to deliver. And I would be far happier if she was safely within our control, if you know what I mean."

"Well, then, I might just be your man." Patrice smiled at him.

"Indeed. I'm glad to see that your new title and fortune hasn't changed you too much, sir." Greed and glee spilled over De Montague's face and into his beard. "I shall contact you with the details soon. I do believe that we will be able to continue to work together for our mutual benefit, don't you?"

"Oh, absolutely, and I thank you for your time, sir." Patrice wrestled himself up from his seat. "Now, if you'll excuse me, I have some unfinished business to attend to. Please stay as long as you wish. Ask Marilique behind the counter for anything you might need."

De Montague put out his hand. "I look forward to hearing from you, then."

Patrice just gripped his walking stick, and limped past De Montague.

Downstairs, Patrice crossed the café with a brief nod at the bar. The girl nodded back. She knew better than to trifle with her new master, especially when he had that look about him. He had a proper temper when he was like that.

She went back to the task of wiping the sticky patches

from the counter as two drunken sailors stumbled in through the door and started singing.

Around the corner from the café, a black steam-carriage waited in the dark. Patrice stepped up to the carriage and got inside.

"Where to, sir?" the driver said.

"The airfield, Chunk. I have a passage booked to Manchester. I need to see to the factory."

"Right on, sir." Chunk started the engine and the motor took off with a rumble. Patrice sat back against the leather seats of his plush new conveyance. With Eustace Abercrombie and the Nightwalker Aleix both sucked into oblivion, it had not been hard to forge the necessary documents that allowed him to inherit the lot—lock, stock and title. And the possibilities his new wealth and power presented made him dizzy when he thought about it. The Warlock's money felt warm and heavy in the pouch inside his pocket. He patted it and smiled. He had work to do.

HISTORICAL NOTE

One of the greatest challenges of writing historical fantasy and science fiction is marrying up that which is fact and that which is fiction with a sufficient degree of competency, so that the work becomes a coherent whole. And thus I take a moment to apologize to those historians who might read this book and feel a sense of outrage. Any liberties taken with historical fact were done mindfully and with the intention of creating fiction rather than a work of academic reference. The world of Shadow and Light is not this world and so there must be differences.

Creating historical fantasy is not a task that can be achieved successfully without the requisite amount of research and for those who are interested in the facts, I mention a few:

The Wright brothers made their historical flight in December 1903, but hot air balloons, dirigibles and other flying machine prototypes were in existence for many years before then. Croydon Aerodrome really was a dirigible airfield and the giant hangars and art nouveau building can still be seen today; it operated as such until the hydrogen gas explosion that was the *Hindenburg* disaster in the 1930's all but put an end to the dirigible industry as it was then.

Stanley produced steam cars until the electric starter motor changed the industry, and I must say a big thank you to the British Car Club of Great Britain for their wonderful photographs and entertaining video footage of these cars in action. I am forever smitten.

The Orient Express is not just one train route, but it was possible to travel from Paris to Istanbul in three days, as can be evidenced from train timetables of the day. The Venice branch of the route was added a few years after the time of this book and so I amalgamated the train route for the sake of the narrative.

Thank you to the British Library for allowing me access to their rare and fragile nineteenth-century newspaper, patent and ephemera collections. I can honestly say that I found things there that no author would ever be able to make up.

Thank you also to the Brooklyn Museum for their wonderful online collection of black and white survey photographs of Istanbul from 1903.

And lastly, I tip my brass-goggled hat to those women who fought for the rights of women and suffrage. From Mary Wollstonecraft to the Pankhursts and beyond. The faces of the past bring history to life.

ACKNOWLEDGMENTS

For most debut authors, the path to publication is a hard journey that is often lonely, but I was deeply fortunate to have met so many wonderful people along the way. To Celia Brayfield and Danuta Kean, who are both Oracles in this world: Without your wisdom and guidance, this series would never have seen its way to completion. To my dear friends: Mareen Goebel, who spent hours reading and who helped me heal the scars; Catalina Buciu, my PhD research partner, who always has time to listen to me bemoan the injustices of this world; and Siobhan McVeigh, who has been writing with me for the longest time. To all my friends at Brunel, who went through the painful process of turning a tiny ember of an idea into a big roaring work of fiction with me. To my agent, Oliver Munson, who has supernatural powers when it comes to books. To my editors Tricia Narwani and Michael Rowley and the wonderful people at Ebury and Del Rey: Your wonderful insights and professional, supportive approach made the editing and production process seem almost effortless. And lastly, to my partner, Mark Hunt, who knows so much and who patiently puts up with the unenviable task of living with a writer.

Thank you all from the bottom of my heart.

Read on for a preview
of the next book in the exciting
Chronicles of Light and Shadow,
A Clockwork Heart.

Published by Del Rey Books

CHAPTER 1

The *Water Lily* creaked happily as she surged against the headwinds that heralded landfall. As she prepared for landing, Elle eased the airship to a lower altitude.

Below her, the canals and gingerbread buildings of the city came into view. Amsterdam was as pretty as a picture, but there was no time for sightseeing. Today was a day for business. The Greychester Flying Company was about to collect its first proper freight consignment. Strictly aboveboard and legitimate.

Elle smiled with pride. Her very own charter flight business. It was almost as if an invisible hand had granted every wish she had ever had in one magical sweep. She had so many ideas about what she wanted to do with her new venture that she could hardly sleep at night. She ran her gaze around the wood and glass interior of the cockpit. The repairs and improvements that had been made to the *Water Lily* were superb. Marsh had insisted on installing brand-new navigational instruments and a state-of-the-art balloon-gas relay system. She had protested, but he had been adamant. She was secretly thrilled, though. In fact, one would never have thought the *Water Lily* had been riddled with bullet holes and dangerously close to being scrapped just months before.

Bought with his money, not yours . . . the voices whispered to her.

"Oh, do be quiet you old crones!" Elle spoke out loud. The voices who spoke were the Spirit of the Oracle. An amalgamation of fragments from the souls from each woman who had, over the centuries, held the position. Elle knew that when she died, a little part of her would rise up to join them too. And as much as she hated the fact that they were always watching her, it gave her comfort to know that somewhere within that patchwork of souls that made up the nebula she came to know as the voice of the Oracle, was a bit of the mother she never knew. It was just a pity that they were such a bunch of busybodies who always chose to interfere at the most inopportune times.

Never forget who you are, child, the voices said in answer to her thoughts.

"Yes, yes, I am the Oracle, the source of wisdom; the one with the gift of sight; the force that holds the many folds of the universe together; the one who channels power to those who are deserving," she recited the mantra they had taught her in a bored singsong voice. "Trust me, if there is one thing I cannot do, it's forget who I am. Now please leave me alone to enjoy this moment, would you? Today I am flying and I want none of this Oracle business spoiling it."

As you wish . . . the voices faded away.

Just then, the communications consul started rattling and spitting out a ribbon of tape, clearing her for landing.

Elle brought the airship round portside and lined her up, ready to dock at one of the platforms that lined the docks on the western district. With a shudder and hiss that sounded almost like a sigh of contentment, the *Water Lily* berthed.

"There you go, my dear," Elle said to her ship as she turned the crank handle that released the tether ropes. "All safe and sound."

Almost as if in answer to that, one of the boiler tank pressure release valves opened to release some engine pressure.

Elle opened the hatch and let the ladder rope drop to the ground. With practiced ease, she climbed down and stepped onto the wooden docking platform.

"Miss Chance, I presume!" A tall man with a shock of white-blond hair that was thinning at the top waved at her.

"Ah, Mr. De Beer." She smiled at him.

"Welcome to the fair city of Amsterdam." He spoke in an accent that was a touch heavy and rounded on the vowels.

"Thank you. It's so nice to finally meet you," she said as she shook her new Dutch docking agent's huge hand vigorously.

"And the same to you," he said graciously. "It is an honor to be working with the famous Eleanor Chance."

Elle didn't have the heart to correct him on her new surname. Simply being Elle Chance for the day, not Lady Eleanor or Viscountess Greychester, was a bit of a relief, if she was honest with herself.

She loved her husband, Hugh, with all her heart, but the pomp and ceremony involved in becoming part of his world over the last few months had been more than a little overwhelming.

"I have the papers ready here, to sign if you will. Once it is completed, I will tell the men to start loading the freight. I have told them to be extra careful with our precious tulips." Mr. De Beer pointed to the crates of bulbs that were stacked on wooden pallets and tied down with coarse rope. They were indeed ready to be loaded into the hull and destined to brighten the gardens and huge glasshouses of Kew this summer.

"My men shouldn't take too long. Sign here, if you please," he said as he handed her a wad of papers.

Elle felt a pang of sadness when she signed the docking papers and charter before handing them back to Mr. De Beer so he could tear off the counterparts. Patrice, her old agent, had been such fun.

In the old days, before Constantinople, Patrice would have taken her to some exotic disreputable bar or café for a drink while they waited for the freight to be loaded. He would have had her in fits of giggles with his lumbering charm and silly jokes. Despite his betrayal and all the terrible things he did, Elle found herself missing his massive moustache. She had been told afterward that very few bodies were ever recovered from the Constantinople earthquake that had killed almost every living alchemist and a large percentage of the Nightwalker population. They had all been gathered in an underground amphitheatre when the vortex their leader, Sir Eustace Abercrombie, had created collapsed, bringing a large part of the city down with it. The last sight Elle had of Patrice was of him hanging on for dear life at the edge of the spinning edge of complete darkness . . .

She closed her eyes at the awful memory. Patrice had simply been sucked into oblivion, never to be seen again. She did not think that a funeral had been held for him and the thought of it made her sad. Such a wasteful and futile quest for absolute power . . .

"Miss Chance, is everything all right?" Mr. De Beer asked. He looked concerned.

Elle blinked herself back to the present. "Yes, all is well. I was just remembering something. Silly really."

She shrugged off her dark thoughts. Patrice had betrayed her, and he had betrayed her husband too, by working as a double agent. Even if he were alive today, she did not think she could forgive the fact that he had sold her to the alchemists as if she were nothing more than a means to gain a profit.

But this was the beginning of a new era and she wouldn't allow dark thoughts to taint things. "Say, do you know where the pilots' mess is?" she asked De Beer.

"Ah, yes, it's just over there. Upstairs in that building with the green roof."

"Thank you." She smiled at De Beer. "Take off in three hours?"

He doffed his flat cap. "Will see you then, Miss Chance."

The pilots' mess room was exactly where Mr. De Beer had said it was, on the first floor of one of the administrative buildings adjacent to the landing docks. The smell of meat stew mingled with the odor of tired bodies hit her right in the nostrils halfway up the stairwell. It was a familiar smell that made her feel warm inside. It was the smell of freedom.

The mess was really nothing more than a large, slightly grubby warehouse that had been converted to serve as a canteen and waiting area for pilots and crew between flights. The wooden floorboards were scuffed and gray paint flaked from the walls, but this did not seem to bother anyone in the way that utilitarian buildings seemed to do.

She walked up to the canteen counter and ordered a coffee. It came in a tin mug and had a faint blue-gray film on the surface that hinted at the hours it had been brewing behind the counter.

She had just picked up her coffee when someone called her name. "Ellie!"

Only her father and one other person called her that. She spun round to greet the young man who was, at that moment, bounding up to her like an overeager Labrador.

"Ducky!" She hugged him with genuine affection.

"Or should I rather bow and say, good afternoon, my lady?" In one quick move, he converted her hug into a half nelson that would have made any wrestler proud.

"Arch!" Elle started laughing and dug her fingers into his ribs to tickle him. This was a practiced maneuver she had perfected while they were in flight school. Richard "Ducky" Richardson was the brother she never had.

Ducky, so called because of his prowess on the cricket field, let go of her. "My word, it's good to see you. What on earth are you doing here?"

"I'm flying." She smoothed her hair back into its customary low knot at the back of her neck.

"Is that old tub of yours still in the air?" he said with amazement.

"The *Water Lily* is not a tub. And she's just had a complete overhaul. I'd bet she'd outrun your manky old ship any day of the week."

"Ha! Now that's a wager I'd like to take."

"Just name the day and I'll be there."

Ducky grinned at her. "Oh, Ellie. It's so lovely to see you. I'm so sorry I missed the wedding, but I was in Japan and I couldn't get back in time. You did get married awfully quickly," he said with naughty smile. "I would have thought you would be busy planning christening breakfasts at the moment." There had been more than a few finely arched eyebrows raised at news of her sudden marriage to Marsh and the gossipmongers were all watching eagerly to see if their suspicions were correct.

"Oh stop it!" Elle felt her cheeks grow warm. "When you know something is right, there really is no reason to wait. And besides, you know I'm not the type of girl who fancies elaborate weddings."

"Come, let me introduce you to the crew," Ducky said.

On the other side of the canteen, a group of men had halted their game of cards and were watching her intently as Ducky steered her over to them.

"Lads, I'd like to you meet my very dear friend Mrs. Eleanor Marsh, or rather, Viscountess Greychester to be precise," Ducky said. "Elle, may I present the crew of the *Iron Phoenix*." He made an overelaborate sweeping gesture.

Chairs scraped as the crewmen all rose to their feet, nodded awkwardly and mumbled "my lady," in gruff tones. All except one. He was dressed like her, in a white shirt and brown leather coat.

"Gentlemen, do sit. Today I am simply Elle, the pilot. There really is no need for formalities, please."

"By all means, join us." The man who was still seated spoke with a soft drawl that immediately placed him from somewhere in the New World, America perhaps, she wasn't sure.

She studied the men. Ducky was the embodiment of a clean-cut Englishman. Apple-cheeked, bred from solid stock and good to his bones, his only flaw was his natural sense of adventure. Despite his family's best efforts, he absolutely refused to settle down. It was also one of the things she loved best about him.

Sandy was the word that first came to mind when her gaze slid to the American. He had the gravelly, freckly look of a man who had spent the majority of his life outdoors. He wore a fedora, which he had not bothered to take off. She stared at his hands as they rested on the table. Broad palms, strong fingers. The hands of a man who knew hard work. A soldier's hands, she decided. He was far too suspicious-looking to be a farmer.

He gave her a quizzical look. "Well, are you going to sit down or not?" he asked.

Elle realized that she had been staring. "Why, thank you," she said sweetly. She set her coffee mug down on the table and took the seat Ducky offered her. As she sat, she shoved her new leather holdall between the legs of her chair. The strap was new and stiff and she had to wiggle it around a few times before the finely stitched brown leather would settle.

The holdall had been a gift from Hugh. He had spotted it in the market in Florence on their honeymoon. "For the one that I didn't manage to save in Paris," he had said when she had unwrapped it from the tissue paper.

They had spent that afternoon curled up in front of the massive medieval fireplace in their room while the gray winter rain slipped down the windows outside. A honeymoon in the middle of winter did have its advantages, for it was far too cold to be traipsing about outside sightseeing for too long.

"Do you play cards, Mrs. Marsh?" The American spoke, interrupting her thoughts.

Elle looked straight into the bluest eyes she had ever encountered.

Without thinking, her fingers went to the place between the buttons of her shirt to the slim hilt of the stiletto she carried inside the laces of her corset.

"I've been known to play the odd hand," she said.

She lowered her hand unobtrusively, feeling silly at her sudden reaction.

He smiled. "Well, then. Mr. Richardson, why don't you deal us a fresh hand. The rest of you men have three hours' shore leave. But don't make me have to come and collect you later."

"Aye, aye, captain," Ducky said and picked up the cards as the remainder of the crew took the hint and went off on their own business.

"Captain?" Elle looked at Ducky.

He laughed. "Dashwood. Logan Dashwood. He pilots our crew. I am first officer on the *Phoenix*," Ducky explained.

"At your service, ma'am." He touched his hat. He wore no collar and she noticed that his shirt was unstarched and unbuttoned at the top. A long strip of leather darkened from wear was wound loosely around his neck. A small amulet carved from what looked like black stone was threaded through the leather, just visible above the place where the buttons met. Elle could feel the dark hum of power from the Shadow side emanating from it.

There was something oddly familiar about this man, but she could not say what. "Well, Captain Dashwood, let's play," she said.

She picked up her cup and took a sip of the lukewarm liquid. It tasted tinny and so foul that she could not help making a face.

"That coffee looks like it could strip-clean the tanks of a spark engine," Ducky said.

"You are not wrong." Elle put the mug to the side. The wedding band she wore on her left hand glinted in the watery light of the mess hall.

Dashwood's smile broadened. He reached over and took her hand in his. "Not married that long then, I see?"

"Long enough," she answered, drawing her hand away.

"That wedding band is still very shiny. Does your husband approve of you gallivanting around the world in the company of men, Mrs. Marsh?"

Elle glared at him. "I am not gallivanting. I am working. There is a big difference between the two, *Captain* Dashwood." She used his title with extra emphasis, but the subtlety of the *faux pas* he had just made by not addressing her by her correct title was completely lost on the man.

He held up his hand. "I was just trying to be friendly. No need to be so prickly."

She could tell that he was laughing at her, but she was no stranger to the reaction. She had spent years fighting the perception that she was some spoiled rich girl who took to flying because she was bored.

"So, Ducky, how was Japan? You must tell me all about it." She turned to her friend, ignoring Captain Dashwood entirely.

Ducky's eyes lit up. "Japan is like nothing you have ever experienced. Had to get out of there in a hurry, though. All the signs are that there is serious trouble brewing out there."

"It's all over the London papers," Elle said. "Such a worry, isn't it?"

"I found myself without a commission. That was until I heard that the good captain over here was in need of a first officer, on account of a slight problem with crew . . ."

Ducky broke off what he was saying, for Dashwood gave him a very stern look.

"And so Mr. Richardson found himself stationed on the *Phoenix*. And a finer first officer no captain could hope for," Dashwood finished Ducky's sentence for him.

Ducky swallowed and picked up the deck of cards. From the looks of things, they had been playing that American card game called poker, which had recently become all the rage.

Captain Dashwood placed a small stack of matchsticks in front of her. "Shilling a stick? Or is that too rich for your blood?"

"Wager accepted, Captain Dashwood." Elle gave him

a slow smile. Her friend the Baroness Loisa Belododia had taught her how to play when Elle and Marsh had stopped by to visit her at her winter castle in the Carpathian mountains. Loisa was an excellent card player and Elle had learned a few tricks from her.

Ducky dealt the hand for them.

Elle felt the soft hum of magic from the amulet around Captain Dashwood's neck the moment she checked her cards, but she said nothing.

He won the first two games easily as Elle observed him play. Each time she looked at her hand, the amulet strummed with an energy that could not be ignored.

So the good captain was cheating. Well, she had a few aces up her sleeve too.

"Another game?" He sat back in his seat with arrogant satisfaction.

"Why not? You seem to be on a winning streak, Captain."

He laughed softly as Ducky dealt again.

Elle closed her eyes and thought of two cards that would make up a bad hand on the table. Carefully she reached out with her mind and sent the image along the trail of energy back to the captain. His eyes narrowed for a fraction of a second and then he gripped his jaw with glee.

Elle glanced at her cards again. She had an ace.

She bet her matchsticks to the growing pile in the center of the table. The game was on.

Expressions grew serious as they concentrated on the cards.

Ducky bet. Elle took another card.

Dashwood drew a card and bit the corner of his lip.

Ducky placed his cards on the table, facedown. "That's as far as my bravery allows me to go," he said shaking his head at the small fortune in front of him.

Elle and Captain Dashwood stared at each other for a

few long moments and Elle felt the crackle of energy from the Shadow side course through her.

"What about you, Mrs. Marsh?" the Captain said.

"Oh, I am still very much in the game, Captain." She added more matchsticks to the center of the table.

"Hmm, a woman with gumption. I am impressed. But let's see what you are made of. I raise you," he said as he pushed all of his matchsticks into the center of the table. Then he looked up and gave her a sly smile.

Elle felt the strum of his amulet and fought against it.

"Very well, Captain." She put all her matchsticks onto the pile. "What else have you got?"

Dashwood scratched his chin and a look of uncertainty flashed across his face. "What did you have in mind, Mrs. Marsh?"

This time it was her turn to give him a sly smile. She leaned forward and pulled the docking papers out of her holdall. "The *Water Lily* for the *Phoenix*. Winner takes both ships."

Dashwood's eyes widened in surprise for just a second, but it was enough to tell her that he had not expected her boldness.

"Elle, no! Dashwood never loses," Ducky put his hand on her arm to stop her.

"There is a first time for everything," she said without taking her eyes off the captain. "What do you say, Captain Dashwood?"

"Very well then, if you are so eager to part company with your ship. I'll take that wager. Perhaps you could even ask your husband to buy it back for you later," Dashwood said.

Elle kept her features neutral, but she was sorely tempted to put him in his place. The arrogance of the man was absolutely incredible. And to think, he had been cheating all this time without anyone knowing.

"Show us what you've got," she said.

"Full house," he said as he laid the cards down on the table. "Three aces and two kings."

Elle stared at his cards without saying anything.

He hooted and lifted his arms in the air. "I win and you, madam"—he pointed at her—"owe me a ship."

"Perhaps, you celebrate a mite too quickly, Captain," she said.

He sat forward in his chair. "What do you mean?"

"Well, you see, there are four aces in a deck of cards. And I happen to have the fourth one right here. Along with a king, a queen, a jack and a ten. Of hearts." She laid the cards out one by one as she named them.

"Blimey," said Ducky before he burst out laughing. "I think they call that a Royal Flush. Is that right?"

Dashwood blanched. He stared at the cards before him. "How is that possible?" he muttered.

Elle shook her head. "Well, Captain, I would recommend that you check whether your opponents have special abilities before you start cheating at cards." She waved her hand over the table. "See?" she said.

Even in the harsh spark lights of the canteen, Elle's arm cast no shadow on the table. It was one of the many peculiarities that being the Oracle brought, for she was the one who walked between the two worlds.

She turned to Ducky. "Ducky, how would you like to come and work for me? I suddenly find myself the owner of an extra airship in need of a pilot," she said sweetly.

Ducky gawked at her.

"You dirty cheater!" Captain Dashwood slammed his fist down on the table with such force that it made the matchsticks jump.

"Oh no, Captain. It is *you* who are the cheater. I just happened to spot that little mind-reading amulet the moment we sat down. You really should be more circumspect about these things. Now, if you'll excuse me." She gathered her holdall and rose from the table. "Ducky, will you bring the *Phoenix* to Croydon? Greychesters has rented a hangar there. Take on whichever crew members you consider to be good men and necessary in order to fly her home safely. I will ask Mr. De Beer to arrange the papers for us." She turned and inclined her head at Dashwood. "Good day to you, sir."

Ducky rose and gave Dashwood an apologetic shrug. "A wager is a wager, Captain. I'm sorry."

Dashwood said nothing, he just stared ahead of him as Ducky followed Elle downstairs.

Mr. De Beer looked up from his desk when Elle strode into his office with Ducky at her heels. "The *Iron Phoenix* is now part of the Greychester Flying Company Fleet," she said.

"Is she now?" Mr. De Beer said in surprise.

"Yes she is indeed," Elle said with a little nod. "Can you arrange her papers for Croydon please? Mr. Richardson will pilot her as soon as she is cleared for take off."

"But what about Captain Dashwood?" Mr. De Beer said.

"What about him?" Elle said.

Her docking agent dabbed his thinning hair with his handkerchief. "Captain Dashwood is not a man I would like to have for an enemy, madam. Are you sure you want to do this?"

"We had a bet and I won. Fair and square. Now the ship is mine and I make no apology for it."

Mr. De Beer shook his head in dismay. "Very well, then. I will arrange it. You had better get ready for cast off, Mr. Richardson. As luck would have it, I have a departure opening right after the *Water Lily*. You had better take it before the captain decides to change his mind. We don't want any trouble, now do we?"

"I think that is an excellent idea, sir," Ducky said. He

too was looking slightly out of sorts. Elle noticed him glance over his shoulder at the direction of the mess as he spoke.

"Come, Ducky, you had better show me my new acquisition." She smiled in triumph as she left De Beer's office. Today was truly a great day for the Greychester Flying Company indeed.